THE
WAKING
OF
ANGANTYR

T0347170

Also by Marie Brennan and available from Titan Books

The Memoirs of Lady Trent series
A Natural History of Dragons
The Tropic of Serpents
Voyage of the Basilisk
In the Labyrinth of Drakes
Within the Sanctuary of Wings
Turning Darkness Into Light

The Onyx Court series
Midnight Never Come
In Ashes Lie
A Star Shall Fall
With Fate Conspire

THE
WAKING
OF
ANGANTYR

MARIE BRENNAN

TITAN BOOKS

The Waking of Angantyr
Print edition ISBN: 9781803363394
E-book edition ISBN: 9781803363400

Published by Titan Books
A division of Titan Publishing Group Ltd
144 Southwark Street, London SE1 0UP
www.titanbooks.com

First edition: October 2023
10 9 8 7 6 5 4 3 2 1

A CIP catalogue record for this title is available from the British Library.

Printed and bound by CPI (UK) Ltd,
Croydon CR0 4YY.

A NOTE ON LANGUAGE

The character ð is pronounced like a soft th, as in the word "then" (not as in the word "thick").

The various accents and other diacritical marks have been removed from the names for the sake of simplicity and reader ease. My apologies to my Old Norse professor and other linguistics nerds for the sins I have committed against the language.

1

WHISPERS FROM THE WELL

Dead men had whispered to Hervor in her sleep for so long she'd almost gotten used to it.

As a child she'd been foolish enough to say what she heard; later she grew smarter, but by then it was too late. The other bondsmaids shunned her, told tales about her over the cooking-fire. *A breech birth, they said, came out of her mother wrong end first and killed her in the coming, and you know what that means.* Ill-omened, ill-starred. No wonder she claimed to hear ghosts.

But over time, the fear's sharp edge dulled. Life went on in its daily routine, much as it always had, and there was a new herdsman who despite the tales kept looking at Hervor with an interested eye, until she truly began to forget it wasn't normal to hear voices that spoke always of murder and betrayal, ravens and blood.

Until the day came when they beat the drum to summon everyone to the garth in front of the hall, and Hervor put down her bucket and ran with the others to stand in a ragged line. Men on one side, maids on the other, and then they waited, and waited; the boy who'd been assigned to keep a lookout ran much faster than a cart moved, and a long time passed before the new arrivals crested the ridge in front of Rognjeld.

At last a small cloud of dust rose above the ridge – it had been another dry spring, sparking fearful whispers of drought returning – and a cart lumbered into view. As if by magic, Gannveig appeared, and the bondsmaids fell silent. They'd all catch it, if the jarl's wife got angry. Feigald was with her, their son Ungaut at their heels, and together the jarl and his kin waited for the carts to pass through the outer fence.

Hervor studied the procession with a jaundiced eye. She was supposed to be burningly excited about the young woman who sat on the front seat of the lead cart, for Anfinna was to marry Ungaut and carry the keys to the holding on her belt. The cart's bed was piled high with her dowry, cloth and tapestries and fleeces and more, and behind that one came a second cart similarly loaded. Anfinna was quite a prize.

The people with her interested Hervor more, simply because they were new. Rognjeld didn't get many visitors. Anfinna's father, Storleik Geirriksson, was far more powerful and wealthy a jarl than Feigald; the disdainful sweep of his gaze around the holding seemed to question why he was sending even a fourth daughter off to a place like this. Half a dozen armed housemen rode at his heels – half a dozen! When Feigald's only followers were freeborn farmers and herders, permitted weapons by law, but hardly well-trained warriors. One houseman even carried a sword at his hip, instead of the more common axe. Hervor didn't like the way his attention snagged on her, the appraising look in his eye. She squared her shoulders and looked away. Behind him…

One of Storleik's servants was helping an old woman down from the second cart. She had a face like weathered stone, seamed and stained with age, but her wits didn't seem to have wandered any. She was looking at Hervor, too, with the unblinking, predatory focus of a hawk.

An old woman couldn't cause the same trouble for Hervor as a sword-bearing houseman. This time Hervor stared back, not caring if Gannveig thumped her for it.

Then someone touched the old woman's shoulder, and like a soap bubble popping, the intensity was gone. She hobbled to join Anfinna and the others, and Hervor fought the urge to scrub at her arms. Why stare at her like that? True, she was the tallest of the bondsmaids by a good handspan, and broader in the shoulders than some men, but that didn't justify such a stare.

Feigald was droning through a thunderously dull speech welcoming Anfinna to Rognjeld. By the time he was done, Hervor's unease had given way to yawning boredom. She almost welcomed it when the bondsmaids were dismissed with a look from Gannveig that said they'd better not think of lingering to gape at the new arrivals.

Hervor retrieved her bucket and joined the others in line at the well to draw water for the guests' baths. They were chattering on and on about Anfinna, of course, how lovely she was, how rosy her skin, how long her braids, until Hervor could no longer stand it. "Who'd want to be a soft flower like that?" she asked scornfully, interrupting the other bondsmaids. "She's from the south. Come winter, she'll be huddled indoors by the fire, crying for home."

"You're just jealous," Isrun said. "You won't be anywhere near the fire, and you know it."

"I don't *need* the fire," Hervor boasted, tossing her own braids back. They might not be so long as Anfinna's, but they were more blonde; let Anfinna be jealous of *that*. "I've got ice in my blood. Come winter, I'll dance naked in the snow."

Isrun rolled her eyes. "We can only hope you'll catch sick and die. Try it, Hervor."

"I will!" Hervor shouted as the others walked away, leaving her alone at the well. "I will." This she repeated in a quieter voice as she knelt to tie her bucket to the rope and lower it until it hit the water with a splash. She placed both hands on the low stone edge and leaned forward, putting her head right into the shaft to hear the echoes. "*I will!*"

Her voice rang against the stones, but when it came back it was no longer hers.

MURDER
traitors
blood bright on the sand
ravens feast
rending our flesh

For one dizzying moment, Hervor thought she would pitch head first down the well. Her hands scrabbled at the stones, trying to catch hold, and then she managed to shove herself backwards, onto the trampled grass.

She sat there, panting, and stared at the well in horror.

Nothing rose out of it. She cast a quick glance around, but nobody was nearby. No one to see her act like a fool – but no one to whisper those words at her, either. Reluctantly, Hervor shifted to her knees and peered over the well's edge.

Nothing but stone, water, and her bucket on the rope.

She squeezed her eyes shut and growled a curse that would have spurred Gannveig to beat some manners into her. Of course there was nothing. She knew those voices. They'd been with her since childhood.

But they'd never spoken during the day.

"That's not fair," she whispered, opening her eyes again. It didn't matter if someone came up to the well and saw her talking to the stones; they all thought she was mad, anyway. "Bad enough that you talk to me when I'm asleep; I've gotten used to that. But it's broad daylight!" Her voice rose, but this time the echoes that came back were her own. "You're not supposed to be talking to me *now*!"

The voices weren't supposed to be talking to her at all, whoever they were. They were supposed to go down to Slavinn with the rest of the dead, not torment a bondsmaid who didn't even know their names.

Hervor dug her fingers into the stones and glared into the well as if the dead men who spoke to her lay under it. "You'd better not play with me like that again. Gannveig already loathes me; I don't need to give her an excuse to put me outside the fence. Stay in my dreams, where you belong."

As if she could stop them, should they decide to wander into her waking thoughts as well. But Hervor hoped that speaking firmly might have some effect. Maybe ghosts were like children, and needed a stern hand.

Or maybe she was going even madder than she already was.

Hervor hauled her bucket out of the well and went back to work before Gannveig could find her dawdling.

The hall of Rognjeld was decked out in its finest for Ungaut's wedding feast. He and Anfinna had spent the afternoon closeted with the priest – not Eyulf, but some old man Storleik had brought with him – having rune-staves of good fortune painted on their skin and being lectured on their new roles as husband and wife. That part, fortunately, nobody else had to suffer through. But between the lecturing and the bedding came the feasting, and that was for everyone, from jarls like Feigald and Storleik down to the lowest bonders.

And when the mead flowed freely and laughter rose into the smoky, shadowed upper reaches of the hall, people tended to loosen up and forget certain things, like shunning the local madwoman. So Hervor wolfed down her share of the meat – maybe more; bonders so rarely got meat that everybody was fighting for as much as they could grab – and laughed along with the others, and for a little while it was as if there wasn't any big difference between her and them. Whispers from the well notwithstanding.

But much of the talk was of Anfinna's lovely clothing, her jewellery, her fine hand with embroidery, and even with enough mead inside her to float a longship, Hervor still found that dull beyond bearing. So after a while she nudged Melbjorg and nodded up at the high table, where the housemen and the priests sat with the two families. Melbjorg had helped prepare Anfinna for the session with the priest; she might know things. "Who's the shrivelled old dug up there, anyway?"

Melbjorg followed Hervor's nod and saw the old woman from the cart. "Anfinna's nurse. Saeunn. I get the feeling she's useless, but she came along because Anfinna dotes on her."

"She looks half-mad."

"Bondsmaid calling the bondsman dirty, aren't you?" But Melbjorg's gibe was amused rather than cruel. "Half-mad's better than half-shrew, like Gannveig."

Hervor wasn't so sure about that. Any time Anfinna's attention was on the old woman, Saeunn seemed like a doddering sweetheart. But when nobody was looking her way, her manner sharpened into a measuring regard Hervor didn't understand – and didn't like in the slightest.

A platter went by, and Hervor lunged across Melbjorg to snag a piece of meat before it passed out of her reach. The piece turned out to be a sheep's shank that had already been gnawed mostly clean, but Hervor stuck it in her mouth anyway, scraping off the last few shreds.

"She keeps staring at me," she told Melbjorg around the bone. "Ever since she got here."

"Everybody stares at you."

"Not till they get to know me," Hervor said cheerfully. "I look normal enough. No limp, no cast eye."

"Normal, hah," Melbjorg muttered. "You're as big as an ox. Dress you up in armour, and you'd be a man."

"Give me armour any day, over this shite." Hervor tugged at her frayed overdress with greasy fingers. "I heard that where Anfinna comes from, they dress their *sheep* better than this."

"That's because their sheep are prettier than you!"

Isrun had overheard the conversation. Hervor glared at her, while all around them the others began to giggle. The smug expression on Isrun's face was simply too much; Hervor snarled and threw the leg-bone at her. Isrun ducked, and the bone landed among the rushes, where three dogs leapt on it.

"Might want to get that before they finish it off," Hervor said in a sticky-sweet voice. "You could use a bit more flesh on your bones, Isrun. Yesterday I heard Bardnor saying you looked like an underfed dog."

Isrun spat a curse at her, but Hervor was already leaving; she'd long since learned to withdraw while she had the upper hand. With a half-hearted nod to the high table – Gannveig caught it, and looked angry – Hervor went through the snow-room and out into the cool night air.

The bite of the wind against her cheeks enlivened her, but something – maybe Isrun's sniping; maybe just a bit of bad meat – had started Hervor's stomach churning. She crossed the garth, hoping the fresh air would help, but in the shadow of the pig-shed she fell to her knees and puked.

"Damn," Hervor muttered, wiping her mouth with the back of her hand. "Good food gone to waste."

She spat a few times to clear her mouth, but a nasty sourness remained. Drinking something would help. She didn't want to go back into the hall just yet, though, so that ruled out more mead.

Hervor turned reluctantly and looked at the well, its low circle of pale stones gleaming in the moonlight.

The thought of water made her desperately thirsty, which only made the taste in her mouth worse. Still, Hervor remained frozen by the pig-shed. The well, a familiar, everyday sight, was suddenly sinister. What if the voices of the dead waited for her there?

She slammed one fist onto the ground, pushing herself to her feet. "Fuck that," she muttered, both to herself and to the well. "I'm not afraid of any damned ghosts. Puke on *them*, I will."

A hide cover had been thrown over the well when the day's chores were done. Hervor pulled it off and stared down into the darkness, hands half-formed into fists, as if something might jump out. But nothing stirred in the blackness, and after a moment she picked up a bucket from the ground and tied it to the rope.

The water came up normal; she drank it in gulps, after spitting the first few mouthfuls onto the grass. Thirst sated, she tugged the hide cover back onto the stones, put the bucket down, and sank onto the well's rim with a weary sigh.

It had been a long day, and the days to come wouldn't get any shorter. And not just because they weren't yet to the summer solstice. Anfinna, sitting at the high table in the hall, now had keys on her belt. Which meant that come tomorrow she'd be there alongside Gannveig, sending bondsmaids running to every corner of the garth and hall, fetching this, disposing of that, carrying out the thousand tasks that kept the holding on its feet. And because she'd want to impress Gannveig, Anfinna would run them ragged.

Hervor rolled her head around, cracking her neck in three separate places, and looked up at the stars to gauge the time. The Hart had nearly set; later than she'd thought, then. Hervor shoved herself to her feet again. Back into the hall for the last scraps of food, before they were all gone.

Halfway across the garth, the voices drove her to her knees.

BLOOD
arrows like wasps
screaming pain, screaming crows, screaming blood
MURDER
we lie betrayed
MURDER
lie unmourned
MURDER
lie and ROT

"No, no, *no*!" Hervor buried both hands in her hair, pulling hard enough to rip strands from her scalp. "Don't *do* this to me! Once was bad enough—"

"Hervor?"

For a moment she thought the ghosts knew her name now, too. But it came from outside her skull, and had a resonance the whispers lacked. Hervor looked up and saw a looming silhouette in the light spilling from the hall. Then the figure knelt, and the light reached the edge of his face, and Hervor recognised him as the person she least wanted to see.

"Are you all right?" Rannvar asked.

Hervor swallowed down curses. Why Rannvar? Why not Melbjorg, or even Isrun? Shite, why not Gannveig? At the moment, Hervor would have preferred to be thrown out of

Rognjeld than humiliated in front of the one man still new enough to the holding not to shun her.

Saying she was fine would be a blatant lie. Hervor managed a twisted grin. "My stomach isn't. I threw up once already—" She gestured in the general direction of the pig-shed. "Something I ate. Or maybe just Isrun's ugly face. But it was such a good feast; I'd rather not lose it all to the ground."

She was proud of that excuse. It even accounted for what she'd been saying – as if she'd been talking to her stomach, and not dead men. Not particularly sane either way, but better this than the alternative.

Rannvar grimaced in understanding. "I think some of that mead was off." His teeth flashed in the moonlight, a quick grin. "Or maybe it *was* Isrun. Her talk's enough to turn anyone's stomach."

He helped her to her feet. Melbjorg might say Hervor was as big as a man, but Rannvar was bigger; he stood a good half-head above any of the other bondsmen, and even a bit above Feigald. He must have been fed well wherever he'd lived, before Feigald bought his bond.

Hervor brushed dust off her knees as Rannvar went on. "Better watch out, coming out here alone."

"Huh?" She stared at him. "Why? You think Isrun's going to attack me?"

"No, that swordsman. Well, not *attack*. More like…"

Hervor saw where he was aiming and snorted. "More like bed. He's been staring at me, hasn't he?"

"Like you're a sheep he's thinking about buying."

"Let him go fuck a sheep, then. I'm not for sale." The words came out harsher than Hervor meant them to, and Rannvar looked taken aback. She fumbled for words to reassure him. "It's just – the way I get treated, here – I'm a bondsmaid, not a *thrall*. Not that I think Gannveig can tell the difference. She's got less honour than the pigs."

Rannvar grimaced. "I wouldn't go saying that too loudly, if I were you."

His concern warmed Hervor. She didn't give a damn about Gannveig, but that Rannvar cared… "It's all a part of my plan," she said with an impudent smile. "Haven't you guessed?"

"Plan?"

She leaned towards him with a conspiratorial air. "I've got Gannveig fooled. She thinks I'm mad, you see. But it's all an act."

Rannvar eyed her askance. "Dangerous act. Everybody says she'd like to put you outside the fence."

"But that's just it! Don't you see? Gannveig will shave her own head bald before she'll admit I've worked off my bond. So if I want to get out of here…" Hervor spread her hands and grinned with all the bravado she could muster. "I have to make her *throw* me out."

She startled a laugh from him. "You *are* mad. What will you do, when your plan succeeds? Wander around as a beggar? You won't be a freeholder; you'll have no land, no money—"

Hervor dismissed this with a wave of her hand, as if it were less important than last year's shearing. "Don't you ever listen to tales? I'll be an adventurer. I'll go kill bears in the Ice Knives. I'll waylay bandits on the roads. Sail the high seas like Enjarik Enjakilsson, hunt monsters in the dark forests of the south—"

"With no weapon?"

"Barrows're full of swords. I'll take one of those."

The humour began to drain from Rannvar's face. "You'll steal from the dead?"

"Why not? What can they do to me?" Hervor said it boldly, but the words put ice in her stomach. What *could* they do to her? Dead men were all talk.

But talk could be bad enough.

She looked into the distance, where the light seeping from the hall didn't reach. The fence around the garth was invisible in the darkness. She liked it that way; with the fence hidden in shadows, she could pretend it wasn't there, pretend that nothing stood between her and the world. Pretend she could just walk off now, tonight, and never come back.

Rannvar touched her arm. "You dream about this a lot, don't you."

Something – the mead, the late hour – made Hervor indiscreet. "All the time," she said grimly. "What else can I do? But it's more than just a dream, Rannvar. I *will* do it. I'm damned if I'll rot out the rest of my life here at Rognjeld, never going anywhere, never doing anything but what Gannveig and Anfinna tell me. That's no kind of life."

"I agree," he said quietly. "But you don't want to end up an outcast, alone, not belonging any place. Do you?"

His tone wasn't condescending, but Hervor bristled anyway. She pulled away from his touch. "You think I belong here?" she demanded, glaring up at him. "Beggar's better than thrall, and belonging no place is better than being trapped in a pen."

He held up his hands defensively. Then a burst of noise from the hall made them both turn. The moment was gone; Rannvar sighed. "We should get back inside."

Hervor shrugged, looking at the ground, until he sighed again and went back without her. She waited several minutes, so no one would think they were coming in together, then steeled herself and followed him.

Inside, she squinted against the sudden light of the fires that ran the length of the hall, down the centre of the room. The din of voices made her flinch, and she realised she was still on edge. Still afraid that the other voices, the dead ones, were going to speak again.

How did she know they wouldn't? They'd done so twice today. She didn't know what had started it, and so she had no idea if it would end.

The thought of it not ending made her gut twist in fear.

Hervor had been standing too long by the door to the snow-room; she would draw attention. Already had, in fact: Saeunn, at the far end of the hall, was watching her again. And when Hervor met her gaze, the old woman's thin lips parted in a silent laugh.

Years of a pattern Hervor knew and could live with. Then today, with no warning, it shifted. There had to be a reason. And what had changed today?

New people showed up. Like a creepy old crone who acted as if she knew something other people didn't.

Hervor tensed. For a heartbeat, with the mead heating her blood and the echoes of the voices still ringing in her ears, she wanted to fling herself down the centre of the hall, leaping the fires as she went, vault over the high table, and shake the truth from the old woman. Was she somehow responsible for this? Had she made Hervor's curse even more unbearable?

Would have done it, too – would have wrung the old woman's wrinkled neck until answers came out of it – were it not for Storleik. Anfinna's bear-like father rose to his feet at the high table, roaring out words that sounded like gibberish through the pounding in Hervor's ears, and suddenly everyone in the hall was standing. Through the crowd Hervor saw Anfinna being drawn up from her seat, her face alternately red and pale beneath the rune-stave painted on her forehead. Wolf-whistles and bawdy shouts rang out in the high reaches of the hall as the new husband and bride climbed the ladder-like staircase to the loft where the family slept.

With so many people in the way, Hervor lost sight of Saeunn, and the broken contact brought her back to her senses. She couldn't attack Anfinna's beloved nurse, no matter what kind of evil look the old woman had just given her. Not when Anfinna was right there, and Storleik, and the entire family of Rognjeld besides.

But if Saeunn was responsible for this new torment, then Hervor vowed the hag would suffer for it.

2

THE FIRE WITHIN

In the days that followed, Hervor's dislike of Anfinna blossomed into near hate. The only thing that kept it from *being* hate was that Anfinna wasn't entirely to blame; the other bondsmaids were half the problem. They were the ones who kept pointing out that Anfinna's father Storleik had sworn his oaths to the Blessed King himself, and wasn't it wonderful to have such an important father, so rich and powerful, such a noble warrior – on and on, until Hervor wanted to scream.

Anfinna bore her share of the blame, though. Whether it was a desire to impress Gannveig or just the girl's native habit, Hervor didn't know and didn't care. All she knew was that

Anfinna made constant demands on the bondsmaids' time, so that they all had twice as much work to do as before. Of course, Hervor got the brunt of it, because she was stronger than the others and less well-liked, and she didn't fall down to lick Anfinna's embroidered slippers the way the rest did. So it was "Hervor, fetch this," and "Hervor, carry that" – when Anfinna bothered to remember her name at all, and didn't just call her "breech-born". Who'd spread the tale of Hervor's birth to her, Hervor dearly wanted to know.

Four days after her arrival at Rognjeld, Anfinna decided to set up her loom. Summer didn't last long here in the north, and her weaving was fine-work, not the homespun that could be made indoors, during the winter, in the poor light of the hall's fires. If she was to get anything done, she must start right away.

Isrun and the others who'd gained Anfinna's favour were given skeins of thread to carry, but Hervor, as usual, had to carry the pieces of the loom itself. She knew better than to complain; instead she picked up the heavy beams and amused herself by turning so the ends just barely missed clubbing Isrun in the stomach. Then she took them out of the snow-room, where they'd been stowed that first day, and into the sunny brightness of the garth.

Naturally Anfinna could not be expected to work too close by the stench of the pig-shed, nor the noise of the smithy. She could have chosen a spot for her loom before Hervor picked up the beams, but she hadn't, and Hervor bit back several short-tempered comments as she waited for the girl to settle on a location.

They found one at last, near the back end of the hall, but not so near as to subject Anfinna's delicate nose to the smell of the kitchens. Hervor put the beams down in relief and with Melbjorg's silent help began assembling them, smacking the wooden pegs into place with a small hammer. They went in faster when she imagined Anfinna's face on the ends.

That thought was a little *too* satisfying. As she gave the final peg one last whack, the head of the hammer flew off and rolled across the grass.

Titters followed her as she went to pick it up. "Stupid sow," said Hrodis, one of Isrun's cronies.

"She looks like one, doesn't she?" said Anfinna, and Hervor's hand clenched around the heavy iron lump as she picked it up and faced the others once more.

Isrun laughed, sounding like a horse with the wheeze. "That's because her mother was one!"

Fury boiled in Hervor's veins, and her fingers curled over the smooth surface of the hammer head. Its weight tempted her. One throw, and Isrun's face would be reduced to red pulp.

But a prickling on the back of her neck made her turn, and she saw Gannveig watching. The ever-present threat of outcasting couldn't make Hervor's fingers relax, but it kept the hammer in her hand.

"Not her mother," Gannveig said to Anfinna, coming closer with brisk, hard strides. "Her father's where the blame lies." She gave Hervor a look that did nothing to ease the anger tightening her muscles. "Blood will tell. Her mother was a bondsmaid who bedded a born thrall, the pig-keeper on my cousin's holding. You can see the result for yourself. There's nothing worse than mixing like that. Better to be an ordinary thrall-born child than a horror like she is."

"Sired by a *thrall?*" Anfinna said, flinching back in disgust. "I heard only that she was breech-born – and that was bad enough! At Kalstað, we would have put her outside the fence as a babe."

"She's strong," Gannveig said. Her bony fingers darted out and dug into Hervor's arm, and Hervor came within a hair of tearing free and smashing her hammer-weighted fist into Gannveig's face. "Trouble too, for sure, but we're thrifty. I bought her bond from my cousin, when he would have put her out to die. No sense wasting a strong body, no matter how rotten its core." She turned her cold eyes on Anfinna and smiled. "If you find her trying, beat her. She understands the lash as well as any animal."

Hervor's jaw creaked from holding in what she wanted to say. Her mother might have been so reviled no one even bothered to remember her name, but she was still kin. No one should have to stand by and hear their kin insulted.

Gannveig left then, heading off across the garth to shout at another group of women who weren't working fast enough. She was barely out of earshot when Isrun said, "A pig-keeper? A likely story. No, breech-born, I think your father was a pig!"

Isrun was lucky Hervor punched with the hand *not* holding the iron.

◆ ◆ ◆

Anfinna, it turned out, was too soft-hearted to have Hervor beaten. Instead Hervor was dragged inside and locked into one of the half-height rooms that lined the walls of the hall, sharing the space with various odds and ends that weren't needed often enough to be kept closer to hand.

Ordinarily Hervor wouldn't have minded. She might not have enough room to stand or stretch out her legs, but she got to rest, and that was rare in a life like hers. It was a lot better than a beating.

But this time she kicked and fought – silently, for fear she'd draw Gannveig's attention, but no less fiercely for that – so that it took six of them to stuff her inside and close the door.

She feared what would happen when they did.

The door cut off the light, a barrel scraped into place against it, and she heard the others moving off, chattering among themselves, leaving her alone in the dark.

Hervor waited, hands bunched into fists until the rough stubs of her nails dug into her palms.

Nothing.

The silence should have made her relax. But Hervor couldn't trust that it would last. The moment she began to believe she'd be left alone, they'd come. Just like she used to think the voices would never speak to her in the day.

And yet they were silent.

"Speak, damn you," Hervor snarled. "I know you're there. You're always fucking there. Speak!"

Still nothing.

Wild hope began to bloom in Hervor's chest, even as she tried to kill it. Maybe they wouldn't come. Maybe they weren't there. Maybe, if she just sat here quietly, and waited to be let out—

She flung herself bodily at the door before that thought was finished. With one fist she pounded the wood, even though she knew no one would come. "Let me out! Please, I have to get out of here…"

no one comes
no one hears
no one will ever let us out

She felt the choking weight of dirt pressing down on her, the cold of the grave chilling her flesh. Her hands bruised against the hard panels and she started shouting, sometimes at the voices, sometimes at anyone who could hear. "Shut up! Shut your gods-damned dead faces — I'm not trapped! I'm not like you! I'm not mad, I swear it, just let me out of here, don't keep me in here with them—"

here in the dark
with the dirt

and the worms
and the blood

The sudden flare of light blinded her. Hervor fell forward onto the boards of the hall's raised floor before she could catch herself. She landed face down, and it took her a moment to realise that someone had opened the door, that she was out of the closet.

She gasped in the sweet, light air of the hall before mustering the will to roll over and see who her saviour was.

The old woman's shrivelled face swam into focus.

Hervor stared. She remembered the thought she'd had the night of the feast, that Saeunn was somehow responsible for this new torment, and for a moment she thought about leaping up and strangling the old woman, bashing her head in, putting an end to it all right now, while no one was around to stop her.

She might have done it, too, if Saeunn hadn't spoken first.

"Noisy lot, aren't they?" she said in a voice that creaked like old wood. "Why don't we go sit down, you and I, and talk about making them stop."

Saeunn led Hervor down the hall and up the ladder to the loft. Hervor had never been up there before; serving the family in their private rooms was a privilege, one not likely to be given to a bondsmaid as ill-liked as her. The loft was divided into three rooms. In winter the family all slept in the central one, which shared a wall with the chimney from the bread-oven below; the heat from that kept them warm. The two side rooms were sleeping quarters in the summer, and work rooms all year round.

Saeunn picked up a stick as she entered the left-hand chamber and used it to lift a shutter in the sloping roof, so that a narrow shaft of light stabbed into the murky room. Hervor stood in it and breathed gratefully of the fresh air.

The old woman settled herself onto a low, padded stool in the shadows, outside the beam of light. "Now," she said in that creaky voice. "Don't think I'm doing anything out of charity, girl. I don't give a damn about the ghosts bothering you, so long as they stay with you. But they're bothering me, too. So we have to do something about that."

Hervor was tall enough that when she turned she almost cracked her head against a roof-beam. "I don't care why you're helping, old woman. Just tell me what to do."

Saeunn sucked on one of her remaining teeth for a moment, then asked, "Whose grave did you dig up?"

"Whose—" Hervor gaped. "No one's. I didn't dig up any graves."

"Don't lie to me, girl. Dead people don't talk without reason. You must have disturbed them."

"I haven't."

"If you're going to lie to me—"

"I'm *not*!" Hervor's voice was too loud in the small room. She made herself speak more softly, so as not to draw Gannveig or someone else up here. "I swear it. On Bolvereik's bloody sword. I was born breech; that draws spirits to you."

More sucking on teeth. Standing in the light, Hervor could barely see Saeunn in the darkness, but she refused to move into the shadows herself. She could feel the old woman watching her.

"Restless dead," Saeunn said at last. "Something's disturbed them, if not you."

"Who? What?"

The old woman shrugged, a barely perceptible motion in the murk. "How should I know?"

Hervor gritted her teeth. "You said you'd help."

"My knowledge only goes so far, girl. I can't make them talk to me; I'm only overhearing what they say to you, and not all of that. If you knew who they were, where they were buried, any of that – then, I maybe could help. But right now?" She laughed, a dry, rustling sound like dead leaves. "I might as well tell the wind not to blow."

As much as she wanted to hit the old woman and leave, Hervor made herself think it through. "So if I found out what you need to know—"

"I promise nothing."

But the alternative was worse than nothing. Just more days and more nights of haunting. The prospect hadn't always scared Hervor; when the voices had stayed in her dreams, she'd been able to manage. But unless someone helped her, they'd be in her waking thoughts, too, and she knew with cold certainty that they'd destroy her. She'd be mad in truth, then, and all her dreams of leaving Rognjeld and making a life worth living would be nothing more than dust.

"Tell me what to do," she told Saeunn, keeping her voice low so it wouldn't shake.

Saeunn shifted in the darkness, drawing her tattered shawl closer around her bony shoulders. "You've heard of drauðr."

Hervor's blood turned to ice. Now, more than ever, she didn't want to step out of the shaft of light. Drauðr was a word meant for dark winter nights, to be spoken in whispers if at all. A word heard in tales, and not tales of bold adventurers, either: tales of trolls, and barrow-ghosts, and ice-witches. She had to try twice before she could speak. "Foul magic."

"*Blood* magic." There were two faint glints in the shadows, the light reflecting off Saeunn's eyes. "Foul or fair is all in what you do with it. Drauðr will help you. It's *all* that can help you."

Hervor opened her mouth to say that she didn't know anybody who practised that kind of magic, then stopped. She was a fool.

Another glint. This time it was the old woman's teeth.

"But drauðr needs certain things to work," Saeunn went on, as if Hervor weren't trembling all over with the need to flee the room. "Blood, of course – but that comes later. First it needs to *know*. Names, certainly, and more than names if you can get it. Where the dead lie. The manner of their death. The more you know, the greater its strength."

The silence when Saeunn paused seemed to stop up Hervor's ears. Through the open shutter she could hear all the noises of a holding at work – the clang of the blacksmith, the grunting of pigs, the chatter of the bondsmaids – but it was distant, distant, as if all of that were happening in another world, a world of light. Saeunn sat in the shadows, and Hervor stood in between.

She focused very, very hard on those sounds, terrified of what she might hear if she listened for anything else.

"You'll have to listen," Saeunn said, as if she'd guessed Hervor's thoughts. "They're the only ones who can tell you what you need to know."

Hervor realised she was shaking her head, a tiny motion at first, then more violent. "No."

"Listen to them now, learn what you need to know – or you'll be listening to them forever."

"No."

"Then I won't help you."

Hervor backed up a step, then two, abandoning the light, leaving it as a razor-edged blade between her and the old woman. She couldn't stay there with this hag, this witch, who spoke in her calm, creaky voice of blood magic and listening to the dead.

"Think well before you choose," Saeunn said.

Hervor whirled, avoiding beams by luck more than anything else, and fled through the low door and down the ladder and out into the hall and the broad, sunlit garth.

❖ ❖ ❖

She was in the hills before she realised it, without quite knowing how she'd gotten there. She'd slipped through a small gate in the fence, but how she'd avoided everyone, kept from being stopped, she didn't know. It didn't matter. All that mattered was getting away from Saeunn and her talk of blood and ghosts.

Hervor moved more carefully now, keeping to the dips between the hills, avoiding the crests where she might be spotted. She wasn't sure where she was going; she'd rarely been outside the garth, for a bondsmaid's duties were of the hearth and hall, and not the wider world. Rannvar, for all that he was new, probably knew these hills like the back of his hand. But he wasn't here, and she couldn't go looking for him.

Instead she ran in a low crouch, looking in every direction to make sure no one saw her. Part of her tried to figure out which way the holding lay, but she wasn't sure whether that was so she could dodge searchers or find her way back. She'd fled the garth, and that wasn't an offence they'd easily forgive.

She could turn around, hope they didn't punish her too harshly. Or she could follow through on her bold vision of fleeing: run away, and try to build a life from nothing.

She'd told Rannvar she'd rather do that than stay, but she'd been drunk at the time. Out here, in the hills, all that talk of running off seemed decidedly less fine.

When she found a small stream she fell to her knees, gulping water gratefully. Once her thirst was sated, she sat back on her heels and looked around, thinking. She'd run west, which meant this might be the stream that fed Olvaið, the little pond where sometimes – in the days before Gannveig became quite so shrewish – they all went skating in the winter, and the men played ball on the ice. It was one of the few landmarks Hervor knew, aside from the dark smudge on the western horizon that was the far-distant Ice Knives.

But what good did that do her? A pond, and a distant range of mountains. Those didn't tell her where to go. Or what to do.

Listen to them, Saeunn had said.

"No," Hervor whispered. "You don't know what you're asking."

She wanted to free herself from the voices, yes. But what good would it do her to be rid of them, if the ridding broke her entirely? She couldn't do what Saeunn asked.

Who said the hag knew what she was talking about, anyway? Saeunn might just be senile, or delusional. There was no guarantee Anfinna's old nurse knew the first thing about blood magic.

Still, it raised possibilities. Drauðr might not be the only solution. Eyulf was old and doddering, and Hervor hadn't thought to speak to Storleik's priest before the wedding party left... but there were other priests in the world, more learned ones. If Hervor went to Hvarlond, where there were real temples, she might find someone who could put an end to the whispers. In a way that didn't involve risking her sanity.

It wasn't the grand adventure she'd boasted of to Rannvar, but it was a start. And once the voices were gone, she could get on with her real dreams.

She wasn't cowardly enough to pass this chance up, was she?

Hervor stood and brushed the mud off her knees as best she could. If this was the brook that fed Olvaið, all she had to do was follow it downstream to the pond. Then she could head south and find the main road, and sooner or later that would lead her to Hvarlond. Probably later, and Hervor spared a moment to wish she'd thought to steal food before fleeing Rognjeld. Well, she'd have to make do. She had good aim with a rock; maybe she could kill rabbits or something.

She began making her way downstream. The brook, though small, ran fast and strong, digging a deep enough channel that Hervor couldn't always walk alongside it. Since she might be seen atop the bank, she had to wade into the water. It was still ice-cold — even come high summer, it wouldn't warm much — and the stones at the bottom were treacherously slick, forcing her to pick her way along one careful step at a time, watching for anything that might cut her bare feet.

Because her eyes were on the water and the stones, not on the hills around her, Hervor didn't realise her danger until she heard the shout.

Then her head flew up, and the rocks shifted underfoot, and she fell into the water. Even from there, she could see the shadow on the hill: a man, silhouetted and distant enough that she couldn't tell who he was, but it didn't matter, because he'd seen *her*.

And now he'd be after her.

Hervor ran.

To hell with keeping track of her direction; she had to get away. She shot to her feet, scattering water everywhere, and flung herself at the bank. Her hands scrabbled for purchase in the stony soil and tough grass, and then she was at the top, running flat out, away from the man—

More shouts, off to her right. Other herdsmen.

She veered left like a spooked horse. Her feet pounded the hard soil like hammers, and she might be a bondsmaid and not that well-fed, but she was tall and strong and had the endurance of an ox, and she believed that she could, if not outrun them all, then gain enough of a lead to find somewhere to hide.

Then one heel landed in a rabbit hole, and her entire weight came crashing down on her twisted ankle.

Hervor didn't scream as she fell; she could be proud of that much. But she swore furiously through her teeth, and tears fell from her eyes to soak the dry earth, as much because of her failure as because of the pain. She heaved herself up anyway and tried to run on, but now she was moving slower than a lamed mule.

The men caught up to her a moment later, and dragged her back to Rognjeld.

This time they didn't lock her in a dark closet. In one corner of the garth there stood an upright post with a beam laid across its top, both pieces of wood as thick as a man's thigh. Hervor had been put to it more than once in the past, for offences that merited a harder beating than usual. Today they kept her tied up at its base until the day was nearly spent, so that everyone could gather to watch, bonders and freeborn alike. Feigald was going to make an example of her.

When the sun was touching the horizon, Berkel came and hauled her to her feet. Hervor almost bit through her lip; her twisted ankle had swollen hugely, and her legs had cramped from being huddled on the ground for so long. The freeholder had to drag her over to where Feigald waited.

"Have you anything to say for yourself?" Feigald asked when she stood before him. "We feed you and clothe you, give you shelter from the cold. You are not overworked, nor are you beaten when undeserving. You have a chance to earn your way free of your bond. But instead you decided to run."

Hervor clamped her jaw shut to keep from saying what she wanted to. Not overworked? Worked harder than the other bondsmaids. A chance to earn her freedom? Over Gannveig's dead body. She'd made the right choice in running. An outcast's life had to be better than this.

But saying so would gain her nothing. So she stayed silent.

"How did you get out of the closet?" Gannveig demanded, stepping forward to glare into Hervor's eyes. "You didn't break the door. What magic did you use?"

"Magic?" Hervor couldn't contain her snort. Saeunn was nearby, hovering just behind Anfinna's shoulder. The old woman wore her usual blank and absent expression, and the sham of it angered Hervor. "That crone over there let me out."

Anfinna's jaw dropped. Hervor wanted to tell her she looked like a dead fish. Then the girl flushed and protested, "Saeunn would never do such a thing!" She put one hand over her nurse's arm protectively.

Saeunn blinked and appeared to come back to her surroundings. "What? Something about me? No, no, I would never let that bondsmaid out. Great hulking thing, she is, terrorising my Anfinna. Mad, too, or so I've heard; breech-born, isn't she? No wonder she's imagining things."

The rush of blood pumping through Hervor's body eased the cramps in her legs enough for her to stand straighter. Were it not for Berkel's hands still on her shoulders, she would've jumped – all right, hobbled – over to the old woman and growled in her face. Mad? The hag knew damn well Hervor's ghosts were real. And denying her own part in this...

She met Saeunn's gaze across the intervening distance and saw, for the briefest of instants, a warning glint in the old woman's eyes: *Don't say anything.*

"Liar," Hervor spat. She wasn't going to let the shrivelled bitch get away with this. "You let me out of that closet. I'm mad? Yes, I hear voices. I always have. But if that makes me mad, then so are you, because you said you heard them too!"

Anfinna let out a dismayed cry, and Berkel's hands clamped down. That didn't stop her speaking, though. "You let me out because the voices were bothering you. And I only ran because of what you said to me about silencing them, because you told me you knew drauðr—"

The roar from the gathered crowd crashed into Hervor like a gale-force wind and carried her off with it. She was still there, screaming at Saeunn and struggling against Berkel's hold, but she couldn't tell any more what words were coming out of her mouth. Anfinna was screaming, too, but at Feigald and Gannveig, and meanwhile her hands fluttered like useless little birds around Saeunn's shoulders, and the old woman's glare could have poisoned Hervor on the spot.

But once the noise died down and people were paying attention, Saeunn showed nothing of the sort. She was the very soul of horrified offence, leaning into Anfinna as if she'd fall down without support, and that was the last image Hervor had of her before Berkel and one of the other freeholders spun her around and slammed her up against the beating post. Hervor fought, but someone else came and leaned against her back so the other two could tie her arms to the thick cross-beam.

When she was bound tight, Hervor twisted her head around in time to see Feigald approach. The jarl was breathing heavily.

"Bad enough you tried to escape," he said. Red mottled his neck and face, clashing with the strawberry blond of his beard. "You know the punishment for that's a beating. But what you've accused Anfinna's nurse of – you've insulted us all."

Hervor's mind belatedly pieced together the memory of what Anfinna had been saying. Ungaut's new wife, too soft-hearted to beat Hervor for punching Isrun, had been screaming for blood.

Ungaut himself appeared at his father's side, carrying something Hervor hadn't seen him leave to fetch. Feigald took it and gave Hervor a murderous look. "You've earned every stroke of this," he said, and gave the thing a shake.

A whip uncoiled to the dirt.

Hervor's gut twisted tight. She'd been beaten before, yes, everything from Gannveig's backhanded slaps to switches and rods – but never whipped.

As if they had minds of their own, her arms jerked against the ropes, but they got nowhere.

Feigald stepped back, out of her field of vision, and then somebody was yanking at the neck of her tattered overdress and shirt, ripping them until her back was laid bare.

"Twenty lashes," Feigald said, and the whip whistled through the air.

Hervor clenched her teeth and vowed not to scream, an instant before red agony exploded across her back.

One, she thought grimly, and her head throbbed where it had struck the wood.

Two, and her muscles ached from straining against her bonds.

Three, and a crimson haze crept over her vision.

Four, and suddenly the pain wasn't getting worse; in fact, that stroke hurt less than the last. Because a fire was burning inside her, burning against the pain, racing down her muscles and flooding her body until there wasn't room for anything else. Giving her strength.

As if from a great distance, she heard something crack and break.

Then there was nothing but the fire, and after the fire, darkness.

3

NAMING THE DEAD

Hervard, first to fall
blood on the sand, blood on the grass
Toki, cut down defending the dead
ravens scream above
steel bright in the sun

◆ ◆ ◆

"Stupid girl. You're your own worst enemy."

The fire was gone, replaced by pain, but the darkness remained.

"You'd better drink this. Though why I'm helping you, the gods alone know…"

A hand touched her and she cried out, but the hand's owner ignored the noise and gripped her hair, lifting her head up as the mouth of a waterskin forced its way between her lips. Liquid flooded her mouth and it was choke or swallow; she did a little of both. The drink was sharp-edged, metallic, carrying warmth as it went down her throat. Then the hand released her, her head struck the ground, and she almost retched up what she'd swallowed. There was a bruise on her head, or more than one; that pain blended with the pain elsewhere. Different flavours of pain, from dull throbbing to red-hot streaks of agony, but when all was said and done, the type didn't matter. She hurt more than she would have thought possible.

Why was it so dark?

"Who would've thought it of you? Makes me wonder if Gannveig's hiding something. If she knows more than she says. But she's not likely to tell me if I ask, and I won't. I've already found more trouble than I want, thanks to you."

Her eyes were closed. That explained a lot.

Hervor prised open her eyes. Or tried to: one obeyed, the other didn't. Still couldn't see anything, though that didn't stop new agony from stabbing through to the back of her skull. After a moment she realised it wasn't totally dark; pinpricks of light solidified in her vision.

Stars. It was night.

That explained more.

She rolled her head to one side, which was a mistake, as it proved there was more than one bruise. But her eyes were adjusting enough that she could see the silhouette next to her: someone crouching, and now standing, looming as if the figure were a god and she no more than mouse-sized, like that tale about the hero Holmdan and how he sneaked into Bolvereik's hall by riding in the god's pocket.

The figure stood for a moment as if studying her, then shook its head. "Tough as stone," it said, and Hervor had come to her senses enough to identify the voice as a woman's, although it creaked like old wood. "Which makes sense. You certainly *act* like your head's solid rock."

The woman turned to go. Moonlight fell on her face, and with a jolt, Hervor recognised Saeunn. She tried to sit up, to say something to the old woman, but the effort made her back scream; she collapsed and blacked out again.

◆ ◆ ◆

what magic is this?
each equal to six
slain as one
we fight but fall
hands heavy as lead
the wanderer's sword

steel bleeds in the sun
Bui's guts, ripped by ravens
they'll glut on us all

◆ ◆ ◆

The next time she woke, the light struck her like a hammer between the eyes. Hervor flinched instinctively, and that set off further pain all down her body, until she couldn't suppress a noise that she wanted to call a groan but was really more of a muffled shriek.

She lay as still as she could, waiting, until the pain levelled out and she had to accept that it wasn't going to get any better. Then she opened her eyes again – they both opened now – one careful bit at a time.

There were shackles on her wrists.

Her gaze rested on these for a long moment. She couldn't quite understand what they meant, not through the steady throbbing that had set up house in her skull where her brain used to be. But then her gaze travelled onwards, from the shackles to the chains, to a thick post, until the separate elements came together and she couldn't hide from the truth: she was chained to the post. *Chained* – not tied.

Part of her wanted to tug on the chains to make sure her eyes weren't tricking her, but her body rejected the very thought. An experimental twitch of a foot proved there were shackles around her ankles as well, and a quiet rattle told her those, too, came with chains. Whether her feet were fastened to each other, to the post, or both, she couldn't tell, and it didn't matter. She was well and truly bound.

Bound, and hurting all over, above and beyond the bone-deep weariness soaked into every corner of her body.

What in Slavinn and its seven sister hells had happened, and why didn't she remember any of it?

Hervor tried to think back, and ran up against the memory of the voices. They'd been in her sleep again, which was normal enough that she was almost grateful for it, except that there had been differences.

Names. For the first time ever, she'd heard names.

There had been more – something other than the voices. A woman. She'd dreamt of Saeunn, as well. Or not dreamt? It might have been real. Except that there had been something about help, and Saeunn had about as much reason to help Hervor as Hervor did to kiss Gannveig.

Something about Gannveig, too, but she couldn't remember what.

It was daytime now, with people up and about. No one on a holding stayed idle for long. Hervor looked past her bound limbs and saw familiar figures moving about. Not Gannveig, or Anfinna – or, for that matter, Saeunn – but bondsmaids, yes.

None of them came near her. Most were trying to behave as if the corner of the garth she was chained up in didn't exist.

Trying, and failing. Their careful determination not to look screamed of their inability to ignore her. Then Hrodis accidentally turned, and in that brief instant Hervor saw that the other woman wore an expression of complete and utter terror.

Given that Hrodis was looking at a bruised and bloodied bondsmaid who'd been chained to a post, it seemed odd. As if the chains held not Hervor, but a monstrous linnorm, or one of the twelve-foot-tall bears said to roam the Ice Knives.

Hrodis fled, and Hervor settled in to wait for answers.

Answers were a long time in coming. The day passed without anything happening other than two more bondsmaids accidentally looking Hervor's way and nearly pissing themselves in fear. No one came near, not even to bring food or water; by midday she was desperately thirsty. As the sun set, cooking smells drifted out of the kitchen, and Hervor's stomach began chewing on her backbone for lack of other fodder. The men returned to the garth, and they treated her just the way the women had, most not looking at her, and the few who did showing fear.

They herded the sheep back into their pens and vanished into the hall, and Hervor was alone in the garth.

She closed her eyes, trying to ignore her hunger and thirst. Thanks to the pounding in her head, she didn't hear the footsteps approaching. When Rannvar spoke, she jumped, setting off fresh stabs of pain all through her body.

"Hervor." The bondsman stood just out of reach, an uncertain look on his face. That was better than fear, but right now Hervor had less interest in his uncertainty than in what he held: a thick roll of bread in one hand, and in the other, a waterskin.

Thirst beat hunger by a league. She tried to demand the water, discovered her throat was too dry to work, and settled for holding her hands out pleadingly.

Rannvar hesitated, then tossed the skin down within her reach. He still didn't come closer.

Hervor was too busy gulping down water to care. In her haste, the liquid spilled over her chin and hands; she scrubbed at her skin with damp fingers, then poured more over her face, washing away some of the dust and blood caked there. Halfway through, hunger reasserted itself with a vengeance; Rannvar tossed her the roll the moment she glanced at it, then stood by as she wolfed it down.

When her stomach rebelled at the sudden arrival of food and drink, Hervor came up for air. She'd managed to achieve a sitting position; now she toyed briefly with the idea of standing, but her injuries argued against it. She settled for staring up at Rannvar with her best imitation of calm. "What in hell is going on? Why am I in chains?"

A strange expression passed over his face. "You can't have expected they'd let you walk free. Not after what happened yesterday."

"What *did* happen?" Hervor asked with what remained of her patience.

"You don't remember?"

"Whoever hit me over the head hit just a little too hard."

Rannvar was shaking his head, though, as if figuring something out just now. "No, it wasn't that. I'd forgotten that one of the... effects... could be forgetting. Especially the first time, they say."

"Effects of *what?*"

Again that wariness. Not the terror Hrodis had shown, but Rannvar was definitely afraid. "Hervor... you went berserk."

She thought he meant it as a saying until she turned to see what he was gesturing at. Behind her, in the corner of the garth, the whipping post was still visible in the fading light.

One arm of the cross-beam was gone. Only a splintered, jagged stump remained.

Hervor stared at what had been a piece of wood thicker than her thigh. *Berserk.* Not just angry; not just something people said in exaggeration. Genuinely berserk. Like someone out of a tale. Thanglif. Valfrik. Angantyr and his sons.

"It took seven men to bring you down," Rannvar said as she turned back to face him. He still hadn't come within her reach, and now she knew why. "You... Hervor, you killed Berkel. And almost killed Garlstein."

She gave her chains a disbelieving tug. The cold, hard iron resisted her easily, especially since her muscles felt like water. Hard to believe she'd really shattered wood, really killed a man

– except didn't they say berserkers suffered from terrible weakness after their fits?

"I slipped out to bring you food," Rannvar went on. "I need to go back before they realise I'm gone. But—" He hesitated, and even in the failing light Hervor could see the conflict in him, sadness and fear and reluctance and more. "They're trying to decide what to do with you. I think… they're going to kill you." That last came out in a rush, as if he'd had to force it.

The words hit Hervor like rocks, but she already hurt too much and was too tired to be surprised. "Last meal?" she asked, lifting the waterskin, the only visible remnant of what Rannvar had brought. She was a bondsmaid who'd killed a freeman: it didn't take a lawspeaker to know what the blood-price for that would be.

Rannvar hunched his shoulders. Standing like that, he looked stupid; he was too tall and too broad-shouldered to hunch well. But his unease was plain. "Gods, Hervor – I wish I could say it wasn't."

"Why'd you bring it?" Now Hervor forced herself to her feet. When Feigald and the others came for her, no doubt they'd come armed; they couldn't risk her going berserk again. This might be her last chance to stand on her own two feet and look someone in the eye. "Why the kindness, Rannvar? When you know they'll be furious if they find out?"

He stepped back, even though she hadn't moved. Did she frighten him that much? Hervor supposed it was understandable. How was he to know that it took every bit of willpower she had to stay upright? She was a berserker, with supernatural strength when a fit was upon her. And for all that Hervor wished she could say he was safe, that she would never hurt him... she didn't know if it was true. She'd never do it knowingly – but she remembered nothing of yesterday's fight. How much were her actions under her control?

Rannvar wouldn't meet her eyes, and he still hadn't spoken. Hervor said, "So you'll give me food and water, but not answers."

"What good can answers do?" Rannvar asked hopelessly. "They won't get you out of those chains, nor convince Feigald not to kill you."

"I'd rather stay in the chains and die than be let out to spend the rest of my life here."

He looked at her then, obviously not believing her. Hervor met his gaze steadily and prayed her knees wouldn't give out. She meant those words this time, with all of her heart – but collapsing wouldn't convince him of that.

"Well," he said, gaze falling again. "I brought you food and water because it was kind, and it's the last kindness anyone's likely to do for you. And nobody's been kind to you before now. You spend your time in the garth and I spend mine in the hills, but bondsmaids talk, and so do bondsmen, and so I hear things. About how you're treated, just because you were born the wrong way round. The things Gannveig and Isrun and the rest do to be cruel, to cut you down to their size. Then I look at you, and I see that nothing they've done, nothing they can do, will *ever* reduce you to what they are. You're a bondsmaid, with dirty hair and bare feet, but you walk around as if you're the equal of any freeborn here – or their better. Because you're not little and petty like they are. And when I see that, I wish you *were* free, and that I were, too, because then maybe there could be something between us." Rannvar's shoulders slumped again, until it seemed he was barely Hervor's height. "But we're not free. So the best I can do is be kind to you when no one else will."

For a heartbeat Hervor forgot about the welts streaking her back, the bruises on her head, the weakness in her knees. Because for the first time in her life, she knew beyond a doubt that someone saw her as more than an ill-omened madwoman, more than a strong back to use and then beat. Rannvar respected her… and it took her breath away.

Then her legs trembled from the effort of standing and her twisted ankle began to throb, and she stumbled back a step to the post that held her chains. She put out one hand to catch herself, hissing as the movement re-opened the cuts on her back.

That brought Rannvar's attention back to her, and she saw tears glimmering in his eyes, touched by the last of the light.

"Hervor—"

She raised her other hand to stop him. If he said anything more, it might undo her fragile calm. "Thank you," she said, her voice wobbling. "For the bread, and the water, and the kindness.

And for telling me what happened." She had to stop to breathe before she could go on, and she told herself it was because of the pain in her body. "Now go."

He didn't move.

"You said you slipped out, right? Go before they find out you're missing."

"Hervor—"

"Go," she snarled. He had to leave before she collapsed, or started crying. He respected her, and she wanted to preserve that.

"The waterskin."

She looked dumbly at the skin in her hand, then understood. He couldn't leave that here with her.

When she tossed it to him, he caught it deftly and left, after giving her one last look she refused to interpret.

Hervor waited until he was out of sight, back in the hall, before she let herself sink to the ground at the foot of the post and shake.

+ + +

weakness, slowness, freezing our limbs
Hrani, young and brave
young and DEAD
with the rest of us
Reifnir's dying words
upon the wanderer, a curse

the curse of the dead
he fell without us
we failed him...

✦ ✦ ✦

"They really don't leave you alone, do they?"

Hervor catapulted into consciousness and was on her feet before she knew it. The sudden action was too much; she staggered and grabbed hold of the post to stay upright, and only then did she see who'd spoken.

Saeunn watched all this with a sardonic eye.

The screams of the welts on Hervor's back were trying to escape past her teeth. She had to clamp her jaw to keep them inside and settle for glaring at Saeunn instead of speaking.

The old woman raised her eyebrows. "Such a look. Keep practising, and some day you'll drop a horse at twenty paces. But for now, stop glaring, and drink this." She held out a waterskin.

Hervor trusted gifts from Rannvar, but not from Saeunn. "What is it?"

"More of what I poured down your throat last night."

So it hadn't been a dream. "And what was that?"

"Something to help you. To restore your strength."

Hervor's knees were trembling already. She snorted. "Much good it's done me."

"If you'd swallowed more instead of spitting it out, it might have," Saeunn told her acidly. "Besides which, it *has* helped you. Otherwise you wouldn't even be on your feet now." She raised the waterskin further. "Come on. Take your medicine like a good little girl."

Hervor realised Saeunn was standing within the reach of her chains. Closer than Rannvar had come, even though the old woman had far more reason to fear her than Rannvar did. "Why help me?"

"Good question." Saeunn lowered her arm. "Maybe I shouldn't, since you're being an ungrateful wretch. How's that, eh? How about I just walk away?"

"Fine." Hervor let go of the post so she could cross her arms over her chest. Couldn't let Saeunn see how much she needed what was in that skin – if the old woman was even telling the truth.

Saeunn cackled. "I like your fire, girl. Maybe that's why I'm helping. Your knees are like a newborn lamb's and your head's pounding as if there's a team of smiths at work inside it, yet you stand there and call my bluff. I spend so much time with Anfinna – who's a dear, but hasn't got a single bone in her body, the little dolt – it's a treat to see someone with a spine." She bared her teeth in what might be a grin. "You've proven you're tough. Now lean on that post again and drink this, before I leave after all."

Hervor stood for a moment longer – so it would look like she was making a decision, not caving to weakness – then did as told.

When the thick, metallic liquid hit her stomach, it sent spikes through her body. Hervor gasped, though she couldn't have said whether the spikes were pain or not. Whatever they were, they raced through her muscles and gave them new strength, until she could stand straight without fear of collapsing. Even her sprained ankle and the lash marks on her back muted their screams.

"Better," Saeunn said approvingly. "Now we talk about your future."

"What future?" Hervor asked, when she'd caught her breath.

"The one you've still got, if you've mettle enough to take it."

"Feigald's going to kill me."

"He's thinking about it, yes. But he hasn't made up his mind yet, and when he does, I don't know what his decision will be. He and Gannveig have been going round and round the subject all day. Now, they don't let a doddering old nurse in on their talk, but I do hear things, and I can tell you this: they're more than a little afraid to kill you."

"Afraid?" Hervor blinked in confusion. "All they have to do is wait until I'm asleep, then bash my head in. Being a berserker won't protect me from that."

Saeunn shook her head. "That's not it, although I can't say what is. More like they're afraid to have you dead. Could be they fear a haunting – and with good cause, I'd say; you're a strong enough soul that I doubt you'd go to Slavinn quietly. But I suspect there's more to it."

"I can't imagine what."

"No more can I. But enough of that." Saeunn chopped one hand through the air in dismissal. "If you stay here they may well kill you, and even if they don't you'll be in a world of trouble. They can't trust you any more – if they ever did – not now that they know you're a berserker. So your choices are die, live out what's left of your life as a beast of burden... or escape."

The word made Hervor's heart leap in her chest. With the strength of Saeunn's mysterious drink in her, she discovered that her resignation at Rannvar's news of her oncoming death had been a fleeting thing, born of weariness and pain. "Get these chains off me, and I'll be gone before they hit the ground."

The old woman bared her teeth again. "Good, good. It may be I can help you on that count. But what then? What will you do? Where will you go?"

Hervor didn't have an answer for "where", but the "what" had become a lot clearer. "I'll get these fucking voices out of my head."

"Oh?" Saeunn feigned surprise. "You didn't seem so sure before."

"That was... before." Hervor touched one hand to her forehead, scraping away flakes of dried blood with her fingernails. "They've spoken to me again – well, you've heard them, I suppose."

"Not so clearly as before." Saeunn looked puzzled by the change. "The voices, yes, but not their words. I think they're paying more attention to you, speaking more directly. As if they have a better grasp on you now than they did."

Not a pleasant thought. But Hervor wouldn't let it slow her. "They've been saying different things. Still all the shite about ravens and blood and rotting, but now there's bits about how they died. Not much, but a little, and they've started using names."

"Names?" Saeunn's attention sharpened visibly. "Tell me."

Hervor hesitantly reached for the memories and found them waiting; for all that she'd been lost in dreams when the names came to her, they'd etched themselves into her mind. "Hervard. Toki. Bui. Hrani. Reifnir."

Saeunn shook her head. "Those mean nothing to me, I'm afraid. Is that the lot of them?"

we failed him…

Hervor shook her head. "There's at least one more. I don't know his name."

"It doesn't change much. You need other things before you can do anything with the knowledge." Saeunn drew her shawl more closely around her. It should have looked like a grandmother seeking warmth by the fire, but the movement was cold and sinister, as if she drew the shadows closer. "Learn more: not just the final name but who they were, where they're buried. Or not buried, if that's why they're unquiet. Once you have that, take what you've learned to someone who knows of such things. She'll tell you what to do."

"Her?" For all that Hervor still didn't trust Saeunn, she preferred the old woman to some stranger. "Why can't you tell me, right now?"

The old woman's eyes glittered like ice. "Because there's no one right path to walk through drauðr, and if I put you on the wrong one we may both fall to its power. I can't guide you without more information, and you can't stay here until you've collected it. You'll have to look elsewhere for aid." She gave a quiet cackle. "It'll be easier than you think. For all that drauðr is a secret thing, spoken of only in whispers, there's more who know it than anyone likes to admit."

Saeunn might well be right. Hervor knew nothing of the world beyond Rognjeld's fence, except what she'd heard in gossip; she'd come to the holding much too young to remember anything beyond what she heard people say. She would have to find her way as she went. "Get me out of these chains, then," she said, lifting her bound wrists.

"Wait here."

Saeunn vanished into the darkness before Hervor could point out that she had no choice *but* to wait. That, and search the impenetrable blackness of the garth with her eyes and ears, so she'd have a little warning if anyone came for her. Only once did she risk a quick glance up at the sky, where she saw that thick clouds had covered the moon. All the better for fleeing.

"Here we are." Saeunn's creaky voice made Hervor jump; in the shadows, it sounded like it belonged to nothing human.

The old woman made her slow way forward, two things in her hands. One proved to be a set of keys. "Where did you get those?" Hervor asked as the old woman fit one into the lock on her wrist shackles. "Those can't be Anfinna's; she wouldn't have one for the chains. If Feigald or whoever finds out you took them—"

"Such a lot of worrying you do. They sleep, never fear, and shall not wake." The chains rattled loose, and Hervor took the keys from Saeunn, then knelt to free her feet. When she rose again, she found that the old woman's second gift was a bowl filled with a liquid as black as the night.

This time Hervor was sure Saeunn's smile was more a baring of teeth than a grin. "We can't have them following you, of course. So I give you this: a bit of real drauðr, just like in a tale."

Not flinching from the bowl took an effort of will. "What's that stuff?"

"Blood. It's always blood. Why do you think they call it blood magic?" Saeunn dipped her fingers into the dark fluid.

Hervor jerked away as the old woman reached for her face. "What will it do to me?"

"Conceal you from watching eyes. You won't be invisible, whatever the tales may say. If anyone could create real invisibility, it was the alfar and them alone, and those creatures are long gone. But it will do well enough, while it lasts; any who look your way will pay no heed and won't remember you when you're gone, and your feet will leave no sign of your passage. Don't push its power, though: if you walk into a man's house and start throwing his belongings around the room, he *will* notice you, and remember you, too. But if you're subtle, it will work. Only take care not to wash it off – the spell will last only while the blood is on your skin."

Holding herself rigid, Hervor submitted to the old woman's touch. Whatever animal had donated the blood had been dead for some time; the fluid was congealed and cold, and it made her skin crawl. Or maybe that was Saeunn's voice, creaking words that Hervor couldn't make out and didn't want to. The old woman murmured as she dabbed sticky smears of blood on Hervor's cheekbones and forehead. Rune-staves of some kind, but Hervor wasn't about to steal Anfinna's mirror to find out what they looked like.

Then Saeunn was done. By the way her eyes stayed on Hervor as she stepped back, it seemed she could see through her own magic. Hopefully no one else could.

"Go, then," the witch said softly. "Go and find the dead."

4

UNSEEN

The night was darker than a witch's heart, and as Hervor ran, head down, lungs burning, stumbling and rising and running some more, she began to think the sun would never rise. She'd left the living world behind and was running through Slavinn, damned to an eternity of terrified flight.

But finally the first rays of light lanced across the sky, proving that the paling horizon wasn't just wishful thinking, and she thudded to a gasping, exhausted halt.

Hervor had no idea how far she'd come. Not as far as she would have liked… but she could have run clear off the edge of the world and it wouldn't have been far enough. No amount of running could leave behind the blood painted on her forehead, or the crew of dead men in her mind. Or the man she'd killed, and the berserker rage that still lurked somewhere inside her, waiting for its chance to break free.

Running could, however, make her hungry enough to eat an entire horse. Hervor bent over, bracing her hands on her knees as she caught her breath. She needed shelter, and she needed food. Unfortunately, she had no more idea how to find either than she did how to find a pot of gold. If she followed the road—

Road?

Hervor straightened and looked around. She'd stopped in a dip between two hillocks, and couldn't see anything from here. Driving her aching legs back into motion, she climbed to the crest ahead of her.

Nothing to be seen except more little hillocks, lots of grass and, in the near distance, the diamond twinkle of a stream.

Surely she'd gone far enough to hit the high road near Rognjeld. Had she passed it in the night? Not a chance; people claimed it was paved with huge blocks of stone put there by giants. Even in the darkness, Hervor would've noticed crossing that barefoot.

Then her gaze shot back the way she'd come, and then to the sun, and she dropped onto the grass and swore.

She'd meant to run south-west. She'd thought she *was* running south-west. But when the sun came up, she was headed due east.

She'd spent the whole night going in the wrong fucking direction.

Hervor sat in the grass, developing new curses. Once those ran dry, though, she had no choice but think. She closed her eyes and tried to scrape together the details she'd heard over the years, about what lay outside Rognjeld's fence. If she went far enough east, she'd hit the coast. Which gave her something to aim for – except she didn't know how far away the sea was, nor what lay between her and it. There might be towns. There might be farmland. There might be ancient forests haunted by linnorms and bears and the walking dead.

Probably not that last. She'd have heard tales, if such a forest were there.

Still, that wasn't much comfort. To the south, on the other hand, she *knew* there was Hvarlond, and in Hvarlond there were people. Priests, even. She'd thought before about asking someone for help. Saeunn had told her what she needed was a witch, not a priest... but maybe Hvarlond had witches, too.

A witch wouldn't do her any good yet, though. Not until she knew more about her ghosts. Besides, for all that they haunted her sleep and her waking days, the ghosts weren't even her immediate problem. Feigald was. It was dawn; by now someone would have noticed she was gone from her chains. If things had been different, it was just barely possible that Feigald would have let her go; surely chasing a berserker bondsmaid wouldn't be worth the risk. But she'd killed Berkel, and the murder of a freeholder couldn't go unpunished.

Hervor opened her eyes and bit her lip in indecision. Not

back west. That would bring her too close to Rognjeld. North would take her into less and less populated areas until it got to giants or land so cold she'd freeze to death. That left her with south or east. Hvarlond – assuming she could find it from here – or the gods alone knew what.

She wanted to go to Hvarlond. She didn't know what lay to the east; the sea could be three days' journey away, or three hundred. East was unmarked territory. The great unknown.

East scared her.

Hervor clenched one hand and slammed it against the dirt. This was fucking ridiculous. How could she be scared? After all her dreams, the things she'd told Rannvar—

But those were dreams. Not the reality she faced now.

She was alone, and barefoot, and starving, with nothing to help her but a witch's dubious spell. This wasn't how it was supposed to go. She should have a horse and a sword, or at the very least some boots. This wasn't adventure; this was misery.

But it was all she had to work with. And she sure as hell didn't want to go back to Rognjeld. So that meant staying away from the road, no matter how comforting it would be to have something to follow.

"Stop snivelling and get to it," Hervor said, shoving herself to her feet, and started limping east.

She awoke in the late afternoon at the edge of a small stream. She hadn't meant to fall asleep there; after scrounging up a few reeds whose roots were safe to eat, she'd filled her complaining belly with water, while planning how to find shelter. Seemed her body had other ideas, though. Hervor stretched where she lay in the dirt and was startled to find that she didn't hurt much at all. What had been in that drink of Saeunn's? She felt her back as best she could and found that the lash marks, for all they weren't even two days old, were thoroughly scabbed over and healing.

The self-examination reminded her that her clothes had been torn from her back. Even if the rune-staves Saeunn had painted on her worked, they wouldn't last forever, and a bondsmaid in a torn dress would be a memorable sight. Someone might guess that she'd run away. So in addition to food and shelter, she needed new clothes.

She'd eaten all the edible reeds that morning. Hervor drank more water and told her belly to quit its grunching. Water was useful in more ways than one; if she followed this stream – and it ran more or less east – then she might find people. People with food.

She began making her way downstream, hissing curses as her feet joined the general complaint. A night of running had left them feeling like pounded meat, and her ankle still throbbed faintly, though not so much as it should have. But she found some more reeds as she went, albeit few enough that they only served to remind her how hungry she was.

Nightfall came without her finding any sign of human habitation. Hervor climbed to the top of a bank for the tenth time and looked about, hoping to see the telltale glow of a fire in the darkness. But there was nothing, and she was tired enough that she couldn't face the thought of walking further. She slid down the bank, hoping that would protect her from the night wind, and huddled in on herself until she fell asleep.

Hunger woke her before dawn. Her stomach was screaming bloody murder; water was a poor substitute for food. She was more than half-tempted to eat some grass. It probably wouldn't poison her – after all, sheep liked it fine – and while it might taste awful, at least it would give her stomach something other than her spine to chew on. She couldn't quite bring herself to do it, though.

Not yet, anyway. Given another day without real food, she might well change her mind.

Hervor forced herself to her feet and slogged on.

By midday she was trudging along in a daze, her mind not on anything besides putting one foot in front of the other. She only stopped because something other than dirt, grass, rocks, water, or her own feet appeared in her field of vision.

A bucket.

She jolted back to awareness with a thud. A bucket! Those didn't usually wander off on their own. Hervor looked around and found the bank was quite low here; to her left she could see a fence, and above it the steeply peaked roof of a longhouse, a curl of smoke rising from its chimney.

Standing in plain sight made her uneasy, despite the supposed protection of the rune-staves. Further on, though, the bank rose more sharply. Hervor hid behind that and peered over the edge at the farm.

The main gate in the fence faced more or less in her direction, and it stood open, giving her a clear line of sight into the garth. Bondsmaids moved about inside, busy at their familiar tasks; one holding was much like another, Hervor supposed. This might even be Garlstein's place. It was certainly smaller than Rognjeld, and close enough to be beholden to Feigald.

But who it belonged to mattered much less than what she could get from it.

Hervor slid down behind the bank to think. Saeunn had told her not to push the limits of the spell. That made her inclined to go in at night – but then she'd have to deal with the fence. She held up one hand and grimaced as her arm shook. She could hardly climb the fence in this condition. Besides, the wind was carrying the scent of baking bread to her, and it might take more willpower than she had to wait—

A sudden whoop sent her jumping nearly out of her skin.

Someone came bounding down the low, gentle slope to her right and took a flying leap through the air. His landing in the water sent a tremendous splash everywhere, barely missing Hervor, and she froze in absolute, paralysed horror.

"Garldor! You almost got me soaked!"

A young woman stood on the bank, stripping off her overdress and folding it neatly atop a flat stone nearby. Scattered around her were other bits of clothing, presumably shed by

Garldor, who certainly didn't have any left on him as he lay back in the water. It was deeper here than Hervor had thought, deep enough to swim in, as these two were clearly intending to do. Which left her with no chance to run. They hadn't seen her yet, but she was right there against the higher rise of the bank, out in plain sight. Spell or no spell, she was too obvious to miss.

When the young woman was naked, Garldor held out his hands, and she went to him willingly, yelping at the chill shock of the water. Hervor squeezed her eyes shut and tried to think—

"Look out! It's Feigald's berserker bondsmaid!"

Her heart stopped dead, and in that sick, frozen instant, Hervor wondered what would happen when men came to take her prisoner. Whether she'd go berserk again. How many she would kill. But her eyes flew open and she saw that Garldor and his girl weren't even looking at her.

The young woman exclaimed in annoyance and smacked one hand against Garldor's chest. "You beastly thing, you scared me half to death!"

He laughed and tickled her, and Hervor stared at them without breathing as she tried to convince her heart to start beating again. He hadn't seen her. Even the blind god Valnarath would have seen her. But he hadn't; he'd turned directly toward her now, and his eyes swept over her as if she were so much grass. He'd just been trying to scare the girl.

So the rune-staves really worked. Hervor might even be able to move without Garldor or that silly teg noticing her, but better not to try. Though she didn't want to sit there and watch them feel each other up in the stream, it was a damn sight better than being captured.

"Garldor, do you truly think she'd come here?"

This was delivered in a small, timid voice, and it gave Hervor a tremendous desire to leap up and scare the living shite out of the girl. Probably stop her heart on the spot. The voice worked perfectly on Garldor, though, who cradled her close. "Oh, I doubt it. She's gone south to Hvarlond, or else to the Ice Knives, where she can run wild. But even if she does, I'll protect you."

"But what those men said – what happened to Berkel's poor body, after she—"

"She's no more than a beast, dear," Garldor said. "And we'll shoot her down like one, if she comes anywhere near here. Even berserkers die, when you fill them with enough arrows."

There was more, delivered in a lower voice, but Hervor didn't bother listening. She was too busy feeling sick over what the girl had said. Rannvar had told her she'd killed Berkel, but nothing more. What had she done to his body?

What kind of animal had she *become*?

Then her stomach growled, reminding her to take one thing at a time. Hervor looked away from the couple in the water, who were getting very friendly with each other, and eyed the clothing they'd left behind. Pity the girl was such a stupidly small thing. If Hervor tried to put on her dress, she'd rip the shoulders out.

But Garldor's clothing...

Hervor looked back at the young man and tried to gauge his size, what she could see of him past the twining embrace of the girl. Not a runt, at least. And dressing like a man was one way to disguise herself.

By now Garldor and his little toy were so busy with each other, they wouldn't have noticed Hervor even without the spell. Still, it took an effort of will to convince her body to creep forward. She gathered up the breeches and shirt, keeping one eye on the pair in the stream.

While she was trying to decide whether to change now or run first, a gust of wind brought the scent of bread to her again.

Her stomach abruptly had the reins, and Hervor was just the horse. Never mind how stupid this was; she went anyway. Across the grass, with Garldor's stolen clothing tucked tight under one arm, first at a hesitant walk, then at a run like a scared rabbit, until she was pressed against the outside of the fence. After a quick glance inside she bolted through the gate, looking for somewhere to hide – there, the pig-shed, and the bars creaked as she slid herself through the fence around the pen, but she dove into the darkness of the shed and hoped no one had heard.

There was a girl in the shed, not more than ten years of age, mucking out one corner. But she hummed tunelessly to herself and showed no sign of noticing Hervor.

Hervor let out the breath she hadn't realised she was holding, and tried to plan her next move.

For all that this was terrifying – part of her refused to believe the spell was actually working, or would go on doing so – her heart had quickened as much from exhilaration as fear. She could do anything. Well, not *anything*; Saeunn had warned her. But no more would she have to starve and live off stream-side reeds.

That bread, wherever it was, was *hers*.

Hervor slipped out of the shed again and began to flit through the garth. She found a basket of turnips near the hall and pinched a good half-dozen, stuffing them into the bundle of clothing before moving on. The bread was laid on a table to cool behind the hall; through the kitchen door, Hervor could see women moving about, putting more loaves into the oven. She grabbed one for herself, burning her fingers on their piping-hot crusts; then hunger reared up again and she scooped several more into her arms, even shoved one into her mouth. She was chewing even as she bolted out of the garth, laughing all the way.

Hervor made it a little distance from Garlstein's holding before the last of her self-control broke. Then she sat down on the stream's bank and began stuffing food into her mouth as fast as she could. A loaf of bread was gone instantly, and an entire raw turnip. She gulped water between bites, and then, feeling more sated than she'd been since the wedding feast – and hoping she wasn't going to spew everything back up – she surveyed her haul.

Garldor's clothing was a little big on her, but it would do. Hervor found a flint near the water and beat at it with another rock until she broke off a sharp edge, then used it to cut her old clothing into pieces. Most of it became a bundle for carrying the rest of her stolen food, but some she wrapped around her feet to protect them from rocks, and one band she used to bind her breasts as flat as they would go. Which was pretty flat; with Garldor's loose shirt on, she could fool the casual eye.

Not with her long braids, though. Hervor was surprisingly reluctant to touch them, even though she knew they had to go. They were one of the few things she'd ever been proud of; she might be a bondsmaid sired by a thrall and born breech besides, but her thick, white-blonde hair was the envy of many a freeborn girl – or would be, if they'd ever admit it. She hated to lose her braids. But in the end necessity won out, and so she took the sharp stone and hacked at them until they came free, leaving her with a man's ragged shoulder-length mane.

In fact, now that she was wearing the clothing of a freeholder...

Hervor stripped again and waded into the stream. She had no soap and no sand, but she scraped at the worst of the dirt with her fingernails and soaked her hair thoroughly, only at the last minute remembering to keep her face dry, so Saeunn's rune-staves wouldn't be washed away.

When she came out of the water she was almost clean, aside from the blood-painted markings. She lay in the last of the sunlight until she was dry, then dressed again and picked up her bundle. Someone had probably noticed the missing food, and she'd tested the spell as much as she wanted to today. It was time to move on.

5

HERVARD

The stream continued to guide her as she travelled. Eventually it brought her to another holding further on, one far enough from Rognjeld that Hervor didn't know if it belonged to one of Feigald's men or not. This time, nervous that the rune-staves might have worn away enough to lose strength, she waited until nightfall and climbed the fence. Two days after that the stream joined a larger river, with a fairly large holding nestled in the fork; this place was much busier, and getting food there tested Hervor's nerve to the limit. But it seemed the spell was still working, and she slipped away without trouble.

The river descended through a rocky set of hills, then plunged into a thick forest. By now Hervor was confident enough in herself that she almost hoped there'd be linnorms or something equally interesting. But she found nothing more exciting than a broad lake, though in skirting its shore she came across a lone fisherman from whom she stole two trout. She also stole a knife when he left it unattended, and hid in the bushes to listen to him swear at the alfar he thought responsible for its disappearance. Then she went a safe distance away and used the knife to gut the fish and strike sparks until she had a fire going, and for the first time since being locked in that damnable closet she had a proper hot meal. The sheer, greedy pleasure of eating the trout put her in a daze.

But it wasn't all sunshine and stolen fish. Not long after she broke free of the forest once more, it began to rain. Hervor trudged on, reduced to wet bread and what she could scrape from the land – more here than around Rognjeld, fortunately – and invented more new swear words.

Until she reached the coast.

The rain had stopped up her nose and so she didn't smell it until she was almost there: the tang of sea air, heavy with salt, which before she'd only known from the muted scent of the salt they used to preserve fish and meat back at Rognjeld. Hervor followed her faithful guide, the river, until it emptied itself into the sea, and there she stood on the beach, heedless of the rain, hardly able to believe the sight. She'd done it. A minor adventure, maybe, hardly enough to interest even the most desperate of storytellers, but to her it was a victory. She, a mere bondsmaid, had escaped from captivity and made her way across the land to the sea.

Hervor threw back the wet tendrils of her cropped hair and crowed in victory.

But the grey sky was dimming with sunset and the damp wind carried a sting. The rain showed no sign of abating. Hervor imagined spending the night with nothing but wet sand to protect her and shuddered. There had to be something better.

She squinted in the fading light and saw, through the misty air, a shadow to the north. Since there was nothing to the south, she headed for the shadow, slogging through the sand. The shadow proved to be a bluff, rising above the narrowed beach, and Hervor eyed it dubiously. Not much help. But there might be a crevice she could shelter in, something between her and the wind.

The bluff blocked what was left of the light, so Hervor made her way along in grey darkness, feeling spray from the waves lashing her skin. If this failed, she'd have to go around the back edge of the bluff and hope that would afford at least a little protection from the sea. If she'd known the coast was this unpleasant, she might have gone in a different direction.

But there was indeed a crevice. Hervor squeezed herself into it, hoping that it widened; otherwise, she'd have to sleep standing up.

It did more than widen. The crevice turned out to be the entrance to a cave. Hervor stood at its mouth for a moment, staring in disbelieving relief. The place was as large as a hut, and a break in its roof allowed in the faintest trickle of grey light. Enough to let her make out the pile of wood laid along one side wall. Even a firepit, carefully positioned to avoid the rain.

This had to be the haunt of local fishermen, but Hervor didn't give a damn. The firewood would have decided her, even if the simple fact of shelter hadn't. She fumbled out her stolen knife and, as the last hints of light faded, struck sparks from a flint to light the fire.

Once it caught properly, the cheerful yellow glow made Hervor smile in pure satisfaction. Not so bad, was this? Throw a problem at her, she'd find a way to fix it. She had light and warmth, and her food might be down to one last heel of bread, but that was all right. She'd sleep soundly, tucked away in here, and in the morning she'd see what her next steps should be.

◆　◆　◆

the cold of the grave
cries in the dark
where we lie betrayed
BLOOD
the end of blood
swift death, slow decay
worms alone for company
the ravens gorged
alone in the dark with the worms and the cold and the shame

✦ ✦ ✦

Hervor woke gasping. Her heart was trying to leap out of her mouth, and so were the meagre contents of her stomach; she clapped one hand over her lips to keep herself from retching. Fucking Valnarath – she'd honestly forgotten about the gods-damned ghosts. They hadn't spoken to her since Rognjeld! The silence should have been strange, but she hadn't even noticed it, too wrapped up in staying fed, staying free, to wonder why they hadn't said anything. Now they were back, and worse. She could *smell* the blood, the rotting flesh, the cold damp earth of the grave. Not just voices, any more.

Her gorge subsided at last, and she lay on her back beside the smouldering embers of the fire, opening her mouth to curse.

Voices stopped her.

For one terrified instant she thought they were *her* voices, the voices of the dead. She couldn't take that again, not now. But no, these came from outside the cave.

Torchlight flickered in the crevice.

Hervor scuttled backwards instinctively, stopping only when her shoulders smacked against the stone. Stay calm, she told herself. Judging by the near-darkness in the cave, it wasn't dawn yet, but the rain seemed to have stopped; she would take her chances outside. Once whoever was coming in got out of the way.

A man stepped into the cave, torch in hand. Hervor squinted against the sudden light, trying to stay perfectly still.

"Who the fuck are you?"

It had been so long since anyone had spoken to Hervor that she assumed the man was like Garldor, talking to someone else nearby. But as her eyes adjusted, she found that the man was looking directly at her – and now he had a sword in his hand.

Fuck.

Too late, *far* too late, Hervor thought of what the rain must have done to the blood that had protected her for so long.

More men pushed into the cave, all of them armed. Twelve already, maybe more, in boiled leather and even some chain mail. These were no fishermen. Then the first one came closer, drawing Hervor's gaze to him. His cheekbones were strongly carved, and the light of the torch made his hair and beard look like flame.

Hervor opened her mouth to say something, and came up with absolutely nothing of use.

"What are you doing in my cave?" he demanded.

She put her hands against the damp stone and hoped it wasn't too obvious that she had to push herself to her feet. Better to face him standing. Not that it would do much good against a sword. The man was taller than her, Rannvar's height, but a damn sight more dangerous than the bondsman. He radiated violence.

Hervor licked her lips nervously, then went for boldness. "Your cave? I didn't see your name anywhere on it."

That got a laugh from the other men, but not a friendly one. The one with the torch smiled at her, like a wolf baring its teeth. "I'm Enjarik, and these are my men, and this cave's mine because I say it is. Now why don't you answer *my* questions, like a good lad? What's your name, and what are you doing here?"

Lad? Bolvereik's blood. She'd forgotten about Garldor's stolen clothing. Hervor floundered for a male name and blurted the first thing that came to mind. "Hervard."

The instant it left her mouth, she shivered. She tried to convince herself she'd chosen the name simply because of its resemblance to her own, and failed. Now she was naming herself after a ghost. How much more would they seep into her life?

Enjarik raised a sardonic eyebrow. "Still waiting for my other answer. I know you can manage more than one word at a time. Speak, before I lose my patience."

And then the bottom dropped out of Hervor's stomach, because she looked at Enjarik, and looked at his men, and suddenly she realised she'd heard of this man. Enjarik Enjakilsson. A viking, a raider, infamous enough that his name was known even at Rognjeld, far inland where no longship could reach.

The tall raider scowled at her, then turned to face his men. That put his back to her, but Hervor knew he had nothing to fear, and knew that *he* knew it, too. Her stolen knife was still lying on the ground by the fire, and this man killed for a living.

"I think we have a problem," he said to his men.

One of them spat. "What problem? Slit his throat and chuck him in the sea. Problem solved." Murmurs of agreement came from the others.

Enjarik turned back to Hervor and smiled that wolf-smile again. "Well, there you have it. We can't let you go running off to tell someone we're anchored here. So that doesn't leave us much choice."

"You've got a choice," Hervor said desperately, trying to pitch her voice low, like a man's. An idea came to her, and she found herself speaking it before she could question whether it was a *good* idea. "You're Enjarik Enjakilsson, right? I came here looking for you. I… I want to be one of your men."

Silence in the cave, except for the faint sound of the torch flame.

Enjarik's smile sharpened, showing teeth. "You want to join me, Hervard? Want to be a viking, do you?"

Hervor nodded, not trusting her voice. Fuck. This was the worst idea she'd had since publicly accusing Saeunn of blood magic.

He tossed his torch to one of the other men, then spread his arms, sword still in one hand. "Pick, then."

"Pick?"

"Sword, axe, knife, or fist? Raiders have to be able to fight. Let's see how you do."

Hervor had never used a knife for anything other than household tasks, and she'd never used a sword at all; few people could even afford one. But she'd been in more than her share of fistfights. "Bare hands."

Enjarik resheathed his sword with a movement as easy as breathing and unbuckled it from around his waist. Another man came forward to take it, and then Enjarik said, "Let's see what you're made of."

It felt like there was a rock in Hervor's throat. She didn't want to step into the open space the men had made; she wanted to melt into the stone at her back. She tried to goad herself forward by calling herself a coward, but that did no good. This wasn't cowardice; it was common sense. Enjarik was huge. He could pound her into mash without trying.

Then Hervor realised the true danger.

Pain had sent her berserk before, and she was willing to bet it could do so again. If Enjarik hit her – and he would – no, no, she *couldn't* go berserk, not now. They'd kill her. Enjarik himself would run her through, if she turned into a real threat.

She'd be killed if she didn't fight, and she'd be killed if she went berserk. Hervor didn't know how to get out of this alive. Except to fight, and hope she could keep herself under control.

Enjarik waited, relaxed, half smiling. Hervor put her hands up to guard her face and approached, warily. Keep calm. Had to keep calm. Had to—

The viking melted out of the path of her first punch and delivered a ringing slap to the side of her head.

Hervor staggered away, caught her balance. One of the raiders was laughing quietly. She moved in again, and again Enjarik just vanished; this time he tripped her so she went sprawling to the hard ground. She got to her feet with a snarl – but the fire building in her was frustration and embarrassment, not berserker fury, and it did no good. Enjarik slipped aside each time she hurled herself at him, and the most humiliating part of it was, he didn't really hurt her. She wasn't even worth that kind of effort. He could have taken her apart in three moves, but he settled for making her look like a fool.

Then Hervor saw an opening, and she threw her entire weight behind her fist.

Enjarik's head snapped back at the impact. He leapt out of her reach, and Hervor stood where she was, panting for air, staring in shock.

She'd actually hit him. A solid blow, too; Hervor's entire hand hurt. Enjarik rolled his head around, cracking his neck loudly, then spat into the sand. "Enough of this."

No point asking whether she'd passed. She hadn't.

"You don't know the first thing about fighting," Enjarik said bluntly. "Why don't we have some truth from you?"

Hervor's voice cracked on the word. "Truth?"

"You've been lying since I came in here. You're not a fighter. You're not even a man."

For a moment she tried to believe he meant she was a boy, an untried youth. The look in his eyes stopped her. This man wasn't just a raider, ignorant of anything but how to sail and swing a sword; he had a sharp mind. And he knew she was female.

Her hands were still up in a sad imitation of a proper guard; now Hervor let them fall to her sides. They wouldn't protect her from anything. "I didn't know you used this cave. I found it just before nightfall, and it was raining, so I came inside for shelter."

"And?"

She managed to find enough boldness to glare at him. "And nothing. My business is my own. Especially since you're going to kill me anyway."

Enjarik laughed. It made Hervor want to hit him again. "Oh, I think we can pass on that. You're hardly a threat – half-starved, barely full-grown, for all you're so big. We'll keep you tied up tonight, let you go tomorrow; by the time you make it anywhere to warn anybody, we'll be long gone."

Hervor didn't want to be killed. But she was surprised to find that she felt disappointed, too. That made no sense.

Except that it did, once she stopped to think. She'd left Rognjeld, the only place in the world where she had a place. A shitty place, but at least she'd *had* one. Now she was on her own. No money, no kin, no possessions except a stolen knife. What was she going to do – sell herself back into bondage? No respectable people would take in a wandering, penniless stranger like her. Which meant she either stayed on her own, or…

"I still want to come with you."

Enjarik stared at her in surprise. Hervor would have stared at herself if she could. The words had popped out as if of their own will.

"What would you *do?*" one of the other men asked. She turned towards the cave entrance and, for the first time, really looked at them. There were at least twenty now, all with axes or spears, and several were grinning in a way she could interpret all too easily.

"I won't whore," she said coldly. "And I once ripped the balls off a man who tried to make me." She hadn't actually ripped them *off*, but it sounded better that way. Hervor looked back at Enjarik; he was the one she had to convince. "I'm strong, though. I can… I can do whatever needs doing. Cook. Take care of your armour." Better not to mention weapons; she didn't want them thinking she might stab them in their sleep. Hervor had no real idea what sort of menial work there was to be done on a ship, but there had to be some. There was always menial work.

If respectable people wouldn't take her in, then she'd just have to find a place with people who weren't respectable.

Enjarik's eyebrows rose again. She couldn't read anything off him other than mild surprise, though, and even that might be a sham. "You think that would be fun?" he asked, his voice dry. "Being a servant to vikings?"

Hervor snorted. "Fun, hah. Right now, I care more about staying fed. And I'd rather be a servant on a ship than a servant on a holding. At least this way I'll see more than the inside of a garth."

Laughter from one of the men. "What are we now, fine lords, with servants to wait on us hand and foot?"

"If it means not eating your cooking, Thurlang, I'm all for it!"

More laughter. Maybe it was Hervor's imagination, but it sounded friendlier than before. But Enjarik was still holding her gaze, and his expression hadn't so much as flickered.

"You're running from something," he said.

He would know if she lied. Hervor nodded.

"I don't want trouble coming down on us."

"It won't," she said quickly. "I've run far and long enough to leave it behind." Surely that had to be true by now. Well, except for the voices – but they were her problem, not anybody else's.

Silence again. Everyone was waiting for Enjarik's decision.

"What's your real name?" he asked.

Hervor realised she'd stopped breathing, and made herself start again. She opened her mouth to answer him, thought about it, then shook her head. "No. Better if you try to think of me as a man. Nobody's looking for Hervard."

Enjarik's eyebrow quirked, but he accepted that. "All right, Hervard. We'll try your idea. But one word of complaint from you, and you'll be put ashore. Understand?"

"Yes," Hervor said, and hoped they'd let her sit down before her legs gave out entirely.

6

DISIR'S FURY

They did let her sit, or at least kneel, because her first task was building up the fire again to cook a meal. The vikings devoured it, leaving her the scraps, then went to sleep; she barely managed to finish eating before falling asleep herself. Her previous rest had been cut short, and once the tension of dealing with Enjarik was over, all her energy drained away. And the voices were silent this time – even Hervard, whose name she had taken.

She awoke early, before dawn. The men were dark shadows on the ground, and someone was snoring. Hervor's stomach growled loudly, but she knew better than to steal food right now. Later she could pinch enough to keep herself from starving, but if she did that from the outset they'd never take her anywhere.

Instead she picked her way between the sleeping bodies and out onto the beach.

Dawn was just a wash of light on the ocean horizon. Hervor stood for a moment, looking out at the sea. Her whole life in Rognjeld, and now not only had she crossed the land, she'd be going to sea. With vikings, no less – and if she was nothing more than a servant to them now, well, who could say what would happen in time?

A prickling at the back of her neck interrupted her dreams of adventure and glory and made her turn.

Enjarik was awake, too; he sat on a rock further down the beach, looking at her. Hervor hesitated. Just because he was watching her didn't mean he wanted to talk.

But if she started out being timid, it would just make it that much harder to be bold later. She'd learned that lesson as a small child, among the bonders at Rognjeld; she couldn't afford to forget it now.

So she walked down the shore towards him, trying to look bold. Trying to *be* bold. It was hard, with Enjarik's wolf-fierce gaze on her. His features, seen in steadier light than a torch's, were striking; the sea weather had taken its toll, as if the wind and storms had stripped away everything unnecessary, leaving behind the core of the man himself. His eyes were the blue-green of the sea's shallows.

She tried to decide which of her questions to ask first. His gaze, which seemed to see more than it should, decided her. "How did you know I'm a woman?"

"Was I the first to guess?"

"You were the first one to see me." Because of Saeunn's rune-staves – but he didn't need to know that. "I want to know how to disguise myself better."

Enjarik shook his head. "It's not the disguise – although when you get nervous, your voice goes too high, and you walk like a woman. But did you honestly think I could get that close to your body and not tell?"

Hervor remembered exactly how close he'd gotten, and flushed.

"If you're hell-bent on going about as a man," Enjarik said, "you can do it. Be careful with your voice, and don't swing your hips when you walk. You're big enough to pass for a youth. But it's not just how you look. You don't know the things a man knows."

Like how to fight. "So teach me."

"Earn it," Enjarik said, "and maybe I will."

It was more than she'd expected to get. Hervor decided not to push her luck any further and confined herself to asking what he wanted her to do. Enjarik told her to get the fire going again, make gruel, then do whatever anybody else told her to. Hervor tensed, but he said it matter-of-factly, without so much as a hint of a leer. She wondered what he'd do if somebody *did* try to rape her. No matter what anybody said, that was one order she wouldn't follow.

Nobody tried, at least not this morning. Turned out they were in a hurry; Hervor barely had the fire up when Enjarik came in and started kicking his men awake. She ladled out gruel, gulped down a ladleful herself before anyone could tell her not to, then killed the fire and did her best to hide that it had ever been there. Someone told her to grab the last few unburnt logs, and then they all trooped out into the pale sunlight.

Hervor hadn't thought about it before, but the ship was nowhere in sight. Everyone walked along the beach in silence, though, so she could only flounder through the sand after them, clutching the logs. They went a little way north along the coast, and then there was a stand of rushes, which turned out to be growing from a small rise in the land and concealing an inlet just big enough to hold a ship. Of course; they wouldn't leave it in plain sight.

Another set of men had been left to guard it in the night, which must have been miserable. Enjarik explained Hervor's presence to them while she studied the ship. It was much bigger than she'd expected: easily more than twenty paces long, but narrow for its length, like a floating blade. The outside was painted, alternate planks in red and white, and the posts at both ends were not only painted but elaborately carved. Hervor wanted to look at them more closely, but before she could move, one of the men spoke to her. "Drop those logs in the aft bilge and help us step the mast."

When Hervor didn't move, the viking scowled at her. "You deaf, or stupid?"

She hadn't found an answer to that when one of the other men swore. "Geirrankel's balls. She doesn't know the bow from the stern!"

"He," Enjarik said dryly, pushing through the crowd. Hervor's hands tightened on the logs. "This is our new friend Hervard, remember?"

"Boy, girl, dancing bear – what matters is that 'our new friend' is as dry as they come!"

Enjarik came close enough to Hervor that she'd have to crane her neck to look him in the eye. She backed up instead, then realised it looked like she was retreating. "Tell me Arvind's wrong," he said. Quietly, but everybody else was silent; they could hear every word he said. "Tell me you know your way around a ship."

Hervor thought back desperately to their earlier conversation. "You said you'd teach me things."

"After you've earned them," Enjarik said. His voice sank to a growl that made the hairs on the back of her neck rise. "Not before."

She couldn't make herself hold his gaze; her traitorous eyes darted to the crowd of men. Looking for sympathy? She didn't find it. One man in particular glared at her – a hideous fellow, with scars at the corners of his mouth that twisted his expression permanently – and his face sparked a memory.

Last night, the vikings talking while she cooked. Making jokes. Mocking each other. Mocking *him*.

Hervor faced Enjarik again and squared her shoulders. "I'll earn it by how quick I learn. I mean, it can't be that hard, right? After all, Vigmand learned. If he can manage it, anybody can."

A disbelieving silence greeted this declaration, followed by hoots of laughter. A snarl of anger, too; that would be Vigmand, and the scuffling noise was probably men keeping him from beating her bloody. Hervor held Enjarik's gaze, though, and even managed a cocky grin. The viking's expression twitched, but she couldn't read it. There was no way in any hell she'd actually convinced him. The real question was, had she amused him?

"You may eat those words someday soon," Enjarik said at last.

Hervor's stomach growled, loudly enough to hear, and the timing made her laugh outright. "I win either way, then. Gods know I haven't had enough to eat lately."

Someone clapped her on the back, making her stagger; then she was pushed towards one end of the boat, and that quickly, her lessons began. The mast had been laid lengthwise along the ship, and everyone lent a hand in raising it until the tip pointed skyward. Then a few of the biggest fellows, Enjarik included, wrestled it into place against a structure in the middle of the boat that looked like it had been carved out of a whole tree trunk, and whose surface was carved with rune-staves. Hervor watched them fix it into place and tie off its supporting ropes while she fished the long, slender oars out of the bilge below the deck planks and handed them to men who slid them through small openings in the boat's top edge.

"Wale," a voice said in her ear. Hervor tried to spin around, lost her footing, and sat down hard on a chest placed for use as a bench. A bald man grinned down at her. He wasn't good-looking like Enjarik, but there was a friendliness about him the viking leader lacked. "Wale," he repeated, slapping his hand against the top edge of the boat. "Bilge. Mast, on the mast step. Bow's the front end, the fore end. Aft is the stern, the back. Steerboard's right, larboard's left. That thing you're sitting on's called a chest."

"I know *that*," Hervor growled, pushing herself to her feet.

The raider held up his hands, still grinning. "You want lessons, don't snap my nose off. I'm teaching. It's more than most of them'll do."

The hard knot of suspicion that had formed inside her relaxed. Hervor nodded. "Thank you."

"Heiðelt," the man said. "Now go to the bow, Hervard, and get the sail. Big piece of cloth. You can't miss it."

She muttered a rude answer to that, but only once she'd slipped past Heiðelt to the front – the bow. Oh, she was grateful for the lessons… but she had a feeling they would come at the price of endless jokes about her ignorance.

The inlet was narrow and shallow, and getting out of it was difficult. Part rowing, part pushing with oars against the banks, and part men in the water pushing by hand. The ship backed out slowly, and more than one viking muttered in relief when it floated free at last. The ones in the water were dragged on board, and then half of them sat down at the oars and began to row.

The ship headed south and out to sea under the power of oars, with the sail hanging slack from the mast in the quiet, nearly windless air. Heiðelt had showed Hervor how to coil a rope neatly, so she was supposedly able to handle that task; in practice, he'd only showed her once, and she botched it several times before getting the knack of it. She could feel Enjarik watching her from his rowing bench, but he didn't say anything. Several of the other men did, though, and their comments made her ears burn.

They could have moved faster if everyone had been at the oars, but Hervor soon discovered why they weren't. The men rowed for quite a while, in time with a pulse one man beat out on a log drum, but eventually the men on the benches rested their oars, stretched, and rose so others could take their place. Obviously speed mattered less right now than conserving strength. But everyone, from the man beating the drum to Enjarik himself, took his place at an oar eventually.

Everyone except for Hervor.

When the second group tired and the first group moved to take their place again, she stood and faced Enjarik. "I want to row."

"You're the bilge-boy, not a viking."

"I offered to do what needs doing. This needs doing." It looked hot and sweaty and exhausting, not to mention she'd probably get blisters. But that didn't matter. Making herself useful did.

"Cooking and cleaning are things any idiot can do. Rowing isn't."

How much cooking and cleaning had *he* done, Hervor wondered. "I told you, I'll learn."

"Go ahead and try," someone said loudly. Hervor turned and found it was Vigmand. He'd stood up from his bench and held the end of his oar in one hand. "Come on, runt. You want to row? Go ahead."

Hervor looked at Enjarik, who merely raised his eyebrows.

All right, then. Hervor staggered down the length of the ship – she wasn't yet used to the rocking motion – and took the oar from Vigmand, who gave her a smile that might even be sincere. Lazy bastard probably just wanted to get out of his turn. Fine by her. Hervor sat down and wrapped her hands around the wood, worn smooth by others before her. Stroke with the beat, and hope her strength didn't give out so quickly as to embarrass her.

The drummer gave the count, and Hervor leaned forward, sending the tip of her oar sweeping back.

The wood bit into the water, waking up muscles all through her shoulders and back. Waking up – not hurting. She could deal with this. She finished her stroke, leaned forward again—

And flew off her bench as though Bolvereik had reached down from a cloud and swatted her like a fly.

She slammed into one of the other men, who swore and

shoved her off. The ship wallowed in the waves. Hervor lay in the bilge and shook her head, trying to clear it, trying to remember what had happened.

"Stupid bitch, fouled her oar with mine—"

"*His* oar." That was Enjarik, of course, with the ever-present undercurrent of sardonic amusement. So he found it funny that she chose to pretend to be a man? Well, to hell with him.

Hervor staggered to her feet. "I don't know what he's talking about. I didn't hit anybody's oar. I just stroked, and next thing I knew—"

"The fouling came after," Enjarik told her.

"So what did I do wrong?"

Hervor was treated to her first sight of Enjarik lost for words. Plainly he knew what she'd done wrong; he just didn't know how to explain it. Finally Heiðelt tried. "Caught water, most likely. You've got to feather your oar—"

"I've got to *what?*"

Heiðelt started to explain, but Enjarik cut him off with a chop of his hand. "This isn't the time to be giving our bilge-boy rowing lessons. Vigmand, get your ass back on that bench and row. Unless we get wind, it'll take us all day to reach Darrey. Do any of you want to make that landing in the dark?" Mutters of heartfelt denial. "Then *row.*"

In the late afternoon there was just enough of a breeze to lift the sail from its lifeless slump, but the men kept rowing anyway, adding their efforts to those of the wind. Hervor had to admit their endurance was impressive. Then a blot appeared on the horizon that slowly grew into an island, and she found out why they were so anxious to reach Darrey before nightfall.

The island was little more than a pine-studded rock, surrounded by a thick scattering of smaller, more treacherous rocks. The longship barely fit between them, easing through gingerly, the men often lifting their oars out of the water to avoid breaking them on the stone. Enjarik stood in the front – the bow, Hervor reminded herself – and watched the water ahead with his blue-green eyes unblinking. Small motions of his hands guided the efforts of the rowers. Only when the ship had safely passed the treacherous belt of rocks did he relax even a little, and he remained tense until they'd unstepped the mast and slipped beneath a low arch of stone, into a shallow cavern.

As soon as the front end crunched gently into the sand, men leapt over the edge – the wale – with ropes in hand; a heartbeat later, with familiar ease Hervor knew she couldn't possibly match yet, they'd tied the ship up securely. Then someone shoved a bundle into her arms, and she spent the next several minutes clambering in and out of the vessel, lugging things back and forth.

The cavern mouth faced the setting sun directly, so that the interior was bathed in vibrant light. Once Hervor had gotten the fire lit, she sat back on her heels, on the pretext of stretching her back, and took a look around.

Only a dozen or so men were in sight. Her eyes searched the interior and soon found a crevice in the rock that seemed to lead to the island's surface; she wondered what was up there, and if they'd beat her if she went to look. It might be worth it even if they did. Why had Enjarik brought the ship here? Just for a safe place to rest up? Clearly the vikings knew this spot well, and she didn't think there was anyone else on the island.

Curiosity and homesickness gnawed at opposite sides of Hervor's heart. She missed Rognjeld desperately – not out of any real attachment; just because it was familiar, routine, all she'd ever known – and at the same time, she hungered for new sights. She'd spent most of the day crouched on the deck, attending to various tasks where she wouldn't interfere with the rowers, so that when all was said and done she'd seen very little of the sea.

But that would change. It would all change.

rotting earth
rotting flesh
TRAPPED
can't breathe
can't see
screaming in the dark

Thick smells filled her nostrils, cold and sickeningly sweet, the stench of putrid flesh. Hervor clamped one hand over her mouth and shot to her feet, looking wildly about. Trapped –

she couldn't breathe – she bolted for that crevice, praying that it led to the surface, that it led to *air*—

She burst into the dying sunlight and found that the wind had picked up. It whipped the hacked-off ends of her hair into her face, blinding her. Hervor stumbled three steps further and then fell to her knees on the rock, retching her guts out. The smell was still with her, but the feeling of suffocation faded, thank the gods. She sucked in huge lungfuls of air and tried to convince her panicking body that she wasn't buried alive.

"Poor little stomach can't handle the sea, can it?"

The mocking voice cut through her disorientation. Hervor was on her knees with her arms wrapped around her stomach; on the rock before her lay the unidentifiable remains of what little she'd had to eat lately. She wiped her mouth with the back of her hand and looked around.

It was Vigmand, of course. If Hervor had been thinking about anything other than convincing Enjarik to let her stay, back on the shore that morning, she would have realised that no one with pride could take an insult like that and let it stand.

Now he stood not far away, grinning unpleasantly at her.

"The sea's no place for delicate little girls," Vigmand said. "You should be home on dry land where you belong, with a man between your legs and another one in your mouth."

His words started a slow boil in Hervor's veins. Not berserker fury, but her old friend, anger. She was glad for its company, after the terror of ghostly voices.

She stood up, moving slowly so she wouldn't stumble, hoping he would read it as confidence. He'd made a mistake in his approach; he stood to the east and a little below where she'd collapsed. Standing upright, she was taller than him, and backlit by the sun. He wouldn't be able to read shite from her expression. Like any lingering nausea from her fit.

"Your words," she growled, "are like the yapping of a small dog. And I don't listen to dogs."

Vigmand stiffened. "*What* did you say?"

She wasn't sure why she was goading Vigmand again. Maybe it was the shock of the voices, or her humiliating defeat yesterday at Enjarik's hands. Maybe it was just Vigmand's ugly face. But reasons didn't matter; results did, and her words brought Vigmand lunging at her with a howl.

She sidestepped the instant he moved, and the sun struck him full in the eyes. In that moment, while he was blinded, Hervor kicked him in the back of the knees, sending him sprawling full length across the rock.

"Clumsy on land," she said as he fell. A grin was spreading across her face. "Stupid at sea." Vigmand was on his feet again, and he swung a meaty fist at her. Hervor dodged it. He wasn't nearly the fighter Enjarik was – though she wouldn't want to face him if he were armed. "Is there anywhere you *are* useful?"

Vigmand bellowed and charged her, and when Hervor tried to dodge, one rag-wrapped foot snagged against a stone. He slammed into her full-force, and they crashed back down together. Hervor took the brunt of the impact, driving the wind out of her. The viking bent in close, pinning her with his weight. "Goddamn little whore, I'll—"

He'd shortened the range just enough. With her last energy, Hervor rammed her knuckles into his throat.

Vigmand made a choking noise and fell off her, clutching at his neck. Hervor knew she should follow up, but she was too busy breathing; she almost passed out from the unspeakable joy of air. Then a shadow fell over her, and she knew that somewhere along the way they'd gotten an audience.

More than one person, she saw as her vision cleared. Vigmand tried to lunge at her again, but the raider at his side held him back, and the one by Hervor hovered over her, as if to stop her from getting any bright ideas. She didn't want to fight any more, though; as she got to her feet, she found the fall had twisted her bad ankle. Not hard, but enough to hurt, now that the rush of the fight was fading.

"I should leave you both here for the gulls to eat."

That snarl was from Enjarik. At least half a dozen raiders stood around them now, but they all gave their leader a wide berth. He stood with his arms crossed over his chest and his feet planted wide, and in the sun's flaming light he looked like the fire god himself. And angry beyond belief.

"It's your own damn fault, Enjarik, bringing this whore along—"

"Shut the fuck up, Vigmand, or I'll cut your tongue out." The words were as hard as iron, and even Hervor flinched. He'd do it, he really would.

Enjarik looked around at his men, meeting each gaze individually. "I lead this crew," he reminded them. "Because I'm smarter than you; without me you couldn't find a tree to piss on, much less plan a raid. And because I'm stronger than you – there's not one of you who can beat me in a fight. So until one of you finds some brains or some balls, I'm the one in charge. If I say we take on someone new, then we take on someone new. And if I say that person's a man, then he's a man. Anybody who's got a problem with that can take it up with me."

Relief threatened to turn Hervor's limbs to water. He wanted her to stay. Gods only knew why, but he did. He wouldn't just kill her and leave her body for the gulls.

Then Enjarik looked at her, and her blood congealed in her veins.

"As for you," he said levelly, "just what the fuck did you think you were doing?"

She reached desperately for the last, fading scraps of her anger, and the strength they could give her. "He insulted me—"

"You insulted him first. This morning. We all heard you."

"I didn't say anything the others hadn't said," Hervor insisted, indicating those around her with a jerk of her chin.

"They're all a part of my crew."

"But you just said—"

"You're the bilge-boy, Hervard. You're not a warrior. You haven't proved your worth to us; all you've proved is your incompetence. Everyone else here has earned his place – even Vigmand." Hervor thought she heard a muted snarl from Vigmand at that afterthought. "You're here on my patience, and that's wearing thin."

Hervor tried to think of a defence. She couldn't claim that she'd beaten Vigmand as proof that she wasn't totally weak; that had been more of a draw than anything else.

But she *had* beaten someone else once, though it wasn't a fight she was proud of.

Hervor straightened up and lifted her chin. "I understand. But I won't stand for anyone calling me a whore, or weak. I once killed an armed man with my bare hands. I can fight, when I have to." Berkel had carried only a knife, and she didn't dare admit that she'd done it in a mindless fit; berserkers like Angantyr might make good stories, but no one wanted one on a ship. Still, it was her only claim to strength. She had to use it.

Enjarik held her gaze, while the sunset wind flung strands of hair across his face. He ignored these, ignored everything except her, and Hervor fought against the feeling that she was a very small rabbit being eyed by a wolf.

"Well, then," Enjarik said at last. "You'll have your chance to prove you can do more than that, soon enough. We'll see how you fare then."

♦ ♦ ♦

Enjarik didn't explain what he meant, and Hervor wasn't about to ask. She went back down into the cavern, walking squarely on her twisted ankle and grinding her teeth against the pain; she didn't dare show that it was hurt. Back in the cave, she prepared food for the men, ate her scraps, and went to sleep.

Heiðelt kicked her awake before dawn the next morning. Hervor rolled over, spat to clear her mouth of a foul taste, and went bleary-eyed to the fire. Already it was becoming routine. But Heiðelt took her by the shoulder and led her past the embers of the fire, over to where the ship rested on the cavern's sandy beach. The water level was much lower now, but Heiðelt climbed easily up the side and over the wale, then passed an oar down to Hervor. She took it, mystified, and stood working her sore ankle around while he came back down.

When Heiðelt was on the sand again, she asked, "What's that?"

The viking looked where she was pointing, at the runes painted onto the stern. "Ship's name."

Hervor sighed. "I'm not an idiot. But what does it *say?*"

Heiðelt raised one eyebrow at her. "You can't read?"

"Of course I can," Hervor said sarcastically. "I'm asking to see if you can."

"If you can't read, then either you *are* an idiot, or you're not freeborn."

She glared at him. "Just tell me what the damned name is."

"*Disir's Fury*," Heiðelt said, and motioned for her to follow him to the surface.

Hervor turned that name over in her mind as she manoeuvred the long oar through the crevice. *Disir.* She'd heard that word before, but where?

In a story. The memory came to her slowly. Something about a woman – Hervor couldn't remember her name. A woman whose children had been slaughtered. She'd gone insane, or something like that, and then ended up as a dis. The details escaped her, but the disir had stuck in her memory. Female guardian spirits. They were linked to specific families, gave protection, got revenge.

Disir's Fury. She liked it.

In the murky predawn light, Heiðelt led her over the island's rocky surface and down to a spot where the stone dropped to just above the water. "Sit down," he told her, picking up a large rock that lay nearby.

Hervor laid the oar down and obeyed. "What's this?"

"This," Heiðelt said with a grunt as he set the stone on end, "is you learning to row."

"You sure I don't have anything else I'm supposed to be doing? Like kissing Vigmand's ass?"

"Kissing Vigmand's ass won't show Enjarik that you should stay," Heiðelt said, picking up the oar. "This will."

"Assuming Enjarik doesn't get mad that I'm doing this and not working."

"Enjarik told me to wake you up for a lesson." There was a hole bored in the top of the stone; the viking slid the oar through it and shoved the end at Hervor. When she took it, she saw that the angle was almost exactly the one she'd had while sitting on the ship's bench.

For the first time she could remember, someone was actually trying to teach her. Everything Hervor had done at Rognjeld had been menial work, or else tasks she'd seen done so many times she didn't need instruction.

But this, if she mastered it, would be a skill of real value. Something no bondsmaid would know.

Despite the early hour, her mind sharpened, and she gave Heiðelt her full attention.

He showed her how to use her whole body to row, and the correct angle to place her oar at. Without the momentum of a ship, she didn't get knocked on her ass when she got it wrong. She didn't go wrong often; the motions began to feel natural very quickly. And Heiðelt had a patience with her the others lacked. Because of that, once she'd gotten the hang of basic rowing, she ventured to ask him the question she'd left unspoken before. "What's Enjarik got planned for me?"

Heiðelt shook his head. There were troubled lines around his eyes. "I'm not sure. He's clever, doesn't think like the rest of us. That's why we're the most feared crew on the sea since Angantyr and his sons; people can't predict what we're going to do. But whatever he's planning..."

He hesitated, and Hervor prompted him. "What? I'll take any help I can get."

"It's not much help," Heiðelt admitted. "Just that, whatever you think the test is, you're likely to be wrong. Enjarik's that unpredictable."

He was right; it wasn't much help. Hervor sighed. "I'm surprised he's let me stay at all." She chewed on her lip for a moment as she rowed, then glanced back up at Heiðelt. "I don't suppose you know why he did."

Heiðelt snorted. "Not the first scrap. I've seen him stab men for less cause than you've given him."

"Half of that was Vigmand. At *least* half."

"What possessed you to pick a fight with him, anyway?"

Hervor shrugged and bent her attention to making sure her oar bit into the water. "He's not that tough."

"You didn't know that when you started the fight. He could have been like Enjarik. He could have killed you. Did you think of that?"

"Why bother?" Hervor asked. The exertion was beginning to make her sweat. "The thread of my life is already cut; I can't stretch it longer. All I can do is make sure that I spend my time well – doing great deeds, defending my honour. At least then, when I die, I'll be able to go to Slavinn with my head held high, and when Eldaskrid asks me my name, I can say it with pride."

"You can't read," Heiðelt reminded her. "That means you're a thrall, or else a bonder from a very young age."

She yanked too hard on the oar; water splashed high into the air. "Pride isn't something only the freeborn have. When I die, I'm not going to rot in Borguld with the cowards. So if someone insults me, I'm going to answer him."

Heiðelt shrugged and sat down on another rock. The sun was starting to rise, and so was the water level; Hervor wondered how much longer she was supposed to sit here and practise rowing. Soon her ledge would be under water. "Maybe that's it," Heiðelt said.

"That's what?"

"Why Enjarik's letting you stay. He likes it when somebody's got balls."

She snorted. "Well, I sure don't."

"Weren't you listening yesterday?" Heiðelt grinned. "You're a man, Hervard. Enjarik said so, and even the gods don't argue with him." He stretched his back, eyed the water, and stood. "All right, enough of this. Let's go find something else for you to do."

Hervor freed her oar and waited while Heiðelt put the rock where it wouldn't get washed away by the waves. "How did you know about this spot, and that rock?" she asked.

The bald viking grinned at her. "Because this, bilge-boy, is where I taught Enjarik to row, many years ago."

7

THE BOOK

Disir's Fury stayed hidden in the cavern for the rest of that day, and all of the next. Enjarik was plainly waiting for something, although Hervor didn't know what. She soon guessed, however, that the test he had in mind for her, whatever it was, wouldn't happen on Darrey. The knowledge didn't relax her much. She just wanted to get it over with.

So for two days she kept her mouth shut and avoided Vigmand, mainly by spending as much time in Heiðelt's company as she could without annoying him. She got two more rowing lessons when the water was at the right height, and as she practised he taught her more about the ship. Hervor drank it all up and pressed him for more. He'd warned her Enjarik's test wouldn't be what she expected. She had to be prepared for anything.

The third morning, Heiðelt kicked her awake, and they left Darrey.

Everyone moved with quiet urgency, and none of the curses that usually punctuated the morning routine. Hervor hauled herself over the ship's side with the rest and stood uncertainly. Would she be rowing this time?

Not this close to Darrey, at any rate. She'd forgotten about the barrier of rocks outside. Enjarik stood in the stern as they eased the ship out; *Disir's Fury* was almost the same shape fore and aft, and could move in either direction. As soon as they'd floated clear of the rocks, he gave the order to raise the sail.

This time Hervor stepped in immediately and helped push the huge trunk of the mast up. She was still pig-ignorant as the raiders sorted out the mess of lines, but when someone started putting covers over the holes the oars had gone through, she followed his lead. That much, she could do.

The sail ran up the mast, snapped tight in the grip of the wind, and *Disir's Fury* sliced forward through the water.

And Hervor stood as if rooted, one foot on a rowing bench, staring out over the larboard side. Her body shifted instinctively with the movement of the ship, keeping her perfectly balanced, and her breath hovered in her throat as a tide of memories threatened to sweep her away.

This – the sea – the expanse of dark blue, glittering like a tapestry of jewels under the sun – the bite of the salt wind against her face—

Someone shoved past her, and she half fell onto one of the sea chests used as benches. Vigmand gave her a nasty smile and walked on.

Hervor dismissed him from her mind. He didn't matter. What mattered was that rush of memories. How could she remember this, remember flying over the waves in a viking longship? It was impossible; she'd never even seen the ocean until a few days ago. And yet she *did* remember, in body as well as mind; something had given her the casual balance of a seafarer, for that brief moment before Vigmand pushed her.

"Bilge-boy!"

That voice was Enjarik's, and Hervor leapt to answer it, leaving her confusion behind for the time being.

What had they been waiting for? That question gnawed at her as *Disir's Fury* sailed. Not the wind; the men were used to rowing.

The tension in the air gave her an idea, and she didn't like it one bit. While under sail, the men had little to do and lounged about on the chests looking relaxed – but they weren't. They were just saving their energy. And she had some notion what they might be saving it for. She was sailing with vikings, after all.

Hervor's stomach began to knot.

They were heading west, towards land, but also slightly south. Not to where they'd come from, then. Hervor tried to make herself rest; whatever was going to happen, wearing herself out with worry wouldn't do any good. But she was painfully aware of Enjarik as he moved about the ship. He didn't seem to be paying particular attention to her, but she hadn't forgotten that he intended some kind of test, and she doubted that he had, either.

Disir's Fury raced on, and before midday the coast was in sight.

The men began to rouse from their false relaxation. Hervor's pulse quickened as she saw them reaching for weapons, sliding axes into belt loops, shields onto their arms.

"Take this."

She turned around and found Heiðelt behind her with a sheathed knife in his hand. Hervor took it without hesitation. She might not know how to fight, but if they were going into battle, then she wanted to be armed. However pathetic her weapon might be.

Was this Enjarik's test? How she did in a real fight?

But Heiðelt had told her not to trust her instincts.

Disir's Fury turned as she approached, until she was skimming along parallel to the beach, still a good distance out. Only the occasional spruce tree broke the flat sweep of the shore. Then there was a shift in the monotony: a small bay. At its mouth they dropped the sail, coasting in on their remaining momentum and easy rowing.

The bay closed in around them, and then there was a town.

Enjarik muttered a quiet command, and *Disir's Fury* ran aground a short distance from the town. Most of the men leapt overboard immediately. Hervor wondered briefly about the ship; someone would need to watch it, after all, and maybe that was her task.

"Bilge-boy," Enjarik said from behind her, and when Hervor turned he shoved a rectangular bundle into her arms, heavy enough to require both hands. She didn't have a chance to see what lay under its burlap wrapping before the raider vaulted down onto the beach and she had to follow, landing awkwardly with her burden. Heiðelt glanced at her, then at the bundle, but he said nothing as they headed for the town.

The place was sufficiently bigger than Rognjeld to make Hervor uncomfortable. Though she suspected this wasn't that large a settlement, the vikings were distinctly outnumbered. Of course, most of the people peeking out at them from behind cracked doors looked like peasants, not warriors. Enjarik alone could cut down ten without breaking a sweat. But this wasn't a battle, at least not yet; the vikings didn't charge in screaming, but rather walked down a muddy lane between buildings as if oblivious to the peering eyes.

Ahead, the lane opened out into a grassy square, where about a score of people waited.

None of the vikings looked surprised. This was a planned meeting, then, between Enjarik and the grey-bearded man who stood at the front of the small crowd. More than a few of the men with him were armed, but with pitchforks and clubs. They didn't have the look of warriors.

Still, her pulse sped up, until she could hear it beating in her ears.

Enjarik stopped, and so did his raiders. "Do you have the ransom?"

The grey-bearded man came forward a step. "Do you have our treasure?"

Enjarik snapped his fingers. Hervor suddenly realised what the bundle in her arms must be. She almost darted forward, guilty over the delay, but she thought of what that would look like and made herself walk calmly.

Once at the viking leader's side, she held out her bundle, expecting him to take it. Instead he flipped the wrappings open, revealing what lay inside.

A book.

Hervor stared at it stupidly. A book? All this was over a *book*? It didn't even have gold on the cover! Just leather, tooled with an interlaced design, worn down by countless hands. Sure, books were valuable – she'd only ever seen two in her life – but who in all the hells would go to this kind of trouble for a bunch of vellum wrapped in leather?

The people of the village gasped when they saw it, though, as if it were indeed the treasure the elder had named.

"The ransom," Enjarik repeated. He spoke softly, but his voice carried through the still air. The wind had died to almost nothing.

The grey-bearded man shifted on his feet. His eyes seemed glued to the book. "Yes. Well. You haven't given us much time—"

"I gave you two moons." The edge in Enjarik's voice made Hervor tense.

"To raise a very large sum," the elder protested. He held up his hands placatingly. "We've done our best. But we haven't had a good harvest in *years* – no one has! We don't have much to spare. Bersulf here has what we've gathered. Ten silver eyrar."

"The ransom," Enjarik said, "is twenty. Plus four casks of salted meat and ten ells of dyed cloth."

The elder licked his lips. Hervor, watching him, felt the hairs on the back of her neck rise. Something else was going on. He was nervous, yes, but not the way he should be.

She glanced to the side, as surreptitiously as she could, and saw shadows moving between the buildings.

"Enjarik—" she whispered.

"I see them."

The calm, quiet response startled her and steadied her at the same time. Hervor wanted to ask what she should do, but she kept her mouth shut.

"I'll take the ten eyrar now," Enjarik told the village elder. "But I'll keep the book. In one moon's time, I'll come back, and when I do, you'll have the rest of the ransom – plus two eyrar more for the delay."

"We can't raise that sum!" the grey-bearded man insisted.

Enjarik shrugged. "Then we keep your book."

All eight hells broke loose.

A yell came from behind Hervor. She ducked instinctively

as she turned, clutching the heavy book to her chest, and saw that at least ten men had charged from their hiding spots to attack the vikings. Metal rang as they crashed in; these had axes, unlike the ones who stood with the village elder. Next to Hervor, Enjarik had drawn his sword.

She went for her borrowed dagger and nearly dropped the book. Shite. How was she supposed to fight while holding on to this thing?

"Back to the ship," Enjarik said to her, then raised his voice to a deafening bellow. "Arvind! Heiðelt! To me!"

The two vikings detached themselves from the brawling clump and ran past Hervor to join Enjarik as he headed for the other side of the common. Hervor was left standing there, the book clutched in her arms, a battle between her and the ship.

Her first instinct was to look for another path. There were gaps between the buildings – but she'd be easy prey for anybody who wanted to ambush her. Or she might get turned around, find herself heading in the wrong direction. She *definitely* didn't want to be stranded here—

A wordless roar was her only warning. Hervor leapt to one side out of pure instinct, so that the man charging at her back flew past instead. He skidded to a halt on the grass, and she saw there was a small wood-axe in his hands. Fuck!

She did the first thing she could think of: she slammed her foot into the side of his knee.

The man screamed and fell to the ground. She'd struck *much* harder than she ever had before. He was sprawled on the grass, clutching at his knee; his axe lay forgotten at his side. Hervor eyed it longingly, but if she couldn't use a dagger while holding on to this stupid, heavy book, she certainly couldn't use an axe.

How in hell was she supposed to make it through this fight if she couldn't defend herself?

Only one answer to that: *run*.

She put one shoulder down and threw herself at a gap between combatants. Someone's hand clamped onto her arm; she ripped free and slammed her elbow into his face. A raider's axe sliced through the air, just missing her head. She stumbled over something unseen. Almost to the edge—

Hands wrenched the book from her grasp. Hervor staggered, but the villager hung on. Her back slammed into the rough stone wall of a building; she was at the edge of the lane. She twisted, trying to get loose, and then the book tumbled free and fell to the ground. The villager tried to grab it. She kneed him in the stomach. He pulled at her, and in the mud of the lane they both lost their balance, collapsing in a tangled heap.

They grappled in the mud by that wall, elbows and knees jabbing at anything vulnerable, and deep inside Hervor the fire was rising.

fury fuelling the fight
bestows the strength of ten

Could her ghosts feel what was happening? The question distracted Hervor enough for the villager to get his forearm across her throat. She writhed out from under it, panting. No, *no*, she couldn't let this happen. Couldn't do to this man whatever she'd done to Berkel.

Desperation to avoid that, rather than berserker strength, drove her fist into the side of the man's head. He went limp. Hervor shoved him off her and looked for the book. There it was, not far away. She reached for it in relief.

A scrawny girl darted out of nowhere, snatched the book an instant before she could grab it, and ran.

Fuck the book; this was sheer stupidity! But even as that thought flashed through her mind, Hervor was on her feet and running. Not towards the ship, even though that would be smarter. After the girl who'd stolen the book.

She wasn't anywhere near fully grown, and Hervor's legs were longer. Catching up, Hervor took her down in a flying tackle. The book smacked back into the mud. Knocking the girl out was easy, once Hervor got past the flailing limbs; then she grabbed the book and lurched to her feet once more. Her breath rasped in her throat as she looked around, but for once she had a bit of luck; the only people nearby were two smaller girl-children, who stared at her with wide, frightened eyes. Hervor grinned at them and stuck her tongue out.

The rising tide of her berserker fury had vanished – and so had the voices of the ghosts.

Not just faded; they were *gone*. The realisation froze Hervor where she stood. How could the rage just vanish, in the blink of an eye? It didn't seem possible. But eight hells, she didn't have time to worry about that. The chase had taken her down a side lane; now Hervor retraced her steps. The fight looked to be over, with many villagers down and the raiders retreating back to the ship.

The pursuit was half-hearted at best. By the time they reached *Disir's Fury* the villagers had given up. Hervor didn't blame them. Some of the raiders were wounded, but none seriously, and the two who'd stayed behind to guard the ship would have been more than happy to fight.

The ship was floating free in the water before Hervor looked around and realised they were missing three men.

Where were Arvind, Heiðelt, and Enjarik?

Surely the vikings must have noticed that three men were absent, when one of them was their leader. Yet no one said anything, and there was no one Hervor dared ask, not with Heiðelt gone. She shoved the book under a bench and silently helped where she could, doing her best to blend in. Vigmand was still there, after all.

As soon as the ship had backed off from the shore, the men began to row north. Hervor, at the stern, pretended she was watching the coast, but her thoughts were all on what had happened after the fight broke out. The book, banishing ghosts and rage alike, and before that...

Were her ghosts those of berserkers?

Was that why they haunted *her*?

Those changes at Rognjeld, after Anfinna and Saeunn arrived, with her ghosts suddenly talking in the daytime. And Hervor had been beaten before, but it never sent her berserk – never anywhere close. Not until a blood-witch arrived. But the possibility must have always been there, the mark of Bolvereik on her soul… a mark shared by her host of dead men.

There weren't that many berserkers in the world. For all Hervor knew, right now she was the only one. But asking around about the ones in her head would be dangerous; most people liked berserkers even less than vikings, and anything that might hint at her connection to them could put her in danger.

Still. It was more than she'd known before – assuming, of course, that she was right.

Then Hervor jolted from her thoughts as she realised the ship was heading for shore again.

They didn't beach *Disir's Fury* this time. There was no need. When they reached shallow waters three figures emerged from a copse of spruces: Arvind, Heiðelt, and Enjarik. They were spattered with small amounts of blood, but none of it seemed to be theirs, and Heiðelt was grinning broadly. He snatched a small leather sack from Enjarik's hand and tossed it into the air; when he caught it again, a metallic clink carried over the water. Whistles and cheers rose from the men on the ship. "Only half what it should have been," one man said, and was answered with: "Half is a hell of a lot more than what we had before."

Half. Ten silver eyrar. Enjarik had gotten that much of the ransom, at least – and more, counting what the vikings had carried off with them.

The three men waded into the surf and were pulled aboard amid much backslapping and cheerful cursing. Hervor gathered that the whole thing, from the first landing to this northern pickup, had been planned in advance. They'd expected the ambush all along.

Not your average stupid vikings, she thought.

Then someone pushed his way through the crowd, and Hervor stood to face the man behind the cleverness and planning. Enjarik looked her over with an eye that seemed to be weighing her to the last quarter-stone.

"I fought," she said, before he could ask. "Even though you—"

"Where's the book?"

He cared more about the bloody *book* than he did about her fighting? Hervor, seeing him scowl, figured she'd better produce it before he did something painful to her. She bent and retrieved it from under the bench and handed it to him, glad to be rid of it.

"You brought it back?" he asked.

"It's here, isn't it?"

"*You* brought it." His gaze bored into her. "You didn't drop it, to be picked up by someone else."

One of his hands was running over the dried mud on the cover. "It got dropped twice," Hervor said. "Once when someone knocked it out of my hands, a second time when I tackled the girl who got the bright idea of running off with it. But no, I didn't abandon the gods-damned book." The thing was apparently worth a lot of money, but his concern for it seemed far too—

Hervor almost swore in disbelief. *This* was his test?

Enjarik tossed the book to one of the nearby men and clapped her on the shoulder, grinning for the first time she could remember. It brought his face to life, power and violence suddenly transformed into charisma, and something throbbed inside her. "Not bad, Hervard. You've got a cool enough head to think about more than saving your own skin, or grabbing for glory in battle. You can't sail or fight worth a damn, but those things, you can learn. If you were stupid or greedy... that, I couldn't fix. You get to stay."

He didn't wait to see her stare at him like a poleaxed sheep. The ship was still wallowing in the shallows, and he turned his attention to getting them back out to open sea. With the wind against them, they had to row, and this time Hervor found herself on a bench with an oar in her hands.

Stupid or greedy, Enjarik had said. By the latter he might have just meant a desire for glory, but she suspected there was more to it than that. She'd had a valuable treasure in her hands – though hell if she understood its value – and no one to stop her if she decided to hide among the houses and surrender to the villagers when the fight was over.

A test of her nerve, yes. And a test of her loyalty as well.

But she'd passed. She truly was part of the crew, and now the beat of the rowing-drum called her to her task.

8

WITCH-HUNTING

"Two points to larboard!"

Hervor unwound a line with quick, deft motions and braced her feet to haul on it. The yard swung slowly towards her, creaking in protest as the wind tried to force it the other way, but there were more hands than just hers on the rope; together they fought it into its new position, then tied it off once more.

Disir's Fury had shuddered under the force of the sail change, but now her motion smoothed out. Hervor made her way forward, back to the pair of chests where she'd been napping before being called to her feet. Heiðelt was headed for them too, but she beat him there, and grinned unrepentantly as she lay back down on her folded blanket and stretched out to her full length.

That length was longer than it had been, though it had taken her a while to notice. Where once Garldor's stolen clothing had been a little big on her, now it fit fine – almost too small. Hervor had thought she'd already reached her full growth, but in the three months she'd been on *Disir's Fury* she'd gone up nearly another thumb-length.

Maybe it was a reaction to her new life, standing tall under the sun as a free viking, instead of hunching as a reviled bondsmaid.

More had changed in those three months than just her height. She knew how to sail, for one thing: while that moment of utter clarity and remembrance had never come back, she'd taken to sailing as if born to it. Heiðelt had taught her other things as well, like fist-fighting. Her scuffles as a bondsmaid had always been short, so she'd never bothered to learn much about defence; that was why Enjarik had beaten her so easily. She could at least stand against the viking leader now, even if he still won without breaking a sweat. And Heiðelt had started showing her how to use an axe.

Three months. She no longer found it odd to live on a longship, or stick her ass over the wale when she needed to relieve herself – she realised now that her pretence at being a man wouldn't have lasted long, not on board a ship – or to stride into towns demanding money from their sheep-like inhabitants. Viking life, at least under Enjarik, involved much less fighting than she'd imagined, and much more simple intimidation. After three months, she was used to thinking of herself as a viking named Hervard.

And she was hanging on to sanity by her fingernails.

The voices didn't always hit her like a charging ram, the way they used to, but hardly a day went by now that she didn't hear them. Sometimes their whispers were relevant; sometimes they weren't. The former frightened her more.

The others knew something was wrong with her. They could hardly have missed it: a holding might have few secrets, but a ship had even fewer. There just wasn't room for them. So the men suspected, even if they didn't know exactly what ailed her.

But what could she do about any of it? The book held the ghosts at bay, but Enjarik kept it close. He'd find it suspicious if she asked to carry it around by day, cuddle with it at night.

At least she'd gleaned a few more scraps of information from their ramblings. Two more names, Brami and Saeming, and Hervor was more sure than ever that her ghosts were haunting her because they'd been berserkers too. A connection forged through Bolvereik's touch.

But she'd yet to find anyone who could tell her what to *do* with that knowledge. For all Saeunn had said a fair number of people knew drauðr, Hervor hadn't met a single one. And not for lack of looking.

The summer sun was warm on her skin, but a core of cold stayed inside her. Hervor never knew when she was going to hear someone muttering about blood, or find her nose full of the smell of rotting flesh. She couldn't take much more of this.

"Hervard!"

Enjarik's call brought her to her feet immediately. No more stumbling about the ship like a dry-land fool; she'd learned to move with the rocking, except when dead men put her off balance. She made her way towards Enjarik in the stern with the ease of any sailor.

He had a bundle on the bench next to him. Hervor looked at it and rolled her eyes. "Not that bloody thing again."

"That bloody thing," Enjarik said, his sea-coloured eyes lit by the sun, "has made us more money than anything else we've gotten our hands on."

"Where are we trying to sell it this time?" Since that first ambush near Darrey, Enjarik had made two further attempts to ransom it off. Both had ended in fights, with the book still in the vikings' possession, along with a fair bit of loot. Hervor couldn't believe anybody wanted a simple book that badly. Even knowing that it was a holy book, sacred to Alfrenvald, failed to explain the amount people were willing to pay for it.

She'd asked some discreet questions about Alfrenvald and found out he was that rarity, a god not much interested in fighting. He concerned himself with learning instead, which explained why Hervor had never heard of him. Maybe it also explained the quenching of her rage; he was enough of a pacifist that anything sacred to him did its best to stop people from fighting. Or something. Hervor cared about that even less than about why people were willing to pay fortunes for the book. What mattered was that she didn't go berserk, slaughter people and defile their corpses, as she had Berkel's. As her ghosts had no doubt done to countless others.

Enjarik had answered her question, and she hadn't even paid attention. Hervor didn't ask him to repeat himself, though. She just listened as he outlined the plan for this next ransom attempt. Her respect for him had done nothing but increase in the three months she'd been on *Disir's Fury*: he was intelligent and cunning, well worthy of the stories told about him. She had no idea what gods he named in his prayers, but she wouldn't be surprised if one of them was Iskoti, the trickster fire god he sometimes resembled.

"How much do you think they'll actually have for us?" she asked when he was done.

"Maybe all of it," Enjarik said, surprising her. "We should be prepared for things to go wrong, but they might not. Gilvind's a wealthy jarl, wealthy enough to pay the whole ransom he's promised. And he might do it, if he wants the book badly enough."

"If he does, we don't fight?"

"Of course not." Enjarik looked at her, his blue-green eyes hardening. "We can't take the full ransom *and* keep the book. If we do that, word will get around, and then no one will want to pay, for fear we'll just betray them anyway."

Hervor muttered her agreement, her heart not behind the words. He was right, of course. But for all that she was sick of trotting into town at his heels, book in her arms, she didn't want to see it go. Without it, she had no way of pushing back the ghosts and the rage.

Maybe she'd become a worshipper of Alfrenvald. Wouldn't *that* be a laugh: an illiterate, breech-born bondsmaid disguised as a viking, praying to a god of books and peace.

Enjarik stood and began calling out orders, and Hervor, putting her thoughts away, went to help adjust the sail again.

Two nights later, everyone but Hervor was celebrating. Gilvind had come through with the entire ransom, and no trickery. They'd exchanged the book, clasped hands, and left without a fight. It meant their golden goose was gone at last, but Gilvind had paid enough that no one else really cared. They could live for months on what he'd given them.

That was, if the vikings didn't piss away half their wealth on the spot. Enjarik had sailed them south, to a small town ruled by a jarl who, while not exactly a friend, wasn't hostile to Enjarik or his men. They'd beached *Disir's Fury* in plain sight and were spending a few days enjoying the jarl's hospitality. Which meant drinking, and dicing, and enjoying the company of various bondswomen and lesser freeborn, wooing them with the trinkets that had made up a good chunk of the book's ransom. Half the vikings had already lost their share to the other half, or to some of the jarl's men, and the women were doing their best to coax what they could from those who still had anything to give.

Hervor had no heart to join in. The loss of her one defence against going berserk depressed her, and she wasn't in a mood to flirt with any of the women – though it had amused her in the past, pretending she was the man she appeared to be.

Instead she sat and watched the rest of the men with a sardonic eye. Even Vigmand had found someone who'd have him, but Hervor had a private bet with herself that he was too drunk to do anything with the woman he'd managed to hook. Most of the men were that far gone; it was a good thing this jarl wasn't likely to try and murder them. Counting Hervor, there were probably four vikings sober enough to pick up a weapon by the right end.

Enjarik, as usual, was one of the four. He was drinking, but not much; he was too canny to leave himself vulnerable when surrounded by strangers. And although two of the jarl's daughters were doing their best to draw his eye, so far he'd ignored them both. That was usual, too.

Hervor elbowed Heiðelt – who was not one of the sober ones – and nodded towards Enjarik. "What's the story with him, anyway? I don't think I've ever seen him tumble a woman."

Heiðelt let loose with a prodigious, beery belch. "Keeps his trousers laced, our Enjarik does."

"But why?" Between the glamour of the viking life and his own weathered good looks, Enjarik certainly didn't have trouble getting attention. And most of the raiders were glad of a chance to bed someone, after long days at sea. Why not him? "Is he not capable, or something?"

That provoked a howl of laughter from Heiðelt. "Don't gone – go saying that where he c'n hear!" He took another pull on his mead, as if he needed more. "Nah, he's capable, right 'nough. Think 'twas something some wench did t'im, though. Not to his body – his—" Heiðelt gestured vaguely at his head. "Y'know."

"Mind?"

"That's it. Tol' me she tried t'knife 'im in his sleep. Made 'im jumpy. I tol'im he should just make sure they don't got knives handy from now on. Didn't listen." Heiðelt shook his head at this folly. "His loss."

Not just his, Hervor thought. With those eyes, and those muscles… these days her fear had faded enough for her to see the man who once sparked it. And yes, all right, she'd noticed that he was damned attractive. The other day, when he'd stripped to the waist to sluice himself clean…

For one brief, mad instant, Hervor imagined going to him now. Handing over her knife. Running her hands through that red-gold hair.

It was a terrible idea, for so many reasons. Not least of which was that Enjarik would probably return the knife to her, between her ribs. There was a time or two, when she'd caught him watching her… but even if she was right and she'd seen desire in his eyes, Enjarik wasn't about to bed one of his own crew. And if she tried to sidle up to him tonight, the others would never let her live it down. Not to mention that Hervor would make a fool of herself trying: she didn't have the first clue how to flirt, how to make herself appealing to a man. It wasn't a skill she'd seen any value in, before.

"Too much beer," she mumbled to Heiðelt, betting he wouldn't remember a word of it. "Need some fresh air." She set her mug down and walked with deliberate casualness into the shadows of the town.

It had become well-practised habit. Every time they stopped at a holding or a town, she searched for someone who could help her. She had the steps down pat. Find a kid, ask them what woman they were afraid to go near, then talk to that woman once the vikings were too drunk to care about her absence. She'd thought about asking after men, too, but dismissed the idea: men were more likely to gossip about her visit where the vikings might hear. Besides, what did men know of blood, besides the spilling of it?

The house she sought was little more than a hut, out on the fringes of the town. Hervor loosened her dagger in its sheath – one woman had been dangerously unstable, attacking her on sight – and went inside.

The interior was full of smoke that had failed to escape through the uneven thatching. Hervor coughed and was still trying to orient herself in the murk when she heard a weak voice from the back of the hut. "Sigunn? Have you brought me the stars, like I asked?"

Great, another madwoman. Keeping one hand near her dagger, Hervor said, "I'm not Sigunn. My name is Hervard. I've come to ask for your help."

An old woman who resembled nothing so much as a bundle of sticks with a wispy cloud of hair on top came shuffling out of the smoke. "I need the stars for my spell," she said petulantly. "Where is Sigunn? Why is she taking so long?" Then she noticed Hervor, and cocked her head to one side. "No, no, you're not Sigunn. Not Sigunn at all. Not Sigunn, nor Hervard, are you?"

Hervor's breath caught in her throat. "What do you mean?"

"Hervard is a man's name," the old woman told her patiently, as if speaking to a rather slow child. "Surely your mother knew better."

For all that this woman looked like she wouldn't notice the gods if they did a fair-day dance in front of her, she was clearly more alert than she seemed. Hervor allowed herself a little hope. "I need your help."

"Sigunn hasn't brought me the stars yet," the old woman reminded her.

Staying patient took real effort. "You don't need the stars for this. I'm told you know things. Do you know how to quiet the dead?"

Silence descended in the hut, except for the quiet crackle of the fire, putting out more smoke. Hervor's head was already beginning to hurt. But she stayed where she was, meeting the old woman's clouded eyes, clenching her hands and praying. Please. After three months of searching, she had to find *something*.

The old woman sank down onto the floor, still staring. Hervor crouched in front of her. In the dark shadows of her mind, the voices stirred, but said nothing she could understand.

At last the old woman shifted and seemed to wake. "That's not of the gods," she said, her voice crackling almost as much as the fire. "Not the kinder ones. Not Valnarath's dreams, nor Alfrenvald's secrets, nor Melsafny's gentle rains. Nor the power of the stars, bright and clean. That's blood you're talking about. Eldaskrid and her hells. Bolvereik."

"Yes," Hervor said, the word rasping from her throat. "I need someone who knows about that. I know the names of the dead, and something of how they died. What must I do to silence them?"

"No," the old woman said and, before Hervor could react, she got up and shuffled towards the back of the hut.

Hervor pursued her. "You have to tell me! They're driving me out of my skull. They see through my eyes, but they don't hear me when I tell them to leave me be. If I don't get rid of them, I'm going to snap. And you've got no idea what will happen if I do. I—"

The old woman had retreated behind a ragged scrap of curtain, but at Hervor's words she emerged again and stabbed one bony finger at her chest. "I smell the blood on you," she hissed, and Hervor fought not to retreat from her burning gaze. "I know what you are, girl. Blood-mad, blood-drunk. Oh,

I know what you can do. But do you know what the *blood* can do? Dangerous enough on its own, yes, that's why people fear it, but it's worse for such as you. The blood calls to you, knows you as its own. I'm an ordinary woman, and so was my Sigunn, but drauðr killed her anyway, all because we made a little mistake. Do you think I would risk that again, with someone like you? It would eat us both alive!"

Hervor's hands were useless fists; hitting the old woman wouldn't get her anything. Was the crone telling the truth? Was she in special danger from blood magic, because she was a berserker? Or were these simply the rantings of a woman driven mad by the loss of her daughter?

"Go away," the old woman said, turning her back on Hervor. "I'm old and alone and my life isn't much, but I won't throw it away to help one like you. Bolvereik laughs while you kill. Ask him to help you kill your voices."

"They're already dead," Hervor snarled, but the old woman merely crouched with her face to the wall and began rocking back and forth.

She stayed there a moment longer, but the crone was humming tunelessly, oblivious once more. Blinking away tears of despair, Hervor went back out into the night.

9

BERSERKER

"Hervard!"

"What?"

"Where's Enjarik?"

"Hell if I know," Hervor said, closing her eyes again. She was lying on a grassy bank next to where *Disir's Fury* was beached, with the late-afternoon sunlight beating down on her, and it felt great.

"Well, go find him," Heiðelt said.

"Find him yourself!"

Hervor opened her eyes again and saw Heiðelt grinning at her in the way that said he was in a mood to throw his weight around. "Uh-uh, bilge-boy," he said. She didn't get called that often any more – except by Vigmand – but Heiðelt didn't say it as an insult. "I've been on the *Fury* longer than you have. That means I get to tell you what to do. And I'm telling you to go find Enjarik and let him know that I've caulked the garboard for now, but we should get it properly fixed as soon as we get the chance. Before the autumn storms, certainly."

"Can't we just tell him when he comes back?" Hervor snuggled deeper into the thick grass.

Heiðelt's grin widened. "You don't want Enjarik to think you're lazy, do you? Move your ass, bilge-boy."

Hervor spat a few well-chosen curses at him and heaved herself to her feet.

Enjarik had wandered off on his own shortly after *Disir's Fury* put to shore in this sheltered inlet. His expression had been less than pleasant; Hervor wondered if he was suffering after-effects from the celebration with Gilvind's ransom. Certainly a few of the other men were still acting like the walking dead, two days later. Whatever the reason, she would have preferred to give him the distance he wanted.

At least he'd had the decency to leave a track she could follow. For someone who lived most of his life at sea, he was unreasonably good at hiding his traces when he wanted to. Hervor followed his footprints up the muddy bank of a small stream, into the thick birches that crowded down close to the beach. They were yellowed and drooping from lack of rain, but even so, being among their white trunks made her smile. Sometimes it was nice to get away from the crew for a while. She liked the company of vikings more than that of bondsmaids, but they still grated on her nerves at times.

The green silence closed in around her, broken only by her breathing, the occasional call of a bird, and the trickling of the stream. Hervor, kneeling to splash water over her face, realised the prints she'd been following had faded away like mist.

Damn. Well, they were in an isolated area; she could risk yelling. "Enjarik?"

No answer.

"Where'd you go, you slippery bastard," she muttered, then raised her voice again. "Enjarik? Heiðelt's got a message for you!"

"What is it?"

She spun and slipped on the moss; for a moment it was all Hervor could do to keep her feet. Enjarik watched this with his usual sardonic patience. He was only a few paces away; had he heard her calling him a bastard? Probably. "He's caulked the garboard," she said when she'd regained her balance. "But it needs better mending than he can give it, or come some autumn storm, you may find yourself swimming."

"He sent you out here just to tell me that?"

Hervor snorted. "Wasn't my idea. I figured you could find out when you came back. I don't care what stories the old fathers tell about the weather getting worse every year; it's not like an autumn storm's going to sneak up on us by sunset."

That got a hint of a smile from the viking leader, the first she'd seen in a while. He'd been sour as hell lately – since getting the ransom from Gilvind. Or before that? It had been worse since the celebration, certainly. "For a man who didn't go on a four-day-drunk, you sure don't look lively," Hervor said.

Enjarik, crouching to drink from the stream, dismissed this with a shrug of his broad shoulders.

Curiosity had been gnawing at Hervor since she'd asked Heiðelt about Enjarik's behaviour with women. She couldn't pass up an opportunity to pry. "Come on, even Vigmand's in a good mood for once," she said. "Probably because he had enough money to bribe someone to ignore his face. You wouldn't have had any trouble; why didn't you take up with one of the jarl's daughters? They were certainly willing."

The viking leader ran wet hands through his hair, raking it back from his face. Droplets of water glimmered like jewels in his beard. "They were stupid tegs, both of them, and nothing special to look at."

The words were plausible, but their harshness rang false. "Heiðelt told me a woman tried to knife you in bed once," Hervor said. "Is that why you never take any woman now?"

Enjarik paused, eyes on her. And Hervor never got a chance to find out what he would have said, because she saw that flicker again, like desire suddenly suppressed – and without warning, something slipped into place.

It was like one of those blacksmith's puzzles Ungaut had always been fiddling with back at Rognjeld. Turn it this way, turn it that way, and suddenly the tangled mess of metal came apart into simple shapes. Hervor stared at the shape that had appeared in her mind, and was shocked enough that she blurted it without thinking. "No, that's not it. You want men."

Fury descended over Enjarik's face, but it came just a hair too slow; for one lightning instant, Hervor had seen the shock it replaced. Her mouth ran on without her, even as she backed up a step. "Shite, I should have seen it before! The way you look at me – it's not *me*, it's because I'm dressed like a man—"

Enjarik lunged for her. Hervor leapt clear just in time, to the other side of the stream. She held up her hands in self-defence. "I won't tell anyone, I swear! Hells, I've got secrets enough of my own; I can keep one more!"

He stood, divided from her by the stream, hands clenched into fists, breath coming fast. Hervor tried not to think of what those fists could do to her. Or what that sword could do, if he drew it. Sure, Heiðelt had been teaching her – but Enjarik could still gut her, skin her, and hang her out to dry.

But he hadn't killed her yet.

"It's true, isn't it," she said, more softly. "Most men would've been screaming about the insult to their honour. You – you just went after me like you needed to me to stop."

"You talk too much," Enjarik snarled. His sea-coloured eyes glittered with a tangle of emotions. Anger, yes, but also fear… and in with it all, that peculiar lust. Because when he looked at her, he saw someone he could pretend was a man.

"Have you always been like this?" Hervor asked.

He gave a short, harsh laugh. "You're one to be asking prying questions, *Hervard*. Where are you from? What are you running from?"

Hervor pressed her lips together. Shite. She'd gotten *him* asking questions now. Not a good move.

Enjarik grinned wolfishly, enjoying her discomfort. "You expect me to answer your questions, when you don't answer mine? How do you know how to sail, *Hervard*? You'd never set foot on a ship three months ago, but within a fortnight you could've made your way around the *Fury* blindfolded. Where'd that come from, bilge-boy? And what's nipping at your heels, that has you running scared? Don't think I haven't noticed you sneaking off in towns, when everyone else is drunk. What do you go looking for, when you think no one is watching?"

Hervor's back slammed into a tree. Only then did she realise she'd been retreating, instinctively, trying to put more distance between her and Enjarik's probing.

"You've got your secrets," Enjarik said, crossing his arms over his broad chest. "I've got mine."

Afterwards, Hervor couldn't have said why she did it. Maybe because her back was against the tree, and it gave her the spine she'd been lacking. Or because she was sick of running. Sick of hiding. Or because of the look on Enjarik's face – like someone had torn away his shield, and he didn't know which direction the attack would come from.

"Fine," she said. "Let's trade."

Enjarik stared at her.

"I'm a bondsmaid," Hervor said. "I ran away because I was treated like shite, and besides which I'd killed a man. I know how to sail because there are dead men in my head who knew how, and they talk to me. I puke my guts over the rail every other day, even after three months at sea, because sometimes when they talk I can smell their rotting flesh. And even though I know how dangerous drauðr is, it's the only hope I've got, so I'm trying to find a witch who can send their souls to Slavinn where they belong."

The viking's crossed arms slipped free in shock. Hervor gave him a smile every bit as wolfish as his own. "Your turn."

"Fuck *me*," Enjarik whispered. The oath lingered in the still air of the wood. "Are you serious?"

"Would I make that up?"

"How should I know?"

"You've seen how I act. You think I'm puking for fun?"

Enjarik shook his head slowly.

"I answered your questions," Hervor said. "Now you answer mine."

"I never agreed to that."

"You don't want to answer. That tells me everything I need to know. So, since I know, and you know, and we both know the other knows, why not just admit it? You lust after men."

She understood his reluctance. Feigald had once caught two bondsmen together with their breeches down; he'd whipped them both, then sold them as thralls. Hervor had always wondered if he knew Ungaut did the same from time to time – if he'd taken out on those bonders the anger he couldn't unleash on his son.

Nobody could sell Enjarik into thralldom… but he could lose his crew, his ship, everything that mattered to him.

He turned half away and stopped. Hervor could see the muscles in his forearm tense, as if he wanted to clench his fists again but wouldn't let himself. The golden sunlight that filtered through the birches gilded his head. The potential for violence hung in the air – violence, or something else.

"Yes."

He delivered the word through his teeth, so quietly she almost didn't hear him. Even though Hervor had known the truth, hearing it still made her want to laugh in disbelief. He drew women like honey drew flies, and he didn't want any of them. He wanted men.

Or Hervor.

"That's why you stare at me that way, isn't it?" she asked. "Because I look enough like a man to draw you. But underneath the disguise, you know I'm a woman, so I'm 'safe'. You don't have to feel guilty about wanting to bed me."

Enjarik faced her again, and the look in his eyes made Hervor's blood heat. Violence, or something else: she knew which one she preferred.

"Why not do it?"

His body jerked.

Hervor licked her lips and came forward a few steps, until she was back at the stream's edge. Only a thin ribbon of water separated them. "We both want to. And nobody but us has to know you're pretending I'm a man."

"You're mad."

"Told you that already. Come on, Enjarik; stop stalling. I'm offering; enjoy it while you've got the chance." Hervor stepped over the stream, and had the very satisfying experience of seeing *him* retreat from *her*.

But there were trees everywhere, and soon he ran up against one, as she had a moment ago. That was enough to stop him. He wasn't really interested in running.

And she didn't want him to run. She'd only bedded one man before, a fellow bonder; she would have taken Rannvar, if she'd ever gotten the chance. But Enjarik drew her in a way no one had, not even Rannvar. It wasn't love – or if it was, all those songs were lying – but it didn't have to be.

Hervor put one hand on his shoulder, ran it down his arm, feeling the tension binding his muscles tight. "Just think of me as Hervard."

When they were done, Enjarik laced his breeches up and left without a word.

She wasn't surprised. When was the last time he'd bedded

anyone? Had he ever actually lain with a man? Or was this the closest he'd let himself come?

No way in *any* hell could she ask him that.

Hervor wiped herself clean and pulled her breeches back up. As long as she waited here a few minutes, then returned to the ship from a different direction, no one should suspect anything. But it was dusk now – they'd taken longer than she realised – so she'd need some answer ready if anyone asked her what she'd been doing all this time.

"Just a whore, after all."

Hervor spun around. Vigmand stood not far away, almost invisible in the thin twilight, and her heart leapt into her throat.

"How long have you been doing it, bitch? How long have you been spreading it for Enjarik?" Vigmand spat onto the moss. "Since the beginning, I bet. He wouldn't let a woman on the ship unless she was his whore."

Oddly enough, her first fear had been for Enjarik, that Vigmand had been spying long enough to hear Enjarik admit he desired men. From the sound of it, though, Vigmand had only caught the end. He thought Enjarik wanted her as a woman.

With that risk out of the way, Hervor was free to be angry. "I said months ago I wouldn't whore for my keep," she said coldly. "I meant it. I've earned my place on the *Fury*. I'm a better sailor than you now."

His scarred face twisted. "You think knowing which rope to grab makes you better, bitch?"

"You know what, Vigmand? I think you're afraid. I'm a better sailor than you, and you can't forget how I kicked your ass on Darrey." It had been more of a draw, but there was enough truth in the taunt to hurt him. "One day you'll turn around and find I'm a better warrior than you are. I'm already smarter, and I've got twice the balls you do." Hervor grinned, baring her teeth like a snarl. "You're afraid I'm more of a man than you are."

She knew he would attack, but the grey light deceived her, making her misjudge his speed. Vigmand shoved her backwards and she stumbled into a tree; her head slammed into the trunk and for a moment she saw stars. She threw a punch blind, more to keep him back than to do any real damage. Her fist found only air, and then his slammed into her stomach, driving all the breath from her lungs.

"Just a whore," Vigmand snarled, knocking her to the ground. Hervor gasped for air, but her lungs had stopped working. She'd just managed to inhale when he kicked her in the ribs.

Bones cracked. Hervor couldn't even scream. And even if she could, they were far from the *Fury*; no one would come to her rescue. Fear wrapped a cold hand around her, in the wake of the stabbing pain. Fear of him… and of what he might push her into.

Her vision cleared just enough to let her make out Vigmand in the fading light. One leg was within reach. She grabbed his ankle and yanked as hard as she could.

He crashed heavily to the forest floor. But Hervor didn't linger to press that advantage; she shoved herself to her feet and ran.

The forest was nearly dark, Hervor smashing past half-seen branches, hoping she was going in the right direction. If she wasn't, she was fucked. Therefore, she *couldn't* be running the wrong way. She was headed towards the ship, and in a moment she'd clear the trees and—

Vigmand hit her from behind, carrying them both to the ground. The impact made her chest shriek with pain. Then Vigmand was rolling her over onto her back, tearing at her clothing, snarling that if she'd whore for Enjarik, she'd whore for him.

Despite her broken ribs, Hervor fought back. She thrashed and punched and kicked and bit; anything to slow him down. For an instant he drew back and she thought she'd gotten an opening – but he struck her once, twice, more, until she'd lost count and could see nothing but red.

And with the red came fire.

This time she felt it coming, knew what was happening. Knew – but couldn't do anything to stop it. Vigmand's touch faded into the distance, as if he held someone else pinned. The pain faded, too, replaced by that internal heat. And with it came the voices of the dead, howling for blood.

Her hands found his shoulders, and from flat on her back, with no leverage at all, Hervor threw Vigmand off. He slammed into a tree and fell to the ground. By the time he was on his feet, she was on hers, and Hervor couldn't see his expression through the red haze over her vision, but the

snarling beast that ruled her now hoped it was one of fear.
His punch seemed laughably slow. She stepped clear and
then struck back, raining blows on his head, his stomach, his
groin, anywhere vulnerable. When his hands came towards
her she slapped them away, then flung him against another
tree. This time when he began to fall she grabbed him,
bracing him against the trunk so she could hit anywhere she
wanted. He no longer tried to defend himself; his arms
flopped limply at his sides. Bones cracked under her fists.
She could smell the blood now, filling her nostrils, stinging
in her throat, and the scent drove her on, drowning out all
thought. When one of his arms rose at last she seized it and
slammed her hand against his elbow, shattering the joint.
His scream was a weak, pathetic thing. He collapsed to the
ground, too beaten to stand, and now it was her turn to kick,
to strike him as he had struck her, her feet thudding into
every available part of his body.

She finally became aware of other things. Noise. Pressure
on her arms. Someone was holding her, trying to drag her back
from her prey.

They were hitting her. Had been for a while. She hadn't
felt it. Now she turned and saw them, some armed with clubs,
others just with fists, steel glinting here and there. It was
almost full dark and she couldn't see how many there were,
but it didn't matter. All of them together couldn't stop her.
She waded in, fists flying, and one struck her hard enough

with a branch that it splintered. The ghosts laughed as Hervor threw him to the ground. She'd deal with them, and then she'd go back to Vigmand, tear him apart until she was painted with his blood.

Something heavy and solid crashed into her head, and for a brief instant she felt pain, *real* pain, before the blackness took her.

Hervor awoke to agony. Agony, and exhaustion that surpassed anything she'd ever known. This time there was no Saeunn to force concoctions down her throat, and she felt for the first time the true, debilitating weakness that followed a berserker's fit.

The faintest of whimpers escaped her lips as she prised her eyelids open. Firelight stabbed through to the back of her skull. Only after her sight cleared did she realise she was on her feet – but not standing. Chains bound her body to a tree, holding her up. She would have collapsed without them.

They weren't a kindness. She wanted to collapse. She was bound because—

The memories swam up piecemeal from the shadows of her mind. The vikings surrounding her, blows raining down, because—

Bones shattering, flesh pulping. Vigmand breaking under her hands, her feet. The vicious, ugly *thing* within her not stopping at mere defence, not even at defeat, because it wanted him to scream and bleed and die. As Berkel had.

But this time she remembered doing it.

this was our weakness
and yet it was not
we should never have been weak

"Fuck you," Hervor whispered through lips that felt like raw meat. "I've got my own problems."

Even speaking hurt, as if she'd been screaming without knowing it. She could taste blood in her mouth, and she hoped it was her own.

sweet, sweet blood
we remember the blood

She would have cursed Bolvereik, but what was the point? He'd marked her as his own, and no amount of pretending she wanted to follow Alfrenvald instead would change that.

traitorous Bolvereik
abandoned us
was it he who stole our strength?
did we fail him as well?

"Fuck Bolvereik, too," she croaked, and at last she lifted her head.

Enjarik leaned against a birch not far away, on the other side of a small fire, arms crossed. His sword was ready to hand, point-first in the dirt in front of him, and she knew what that meant.

"So much for confessions," he said in the low growl that never failed to make her want to bolt for cover. "You left a few things out."

Pain and exhaustion and shame at what she heard in his voice made tears slip from Hervor's eyes. "I'm sorry."

"You're *sorry?*" Enjarik straightened explosively from his slouch. "You're a fucking berserker! You killed Vigmand – Geirrankel's balls, Heiðelt's been teaching you to fight. If you'd been armed, you might have killed us all."

No surprise about Vigmand. Hervor thought he'd still been alive when she was knocked out, but after what she'd done... nothing short of a miracle could have saved him.

And nothing short of a miracle could save her now. She was chained to the tree, and if she weren't she'd fall in a heap on the ground. Her life depended on Enjarik's mercy, and Hervor's mind relentlessly listed the reasons he had for killing her. She'd murdered one of his men. She was a berserker, unreliable, like a rabid dog. She was a liar and a fugitive. She knew his secret, could betray him to the others.

Not even a miracle.

She wanted so badly to be able to straighten up, face him proudly, take her death like a warrior. She might not be a man, but she *was* a viking. If not a very good one.

But there was a weakness in her. Not just her exhausted

body, but something that refused to face death with pride. Something that desperately wanted Enjarik's good opinion, and couldn't stand the way he was looking at her now. She was a killer, but not without cause. "Vigmand tried to rape me."

"And for that, you broke almost every bone in his body."

I didn't mean to. That was what she wanted to say. But it would sound stupid, childish. Besides, it wasn't true. She *had* meant to. She'd been berserk, but she didn't get to disown that part of herself, as if it were some other person who'd pinned him against the tree and kept on punching.

Even so, the words limped out of her mouth. "He triggered the fit. Pain does it. He broke my ribs, hit me until I couldn't see straight. That sounds like an excuse; I don't mean it as one. It's… an explanation. Part of it. Because part of it was my choice." Here she had to stop and spit; blood had been pooling in her mouth, muddying her tongue. "I don't know if I could have chosen otherwise – chosen not to go over the edge. They say some berserkers can, but this is only the second time I've slipped; I have no idea how they control it. But it doesn't matter, because I didn't try. I gave in."

"Is that supposed to make me trust you?"

She heard the fear in Enjarik's voice. He was no craven; it wasn't that kind of fear. But no one could trust a berserker, and it frightened him that he had.

He *had*.

For the first time since seeing the unsheathed sword, Hervor began to hope that she might yet live.

Fear, yes... but also pain. Betrayal. He'd liked her, and as she dragged her sagging head up again she saw the regret in his eyes. He didn't want it to end like this.

"No," she said, answering his question. "I can't make you trust me; there's no reason you should. I don't expect you to let me back on the *Fury*. But – you don't have to kill me."

"You beat one of my men *to death*."

"What was I supposed to do? Let him rape me, then come to you for justice?"

The muscles in Enjarik's neck tensed. She believed he would have punished Vigmand – but it would have been too little, too late. In the moment, the only defence she had was overwhelming violence.

Enjarik said, "For the others, it won't be about that. They didn't see it happen, and some of them wouldn't care. They may not have liked Vigmand much, but they didn't hate him enough to wish that end on him. If you don't pay for that..."

Hervor coughed, sending knives through her whole body. Knocking out a berserker wasn't easy. "So what – we go to a lawspeaker, get him to declare the weregild?" Hervor knew very little of the law, except that the blood-price was supposed to be paid to the dead man's kin. Vigmand was a raider, an outlaw. Did he even have any kin to pay?

No. For vikings living outside society, the blood-price could only be paid in blood.

"There's little mercy in them. They want you dead." Enjarik spoke of the others, and his blue-green eyes held regret... but his voice was as unforgiving as Eldaskrid passing judgement.

Who could Hervor pray to for mercy? Why should the gods listen to a bondsmaid like her?

Enjarik touched the hilt of his sword – hesitated – then pulled it from the dirt.

Hervor sagged in her chains. Yes, he felt pain, but since when would that stop him? He was the most ruthless man she'd ever known. He had to be, for the life he led. Killing her would hurt him, but he'd do it anyway.

She sent an inarticulate prayer to Bolvereik, dragged together the tattered remnants of her strength, and threw herself against the chains that bound her. Fire screamed through her body, but it didn't bring on the rage; she collapsed once more, trying not to weep, and felt the blackness coming for her again.

"You're a good man," Enjarik said. His voice sounded like it came from very far away. "Woman. Warrior. I'm sorry it's turned out this way."

Her vision was fading, but Hervor forced her chin up and met his gaze one last time. "I'm sorry too," she said, and bit down hard as he raised his blade. She would not cry.

Enjarik's arm came sweeping down, and the pommel of his sword crashed into her temple.

10

AETTARSTAÐ

She was cold – a damp, bone-deep chill whispering that she might never move again. Hervor had drifted in and out of awareness for what felt like forever, but now light was pressing against her eyelids, dragging her back towards reality. What she was lying on felt like leaf-mould and dirt, and when Hervor forced her eyes open, she saw trees. Dawn was breaking, and she was still in the forest.

Enjarik had left her alive.

Alive, and unchained from the tree, but that was it. The sea wind and the earth had leached all warmth from her body, and her shivering flesh hurt like a bastard. Gods, what had they *done* to her?

She put one hand against the dirt and pressed experimentally, trying to push herself up. It hurt badly enough she choked back a scream. Enjarik had left her alive, but much good that would do her if she couldn't move, just lie here until she died of exposure or starvation.

the earth weighs us down

Exposure or starvation, with only dead men for company.

But with the dawn came a tiny fragment of warmth, and a tiny fragment of hope. She was still alive. That was something.

we thought we had hope

"Bugger off," Hervor mumbled. "I haven't given up yet."

She began to move, a limb at a time, systematically. Something in her right knee hurt, and one or more toes on that foot – hard to be sure how many – screamed bloody murder, but her left leg seemed more or less intact. Bruised foot; that might be from kicking Vigmand. Her gut had taken a real pounding, and there was a slash along her lower back, but worse than that were her cracked ribs. Two broken fingers on her left hand, and another slash on her arm, deeper than the one on her back. Since she couldn't breathe through her nose, she assumed that was broken, too. Black eyes, certainly; she could barely see out the left one. And her head felt sick and swimmy whenever she moved it.

But lying here longer wasn't going to make any of those things better. Hervor rolled carefully onto her left side and gritted her teeth. Here went nothing.

There were pauses where she almost collapsed back into the dirt, but she didn't let herself quit until she'd risen to her knees. There she stayed, panting and weeping, the salt of her tears stinging the scrapes on her face. When she had her breath back, she reached out for a nearby sapling and used it to pull herself the rest of the way up.

She'd made it to her feet. If she could do that, she could manage the rest.

In truth, though, she didn't know what the rest was. She still had her old goal: shut the voices up. But for three months now she'd had a way to do that, and a way to keep herself fed while she did. She'd had an identity, as a viking named Hervard on the *Disir's Fury*. She'd had something she might even call friends.

Now she was nothing more than a runaway bondsmaid again. Friendless and alone.

Hervor flung that thought away. Now that she was on her feet, the next task was to see if she could walk.

She could, with the help of a branch long and straight enough to work as a walking stick. And even though it was stupid, Hervor went to the beach first.

Disir's Fury was gone. Only a gouge in the sand marked where it had been, rapidly washing away in the tide.

"So now what?" Hervor said to the empty beach.

we were unworthy sons

"I wasn't asking you."

She hadn't been on the *Fury* long enough to learn the coast the way Enjarik had, but she knew a lot more about the land than she had back at Rognjeld. Gilvind's holding was north of here. The friendly jarl was south. But he was friendly to Enjarik, not to her.

Nobody would welcome her anywhere. She might as well pick a direction and go. And in the absence of any better target, she figured south was at least warmer.

She was gathering her strength to start walking when something caught her eye.

It lay under a bush, almost too hidden to see. Hervor made her way slowly over, one careful step at a time, and dragged it out from under the bush with the end of her stick.

A leather sack.

Bending over to pick it up offended every injured bit of her body, but at last the sack was hers. Hervor staggered over to lean on a tree and pulled at the ties until she could see inside.

The smell of food hit like a club, almost knocking her over. When she had herself under control again, she stared at the food in wonder. This couldn't be an accident. Bread, dried meat

– gods, trying to eat that would probably make her teeth fall out; some of them felt loose. But it was enough food for a couple of days, maybe.

A parting gift from Enjarik? She hadn't expected that. Not after he'd left her lying unconscious on the forest floor. Tears stung her eyes again, but suddenly the world was looking a lot better.

Hervor slung the sack over her shoulder, gripped her stick, and began to hobble south.

It was bad luck to turn beggars away empty-handed from your gate, but when the beggar was covered in dried blood, people gave as little as they could get away with. Hervor tried to wash her clothes in a stream once, but removing them hurt too much. And with no company on the road as she worked her way south, she fell into the habit of talking to herself, talking to the voices, cementing the opinions of those she met that she was mad. Sometimes that was good: they gave more food to lunatics than simple beggars. Sometimes it wasn't: they chased lunatics off.

She'd been on the road for days when the first storm of autumn caught her.

It came howling up with no warning, or maybe she'd been too wrapped up in herself to pay attention to the signs. The rain caught her out in the open, with no shelter in sight. Drenched to the skin within minutes, Hervor knew she had to keep walking to stay warm. At least this would wash some of the blood from her clothing; she tried to take comfort in that.

Then, when exhaustion had her lurching badly enough that she risked falling, she saw something ahead, almost indistinguishable in the grey smear of rain.

It looked like a fence, like a holding – maybe even a town. Towns cared less about beggars at their gates than holdings did, might even drive her away, but the leaden sky was dimming towards dusk with no sign of the rain letting up; she had to try. Hervor slogged on.

The road led right to the gate. It *was* a town, a pretty big one. Hervor began planning what she would say to the guards. She had a couple of stories to explain her condition; which one should she use?

A few paces short of the gate, one foot slipped in the mud.

She wasn't in good enough shape to catch herself. Her injured knee gave out and, with a strangled scream, she fell in an inglorious heap. And once down, she couldn't make herself get back up. She hurt too much, and she was too damn tired. Hervor lay in the mud with the rain pounding down on her, vision going grey.

The last thing she heard was hoofbeats.

Hervor had no idea how long she was out, but when she woke it was with a feeling of being more well-rested than she'd been since she'd left *Disir's Fury*. She still hurt, but not as much, and—

She was lying in a bed.

The strangeness of that brought her to full wakefulness in an instant. She'd never been in a bed, not in her entire life. Just a pallet on the floor, or a bench on the *Fury*.

Sitting upright proved she hadn't slept the year away like Torgrim in the tale; her ribs still made their usual complaint, though it was softer now. But that made her look down, and she saw to her shock that her old clothes, stolen from Garldor, worn on the *Fury*, torn, dirtied, and soaked with blood, were gone. In their place she wore a loose shirt and leggings – and no bindings on her breasts.

"You're awake."

She hadn't even noticed she wasn't alone. Now Hervor's head jerked up, and she saw a woman sitting in a chair on the other side of the small but well-built room. No peasant hovel, this – hells, no peasant could afford this kind of bed. And the woman was no peasant, either. She wore a dress with embroidery on it, and jewelled brooches, and her greying reddish hair was not just braided but pinned up onto her head. In her hand was a hoop with more half-finished embroidery, and on her face was a level look that bordered on hostility.

Hervor quickly reviewed her memory. How in Bolvereik's name had she gotten here? She'd collapsed in the mud outside town: hardly a good entrance. Obviously this woman had taken her in, but why? And why glare at her as if she'd done something wrong?

"What is your name?" the woman asked.

"Hervard." It came out reflexively; then Hervor remembered her unbound breasts and flushed. "I mean – that's the name I've been using. I… I've been dressing as a man."

"I know." The woman set down her embroidery hoop and frowned. "I tended you when you were brought in. Why were you disguised as a man? Who are you?"

Hervor wasn't about to tell this stranger that she'd been a viking until a little while ago, nor that she was a bondsmaid on the run. "I'm a wandering warrior. I wear men's clothing because it's more practical, and I bind my breasts because an armed woman attracts too much attention."

Enjarik and this woman in a staring contest would be a sight to see. "I have brought you under my roof. I have washed you, clothed you, and tended your hurts. Are you aware of what the gods do to those who repay hospitality with lies?"

The accusation outraged Hervor. "I'm not lying!"

"You carry no weapons. And why are you so badly injured?"

Hervor did know the punishments that awaited those who betrayed hospitality; she hastily chose the story with the most truth in it. "Friends of mine had to take down a berserker, but I was badly hurt in the process. Since I'm no good to them injured, they took everything that was mine and abandoned me." Her sole possessions the vikings had taken were her dagger and a few coins, left on the *Fury* before she went looking for Enjarik, but it was true enough to pass.

The woman seemed to be weighing this story, her expression still flinty. "Not very good friends, were they?"

A lump formed in Hervor's throat. "Not as good as I'd hoped." She sent a mental apology to Heiðelt, who she believed *had* been a friend, and to Enjarik, who'd been friend enough to spare her life.

"So what are you doing here?" The near-hostility was back again. Hervor didn't know how she'd managed to offend this woman while out cold – nor why, despite that, someone had decided she merited washing and clothing and wound-tending. But it might mean she stood a chance of getting more than just food and a wish of good fortune on her journey. Given what little she'd seen of this place in the rain, she knew it was more than a simple holding. The jarl of a town like this had to be powerful, much more so than Feigald. "I told you, I'm a warrior. I'm looking for a jarl to take service with."

The woman seemed to find this funny. "Why should my lord hire a woman who lacks even weapons?"

Hervor bristled. "I may have lost my axe" – she wasn't saying she *had* lost one; it wasn't a lie – "but put one in my hands and I'll show you why." A gamble, but worth taking. Hervor knew she wasn't bad with an axe, after Heiðelt's teaching. The only reason she didn't have one of her own was because Enjarik didn't give her more than a pittance from the treasure they took, and she hadn't been able to afford one yet.

Oddly enough, that seemed to melt the ice in the woman's gaze. As if she'd been expecting a different answer, and Hervor's reaction laid some fear to rest.

Ah, to all eight hells with it. Why tiptoe around the subject? "You've been glaring at me since I woke up. Did you expect me to say I was here to burn the town to the ground?"

It was like walls slammed up in the woman's eyes. "You were not aware when my lord found you in the road."

"Dead to the world."

"You did not hear what he said."

"Not a word of it."

"Do you know what happened to my lord's son?"

Hervor was getting impatient. "Lady, I don't know who your lord *is*. I've only got the faintest idea where I am; I've got *no* idea which holding this is. For all I know, your lord's son could be a troll or an incarnation of Alfrenvald."

The woman looked down at her hands for a long moment. When she lifted her head again, the walls had cracked. "My lord is Bjarmar Bjarmundsson, and he is... old, and his mind is not always what it was. When he saw you in the road, he... he became convinced that you were his son."

Hervor's eyebrows rose. "Well, I'm not. That should be obvious."

"His son," the woman said, "died nearly twenty years ago. He was of your age, and it's true you look somewhat like him. But no – you are certainly not Bjarrik."

The pieces clicked together in Hervor's mind. "And you thought I came here intending to make your lord believe I'm him."

The woman looked down again. "My lord's health is failing, and fate has seen fit to take all of his children from him. Many have seen opportunity in this."

Serving this jarl didn't sound very appealing. On the other hand, if he was sick and childless, he probably had trouble holding on to his followers; he might not turn his nose up at someone like Hervor. He might even be grateful.

"I'm injured," Hervor said, "so at the moment I'm useless. But if you allow me to stay here until I'm well, I'll prove my skill to your lord, and then I'll repay the hospitality you've shown me. It sounds like he could use a loyal houseman."

The woman's head came up again, and she regarded Hervor with a sharp eye. But this time it was more measuring than hostile. Hervor saw the woman take in her height, the muscle on her shoulders, her strong hands. Injuries aside, she was in excellent shape.

"I will consider it."

Hervor nodded. Then, unable to hold herself back any longer, she asked, "Could I have something to eat?"

11

FLICKERS OF ANOTHER TIME

The woman, Jordis, turned out to be Bjarmar's wife. It made sense; there couldn't be many women this wealthy, even in a town. Although she'd thawed towards Hervor, she was prickly; problems rose up at every turn. Like when Hervor, in between huge bites of food, refused to give a name other than Hervard.

"Look," Hervor said, cutting off Jordis's angry words. "It's not a lie that will offend the gods; I've been using the name Hervard ever since I took to the road. It's mine as much as my old name is – I've made it my own. And if I'm going to be meeting your lord as a man, I ought to have a man's name, wouldn't you say?"

"Who says you'll be meeting my lord as a man?"

"I do," Hervor said, startled into bluntness. "What else would I do?"

Jordis frowned. She did that a lot, and when she did, lines webbed across her face. Her life might not have been as difficult as Hervor's, but clearly it had seen its share of trouble. "Declare yourself as viga-kona."

"As *what?*"

"It's the proper term for what you are. A woman who fights."

Hervor thought about Feigald, far to the north in Rognjeld. Had he pursued her this far, sent out descriptions of his escaped bondsmaid that might have reached Bjarmar's ears? Of course, if "Hervor" had her troubles, "Hervard" had his; there was a whole ship of vikings who probably thought he was dead. But Hervard wasn't such an uncommon name. And Bjarmar's holding lay a good ways inland, far from the coast and the *Fury*.

"Only you and I know I'm a woman who fights," Hervor said. Jordis had kept her presence mostly secret, out of the hope that Bjarmar would forget his belief that his dead son had come back. "To the rest of the world, I'm Hervard, and I'm going to stay that way."

Jordis argued, but Hervor won, which added to her suspicion that Bjarmar was in sad need of warriors. The woman brought her strips of cloth to bind her breasts anew. But not until another day had passed – and even though Hervor chafed at waiting, she had to admit Jordis had a point about facing Bjarmar in the best shape she could manage.

With no weapon and no fame, she'd need to look healthy to convince him to take her into his service.

Besides, resting had done her battered body a world of good. Persuading her to laze around more in the ridiculously soft bed wasn't hard.

But at last, dressed in borrowed clothes and her breasts bound flat, with Jordis at her side, Hervor ventured out to see where she'd landed.

Her first sight of Bjarmar's holding, Aettarstað, impressed her. She'd been in a few larger places, but always as a part of some effort to extort money out of the locals with Alfrenvald's holy book, and then she'd been more concerned with being ambushed than enjoying the sights. Aettarstað could have swallowed Rognjeld several times over, and its orderly lanes were straight and wide.

But Hervor was no longer the wide-eyed bondsmaid who'd been impressed by even the smallest town, and before long she began to notice things. How the lanes had once been gravelled, but no one had bothered to repair them in a long time. How refuse was piling up against the walls. How the walls themselves needed repair, and the people of Aettarstað wore clothing that verged on the threadbare. Times were hard everywhere, and had been so for years – droughts in summer, blizzards in winter, early freezes and fierce storms that decimated harvests, and even the Blessed King unable to avert it all. But Aettarstað was badly off by anyone's standards.

Jordis walked stiffly at Hervor's side, all too clearly aware of her home's flaws. Hervor knew better than to say anything; after all, she was here for work. And luckily they didn't have to walk far. The house where Jordis had been keeping her was very close to the centre of town, which was, of course, Bjarmar's hall.

At the edge of the open garth before the hall, Jordis stopped her. "When you speak to my lord…" she began, then hesitated.

Hervor waited, but the woman said nothing more. "Yes?"

"Be careful what you tell him," Jordis said at last. "About the troubles you've had."

Remembering the story she'd given, Hervor said, "With the berserker?"

"His daughter married one."

"*Married* one?" Hervor's jaw sagged. Of course berserkers were real men, not the fanciful tales she'd thought before she went berserk herself – but still, she'd never thought about them having normal lives. Getting married. Having children.

Jordis's lips pressed into a thin line. "It brought her nothing but tragedy; better for her if she had not. But Bjarmar was friendly to berserkers then, and he remains so now, despite… everything. You would be better off not speaking ill of them."

It finally occurred to Hervor that she ought to express some kind of sympathy for the troubles Bjarmar and Jordis had suffered. "I'm sorry. For all you've lost."

Jordis shook her head. "For me, it is not so much. I am Bjarmar's second wife; Bjarrik and Svafa were not my children. No, I had only one son, who sickened and died as a boy. My lord has lost far more."

Hervor couldn't imagine any of it. Having children or losing them, whether young or as adults. "I'm sorry for you both. And I'll keep in mind what you've said."

Jordis nodded and led her across the open garth – could you still call it a garth, Hervor wondered, when half a town lay between the hall and the fence? – to Bjarmar's hall.

The interior was better lit than she'd expected, with hatches high on the walls letting in light. There was no snow-room; Hervor followed Jordis directly into the hall, where small fires flickered in the long hearth that ran down the centre. It was both like and unlike Rognjeld. This was the central building of the holding, yes, but it was for drinking and feasting and ruling only. People didn't live here. And yet it was far larger than Feigald's hall.

Men lounged around on the benches, sitting in small clumps, and their eyes followed Jordis and Hervor as the two women walked the length of the hall. Hervor studied them out of the corners of her eyes. What she saw impressed her even less than Aettarstað had. If these were Bjarmar's housemen, then they were a mismatched and sorry lot. Some were greying; some were beardless boys. Those in their prime looked like they spent more time with a tankard in hand than an axe. She could outfight half of them with one hand tied behind her back.

"My lord," Jordis said, "the warrior Hervard."

Hervor turned her eyes at last to the man who sat on the dais.

fallen
all has fallen
to age
and dust
and rot
when once this hall was warm with light

The voice rocked Hervor back on her heels. For a moment she didn't see the man in front of her, nor the warriors around her; there was only the hall, and it wasn't the same. It was cleaner. Brighter. Tapestries hung along the walls, shields on every post, and the benches were full of men.

Hervor didn't get a chance to absorb that vision. She felt the stiff, furious presence of Jordis at her side and jerked back to where she was – *when* she was – remembering that she'd just been introduced to a jarl and ought to show some manners. She tapped her fist to her chest in salute and looked up at Bjarmar.

Her first thought was that he was the oldest man she'd ever seen. What was left of his grey hair hung in lifeless wisps around his face, and his wrinkles were as deep as if someone had carved them with a chisel. His hand trembled as he raised it in acknowledgement of her salute. He looked like he was in his barrow already.

But then she saw his eyes, and she changed her mind. For all that the flesh around them was liver-spotted and drooping, his eyes were still clear, and he studied her with a much sharper gaze than she'd expected. Not as old as she'd thought, then. Just a man who'd suffered a great deal, and didn't have much left to make him happy.

"Hervard," the jarl repeated, and Hervor wondered with a moment's sadness what that voice would have been in its youth. It held an echo of power even now. "Just Hervard?"

"It's enough of a name for me. I choose not to acknowledge my father." Nobody would accept the child of a pig-keeping thrall as a houseman.

Bjarmar accepted this with a slow nod, not looking away. If he remembered thinking she was his son, he showed no sign of it. "My wife tells me you wish to take service with me."

"I do."

"Well, Hervard the warrior, you seem to be lacking the tools of your trade."

"I was robbed, my lord, by men I thought friends, when I wasn't in a position to stop them." Summoning up a scowl was easy; she just thought of Vigmand.

"If a blacksmith comes to me with no hammer, I do not give him a forge," Bjarmar said. "The carpenters in my town do not ask me for wood."

Hervor saw the glint in his eye and smiled inwardly. Not in mockery; out of respect. Bjarmar was interested, but not interested enough to welcome her with open arms. That still left her a chance to prove herself. "I can show my strength barehanded."

Bjarmar scoffed. "Shepherds and drunkards can swing their fists. That does not make them warriors."

"Lend me an axe, then," Hervor said. "Just for the moment." She cast her eye over the sorry collection of housemen in the hall and let a smile spread across her face. "I'll fight whoever you want. And if I prove myself, then we can talk again."

A rumble ran through the hall – they'd noticed her lack of respect for them. Didn't matter; Hervor was bigger than half of them. And it wasn't like being hated was anything new for her. Besides, sailing on the *Fury* had taught her that she didn't need to be liked. So long as she had the favour of the fellow in charge, she could hold her own.

Of course, that assumed Bjarmar could keep his men in check. He was lucid enough now, but Jordis said his wits tended to come and go. Deal with one thing at a time, Hervor thought, and raised her eyebrows at Bjarmar. "Well, my lord?"

"I'll fight him."

The new voice sounded like it had been scraped over rocks. Hervor turned and found a bull-necked man had stepped out of the crowd. When he had her attention, the man folded his arms across his chest, as if to show off their size. His beady eyes delivered a blatant challenge as he waited for Bjarmar's reply.

"Do you know the customs?" the jarl asked Hervor.

She thought rapidly. Three shields? No, that was the holmganga. This was a test, not a ritual duel. Damn, she *knew* she'd heard tales about this. Around the fires at Rognjeld – but that seemed so long ago. Hells, Arvind had talked about it, back on the *Fury*!

Memory came back in a blessed rush. "Fought in the circle," she said. "One shield only, no replacements. No killing blows, nor maiming ones. First one forced out or disarmed loses."

Bjarmar nodded approvingly. "Do you agree to it?"

"I volunteered, didn't I?" Hervor cast a glance back at the man she was to fight. He was shorter than her, but a lot thicker. Well, that would just make him slow. And the rules governing the fight should keep her from getting hurt badly enough to go berserk. "I just need an axe."

Everyone came outside to watch the show. Hervor cracked her knuckles and looked on as one man – a boy, really, scarcely more than a stripling – traced out the circle in the dirt. Big enough to move in, but not much more. That was fine by Hervor; Heiðelt had taught her to fight on shipboard as well as land, and this wasn't any smaller than the broadest part of the *Fury*. And it would be steady under her feet.

She ignored the hostile gazes directed her way. Hervor wasn't about to let a bit of unfriendliness put her off. Not when she stood to gain so much.

The general milling began to sort itself out. The men had

armed themselves with axes and shields, and Hervor saw
that they intended to stand around the perimeter of the circle.
Only Bjarmar was still empty-handed. She wondered if the
old man even had the strength to hold weapon and shield
any more.

The youth who'd traced the circle appeared at her elbow,
gear in hand, and Hervor took it from him, ignoring his sullen
glare. The shield was fairly shitty work; good thing Heiðelt had
put a lot of emphasis on dodging. One good blow might crack
this thing in half. The axe wasn't much better. But she doubted
anyone would take it well if she asked for replacements.

Her challenger was in the circle already, waiting. Hervor
stepped over the boundary, and the assembled men closed the
gap behind her.

"I am Auðleif Torbrandsson," the challenger announced in a
loud voice. "I have been a warrior since the age of ten. In the
service of Vandstein Bolskegsson I fought raiders along the coast,
and there I slew the viking Grankel the Wild. I received honour
from the hands of the Blessed King himself, for service to him in
the wars over the sea. I fear no man who walks beneath the sun!"

Hervor watched this performance with an ironical eye.
She'd come late to Arvind's story; if he'd mentioned the
boasting, she'd missed it. Well, what could she say about
herself? Not much.

Not much that was true, anyway. But she technically wasn't
under Bjarmar's roof at the moment.

"I am Hervard," she called out. "At the age of eight I slew a wolf that threatened my sister. I have travelled this land from the Ice Knives to the eastern sea, from the ever-frozen forests of the north to the plains of the south, and been the guest of a dozen jarls. I have hunted bears in the mountains and linnorms in the woods, and I've killed two men with my bare hands when they insulted me. And now I've had enough of talking – let's get to it!"

Bjarmar cleared his throat. "Fight with honour," he said. Hervor heard the unspoken reminder: she was surrounded by more than a dozen armed men. If she fought without honour, they'd show her the error of her ways.

But she had no intention of doing that. Hervor set her feet and put her focus on Auðleif, as all around them the men began to beat their axe-hafts against the edges of their shields in a rhythmic pulse.

Auðleif's axe and shield were of better make than hers. His hands were meaty, and his arms massive, but the latter were stubby; that gave Hervor the reach on him. She probably had the edge when it came to speed, too—

He charged at her with a yell.

Hervor knew without thinking that the charge had to be a feint. If he ran at her full-bore, he'd thunder straight out of the circle, and that would be a hell of a stupid way to lose. Sure enough, he began to slow even as she moved. Hervor took two quick strides forward and to the side, turning as she went, and found his back wide open. Auðleif was faster than she'd given him credit for, though; he was already spinning to meet her, and her axe-blow deflected harmlessly off his shield. Hervor used what was left of her own momentum to leap backwards, out of Auðleif's range as he swiped at her. Then, having taken their measure of each other, they began to circle more warily.

Since her shield wouldn't survive many hits, Hervor did her best to keep her distance, closing in only when she saw an opening. But that was hardly a respectable way to fight, and before long Auðleif was snarling insults, calling her a coward, taunting that if she wanted to run, she was free to go. Hervor ignored him. Harder to ignore was the steady beat of axe-hafts against shields; the pounding echoed inside her head, distracting her.

As much to get away from the pounding as anything else, Hervor charged Auðleif. They ended up at short range; she set her feet and shield-bashed him, trying to knock him out of the circle. It almost worked: he hovered, off balance, just at the edge. Hervor saw her opportunity and moved to take it—

And then she was ducking an axe-blow so close she felt the wind over her head. Even with the blunt side, that would have hurt. Hervor managed to get clear of Auðleif for an instant and blinked in confusion. They were on the other side of the circle now. How had they gotten over here? No time to think about it; Auðleif was coming for her—

Now she was on her back, and only pure instinct made her kick out, tripping Auðleif and dumping him into the dirt next to her. Hervor slammed her shield in his general direction to keep him down while she scrambled to her feet. Fuck! What *was* this? That time there'd been the briefest of flashes—

Auðleif's axe slammed into her shield. The metal rim parted with a shriek, and the wood split clean in half; the force of it nearly knocked Hervor off her feet. She staggered and almost stepped out of the circle. At the last moment she spun away, hoping Auðleif was chasing her fast enough to overshoot, but he wasn't. What were the odds of beating him, with her shield broken? She could hardly concentrate on him, either, what with that relentless beat, and the flashes that kept cutting into her vision.

Like when she'd been in the hall, meeting Bjarmar.

Flickers of another place, another time.

Auðleif came for her, and without thinking Hervor shook off the remains of her shield and gripped her axe in both hands, even though the haft wasn't quite long enough. Heiðelt had never taught her to fight this way, but it felt familiar.

Familiar to someone else.

Hervor dodged Auðleif's first blow, caught his second on the haft of her axe, and then, amazingly, began to drive him back. But then he wasn't Auðleif; he was a taller, thinner man with flame-red hair – no, a man as wide as a troll, pure blond – no, a short man with a shaved scalp—

She was seeing the ghosts' memories.

This fight was blending into ones she hadn't fought. Just like on the *Fury*, when she moved with the familiar ease of a veteran sailor. The ghosts were remembering battles they'd fought before. And her body was reacting with their skill, fighting two-handed because that was how they had fought.

This scared Hervor worse than going berserk did.

The crack of wood brought her back. Her first thought was that her shield had finally given out, but that made no sense; it had already broken, and lay in splintered halves on the ground. This time it was Auðleif's shield.

Memory threatened to swamp her. She knew what to do now, how to lure Auðleif's axe out of line, and then split his head open with a downward swing—

"No," Hervor snarled, and dragged her weapon away from that attack by brute willpower. It felt like someone else was pulling on the axe, on her arm, willing her to strike a killing blow. "No!"

With that second cry she slammed her shoulder into Auðleif, sending him stumbling backwards. Then, blessedly, a new memory came, and she stepped in close and rammed the butt of her axe into a particular spot on his biceps.

Auðleif's axe dropped from his limp hand and fell into the dust.

Hervor took three steps backwards before the dead men in her head could get any more good ideas, then stood, panting from more than just the fight. Fuck. *Way* too close. She had not the slightest doubt that the ghosts, if she hadn't stopped them, would have cleaved Auðleif's skull in half. And what would the men around her have done then?

She prayed none of them realised how close she'd come.

The beat had stopped; her head was her own once more. Hervor thought, with the wild edge fighting always gave her mind, that she missed the simpler days when the worst she had to worry about was voices when she slept and Gannveig when she was awake.

Auðleif was watching her, wringing his numb fingers. He made no move to pick up his dropped axe, and Hervor wondered what was supposed to happen now. Should she put her own weapon down? But she was still surrounded by a large number of armed men.

"Give that back to Kjarvald."

The order came from Bjarmar, and the youth appeared at her elbow, hands outstretched. She stared at him, then at the jarl. He was serious. Shite. But he didn't look angry; she tried to reassure herself with that as she grudgingly handed the boy's axe back to him.

"Kneel," Bjarmar said, and came towards her with his slow, uncertain steps.

Hervor did so, biting back a curse when she saw him pick up Auðleif's fallen axe. He must have heard her snarled denials, or seen how she'd almost killed his warrior.

She glanced around the circle, wondering which direction she should run. If it would even accomplish anything. But she couldn't just sit here and be killed.

When she glanced back, Bjarmar was holding the axe out to her.

"Huh?" she said. Not too clever, but she was tired and confused, and now the rush of battle was gone, her body was reminding her she had some bones that hadn't quite stopped being broken, and they didn't much like the way she'd just treated them.

Bjarmar's eyes glimmered with amusement. "You suggested that, if your skill impressed me, we talk afterwards about providing you with weapons. You've defeated Auðleif. His axe is now yours."

Hervor looked at Auðleif and found he was staring very fixedly at the ground. Damn. On the one hand, she'd shamed him badly enough already; this would just cement his hatred.

On the other hand, she would finally have something more than a dagger to call her own.

She took the axe. "Thank you, my lord."

Bjarmar lifted her to her feet – or rather, put one hand under her arm and kept it there as she rose. Hervor wasn't about to let him take any of her weight; fine sight it would be if he fell over when he'd been nice enough to give her an axe. They stood for a moment in the ring of men, and Hervor saw Bjarmar's eyes glaze over, as if his mind had gone elsewhere. She could guess where. She reminded him of Bjarrik, and now she stood in front of him, holding the weapon he'd just bestowed on her. Either he was remembering the day he'd first armed his son, or he was in dreamland, imagining she were him.

She'd promised Jordis she wouldn't take advantage of that.

The others never gave her a chance to. Kjarvald stepped forward again and touched Bjarmar's shoulder, breaking him from his reverie, and then they all went back into the hall. Bjarmar led the way with Kjarvald at his side and the warriors behind him, leaving Hervor and Auðleif to exchange hostile glances before following the rest.

Auðleif made Hervor precede him into the hall, and she didn't blame him. She was armed now, and he wasn't. In his place, she wouldn't want him at her back, either.

She swore herself into Bjarmar's service that night, with her hands to either side of his unsheathed blade, symbolising his right to slash them to uselessness if she failed him. Bjarmar wasn't enough of a traditionalist to seal the oath in blood, so she didn't have to cut herself; she only had to pray his own hands would remain steady as she recited the oath. They did, and with the formalities done, it was time for a feast.

Such as it was. But if the meat was stringy and tough, reflecting the run-down condition of Aettarstað, at least it was meat, and Hervor got to eat as much as she wanted. No more scraping the last shreds off somebody else's chewed bone; she sat at Bjarmar's right hand at the high table, and got the first pick of everything.

There was mead aplenty, and that at least was tasty. Hervor drank deep and told herself not to worry about the ghosts. What could they do to her, anyway? Speak when they shouldn't? Treat her to the smell of rotting corpses? Take over her vision? Take over her body? They'd done all that already, or tried to, without the help of mead. If they had any other tricks up their non-existent sleeves, she was sure they'd get around to them eventually, whether she drank or not. Her ghosts did mutter during the meal, and occasionally she thought she saw more men at the tables than the paltry score here now, but if she acted oddly, who could tell? She was far from the only one on her way to being drunk.

She regretted drinking quite so much, though, when Jordis helped Bjarmar out of the hall, presumably so the old man could relieve himself. The moment Bjarmar was gone, Auðleif rose from his seat, and so did several of his friends.

Hervor leaned back in her chair and tried to map the best way to get clear of the furniture if one of them came after her. The table would slow them down, at least.

"You've beaten me once already," Auðleif said without preamble. His massive arms were folded across his chest, and his jaw was firmly set. "And I'm sure you could do it again."

"Got that right," Hervor said, trying not to slur her words. She'd expected this, but she hadn't expected it tonight. Would it come to a fight?

A muscle jumped in Auðleif's jaw, but he went on doggedly. "You can't beat all of us up, though, not all at once. So I'm warning you now: if you harm Bjarmar in any way – *any* way! – we'll come after you. Not one at a time; not even two at a time. *All* of us. And we'll make sure you don't hurt him ever again."

At first Hervor thought she was so drunk she'd misheard him. No angry words about the insult to his honour; no threats of how he'd get back at her for shaming him in the ring. Just concern for Bjarmar.

Hervor looked from Auðleif to his friends, then out at the rest of Bjarmar's housemen. She'd assumed that the snot-nosed boys and milky-eyed oldsters were here because they couldn't get anyone better to accept their service, and she might still be right. But she'd also assumed that Auðleif and his friends – the only ones in their prime – were here because they could take advantage of the jarl's failing wits, and get the relative luxury of being his housemen without having to work for it.

But the set of their jaws bespoke loyalty, not arrogance. And that was like someone lighting extra lamps, casting the whole of this hall in a new light.

Auðleif was still glaring, and Hervor realised her silence wasn't making her look very good. "You've got nothing to fear from me," she said quietly.

"We *know* we don't," one of the others said, still full of aggression.

She held up her hands to stop him. "You misunderstand me. I don't mean Bjarmar any harm. In fact…" Hells, why not admit it. "I figured you all for louts, living on his generosity without much caring for him. I was wrong, and I see that now. We've got nothing to disagree over."

Despite her peaceable words, Auðleif's already small eyes narrowed even further in suspicion. "If you're not trying to take advantage of Bjarmar, then why are you here?"

"Why are *you* here?" Hervor countered, partly because she was curious, but also to buy time. She had several answers to his question, but she didn't think he'd like any of them. "You look like you could get service somewhere else. Somewhere better."

Auðleif scowled, as if she were accusing him of something. "He's been good to me," the warrior said, as if daring her to argue with him. "He's a distant kinsman of mine, and he saw to my sister's care when she fell ill. When his wits started to go, men started using that against him, and I couldn't let it go on. So I came home."

Home. The word hit Hervor like a fist to the gut. For one blinding instant she envied Auðleif so badly she could taste it. He had a home, a place he fit in. She'd never call Rognjeld home. The *Fury*... she'd been happy there, until it all went to hell. But that wasn't home, either.

And neither was Aettarstað. No place could be. Not so long as she had dead men haunting her. Once she got rid of them, though...

She couldn't afford to think that far ahead.

She still owed Auðleif an answer. "I came here by accident," she said. "Then Jordis told me about his troubles. I figured, like you, that there were people taking advantage of him, and I thought I had a chance to do something good." Hervor allowed herself a grin, hoping it would unwind a bit of the tension. "Maybe not so much as I thought, though. With men like you to defend him, he doesn't need me. Still, I'd like to stay."

Silence greeted her words. From the tables where the others sat, there was a low hum of talk, but Hervor knew they were all keeping an eye on this confrontation.

At last Auðleif nodded. "You sound like you're telling the truth."

"I am." Part of it, anyway.

"We'll see." Not friendly, but less hostile than he had been. "And if you *are* telling the truth… well, then we'd be glad to have you."

Hervor nodded, Bjarmar re-entered the hall, and the men went back to their tables. And Hervor drank more mead, and tried not to indulge in fantasies of Aettarstað as home.

12

A MESSENGER

"What do you think you're doing?"

Hervor pitched her voice so it would carry the length of the hall. The bondsmaid at the other end jumped, then cowered as Hervor approached. "I'm cleaning!" she yelped.

"You call that cleaning?" Hervor looked down at the table and scowled. There was soapy water on it, sure, but only in swipes, with whole stretches of dry wood in between. "A one-eyed man could do better. You've got both eyes, don't you?" The girl nodded in frightened agreement. "Then wash this *right*."

The girl nodded again and bent her head to her task. Hervor stood over her for a moment, watching her scrub industriously, then sighed and strode towards the door. She couldn't stand watch forever, but unfortunately she knew the girl's efforts would fade again the moment Hervor was gone.

All the servants did that. The decay of Aettarstað was in the people as well as the place. Hervor had been there a bare fortnight, but that was enough to show her that the real insults to Bjarmar's dignity weren't coming from his housemen. No, it was the servants who did a shoddy job of cleaning, the drunkard cook who kept the best cuts of meat for himself, the craftsmen who held back half the tithe they owed their jarl. A thousand little insults, and Bjarmar too feeble to stop them, when he was even lucid enough to notice.

Jordis did her best. In Bjarmar's wife, Hervor got her first glimpse of what it was like to have a decent person in charge of a holding's domestic side. She wasn't cruel like Gannveig, and she didn't play favourites; Jordis's own maid was a former bonder who'd earned her freedom and chosen to stay on. Aettarstað was as well and fairly run as one person could arrange, and if Hervor had grown up here, her life might have been very different. But in the end, Jordis was only the jarl's wife: she didn't have the authority necessary to control and punish those who took advantage of Bjarmar's weakness.

Hervor chafed at it, and so did Auðleif. She still wasn't sure the houseman trusted her, but they were starting to get along; if nothing else, they had a common enemy in the people who insulted Bjarmar. She might not have Auðleif's depth of loyalty, but every time the old man looked at her and saw Bjarrik, she felt sorrier for him.

Especially since she'd heard how he lost his son.

She couldn't avoid thinking of Bjarrik. Every time she walked outside the hall into the garth where she'd fought Auðleif, she remembered that Bjarmar's son had died there.

It would have made a great story, if it had been about someone else. Someone whose father she didn't know. Bjarrik had been thrown from a horse while riding, and after that he could barely walk. His days of riding and fighting were over.

Which Modulf Ordgilsson had known. And so Modulf had insulted Bjarrik, mocking him for being useless, in Bjarmar's own hall. He probably thought there was no downside: either Bjarrik would take the insult without retaliating – because he *couldn't* – or someone else would have to defend Bjarrik's honour for him. Either way, Bjarrik would come out of it looking bad.

Bjarrik had known it, too. Which was why, Hervor guessed, he'd found his own way out.

Looking at the open, hard-packed ground where she'd fought Auðleif, she could imagine it all too well. This wasn't any borrowed memory from her ghosts; if they'd seen a fight like that, they weren't telling. No, this was pure fancy… but that was enough. A young man with twisted legs standing there, sword in hand, facing down Modulf with a glare that would have done Bjarmar proud.

Then the beat would begin, axes on shields.

Then the battle.

Then the dying.

For Bjarrik, it had probably been the best ending within his reach. The world wasn't kind to anyone whose body wasn't whole, and even less so to someone like Bjarrik: heir to his father, but physically incapable of carrying out the duties of a jarl. She doubted Modulf had been the only one mocking him, behind his back or to his face, and far worse would have followed once he took his father's place. Instead of living to see Aettarstað fall, Bjarrik chose to go down to Eldaskrid with his head held high. He died a warrior's death, and for that he would feast with Bolvereik forever.

Him and Modulf both, bleeding their lives out into the dirt. Even mortally wounded, Bjarrik had taken his enemy down with him.

Now he lived on as a cherished memory, instead of a broken reality. Just as he'd no doubt wanted.

Scowling, she made herself look away. This morbid fascination with Bjarrik's death wasn't helping her. As far as she could tell, he was safely in his grave, and keeping quiet there. Would that some other ghosts she could name were doing the same.

Hoofbeats made her look up. That wasn't the sound of a plodding draught horse pulling a cart; that was a rider.

A fancy rider, she saw as the horse pranced to a halt in front of the hall. The man's clothes were finely made under the dirt of the road, and the pin holding his cloak was gold. Jordis was the only one in Aettarstað who dressed like that,

Bjarmar being too apathetic to bother. But this was the kind of messenger Bjarmar should have had serving him, if he hadn't let his hold on everything slip.

The messenger gave Hervor a look of thinly disguised distaste. She stood casually, as if she didn't notice. So what if her clothes were plain? She could break this man over one knee without trying. She'd take that over silly decoration any day.

With no one else in sight, the messenger was forced at last to come to her. "I am here to see the jarl Bjarmar Bjarmundsson," he announced without quite looking at her. "You may take me to him."

"He's not available," Hervor said bluntly. "You can wait." She wasn't about to tell this fop that Bjarmar was sleeping, not when he was so contemptuous of Aettarstað. No sense admitting the jarl's weakness that openly. He napped often, she'd discovered, and it was best to let him; otherwise he fell asleep in front of people, and that was worse.

The messenger met her eyes at last. "I come from Thjostan Svernorsson," he growled. Unfortunately for him, Hervor had been growled at by Enjarik, and compared to the viking, this man sounded like a puppy. "You will not keep me waiting!"

Hervor had no idea who Thjostan Svernorsson was, though clearly she was supposed to. What now? Putting her fist in this man's face, though tempting, didn't seem like a good idea.

In her peripheral vision she saw Auðleif emerge from between two buildings and begin crossing the garth. Hervor didn't want to wave him over and look like an idiot in front of this messenger; she breathed a sigh of relief when he spotted them and came their way.

"Auðleif," she greeted him when he came within range. "This is one of Thjostan Svernorsson's dogs. He seems to think he's important enough to warrant disturbing our lord."

Auðleif definitely recognised the name; his jaw set in the line she'd learned to identify as unhappy. It was the same expression he wore whenever he caught someone treating the jarl poorly. So, Thjostan Svernorsson wasn't a friend. Good to know, since she'd just insulted his messenger.

"You can give me your message," Auðleif said. "I'll take it to Bjarmar."

The messenger puffed his chest out. "The message is for *him*, not you."

"We all know what his answer will be."

Hervor didn't, but she kept her mouth shut.

"I insist," the messenger said.

The muscles of Auðleif's jaw said he was grinding his teeth, but finally he nodded. "Come inside the hall. I'll send someone to serve you, and then get Bjarmar."

"Very well." The messenger straightened his sleeves with a great show of care. "But do hurry. I have other messages to deliver, and will *not* be spending the night here."

Auðleif gave Hervor a look she couldn't read, then led the messenger away, leaving her alone with her curiosity.

◆ ◆ ◆

She didn't get answers until that night, when nearly everyone gathered in the hall. Bjarmar was conspicuously absent; Jordis presided alone at the high table. Hervor sat at a floor table with the rest of the men, as she'd done since that first meal.

Auðleif came in not long after the food arrived. He sat down near Hervor and reached for a hunk of bread.

"Messenger from Thjostan, Hervard says." That came from Holmstein, one of the older men. Hervor had learned to respect him, too; old he might be, but far from weak.

Auðleif nodded and tore into his bread.

Isbjorn sighed. "It's that time of year."

"Time for what?" Kjarvald asked it before Hervor could, which was fine by her. Let the snot-stripling boy look like the ignorant one.

"For the moot," Auðleif growled in the same voice he might have used to say, *For pulling out my teeth.* "The gathering of jarls. Thjostan's hosting this year."

Kjarvald perked up visibly. "We're going to Skersstað?"

Holmstein barked with laughter. "Hells no, boy. When's the last time you saw Bjarmar even do the rounds of his lands? He's not going to ride to Skersstað. He hasn't gone to the moot in…"

"Almost twenty years," Isbjorn said; he too was one of the older warriors. "Since before Angantyr died."

Holmstein thought this over, counting on his fingers. "Every three years… I guess it was eighteen years ago. Angantyr left here the year after that."

A sound of disbelief escaped Hervor before she could stop it. Eyes everywhere turned to her. "Angantyr?" she said. "Not *the* Angantyr."

"What other one is there?" Isbjorn asked. "Not a very common name."

"The berserker? But he's a legend."

"Legendary," Auðleif said, "but not a legend. He married Bjarmar's daughter. Didn't you know?"

Hervor remembered Jordis saying the girl had married a berserker, yes – but this was absurd. "*The* Angantyr. The one in all the stories, with the magic sword and everything."

"Tyrfing," Isbjorn said, nodding. "I don't know how magic it was – never saw him draw it – but it was a damn fine sword. Yes, that's the one."

She might have been willing to believe it if someone had told her Angantyr had once been a real man, but surely that had been ages ago. Not within living memory. People like that just didn't exist any more: famous berserkers with magic swords, sailing the seas with their crew of—

Hervor's breath caught in her throat. For one frozen instant she heard not voices, but the memory of them. *We were unworthy sons.*

"Magic sword, the whole bit," she said, fighting to keep her voice steady. "I suppose he had twelve berserker sons, too?" Isbjorn and Holmstein nodded; they were both old enough to remember Angantyr, if he'd left here seventeen years ago. "Poor sods never get named in any of the stories, have you ever noticed that? It's just 'Angantyr and his twelve sons'. Nobody remembers them."

Isbjorn snorted. "Oh, I remember them well enough. Reifnir used to beat me at dice every night – must have been cheating, but I never figured out how. And Hrani was sweet on my sister, though nothing came of that before he left." He brightened suddenly. "*That's* who you've been reminding me of. Angantyr's eldest was named Hervard."

The floor dropped out from under Hervor. *Reifnir. Hrani. Hervard.* Pieces clicked into place. She'd been right that her ghosts were those of berserkers, that it was the touch of Bolvereik that tied them to her. Breech-born, and a berserker herself: she was the perfect person for them to haunt.

And this place, the memories that kept crowding in on her. The ghosts couldn't hear her, but physical things, familiar actions, the world around her... they were capable of recognising those things.

Had they brought her here? All those days spent stumbling along in a daze of hunger and pain – had they taken over her body, like they tried to do against Auðleif, and brought her to a place they remembered?

"Are you all right?"

Hervor blinked and found herself looking into Kjarvald's concerned face. She was lucky she hadn't pitched straight off the bench in her shock. But now they were all staring at her.

She faked a cough, and got several less-than-helpful slaps on the back. But it gave her time to think. Valnarath's *eyes*. She had names now – *Angantyr's* name – and more than just that. She knew who her ghosts were.

What else had Saeunn told her to learn?

"Whatever happened to them, anyway?" Hervor said when her feigned choking fit was over. "I've heard all those stories about them, but there's nothing about how they died. Or how Angantyr died, at least. I guess the others might still be alive."

Another surge of relief when Holmstein shook his head. "They're all dead," he said grimly. "And if it's not in the tales, I guess it's because it doesn't make a pretty enough story. They got into an argument with someone, decided to settle it by holmganga. Angantyr and his sons lost."

"All thirteen of them? How many were they fighting?"

Isbjorn spat into the rushes. "Not many. Four, five? Maybe less. Nobody really knows what happened. The Blessed King oversaw it, and he said the gods turned their faces from Angantyr and his sons."

"That's how it's supposed to work," Kjarvald said, sounding uncertain but determined to believe. "The gods favour whoever's in the right."

"The gods have fuck-all to do with it, boy. Watch enough fights and you'll know that. Nine times out of ten, the man who wins has the strongest arm, the nimblest feet, the quickest mind. But the tenth…" Isbjorn shook his head gloomily, throwing the bone he held back onto the trencher. "The tenth time, thirteen berserkers die at the hands of a few idiots. Maybe the gods decided to play a trick on them. Bolvereik taking back what he'd given."

Hervor stared sightlessly at her food. She didn't want to eat; she wanted to run out of the hall and get on with silencing the ghosts. If she'd had the faintest clue where to find a blood-witch, she would have tried. Or the dead men, for that matter.

"So where are they now?" she asked. "Angantyr was Bjarmar's son by marriage – did he get buried here?"

Isbjorn glared at her. "Are you stupid, or just pretending to be? The Blessed King himself said the gods turned away from Angantyr. You think he'd have their bodies carted all the way back here, so they could be buried nicely? You think Bjarmar wanted them anywhere around here? Hells, no. They were buried where they fell, on whatever island they took the duel to."

"And where was that?"

"How the fuck should I know?"

Hervor clamped her jaw shut and tried not to scream with frustration. She'd gotten the names, just like Saeunn told her to, but she was still missing that last detail. And without that, much good it did her to know who her ghosts were.

The great doors at the far end of the hall creaked open. Silence fell along the tables, and Jordis rose from her seat, eyes wide with shock.

Hervor turned and saw Bjarmar.

The jarl walked the length of the hall, between the tables of silent men. Hervor couldn't have said what caused them all to stare at him; it wasn't anything she could put her finger on. Something in the way he stood. Something in the way he walked. A light in his eye, the angle of his head... whatever it was, she knew that for the first time she was in the presence of the *real* Bjarmar. Not the wit-wanderer who looked at her and saw his dead son, and not even the old man crushed by tragedy. This man saw clearly, and he moved with energy, with purpose, for the first time she'd ever seen.

When he got to the high table, he went to his place by Jordis, but he did not sit.

"Men," he said into the silence. "I have had a messenger today, from Thjostan Svernorsson, the jarl of Skersstað. He has called me to the moot." Bjarmar paused, and his eyes scanned the paltry ranks of his followers. "The invitation has come rather late, I must say, as if..."

He trailed off, but Hervor could guess at the rest of it. As if Thjostan, knowing Bjarmar wouldn't come, had sent the invitation only as an afterthought.

Bjarmar gave a little shake of his head, brushing this aside. "This leaves us very little time to get to Skersstað. Gather your things. We leave tomorrow at first light."

The silence thickened. Jordis's jaw had fallen open.

"We're going?" Kjarvald's voice cracked on the question.

Bjarmar glared at him. "Of course we are. It would be an

insult to Thjostan not to, and a betrayal of my duties to my people."

No mention of the other jarls insulted in the last eighteen years, or the way Bjarmar's people had suffered because of his neglect. But Hervor doubted anyone would bring that up now. They were too busy looking like someone had come along and individually poleaxed them all.

"Finish your food," Bjarmar said. "We must be ready to leave tomorrow."

"My lord." Jordis laid one hand on Bjarmar's sleeve. "You cannot take everyone."

"Why not?" He scowled at her. "I need a proper following; I can't just show up by myself."

"No, but neither can you strip Aettarstað bare! Someone must stay here."

Apparently this hadn't occurred to him. Bjarmar looked out over the tables again, a hint of pain showing as he saw how few men there were. Then he shook his head. "You'll stay here, of course, Jordis. I trust you to take care of things while I'm gone."

She raised her eyebrows. "By myself? The traders would laugh in my face, and you know it."

Hervor privately thought Jordis would do a better job of it than Bjarmar. Woman she might be, which put her at a disadvantage with the traders, but at least she didn't tend to wander off into trances of memory. If she'd been willing to step on her husband's dignity by ruling in his place, she might have been able to make it stick. But Bjarmar was nodding reluctantly, agreeing with her. "Very well. You may keep… four men here with you."

"I will stay," Holmstein said, stepping over the bench and nodding a small salute to Jordis. After an awkward moment, two others stepped forward and volunteered together, followed by a lad whose name Hervor couldn't remember, who might have been older than Kjarvald but was so small and weedy he looked even younger.

"There's your four," Bjarmar said. "The rest of you, be ready tomorrow morning."

Jordis had another protest lined up. "My lord, there's no way we can get supplies ready in time—"

"We leave tomorrow!" Bjarmar roared. Jordis jumped, searched his face, then nodded. She wasn't cowed, Hervor thought. Just convinced. If Bjarmar was taking an interest in the world once more, his wife wasn't going to stand in his way.

Too late, it occurred to Hervor that she should have volunteered to stay. Far easier to slip away in the general bustle of Aettarstað than on the road to Skersstað. But she consoled herself with the thought that Skersstað might hold someone who knew blood magic; she'd turned up no one here. And once she had the information she needed, she could just run. Hervor doubted they'd chase her far.

But she still needed to know where Angantyr and his sons were buried. And if anyone knew, Bjarmar would.

She just needed a chance to ask him.

13

THE GATHERING OF JARLS

She got no such chance that night, nor the next morning; she hardly got a chance to sleep. Jordis hadn't been joking when she said they couldn't get supplied by morning, and the fact that they managed it anyway was a testament to her skill and strength of will.

While Bjarmar offered sacrifice in Aettarstað's temple for a safe journey, his wife oversaw the more ordinary preparations. They couldn't afford to buy food along the road any more than strictly necessary, so Hervor spent most of the night running around town, waking this merchant to sell her dried meat, rousing that farmer to sell her grain, kicking the town baker out of bed so there would be loaves ready by morning. Plus a cart to carry it all in, and mules to pull the cart, and Bjarmar's riding-horse to be readied. Hervor swore her head had only just touched the pillow when Auðleif shook her awake.

A bleary-eyed bondsmaid offered her porridge, but lack of sleep had made Hervor nauseous, so she turned it down. Men were shuffling around in the predawn light, looking as unhappy to be awake as she was. Then Bjarmar appeared, and they all made at least an effort to straighten up. The old man couldn't have slept any more than they had, but he wasn't letting it slow him.

Jordis stood by as Auðleif helped Bjarmar into the saddle. Then she reached up and took her husband's hand.

"Fair weather and good roads, my lord," she said, loudly enough for everyone to hear. Then, softer – "Be careful. And do not antagonise Thjostan."

Bjarmar whispered something inaudible to her before setting his heels to the horse's flanks. As he rode down the street that led away from the hall, the cart followed him, and his men afoot. Hervor and Auðleif were last. Jordis watched them go.

Few people in Aettarstað were up yet to see them leave. They reached the gates quickly and were soon on the open road. Everyone walked in silence at first, but as the sun rose and the chill autumn air warmed a few men began to chat, and when Isbjorn began singing a walking song some joined in.

Hervor did not, and neither did Auðleif, a short distance

away. Every time she glanced at him, his brow was furrowed in worried thought.

She drifted closer to him. "How long to Skersstað?"

He jumped, as if he hadn't noticed her approach. "Depends on what kind of pace Bjarmar sets. A sennight, at least; maybe a fortnight."

"You don't seem eager to get there."

Auðleif didn't answer immediately. They walked side by side, at the end of the small column but away from the cart's dusty wake, and Hervor listened to Isbjorn's song. He had a powerful voice, if not much sense of pitch.

"I'm not," Auðleif said at last.

"Why?"

Auðleif just shook his head.

"Look, I'm Bjarmar's houseman too. If there's going to be trouble, I'd rather know before it bites me on the ass."

"It's ancient history."

"Ancient like, 'in the days of Holmdan the Bold', or ancient like Bjarrik?"

"Like Svafa."

The daughter who'd married Angantyr. "Go on."

More silent walking. Hervor bit her tongue to keep from pressing Auðleif. She'd learned enough of his moods to guess that if she pushed, he'd shut up entirely.

Finally Auðleif looked out across the surrounding pastureland and sighed. "Eighteen years ago, Bjarmar went to his last moot. The next year, Angantyr and his sons left, and not long after that we got word they'd died." Auðleif glanced up to the head of the column where Bjarmar rode, slumped in his saddle. The sight seemed to pain him, and he looked down at his boots. "It hurt Bjarmar, but it broke Svafa. She went mad."

Hervor still saw no connection with where they were going and why there might be trouble, nor any explanation of Jordis's parting comment. Auðleif seemed about to stop, so Hervor risked prodding him. "Mad how?"

"Any way you can think of. She and Angantyr had a daughter by then, barely old enough to walk; Svafa tried to kill her once. Another day, someone found the two of them outside the hall. Svafa was shoving a sword into the child's hand, telling her to go avenge Angantyr. She talked to him, or to his ghost – hells, she talked to the *walls*. I was a boy then, but I remember. She ran outside without clothes on, wouldn't eat, spent whole days crying. Sometimes she didn't even recognise her own father."

"How'd she die?"

"Ran off. Her and the child. Bjarmar sent people to look for them, but nobody could find them."

"Wait – so maybe she isn't dead?"

Auðleif shook his head. "No, she is. She showed up at some holding in the north, in the middle of winter, her daughter in her arms. The child was dead by then – had been dead for days

– but Svafa wouldn't let her go. She died herself, a couple of days later. The jarl there at least was kind enough to send their bodies back; they're buried south of here."

And so Bjarmar lost daughter and granddaughter both. After losing the son who should have been his heir. Hervor felt bad for him, but that still didn't explain why Auðleif was nervous. "So where's the trouble? Was Thjostan that jarl, and Bjarmar holds a grudge?"

Auðleif spat into the dust. "No. I don't remember who it was. There's a grudge, though – Bolvereik's teeth, is there ever a grudge. Thjostan caught Svafa at one point in her wanderings, not long after she ran off. Bjarmar rode to Skersstað as fast as he could. But by the time he got there, she'd escaped again."

"Well, if Bjarmar couldn't hold her, how could he expect someone else to?"

"Thjostan has too many sons, and his wife is Bjarmar's kinswoman." Auðleif growled the words.

No one cared too much which bonders had children, and with whom; it took Hervor a moment to follow the implication. "He thinks one of his sons will get Aettarstað, since Bjarmar has no heir?"

"Maybe." Auðleif kicked a rock, sending it flying off into a withering hedgerow. "Maybe not. It would have been a long shot at best. But even if he didn't let Svafa go… maybe he just didn't try hard enough to keep her there."

Really, Hervor thought, it hardly mattered what Thjostan had or hadn't done seventeen years ago. It was enough that Bjarmar carried the memory.

This was going to be an interesting trip.

Auðleif grabbed her arm then, fingers digging in hard. Hervor looked at him in startlement.

"Don't bring this up with Bjarmar," he said. "Not with anyone. Not any of it. Not Svafa, not Angantyr. All the questions you were asking last night – just let them lie."

Nettled, Hervor yanked her arm free. "They're just questions."

"No, they're not. They're pain, and Bjarmar's got enough of that." Auðleif glared at her fiercely. "If you breathe a word about any of this while we're on this trip…"

"You'll do what?"

His eyes were like chips of stone beneath his brow. "Remember what I said, that first night."

Hervor hadn't forgotten. And she didn't doubt that Auðleif would make good on his words, even in Skersstað, even with strangers watching.

"I understand," she said at last. Auðleif nodded, and let it go at that.

The man should learn to listen better. She'd said she understood. She hadn't promised anything.

Because she didn't want to tangle with Auðlèif and the others, Hervor couldn't just slip the question to Bjarmar in the middle of a conversation. *I hope the weather holds. Yes, the roads are in surprisingly good shape. Where is Angantyr buried? Here, have an apple.* No, if she wanted an answer without a brawl, she was going to have to ask him privately.

But privacy was impossible to come by on the road. It was all Hervor could do to slip away and relieve herself without anyone seeing. She ground her teeth in frustration, but she wasn't impatient enough to risk trouble with Auðleif.

Not yet.

The ghosts seemed to share her impatience, muttering to her often, occasionally treating her to whiffs of rotting flesh. They'd been dead for seventeen years; shouldn't they be down to bones by now? Hervor only realised she'd asked the question out loud when she saw Kjarvald looking at her curiously. She forced a smile at him and then quickly turned away, sweating. The boy hadn't heard her exact words, she hoped. No one knew about the voices yet, and she wanted to keep it that way.

But between the stress and the phantom stench, her stomach was in uproar. She'd started puking again, usually in the morning, after a night of appalling dreams. There were flickers in them now, as if for a heartbeat she could almost see the dead men, or how they'd died. Like in Bjarmar's hall, or during the test against Auðleif. Voices, smells, sights – how many more of her senses would they take over? Would she feel the touch of fleshless fingers next?

"Don't get any ideas," she mumbled under her breath.

Her surroundings didn't help. Autumn was tightening its grip, and the days were more often grey than sunny. The road north started out in farmland, but by the third day it was beginning to wind in and out of woods, and the dark shadows beneath the evergreen branches seemed to press down on Hervor's shoulders, reminding her unpleasantly of Angantyr in his grave. She began to look forward to the open spaces, and even more to their arrival in Skersstað. Surely she could get a moment alone with Bjarmar then, or at least away from the other housemen.

When she saw the town, though, she reconsidered.

Skersstað was what Aettarstað *should* have been. Maybe even had been, eighteen years ago. Gravelled streets, well-tended; houses whose whitewashed walls showed no cracks and whose thatching was fresh; bronze and silver and even some gold pinning the people's clothes. And the *number* of people! Hervor hadn't realised until now how underpopulated Aettarstað was. Or maybe it was just because of the moot. Either way, people were packed in shoulder to shoulder, with barely enough room to move; getting the cart through was a real pain.

But they could hardly lose sight of where they were heading. The great hall stood on a hill in the centre of town, high enough that it was visible even from the gate. The cross-beams of its roof were carved like dragon heads, rearing against the iron sky, and when Bjarmar's dusty group reached the open space of the garth Hervor saw that the carving continued down the front pillars. This was wealth Aettarstað couldn't hope to match.

They were met outside the doors by a well-dressed warrior who gave them a look that stopped just short of contempt. "Who are you?"

Auðleif stepped forward and drew himself up proudly. "We are the men of Aettarstað, escorting the jarl Bjarmar Bjarmundsson."

The warrior didn't look impressed. "Wait here."

He vanished into the hall, leaving them all waiting impatiently. Bjarmar had sent Kjarvald on ahead the previous day, so Thjostan had to know they were coming. Hervor didn't have any basis for comparison, but she didn't think this was a particularly warm welcome.

"You can come in and present yourself," the warrior said when he returned. "Four men only, though, at your side. The rest stay out here."

By Auðleif's flush, that *was* an insult. But Bjarmar merely said, "Auðleif, Hrofi, Isbjorn, and Hervard." Hervor stepped forward with the other three to help the jarl down from his saddle, hoping no one had noticed her surprise at being named. At least Bjarmar hadn't called her Bjarrik.

The interior of Thjostan's hall was even more magnificent than the exterior. The support posts were carved, too, accented with gilded rings just above head height, and bright tapestries hung along the walls. These might be hard times for farmers and herdsmen, but clearly Thjostan wasn't letting that affect him. The crowd of men inside seemed huge to Hervor, who was used to the way Bjarmar's few housemen rattled around in his hall. It looked like every bench was filled.

Mutters followed Bjarmar as he walked the length of the hall. Hervor, listening to them, realised half the men here had no idea who this new jarl was. That was how far he'd retreated from the world.

Thjostan at least knew Bjarmar, and he stood to greet his fellow jarl with clasped hands. The first words out of his mouth, though, weren't encouraging. "You come rather late, Bjarmar. The moot has been meeting for three days already."

Bjarmar had roused out of the stupor he'd ridden in, but that might not be a good thing. He glared at Thjostan. "Your messenger got lost, it seems. I should have known about this a month ago."

"If you'd been at the last moot, you *would* have known."

"I'm here now," Bjarmar said. "With my men. We've travelled hard to get here, and would like to rest."

"I have ever been a good host to those of Aettarstað," Thjostan said, beckoning a houseman over to describe where Bjarmar's men would stay. Hervor didn't bother to listen; she was too busy seething over Thjostan's deliberate reminder. How dare he drag the memory of Svafa up like that?

She grinned ruefully at her own thought. Bondsmaid calling the bondsman dirty, wasn't she? But Thjostan had said it with the intent of hurting Bjarmar. She looked at her jarl's hands, clenched quietly into fists by his side while he spoke with the houseman, and hoped Bjarmar didn't lose his temper. Then she looked at Auðleif, and wondered why Jordis hadn't given *him* a word of warning.

Auðleif managed to keep himself contained until they were in their assigned quarters. Then he exploded, pacing around the room, gesturing at the walls, and kicking anything that got in his path. Railing at Thjostan's arrogance. His rudeness. Shunting them all off into this out-of-the-way corner, into lodgings far beneath Bjarmar's rank.

"And accusing us of being *late*," he snarled. "People come and go all the time during the moot. He knows that! Hells, Storleik's not expected until the day after tomorrow, and even then he's only staying a few days!"

Hervor, who had been trying to keep out of his way, froze. When Auðleif pivoted to make another circuit of the room, he ran smack into her, and she almost fell.

"Storleik?" she asked, once she had her balance back. The name came out high-pitched; she dragged her voice back down with an effort. The rest of the name floated up from her memory. "Storleik Geirriksson? Of Kalstað?"

Auðleif was swearing again; he didn't hear her. On the other side of the room, Isbjorn nodded. "That's the one."

Hervor turned away to hide her expression. Anfinna's father. Fuck! She should have *thought*. They'd travelled north, to a gathering of important jarls. Storleik was an important northern jarl. They hadn't come that far north, though – they were nowhere near Rognjeld. But Storleik was here anyway, or would be. Day after tomorrow.

She tried to slow her breathing. There was no reason to panic. No reason to think Storleik would recognise her. Why should he? He'd stayed at Rognjeld for all of three days, and she'd been nothing but a bondsmaid. He hadn't been there for her berserker fit. He might have heard about it, but he wouldn't be looking for her.

But what if he recognised her anyway? She stood out, tall as she was. Not among the men, but even so...

Hervor clenched her hands until the ragged edges of her nails bit into her palms. Odds were she was jumping at shadows – but why risk trouble? She just had to stay out of Storleik's sight. That shouldn't be hard, not with this many people here for the moot.

In her dreams that night, though, she ran endlessly through Skersstað, trying to escape Storleik's clutching hands.

The problem with her plan of avoiding Storleik was that she didn't have control over where she went. You couldn't throw a bone in the great hall without hitting a jarl, and they were constantly snagging men – not always their own – and sending them off with a message for someone. By the end of her first full day there, Hervor could recognise and name more than a dozen jarls, and she'd formed a particular dislike for Aglang Gestlifsson, who'd sent her on more errands than any other three jarls put together.

When she complained to Auðleif, she wished she hadn't; he just snarled something about how no one would dare treat the men of Aettarstað this way if Bjarmar hadn't fallen so far.

But the result was that someone could send her to Storleik with a message, and she wouldn't be able to do a damn thing about it. She tried handing a message off to another man, just as a test, and almost got into a fight for her pains. That was the other problem: every last man there was strutting around with his chest puffed out, just waiting for someone to injure his pride. There were twelve fistfights and one serious duel, just in that first day.

Hervor felt trapped inside Skersstað's walls. Too many threats. Storleik coming, and all around her were men eager to fight. She wasn't worried about losing; she was worried about going berserk. She wanted to ask Bjarmar her question and get the fuck out of there. Even the dark forests that surrounded Skersstað seemed preferable by comparison.

Those forests ended up saving her.

Thjostan had provided scores of barrels of mead, and the assembled warriors were doing their best to drink all of it before the moot was over. Hervor, facing the grim prospect of Storleik arriving the next day, was drinking her share and more, in company with Auðleif and a small cluster of other men. They were all busy talking about people she didn't know – though she heard someone grouse about Aglang, and she grinned – but then a word caught her ear, and she began paying attention.

The word was "witch".

"Hallmod was furious, but what could he do?" The warrior at the next table over had his head shaved bare and three scars in his scalp. "I asked him to let me go deal with the bitch, but he was afraid we'd be delayed. He preferred to go around."

Hervor's heart sank. Surely it hadn't been "bitch". Someone had said "witch". Hadn't they?

"Keep talking," a man with his hair in many braids snorted. "She'd've painted the trees with your blood. Hey, maybe you should have gone; then we wouldn't have to listen to you!"

After the brief ensuing scuffle was over, someone behind Hervor spoke up. "What's this you're talking about? There's some squatter out in Thjostan's forest?"

"Squatter, hah," the man with braids said. "If it were that easy, she'd be gone by now. She's a witch, and everybody who's gone after her has failed – or not come back at all."

Hervor tensed. "What kind of witch?" she asked, trying to sound like she didn't much care.

The man with braids gave her a patronising look. "The kind who gives out honeycomb to children. What do you think? She's a blood-witch, idiot. If she's human at all. Some people think she's one of the altar."

Roars of derision greeted this last statement, but Hervor didn't join in. A blood-witch. If that was true...

"So where is she?" Hervor asked when the noise had died down.

"Along the western road," the man with the scarred scalp said. His nosebleed from the scuffle had mostly stopped. "The one going to Vindjeld, the southern route, not the north one to Hvarlond. The north road's the one we took, because Hallmod didn't want to face her."

"How far?"

"What do you care?" the man with the braids demanded.

Hervor smiled widely and leaned back, propping her elbows on the table behind her. "Well, if it's not too far away, maybe I'll see if my lord Bjarmar will let me wander off and see to this 'witch' of yours."

She couldn't tell why Auðleif was glaring at her. This had nothing to do with pestering Bjarmar about the past. Well, she didn't have time to worry about him; people were mocking her boast. "A day west of here," the man with braids said, pitching his voice to carry over everyone else's. "You want to try and deal with her? Go ahead. We've got too many of you Aettarstað peasants here, anyway."

Hervor and Auðleif both lunged off the bench at the same time, but she beat her companion there. Grabbing two handfuls of the man's shirt, she dragged him to his feet. "We are not peasants," she snarled. "And we'll be happy to prove that to you in the circle. I'll meet you there myself, if you like." Oh, hells, that wasn't a good idea, but the words were spoken and she couldn't take them back.

The man yanked himself free of her grip. "Prove it in the circle? That wasn't what you were saying a moment ago. What about that witch?"

She smiled at him, more a baring of teeth than anything else. "That too. I'll go deal with her, then come back here and teach you some manners. And when I'm done, you won't even dare to look dogs in the eye."

The man smiled back, equally sharp. "Let's go talk to the jarls."

Once the heat of the moment had faded, Hervor felt cold. She was going after a blood-witch who, from the sound of it, had nasty surprises set for anyone who tried to find her. And if she survived that, she got to fight a duel and try not to go to berserk. But one problem at a time, the first of which was convincing Bjarmar.

But the man with braids turned out to be Thjostan's houseman – she should have guessed it, from his familiarity with the situation – and Bjarmar was in favour of anything that showed a chance of strengthening his position with the jarl of Skersstað.

"Very well," he said. "After the moot—"

"Tomorrow," Hervor insisted. "Or even tonight. Why wait?" She had a very good reason not to, and his name was Storleik. She'd realised, while she was listening to Thjostan's houseman explain what had happened, that this was a perfect way to avoid him. Only staying for two days, Auðleif had said. She could easily stay in the forest for that long.

"In a hurry to die?" the man with braids said.

She laughed carelessly. "In a hurry to come back here and beat the shite out of you."

"*Hervard*," Bjarmar said. "Thjostan is our host."

And that meant she had to be nice to his dogs. Hervor forced herself to nod.

"Let your man go tonight," Thjostan said. She didn't miss the malicious note in his voice. He expected her to come back shamed at the very least, and maybe not to come back at all. Well, he could rot in Borguld. She wasn't afraid of a witch.

Except that wasn't true. She'd feared Saeunn, and that old woman had been masquerading as an innocent nurse. This witch was rather more dangerous-sounding.

But she couldn't pass up the chance.

"Give me food," Hervor said to Thjostan, "and I'll leave right now."

Bjarmar touched her shoulder. When she met his gaze, she saw sorrow there, and she remembered what Auðleif had told her. Svafa had left this town – maybe even ran off into the same forest she was headed for – and died soon after. Was that why Auðleif was angry?

So she forced confidence into her eyes and smiled at the jarl. "I'll be back in a few days," she said. "And I won't disappoint you. I promise."

14

THE SILENT FOREST

The south-western road showed signs of neglect. Clearly no one had travelled this way for some time, except the warriors who'd gone before Hervor, trying and failing to get rid of the witch.

She'd heard plenty of stories about them, while Thjostan oh-so-generously put together a pack of food for her. Even if half the tales were pure bullshit and the other half were grossly exaggerated, she was going into danger. The witch did not seem to like company.

But the stories contradicted each other. Some people made it through just fine, while the travellers right behind them arrived in Skersstað half-dead with fright. Did the witch purposefully pick her targets, or did she torment them at random? Hervor didn't know, but one thing was certain: anybody who went *off* the road was guaranteed a horrible time.

The farms she passed petered out quickly, giving way to the shadowed weight of the forest. Although no one knew exactly where the witch lived, Thjostan had mentioned a huge split rock that served as a landmark. Not long before sunset, she found it looming just a few paces off the road. Hervor wasn't stupid enough to venture into the forest at night; instead she ate some bread, drank mead from a skin, and curled up on her bedroll to sleep. In the middle of the road, well away from the trees. Given how little-used this route was, she doubted she needed to worry about someone coming along and trampling her.

She awoke to light streaming down, filtering through the interlacing spruce branches. After more food and more mead, she faced the trees. The split rock stood in a small open space, and just behind it the forest began, thick and dark. Some light speckled the ground inside, but not much. The stories said instant night was among the tricks the witch had up her sleeve; with that as her starting material, it wouldn't be hard to create.

    the endless dark of the grave
    never to see the sun again

Why could the dead men sense useless things, like where she was and what she was doing, but couldn't hear her telling

them to shut up? Or were they just not listening? Yet another
thing to ask the witch. And she wouldn't get any answers
standing out here.

Hervor squared her shoulders and marched forward.

The chill, damp air of the forest closed around her instantly.
Hervor resisted the urge to turn and see if the road was still
there, ten paces away. If it wasn't, she didn't want to know.
Besides, she had other things to worry about. Some of the men
who'd gone after the witch came back babbling about ghosts and
unearthly wails and severed limbs hanging from the branches.
Others swore the trees moved, herding them, forcing them away
from the road but never letting them near the witch. Hervor
would have scoffed at that, but some of the men hadn't come back
at all, and one man was found in a tree. Not sitting in it; impaled
on its branches. Ten feet off the ground. As though the tree had
picked him up and run him through.

She cast a tense glance at the spruces around her, but they
didn't so much as sway in the non-existent breeze.

She'd vaguely assumed that the horrors of the forest would
lead her to the witch's lair: head straight in the direction they
seemed to want her not to go in, and she'd find the witch. Right?
Only the horrors weren't obliging her. Hervor's skin crawled as if
icy blades of wind were sliding over it, but that was the worst of it.
No wails, no ghosts – Bolvereik's teeth, not even her own. She
hadn't heard a word from them since she stepped under the trees.
She'd almost appreciate the silence, if she weren't so on edge.

The ground sloped down to a small stream. Hervor knelt at the water's edge, then hesitated. What if it was enchanted? Maybe the lack of trouble had been bait, luring her in, and now the stream was the trap. But she was thirsty and wanted something other than mead to drink. The water looked clean enough. Not that she'd be able to see an enchantment.

To all eight hells with it. Hervor shoved her hand defiantly into the chill water, brought it to her lips, and drank.

Nothing.

She snorted at herself. Enchanted water, right. It tasted fine. And nothing leapt out of the trees. In a way, though, that scared her more. She'd come here prepared to do battle with magic, and all she found was a forest. Gut instinct said that meant something worse was in the offing. But where was it?

Without anything better to guide her, she fell back on logic. People usually lived along water, and witches had to drink like everyone else, right? Unless this particular witch *was* one of the alfar, or a floating spirit. But if that were the case, Hervor might as well give up now.

In the thick shade of the spruces, she couldn't judge time as she headed upstream, but it had to be past noon. She still knew which direction the road lay, more or less; maybe she should head back. Not to Skersstað – just out from under the trees, before the light failed entirely. But what reason did she have to flee? From what she'd seen so far, this witch didn't even exist.

Deep in this argument with herself, she hiked upstream, and not until she smelled wood smoke did she realise there was something up ahead.

She caught a split-second glimpse of some kind of structure before all eight hells broke loose.

Vines shot out from the spruces on either side of her and wrapped around her arms. Hervor tore her left arm loose before the vine had gotten a good hold on her – leaving a bleeding rent in shirt and arm alike – but the right one was trapped. Creepers were emerging from the undergrowth and twining around her legs. She couldn't draw her axe left-handed; she went for her dagger and got it out of the sheath, but an instant later another vine had her left arm again, preventing her from cutting herself free. Hervor kicked and writhed, hoping to snap something, then screamed as a length of green encircled her neck from behind. A moment later her scream ended as the plant clamped down and cut off her air.

Immobilised by the vines, Hervor still tried to fight. But spots were covering her vision, and she couldn't feel the dagger in her hand any more. Her knees were going weak. Only the death-grip of the vines was holding her up. Her lungs screamed for breath—

Through the pounding of her heart, she heard something else. A voice. Something touched her bleeding arm – not a vine – and suddenly air flooded back in.

When her vision cleared, she saw a woman standing before her.

The woman looked like she'd tried to shave her own head, and had done it badly. Patches of stubble spread across her scalp like a skin disease, along with dirt and something that might be dried blood. More dirt and blood caked the woman's fingernails, which were all of different lengths, the shorter ones ragged like they'd snapped off. She was bony, half-starved, and clothed in rags that were literally falling off, baring one breast. How old she was, Hervor couldn't tell, but she wasn't elderly – not like Saeunn. Hervor didn't know why she'd expected the witch to be old. But here this woman was, and there was no doubt she was the witch.

Hervor tried to speak, and found she couldn't.

The witch tapped one filthy fingernail against her teeth, studying Hervor as if she were a rabbit in a snare. The vines still held her, although now they were just a formality. She couldn't so much as twitch a toe. She could blink, and breathe, and that was it.

That tapping finger gleamed with fresh blood.

Hervor's blood.

"Very good." The witch looking the way she did, her voice should have been a rasp, or a whisper, or a raptor's shriek. Not this melodious tone, so at odds with her appearance. She sounded totally sane. "My faithful friends, defending me at the last, when everything else has failed. And why *has* it failed, my sweets?" She wasn't talking to Hervor; she was talking to the vines. Maybe not so sane after all.

The witch began to pace a circle around Hervor. The vines curled out of her way as she went, leaving Hervor's arms still outstretched and frozen. Hervor tried to follow the woman with her eyes, but they wouldn't move. Blinking and breathing; that was it. She was lucky she could do the latter.

"No screams," the witch mused, somewhere behind Hervor. "No running. No fear. Why is that? Because there was no *reason* to scream, or run, or fear. Nothing. Where there should have been horrors, there was a forest. And that means…" She stepped back into Hervor's field of vision at last. "Our guest is not what he seems."

Without warning, the witch ripped Hervor's shirt open down the front. Hervor jerked in her mind, but the movement never reached her muscles. She had to stand there, paralysed, while the witch plucked at the fabric binding her breasts.

"Yes, my friends, this would explain it indeed." She was tugging at the binding now, trying to create enough slack to peer inside. But Hervor had put a good knot in, which the woman seemed oblivious to; the knot held, and the cloth didn't slip. The witch finally resorted to shoving her hand between Hervor's legs, the better to confirm her suspicions. "Our man is not a man at all, is he? And so all the little treats I set out for him slept on, unaware that someone had come to visit. All except you, my darlings." She caressed one vine with a loving hand. "You defend me against everyone."

Now her eyes rose at last, and Hervor saw they were a dark,

drowning blue, like the deepest parts of the sea. But they held an intelligence and alertness that belied her ramblings.

"Has Thjostan the Bastard gotten clever?" she asked, her voice sinking to a whisper, nauseatingly intimate. "Has he realised at last the weakness in my defences? Does he think me that easy to defeat?"

Hervor tried to answer, but her voice still wasn't working.

"The weakness was unavoidable – at the time. All I had was a man, you see, so all I could defend against were men. It worked well enough. Who would have thought Thjostan the Bastard would be clever enough to send a woman? But it doesn't matter." The witch smiled, and Hervor saw with a shudder that her teeth had been filed to points. "He's sent me what I need."

She reached out and ran a finger down the scratch on Hervor's arm again, then held the stained tip before Hervor and smiled wider. "A little of your blood, and here you are, still as a stone. Child's play, really. A *lot* of your blood, and no one, man or woman, will be able to come near me." She licked the red off, savouring the taste.

Hervor renewed her useless struggle. Was it really that simple? A bit of her blood, and the witch had her trapped? No fucking magic could hold her! But it did. All her effort failed to produce any result. She was going to stand here while the witch murdered her to fix the hole in her spells.

The witch pulled the axe from the loop on Hervor's belt and tossed it carelessly into the underbrush. Then she prised the dagger from her frozen fingers. "Lovely work, lovely indeed. Perhaps I'll use this. Now, to business." She faced Hervor squarely, dagger in hand. "I need your name. So I'm going to let you speak. But it has to be your real name! If you lie to me, I'll know. And then things will get very unpleasant for you. You're going to die anyway, but if you behave yourself and don't cause me trouble, it won't hurt a bit." She considered this. "Well, not much. It will hurt a lot more if you try to lie. I can give you agony the likes of which you can't even imagine." Her voice promised it was true. Hervor could hear the echoes of her own howls already, if she didn't do what the witch asked.

She was used to pain. And not at all used to giving up.

"Now. What is your name?"

An uncomfortable tingle went through her throat, and Hervor realised she could speak. She gambled everything on this one chance.

"I came to ask for help."

Agony exploded through her body. If she hadn't been paralysed, she would have collapsed. A scream tore from her throat, raw and jagged. It seemed to go on for an eternity; then it stopped, and her vision cleared, slowly.

"Oh dear." The witch sounded genuinely mortified. "I'm sorry. The first words out of most people's mouths are generally 'you bitch' or something like that. I didn't pay attention to what you said. Are you all right?"

Hervor gasped for air in the aftermath of the pain and

stared at the woman in front of her. Was she *all right?* What kind of question was that?

"Did you say you'd come for help?" the witch asked.

"Yes," Hervor said; the word came out a rasp. Her throat hurt like fury, just from that one shriek. She sincerely hoped the witch wouldn't get confused again and make her scream a second time. Given that the woman was several bushels short of a harvest, the chances weren't good.

The witch looked surprised, and more than a little confused. "What an odd place to come for help."

"You're a blood-witch, right? Not a lot of those around." Hervor coughed; she still wasn't breathing right. "I need a blood-witch's help."

"Thjostan sent you to ask for *my* help?"

"Thjostan doesn't have a damn thing to do with this. He didn't send me. I came here – *me*, by myself – to see you."

"Oh." The witch considered this. "I didn't expect that. Well, that's different, then." She stuck her hands out, then drew them back in as if pulling something to her, and with no more ceremony than that the invisible bonds holding Hervor vanished. She crashed into a heap on the damp ground.

The witch was oblivious to her problems. She'd already turned to the structure Hervor had glimpsed before the vines caught her. It was little more than a lean-to, set against a small bluff, and it looked like it might fall on the head of anyone unwary enough to go in. But the witch was headed for it, saying,

"Come on, then," in a cheerful tone, and Hervor had no choice but to shove herself to her feet and follow. She paused long enough, though, to root around in the underbrush and find her axe. No way in any hell she was going in there without a weapon.

The interior was cramped enough that Hervor had to duck. So did the witch; the two of them were of a height. She had enough power to paralyse people and fill a forest with horrors, but she couldn't build a better home for herself than this? Hervor supposed drauðr wasn't good for everything.

The small fire inside produced more smoke than light or heat, but a pot sat on a flat rock next to it. The witch picked up a small wooden cup, dipped it into the pot, looked around in confusion for another cup, then shrugged and began drinking out of it herself. By the smell, Hervor was just as glad she hadn't been offered any. Who knew what a blood-witch was likely to brew up?

The sooner she asked her questions, the sooner she'd get out of here. Hervor squatted gingerly across from the witch, leaving the smoking fire between them, and began. "How do I—"

"Ah-ah-ah!" The sudden exclamation cut her off. The witch shook a warning finger at her. "Fair trade, fair trade. Mine first."

"Yours?" It was like dealing with a small child. A small, irrational child, with lots of power.

"You have to answer, before I answer." By the witch's tone, *she* was the one dealing with a small, irrational child.

The rawness in Hervor's throat reminded her. The witch had asked her name. They were trading answer for answer, apparently. "My name is..." She almost said Hervard, and swallowed it. "Hervor. Now, how—"

"Meltharkatla."

Already Hervor's head was pounding, and she rather thought it had more to do with this conversation than the smoke from the fire. Did the witch think she was answering Hervor's question in advance?

No, it was her name. Hervor's blood ran colder at the realisation. Meltharkatla – it was like a god's name, with three parts to it. Mel-thar-katla – the "mel" was common; it meant *dark*. Lots of women had that in their names. Hervor had heard of a woman named Ankatla, but she had no idea what that part meant, nor the "thar". She opened her mouth to ask, then shut it again. If they were trading questions, she didn't want to give any more information than she had to; gods only knew what the witch would ask. Besides, if this woman was foolhardy enough to give herself a divine name, Hervor didn't *want* to know what it meant.

She dragged herself back to the task at hand. "I hear the voices of ghosts in my head. How do I get them to shut up?"

Meltharkatla rocked back on her heels. In the dimness of her lean-to, her eyes glimmered like dark pools. "Ghosts, is it."

"Yes. Thirteen berserkers, Angantyr and his twelve sons, betrayed and dead."

After a moment of staring across the fire, Meltharkatla rose to her toes and fingers and scuttled around to where Hervor sat. Before she could react, the witch leaned over and sniffed her.

Hervor almost put her fist into the woman's face before remembering that might not be a good idea. She settled for leaning as far back as she could and hoping the witch would go away soon.

Meltharkatla's face was almost completely in shadow when she spoke. "You've touched it, haven't you."

"Touched what?"

The word growled through the lean-to, deeper than Meltharkatla's voice should have been able to go. "*Blood.*"

Hervor couldn't keep the tremor out of her own voice. That sound hadn't been natural. "I'm a warrior. I've fought people. Killed them, even." The dark pools of Meltharkatla's eyes dragged the truth out of her. "I'm a berserker, too. Like them."

The witch crouched there, still balanced on her toes and fingertips, for a long moment. Then she shook her head, slowly, not taking her eyes off Hervor. "No."

"I am. I swear it."

"*Blood magic.*" She inhaled again, let the air out in a hiss. "You've touched drauðr."

"Oh." At first Hervor couldn't think what in hell the witch was talking about; then she remembered what Saeunn had done. "This woman – she was a witch, too – she made me… well, not invisible, but—"

"Dead."

Hervor froze.

"Dead in the world's eyes," Meltharkatla went on. Her teeth glinted as she smiled. "Blood from a dead man, blood on your face, am I right? I know these things. I know much. But there's more, oh, there's more…" She leaned in closer again. Hervor tried to retreat, pushing herself backwards, but she hit the branches holding up the lean-to. They creaked behind her. If this got much creepier, she might just bash her way through them and run. Meltharkatla was between her and the exit.

But she couldn't run yet; she didn't have her answers. "What about my question?"

Meltharkatla ignored her. She leaned this way and that, sniffing all over Hervor's body. Then her head darted forward, quick as a snake, and she licked the blood from Hervor's arm.

With a cry of disgust, Hervor shoved her away.

Meltharkatla fell onto her ass, but she wasn't angry. She laughed, and the sound dragged across Hervor's skin like fingernails. "Blood without, blood within. Your strength took his; his strength returned yours. Did his blood taste good? I can still taste it in you."

"Taste it?" Hervor whispered, staring at her in horror.

"Berserker-child, daughter of Bolvereik – she showed you the way, showed you how to heal, how to be strong again, didn't she? Clever work, clever indeed—"

Hervor almost went through the roof of the fragile lean-to. "No! You're out of your fucking head – you don't know what you're talking about. I didn't—"

The words died unspoken. She knew what Meltharkatla meant. That girl in the stream, Garldor's doxy, had said it.

Someone had done something to Berkel's body, after he'd died... Hervor hadn't heard the rest of it, or what it was that had happened to him.

Blood from a dead man, Meltharkatla had said. Where *had* the blood Saeunn used for the don't-see-me spell come from? Something that had been dead for a while. And then there was the strength potion, whose thick, metallic taste still haunted her.

Hervor's skin crawled as if Berkel's blood were still on her face, and her stomach tried to heave up the potion that was no longer in it. Twice. Saeunn had done that to her *twice*. That horrific bitch had defiled a corpse, and dragged Hervor into it with her.

She came to her senses and found herself on her knees. Meltharkatla was stroking her hair with one filthy hand, her ragged nails catching strands and tugging them painfully. Hervor flinched away from her touch.

"So much confusion," Meltharkatla whispered. "So many voices. You wish for silence?"

"Gods, *yes*," Hervor said violently. "But—" What if the witch said she had to kill someone else, or commit the crime Saeunn had?

Meltharkatla responded as if she'd heard that thought. For all Hervor knew, she had. "There will be death, yes; there's often death. But a little one, never fear. A rabbit. Or a fox. The ghosts must feed, after all."

Talk of feeding, coming hard on the heels of the truth about Saeunn's potion, made Hervor feel ill. She wouldn't balk at killing an animal, though, not if it would buy her peace. "Tell me what to do."

"You must talk to them."

"I *have*. They don't fucking listen."

"Because they can't hear you," Meltharkatla said. She was back to her talking-to-an-idiot-child voice. "They need blood for that. So you go to where they are, and you give them blood. Dusk is a good time, between worlds as it is. But careful! Berserkers make thirsty ghosts, oh yes, they do. They'll take the blood you give them and then all of yours, too, if you don't stop them. Make themselves strong again on your blood."

Hervor shuddered at the thought. "So how do I stop them?"

"You trap them. A piece of leather, maybe. Pin the corners down with bones; you don't want it to blow away." Meltharkatla cackled in vicious amusement. "That would be bad. You pin it down, you put in little stones, a ring of stones all touching to hold them in – pale stones, pale like the dead. And with the blood, inside the ring, you draw this."

She drew a figure on the floor of her hut, one claw scratching through the dirt. A rune-stave, like the ones carved into the mast step of *Dísir's Fury* for good winds, or the ones Saeunn had painted on Hervor to let her pass unseen. Saeunn's had worked, but the *Fury* didn't always get wind when they needed it. How much could Hervor trust this one?

Or the woman carving it, for that matter. Meltharkatla made Saeunn look downright stable. She could be spinning all of this out of the cobwebs of her mind. The real question was, would that mean the stave did nothing... or would it mean Hervor got herself sucked dry by ghosts?

No. The real question was, was Hervor desperate enough to gamble on the witch being right?

She thought longingly of the chance at a normal life, the chance she'd never had. Even before the ghosts invaded her waking hours, she'd been an outcast because of them. She would take any chance she got to get rid of them.

"That's it, then?" she asked the witch, after committing the stave's shape to memory. "I draw a circle on leather, pin it down with bones, make a circle of pebbles, draw this in blood – and then tell them to shut up?" It sounded suspiciously easy.

Meltharkatla giggled, a high-pitched sound as unlike her normal voice as that deep rumble before. "If they agree."

"What do I do if they don't?"

"Find out what they want." Meltharkatla shrugged as if it didn't matter, moving away from Hervor at last. "Everybody has a price, even the dead."

Hervor took a deep, wavering breath, held it, then let it out slowly. That was it, then. All she had to do was find out where Angantyr and his sons were buried, and she'd be ready to get rid of them at last.

Her gaze rose slowly to where Meltharkatla was rummaging through the debris in a corner of the lean-to, and she remembered her other reason for coming here.

For all that Meltharkatla was an unstable, murderous witch, she'd helped Hervor. Told her some things she would've preferred not to know, sure, but also given her the key to shutting the ghosts up. For that, Hervor was very grateful.

But she'd made a promise. Thjostan had sent her out here expecting her to fail; he wouldn't be surprised if she came back and said she had. Bjarmar, though... he'd lost most of his wealth, his reputation, and his pride. Hervor was in a position to give a little of that back to him.

She'd promised that she would.

Meltharkatla had her back to Hervor as she crouched, digging with both hands through the dead leaves and half-rotted wood and cracked bones. Hervor knew first hand what the witch could do; no way in any hell she'd attack the woman face on.

But hitting her from behind...

She'd *helped* Hervor.

But there was the promise to Bjarmar.

Hervor's hand ran along the haft of her axe, feeling the smooth wood beneath. Attacking from behind was despicable. Then again, berserkers were generally considered despicable. It wouldn't change much about Hervor, one way or another; she was a jumped-up bondsmaid hiding behind a dead man's name. And no one would know what she did out here in the depths of the forest.

But she would know.

And so would the gods.

Hervor clenched her hand, then moved it away from her axe. She might be a berserker, but that didn't mean she had to throw her honour into the midden. There had to be another way.

"Meltharkatla," she said quietly.

The witch spun around so fast Hervor almost leapt for the exit, convinced she was about to be attacked again. But Meltharkatla smiled, looking like a twisted caricature of a friendly farmwife, and said, "My turn."

Hervor's breath hissed between her teeth. "All right."

"Ghosts drink the blood and do not live. What drinks the life and does not die?"

"Uh…" Hervor stared blankly at her. "I'm not very good at riddles."

"It's not a riddle," Meltharkatla said impatiently. "I'm here for a *reason*, you know. I have to find answers. Have to find *it*. Only I don't know what I'm looking for."

"Well, I don't think I know, either. My turn to ask a question now."

"No, it's not." The witch glared at her, all trace of friendliness gone. "Fair trade. You answer. *Then* you ask. Not before!"

Hervor's hand was drifting to her axe again. It wouldn't be dishonourable to kill a woman who attacked her first, and that looked like a distinct possibility right now. She'd hoped to reason with Meltharkatla, to coax her into agreeing to leave this forest, or at least to stop harassing travellers, but no way in any hell could she expect the witch to listen to reason right now. Hervor would have to invent some answer, calm her down, and then try to persuade her. Or else kill her.

"I think..." she began uncertainly – and then inspiration struck.

She smiled, leaned forward, and beckoned Meltharkatla closer. The witch scuttled towards her and waited, twitching.

"I think I know what you're talking about," Hervor whispered, as if for Meltharkatla's ears alone. "I don't know what it's called, but I've heard tales."

Meltharkatla's eyes widened.

"You said you're looking for it?" Hervor asked. The witch nodded rapidly. "It's not around here, you know. It lives up in the Ice Knives, haunts the heights where the snow never melts."

"The Ice Knives?" The words were barely audible, mere ghosts on Meltharkatla's breath.

"West of here. Far to the west. Days away." Hervor looked at her, calculating, and added, "Maybe you don't want to go. It is a long way, after all."

Meltharkatla shoved her angrily. Hervor's nerves were strung so tight she almost ripped her axe from its belt loop in self-defence. But the witch wasn't attacking; she was just offended. "I do not give up easily," Meltharkatla said, biting each word off. "It's been around for a long time, an age and then some. I have to know how. And why."

So she could be like it? The thought of Meltharkatla becoming immortal would have been scary if Hervor thought the woman could hold a coherent thought long enough to manage anything of the sort. "So you're going, then."

"Yes," the witch said, nodding. "Yes." She shot to her feet, crouching so she wouldn't hit the roof, and went outside.

Hervor scrambled after her, into the fading light. They'd been in there longer than she'd thought; the sun was well on its way towards setting. Meltharkatla was already into the trees, heading west. "You're leaving now?" Hervor asked in surprise.

The witch turned and stared as if she were an idiot. "I haven't got time to waste. I'm already old."

She didn't look old, but who was Hervor to argue? "What about your spells?"

"They'll be fine without me," Meltharkatla said airily.

Hervor ran after her. "You should take them down," she said when she'd caught up to the witch.

"Why?"

Hervor had a feeling that "because you're scaring people" wouldn't convince her. "Uh... they're your friends, right? They'll... be lonely without you. Imagine them sitting here, day after day, wondering where you've gone, why you don't ever come say hello to them. They'd be so sad."

That sounded stupid even to Hervor, but Meltharkatla considered it – jerking to such a sudden halt that Hervor went three paces on before realising she'd stopped – and sighed. "They *are* like that," she admitted. "Very well. They can come with me." Then she spun in a circle, shrieking, arms outflung and rags flying. Hervor felt something rush through her, overturning her stomach, and for a moment she didn't know which way was up.

> screaming without end
> we scream without sound
> and curse the gods
> they cannot hear

Great, the voices were back. Hervor, clinging to a tree for support, swallowed a curse. Didn't matter; she'd be rid of them soon enough. The thought gave her strength.

Meltharkatla was looking at her with a knowing gaze. Could she hear the voices, as Saeunn had? If so, she didn't admit it. "Blood has many uses," she said. "Keep yours to yourself, if you can."

"I know," Hervor said with a shudder.

"Knowing won't help," Meltharkatla said. "But it's better than ignorance." She ran her hands over her body, an inch above her skin, as if stroking something that lay thick and soft across her shoulders. "No more questions, no more answers. I'll get my own answers now." With that, she began walking again, towards the setting sun.

"You do that," Hervor said, and didn't follow her again.

15

THE WANDERER

Hervor would have preferred to remove her own toenails rather than spend the night in the forest, but she didn't get a choice. With the return of the voices, her energy went away; the very thought of attempting to find the road again in the rapidly growing dusk made her limbs drag like lead. Besides, even though she'd felt Meltharkatla's spells going home to roost, she didn't want to test it by stumbling blindly through the dark woods.

On the other hand, no way in any hell was she going to sleep in Meltharkatla's lean-to. Valnarath only knew what was living in there, buried in the debris. So despite the wind's frosted bite, Hervor built her fire outside and went to sleep next to it, pursued by the voices of the ghosts.

She awoke in sharp-edged autumn sunlight that made the previous day seem even more unreal. But there was the lean-to – looking even less sturdy than she'd thought – and she could see Meltharkatla's bare footprints, heading west. No sign that the witch had returned. Hervor stretched and smiled to herself. Success after all, and quite cheaply bought at that.

Fed on her dwindling supplies, the edges of her torn shirt crossed over each other and tucked firmly into her belt, her axe in its loop – the dagger was lost for good – Hervor set out for Skersstaŏ once more. She found the road without much trouble and whistled to herself as she walked along it. Even periodic murmurs from the ghosts couldn't dampen her mood. Suddenly the world seemed full of possibility. She could quiet the ghosts, go back to Aettarstaŏ without fearing that the memories of dead men would overtake her vision. She could make her own life, finally, free of that weight. She could—

Her whistling faltered. There was just one problem. She'd lied to everyone there.

They thought she was a man named Hervard. Someone would find her out eventually. She'd be wounded, or someone would see her bathing – hells, all it took was someone perceptive like Enjarík. Or enough time going by that she could no longer pass herself off as a youth hardly in need of shaving. Sooner or later, they'd learn the truth, and then what would they think of her?

As much as the thought of confessing made her stomach twist, she would have to do it. Not immediately; the moot was *not* the place to be admitting such things. But after she laid the ghosts to rest? Yes, that would be fitting. Then she could come back and do what Jordis had urged her to do from the start: admit her true nature, declare herself – what was the term? Viga-kona? – and, well, hope for the best. She'd proved herself as a warrior and gotten rid of Meltharkatla, sending her off on a wild hare chase to the Ice Knives. Hells, Hervor could even tell Bjarmar about the ghosts. Let him know that Angantyr's spirit rested quietly at last.

She began whistling again as she passed the boundaries of the forest and found herself among farms once more. From a farmwife she was able to beg a shirt to replace her torn one; tucked in, the old one showed the outlines of her breasts, even with them bound flat. Disguise restored, she continued on, pressing her pace hard. She wanted to make it to Skersstað by nightfall.

Only when she'd passed through the gates of the town did it occur to her that she might have gone too fast.

She stopped dead in the middle of the street and counted. Storleik had been expected to arrive the day she'd left for the forest. Then a day of wandering around and a night sleeping outside Meltharkatla's lean-to; now it was just past dusk, and she was back in Skersstað. Auðleif had said Storleik would be here for only a few days.

She tried asking people out on the streets whether he'd left yet, but they brushed her off. None of them even knew who Storleik was. Shite. She'd have to go to the hall to find out.

Hervor bit her lip. If she went to the hall and Storleik was still there, she ran a risk of running into him. Common sense told her to leave town again and sleep in a hedge, coming back the next day, when he was certain to be gone.

But her body had been abused lately, and she'd spent the whole day moving fast; her muscles complained loudly enough to drown out common sense. If he was gone, she wanted to know.

Luck was on her side. Outside the hall, she literally ran into a boy even younger than Kjarvald, who was leaving on some errand. She caught her balance, grabbed him, and asked.

"Storleik?" the boy said, wide-eyed. Hervor was twice his size, easily. "Um, I'm not sure—"

"The jarl of Kalstað," Hervor added.

Recognition flashed across the boy's face. "Oh, him. He's not coming after all, they say. Some argument."

Relief washed over Hervor. She grinned broadly and patted the boy on the shoulder. "Thanks." Released, the boy scuttled off on his errand; Hervor went to the door of the hall.

The warrior there looked her up and down. "What?"

"Hervard, Bjarmar's man," she said crisply. "I've come to tell my lord and Thjostan some good news."

Apparently people had been talking in her absence. The warrior's eyes widened almost as much as the boy's, and he opened the door for her without hesitation.

The hall inside was packed to the walls with men, most of them devouring an enormous feast, and the clamour was deafening. But the warrior had been put at the door for a good reason. He gathered himself, drew a deep breath, and bellowed in an impressively loud voice, "Hervard returns!"

Every eye in the place turned to look at Hervor.

once we stood tall
but so swift we sank
our strength had gone from us

In that instant, she wished she'd taken the time to rest and clean herself up. But maybe it was better this way. Looking like she'd had a hard time would lend credence to her tale.

She was still in the doorway. Hervor made herself walk forward, down the length of the hall – which felt like it had gotten longer while she was gone – to where Thjostan sat at the high table.

"Well?" the jarl asked when she came near and saluted him.

Hervor glanced at the rest of the high table. "Where is my lord Bjarmar?" She wasn't about to report to Thjostan without Bjarmar there to be honoured. Thjostan scowled, but glanced past her; when Hervor turned she saw Bjarmar making his way towards them from the Aettarstað table. The look in his eye made her shiver. She hoped he would keep his mouth shut and not call her Bjarrik in front of all these people. She'd worked too hard to bring him some honour for him to squander it by losing his wits in public.

"My lord," she said, before he could speak, "Thjostan – I have done as I said I would. I went into the forest to the west of your town, and I got rid of the witch."

Thjostan gave her a flat look. "Then where is her head?"

Hervor almost swore. Probably no one here had ever considered that she might get rid of Meltharkatla by some method other than killing her. Damn it. And if she said she hadn't tried, they'd think her weak.

Well, boasting was a time-honoured tradition. And she'd never yet heard of anyone being struck down by the gods for exaggerating his deeds far beyond their actual shape, so long as the core stayed true.

"I tried to bring it," Hervor said blandly. "I hunted her down at her lair, and I fought with her, and I cut her head off. But it bit me when I tried to pick it up – she didn't have any hair, so I had to hold it by the jaw – and her body kept attacking me. So I dropped her head and started dismembering her, because I thought that would stop her. No such luck; her arms and legs kept flying back to her body, and pretty soon her head did, too. I finally threw my axe down and wrestled with her, and when I had her pinned to the ground I made her promise to leave the forest."

One of the jarls at the high table with Thjostan slammed his cup down. "So you've sent her off to our lands?"

Hervor glared at him. "I'm not an idiot. I sent her to the Ice Knives. Let her go bother the trolls."

"And supposing she decides, halfway there, that she's tired of walking and wants to stop?"

"Actually, she was flying, but if she stops in your lands, then just send a messenger to fetch me from Aettarstað. I beat her once; I can do it again." Hervor would die a happy woman if she never saw Meltharkatla again, but she didn't think it would be a problem. The witch had been very single-minded; she'd make it to the Ice Knives. Right now, the point was to make Bjarmar look good for having a houseman like her.

She could almost hear Thjostan's teeth grinding. Finally the jarl said, "You've done me a noble service, Hervard."

Hervor sneaked a glance at Bjarmar. What she saw hit her like a punch to the gut – a good one. Pride, wonder… joy. This might be the first time she'd seen the old man happy.

That one sight made all of it worth the trouble. Even the bits where she thought she was going to die.

"Thjostan!"

The shout rang through the hall. Hervor turned and saw a man had risen from one of the benches immediately to her left. He looked familiar, though she couldn't place him. The sword at his side made him more than a run-of-the-mill warrior, but who was he to yell Thjostan's name with such authority? She met his gaze squarely as he advanced, and was surprised to see contempt seething there.

all warriors fall
and feed the ravens in the end

He reached her side, and before Hervor even knew she'd been struck she was on the floor, gasping for breath.

"What are you doing?" Bjarmar roared.

"Thjostan. Bjarmar." The warrior faced the two jarls squarely as Hervor picked herself up. "You have been lied to."

"Satisfaction," Hervor snarled, glaring at him and shaking with fury. "I demand satisfaction. Face me in the circle, whoever you are; you can't insult me like this. It's my right as—"

The stranger threw a fist at her face. Hervor tried to dodge, but somehow she found herself staggering backwards, her vision spinning.

our strength was gone
and so we died

"I know this *woman*," the stranger spat. "She is no warrior. She is an escaped bondsmaid, and a murderer."

The shouting in the hall would have drowned out any response Hervor had tried to make, but she was too horrified to say anything. Who the fuck was this man? How did he know her? He didn't just know she was a woman; he *knew* her!

Thjostan bellowed the room to something like quiet; then he turned to the stranger with an expression that tried to be innocently puzzled but held far too much satisfaction. "That's quite an accusation. How do you know?"

Not, "What proof have you," but, "How do you know." Thjostan believed him. Hervor's gut twisted. She couldn't make herself look at Bjarmar.

The stranger eyed her the way he might eye a rabid cur. "I was of late a member of Storleik Geirriksson's company. I was there when he wed his youngest daughter to Ungaut Feigaldsson, and I saw this woman – this *bondsmaid* – around the holding. After we left, we heard that she'd killed a freeholder and run away. We were asked to keep an eye out for her. I'm not Storleik's man any more, but I told him I'd search for her, and see that she was punished."

Hervor's thoughts had turned into a stream of curses, with the maddened snarls of the ghosts as ominous embroidery. How could she deny it? She remembered him now, the swordsman who'd eyed her so much. And he was right. Every bit of it was true. All they had to do to prove that was strip her.

No. Stripping her would only prove one thing.

She straightened and swallowed, trying to keep her voice from shaking. "My lords." She nodded in a semi-salute to the men before her. "This man – who are you, anyway?" Just a hint of contempt there; good.

"Orvar Grimsson," the stranger growled. "Called the Wanderer."

The name meant nothing to Hervor. "You're right about one

thing; I am a woman." Rumbles rose and fell throughout the hall; she waited until they'd died down. "But for the rest of it, you're dead wrong. I'm not a bondsmaid, and I'm not a murderer. Punish me for lying about my sex, if you like, but that's my only crime."

Now, finally, she let her eyes stray to Bjarmar. His expression almost broke her fragile calm: his eyes were lost, like he wasn't quite seeing the world around him any more. The joy of a moment ago was gone, replaced by the mists that clouded his mind. She cursed Orvar Grimsson for doing that to him.

"This is all very interesting," Thjostan said, and Hervor knew she hadn't convinced him. "Your word against his. Orvar Grimsson is a noble warrior, one who's given his service to many a jarl across the land. You, on the other hand, are an admitted liar."

"I'll prove my honesty in the circle," Hervor said recklessly. Stupid thing to say; she knew first hand that Orvar moved like lightning. But right now she had to behave like a freeborn man – or at least a freeborn woman with an axe – and that didn't leave her much choice.

"I don't think so," Orvar said, his voice cold. "There's one detail I left out. You're a berserker, *bondsmaid*."

"Afraid of berserkers, are you?"

The words didn't come from Hervor; she wasn't about to admit she was one. She turned and found Auðleif was shoving his way through the crowd to where they all stood. Hervor was glad for the support, such as it was, but she wished he hadn't implied the accusation was true.

Orvar smiled thinly. "Not hardly. But who's to say what a woman of this sort would do? I won't give her the chance to cause chaos, here under Thjostan's roof. It would be impolite."

"It's irrelevant," Hervor said, raising her voice so all the hall could hear. Boldness was the only way she stood a chance in any hell of getting out of this. "I'm not a berserker. So face me in the circle, and we'll sort this out. I'll prove the truth of my claims to you. I'm a freeborn woman; I dress as a man by choice, because not everyone accepts viga-kona. I'm not a bondsmaid, and I'm no more a murderer than any warrior here – hells, I've never even been to Rognjeld."

Orvar's smile widened to a victorious snarl, and only then did Hervor realise what she'd said.

Fuck.

The uproar began slowly, with those quick-witted enough to see her misstep. It took few moments to spread to the rest of the hall, to those who didn't recognise the name of a shitty little holding so far to the north. A name Hervor herself should not have known.

She could have tried to cover for it. Hadn't she boasted about her wide-ranging travels? She could have claimed she'd visited Rognjeld, been a guest of Feigald's. But she'd left it too long, looked too appalled when she realised Orvar had never said where Feigald lived. Auðleif was staring at her in horror, knowing that what was left of Bjarmar's hope had just been crushed.

Then Orvar moved, and she pulled her axe from her belt loop, but it was barely in her hands before he closed with her. He seized the haft, twisting it, and her nerveless fingers betrayed her; the butt of her own axe struck her across the face and then she was falling to the floor, unarmed, revealed to all the world as a liar.

Bodies surged around them. Orvar bellowed for them not to strike her. A few fists landed anyway, and Hervor reached desperately for the red fury that might – *might* – get her out of the hall, but it was too far away, and too many hands grabbed her, pinning her arms to her body, making escape impossible. Hervor struggled anyway, but it was as useless as it had been with Meltharkatla. They dragged her to her feet while Thjostan fought to restore order in the hall.

When he had it, he turned to face her again. He was out of breath, but smiling. "Well," he said. "Condemned by your own mouth, it seems." He looked to Orvar, who held Hervor's axe with a loose, easy hand. "I assume they wanted her executed?"

death, the ghosts snarled.

Well, that was one way to get rid of the voices, Hervor thought with acid bitterness.

But Orvar shook his head, slowing the blackness drawing tight around her heart. "They wanted her brought back to Rognjeld."

Thjostan stared; Hervor did too. "Why?" the jarl asked. "If she's a berserker, as you say, then she's a menace."

"It's what they said," Orvar replied. "That's all I know."

If she had to be dragged all the way back to Rognjeld, then that was a few more days of life, a few more days in which to escape. It was more chance than she had right now.

Thjostan looked at Hervor with distaste. Her one satisfaction was seeing a hint of fear in his eyes. "Transporting a berserker all that distance—"

"I'll do it," Orvar said. "My road leads me to Reiðast, anyway."

"I'll send men along—"

Orvar shook his head. "Not necessary. I fear no warrior, man or woman, who walks this land. She will not escape."

Was he planning to murder her along the road? But if that were his plan, he could have told Thjostan to kill her now. Hervor didn't care what his reasoning was; she just knew her odds of escaping had gone up sharply. However fast Orvar was, he had to sleep eventually.

"As you say, wanderer," Thjostan said, clearly glad to be rid of this burden.

"Chain her up for tonight," Orvar said, making his way towards the far end of the hall. Men cleared out of his path in a hurry. "We'll leave tomorrow morning."

"Wait!"

The shout stopped Orvar. He paused, still facing the doors, then turned to see who had called out.

Auðleif.

"That axe," Bjarmar's houseman said, "is not yours."

Orvar's lip curled. "It's not *hers*. She's a bondsmaid; she owns nothing. I took it from her—"

"And she took it from me," Auðleif said.

Murmurs rippled through the crowd, a wave of agreement. Orvar looked at the axe in his hands, then at Thjostan. "The choice is yours," the jarl told him. "You can claim it, or not."

The warrior nodded. "I have no need of an axe." He stepped forward, holding it out to Auðleif.

But Auðleif shook his head. "No. I want it back, but not from you."

Orvar's laugh was short and disbelieving. "You think I'll put this back into her hands?"

"Why not? You're not afraid of her. You disarmed her once; you can do it again. I want that axe from her own hands."

Hervor's muscles tensed. If she got that weapon back—

No. She'd be stupid to do anything, however much she wanted to. Here, surrounded by scores of warriors, she didn't have a chance of escaping, even if armed. Better to wait until they were on the road.

But it tore at her heart to give up the weapon she'd earned.

we lost all, in the end

Orvar held the axe out, his expression contemptuous. "Take it, bondsmaid," he said. "Touch it one last time, and give it back to a true warrior. But swing it, and you will die where you stand."

The hands released Hervor. She stood for a moment, wavering, then forced herself to move. But first she tugged her clothing straight, very deliberately. If this was to be the last thing these men saw of her, then at least she'd behave with pride.

Even bondsmaids had pride.

She walked forward, took the axe from Orvar's hand, and turned to face Auðleif.

His small eyes had gone flat and unreadable. She supposed that was better than contempt. For a while there she'd thought he was a friend; he'd tried to defend her against Orvar's accusations. But if he really were a friend, he would have let Orvar keep the axe – or asked for it privately – or at least taken it from Orvar's hand. Not made her return it so very publicly.

Orvar was watching, waiting for her to do something stupid.

Hervor gave the axe to Auðleif.

"I won it off you," she said softly. "I beat you in the circle. Whatever I am, you can't change that."

Auðleif's jaw muscles tensed, but he said nothing. His hands closed around the axe, and he stepped back, out of reach.

Despite her determination not to cry in front of these bastards, tears sprang to her eyes as she looked at Bjarmar. All the colour was gone from his face; his hands shook visibly. She cursed Auðleif, but she hoped he'd take care of Bjarmar.

Someone had to get the man out of here, back to Aettarstað, where no one could see his shattered face. Let him keep that much dignity, at least.

The men grabbed her again and began dragging her out of the hall. But as they seized her, Hervor remembered one last thing.

"Bjarmar!"

A sharp push almost sent her off her feet. Hervor caught her balance and twisted desperately, not trying to escape, just trying to see – *"Bjarmar!"* In a moment they would pick her up and carry her; she had to do it now.

She gathered all her strength and shouted above the growing noise, "Where is Angantyr buried?"

The briefest of gaps appeared between two men, and through it she saw him.

Saw life spark back into him for just an instant at the name of Angantyr.

Heard his answer, almost unintelligible over the roar that filled the hall.

"Samsey."

16

THE ROAD NORTH

She held on to that one word as they dragged her forcibly outside, as they chained her, as they left her alone save for a single guard. Samsey. An island, judging by that -ey at the end of the name, but beyond that she knew nothing.

First things first, though. If she didn't manage to escape, she wouldn't even get a chance to find Samsey. Hervor wrapped her manacled arms around herself to hold in what warmth she could and tried to come up with an escape plan.

Instead, all she could see was Orvar's contemptuous eyes, Auðleif's hand closing on the axe, Bjarmar's shattered face.

So much work, so much pain, so many lies, to gain the

answers she needed. It was too unfair, that she should make it this far only to be tripped up by a random warrior who'd followed Storleik for a while. Just long enough to be at the wrong wedding.

Bolvereik laughs while you kill, that old witch had said. What she'd left out was, Bolvereik also laughs while you die.

Hervor could hear the god laughing now, while she crouched on the ground, awake and heartsore, through the long, cold autumn night.

She got some sleep in the end, deep enough that she wasn't aware the sun had risen until Orvar kicked her awake. Hervor rose and stumbled after him on feet gone numb from the cold. He'd freed her from the post they'd chained her to, but there were still manacles joining her wrists to each other and hobbling her ankles enough that while she could walk, she couldn't run. That was going to make escaping hard.

So was Orvar's horse. Hervor wondered at it, in a dull and uncaring way: he had a horse, a sword, and enough influence that he could apparently come and go from a jarl's service with ease. Thjostan had treated him like he was legendary. Hervor had never heard of him. But then, what did bondsmaids know of warriors?

The horse was for Orvar, not for her. He tied a rope to the shackles on her wrists, the other end to his saddle. "You can't run," he said, as if she couldn't tell that for herself. "And if you try to attack me, the horse will bolt. I'll stay in the saddle, but you'll be dragged. I don't recommend it."

His patronising tone broke Hervor from her stupor. "Go to hell," she said.

He backhanded her, casually, and she fell to the ground.

rot forever
in the dark

"Get up," Orvar said, mounting. "Unless you want to be dragged to Rognjeld." Then he sent the horse forward at a walk, and Hervor had no choice but to follow.

Few of those around the hall were up at this early hour, but out in the town, people stared as the horse went past with Hervor trailing behind. She ignored them, concentrating instead on observing every detail she could about Orvar. He rode well, as if being in a saddle were as natural as walking, and she knew all too well that he was fast. A dagger stuck out from the top of his cross-laced boot; maybe she could grab that? But his sword rode on his other hip, out of her reach. He could draw and cut her down in a single motion, if she went after the dagger.

She'd have to wait for a better opportunity.

They hadn't fed her the previous night, and Orvar didn't offer anything, although there were packs tied to the back of his saddle. Hervor ignored her complaining stomach, telling it he'd have to feed her eventually, that she'd been a damn sight hungrier before and lived to tell the tale. She'd survive this, too.

She had decided the previous night that she wasn't going to talk to her captor, but before morning had become afternoon she was heartily sick of listening to her ghosts snarl. "How in hell did you recognise me?" she asked as she trudged along behind the horse. "Last time you saw me was months ago, and I was dressed like a woman at the time."

Orvar rode in silence long enough that she began to think he'd made the same decision she had. Then he answered. "You're tall," he said. "You stood out."

"That's it?" Hervor asked in disbelief. "One tall bondsmaid stuck in your memory so well, you recognised her months later?"

"And you reminded me of someone."

Great. Bjarrik again, or someone new this time? Before Hervor could make up her mind whether to ask, Orvar added, "I thought about asking Feigald if I could bed you. I had a right to ask for it, under the laws of hospitality."

Like you're a sheep he's thinking about buying, Rannvar had said. Except that Orvar hadn't even intended to pay. Hervor spat towards his back, wishing she were good enough to make it strike home. "See, *that's* why I ran away. I'm not some fucking pig, to be sold off or given as a gift. I'm not a thrall. I'm a *person*."

"You're a bondsmaid."

"Which means I have a right to earn off my bond! But there would have been a feast in Slavinn before Gannveig let me do that. I worked like a mule for years, and never a word about my bond. I was beaten, and insulted, and treated like a thrall, like I had no rights. That's what you're dragging me back to."

Orvar shrugged. "It's not my business."

"Oh, so when it comes to caring it's not your business – but when it comes to interfering, it is?"

"They asked Storleik for aid in capturing you."

"You're not Storleik's man!"

"I was when they asked. He was generous to me; I'm glad for the chance to repay him. Besides," Orvar added, "you murdered a freeholder. His kin deserve justice."

Hervor ground her teeth. "Very fucking honourable of you. Sorry to tell you, but the people who asked for the help have all the honour of pigs. If they had any decency, they'd have given me a chance to work off my bond. A *real* chance."

Orvar didn't answer, and so Hervor stewed in silence.

The pace he set was merciless. Hervor wanted the trip to Rognjeld to take as long as possible; every day on the road was another day she might escape – or convince Orvar to let her go, although sheep growing wings was more likely. So she slumped, and shuffled, and gave off every sign of being on the verge of dropping from exhaustion. Either Orvar could tell she was shamming, or he just didn't care; he rode on, not even stopping for food, pressing Hervor to her genuine limits before halting for the night.

A farmer gave them shelter in his barn, but Hervor didn't try to run right away. As much as she wanted to, she knew

Orvar would be expecting it. Better for him to think she was too tired or beaten to flee – hells, the former wasn't far off. She hadn't slept much the previous night. When he offered food, she wolfed it down, then curled up on the barn's hard-packed ground with the one thin blanket he provided. She tried to stay awake long enough to see whether he dropped off right away, snored, slept lightly or deeply, but she failed. The next thing she knew, it was morning.

The second night, though, she didn't fall asleep immediately. And when Orvar had been out for a while, she ran.

At first she thought she'd made it. Their lodging that night was a disused shepherd's hut on the edge of a forest, and the lack of a door meant there wasn't anything to creak as she crept away. Across the open ground she kept her pace painfully slow, not letting the ankle-chains rattle any more than they had to. Once under the branches, she picked up her pace to a shuffling run. When she heard nothing but the clank of her chains, she honestly thought Orvar was still asleep, that he wouldn't notice she was gone until she had a good head start.

Then he appeared from behind a tree and let her run straight into his fist.

Hervor crashed to the needles carpeting the forest floor, but despite that she was on her feet again immediately. Orvar was ready for her, though. With the shackles still on her wrists, fighting was a lost cause. He blocked her punches and immobilised her, calmly but efficiently, then dragged her back to the shed, where he dropped her on her blanket and went back to his own without a comment.

He hadn't even tied her up. If she ran, he'd just track her down again.

Despite this demonstration of his skills, Hervor didn't quit trying to escape. They never stopped in settlements, probably because Orvar didn't want her recruiting help, but in the hinterlands and wilderness she made at least one attempt a night, and more than once tried during the day. None of it fazed Orvar in the least. He tracked her or rode her down, and always dragged her back.

She tried taunting him, in the hopes that he would hit her and drive her into a rage. "Do you think I'm delicate? Or are you just afraid I'll go into a berserker fit and kill you?"

"I know you won't," Orvar said levelly, not looking at her. They were on a new road, now, a broad one; she thought it might be the one that led to Hvarlond, for its surface consisted of enormous blocks of stone men could not possibly have put there. She cared less for that proof of giants than for the proof of their position. Rognjeld was somewhere near this road, north of here.

"How can you be so sure?" she asked him. "You don't know me—"

"Berserkers trigger their rages with pain or by going into a trance," he said. "The trance involves preparation; I doubt you even know how. And as for pain, I know how much it takes. You won't get what you need from me."

Hervor stared at him. He spoke so matter-of-factly, as if the ways of berserkers were as well known as sheep-breeding. Most people treated berserkers like legends, and wild ones at that – not something to be talked about rationally. "What if I hurt myself?"

"You can try." Orvar shrugged. "I'll deal with you just the same."

"Very confident, aren't you?"

"I've killed berserkers before."

It wasn't a boast. He made the claim the way Hervor might have said, *I've carded wool before.* His calm tone of voice chilled her.

Still, she stood a better chance berserk than she did sane. Could she drive herself to the rage? It was true that she had no idea what kind of trance he was talking about, though some of the legends said things about berserkers beating their chests, tearing out their hair, frothing at the mouth, howling at the moon. Orvar would notice if she tried.

So that left pain.

She redoubled her attempts to escape, and when Orvar came after her she did everything in her power to make him hit her, reaching all the while for that inner, consuming fire. But Orvar knew what he was doing; he wrestled her into submission, or gave her one or two blows that knocked her silly without bringing on the rage. The result was that she ached all the time without ever achieving the necessary red haze.

Then they left the road, and with a sick wave of horror, she recognised the land around her.

They would reach Rognjeld by nightfall.

No time left for planning, for subtlety. She charged straight at Orvar on his horse and leapt into the air, dragging him from the saddle. She kicked and bit as they fell, clawing bloody furrows down his face with her nails, but she landed on the bottom, knocking the air out of her. After a brief scuffle Orvar had her pinned, and his hands clamped down on her throat. Black spots danced across her vision. Hervor flailed, but weakly; her arms had no strength. She might as well have been a child.

Orvar let go an instant before she would have passed out. Hervor sucked in great gasps of air, responding numbly when he hauled her to her feet. He remounted, the horse moved on, and she followed.

Her feet dragged across the frost-hardened ground. The whispers of the ghosts were no darker than her own mind. She'd thought this journey to Rognjeld meant a chance at escape, but she'd failed at every attempt. Now she had no more hope of avoiding her fate. Had Feigald ordered her brought here just so he could oversee her execution, the blood-price for Berkel's death? Or were they still hoping to get use out of her? Was she doomed to live out her life as a drudge, chained, beaten just shy of rage, with dead men whispering until her sanity broke forever?

She stumbled along behind Orvar's horse, frozen with misery, until the familiar smells of a holding reached her. Baking, and wood smoke, and the woolly stench of sheep.

Hervor looked up and saw the fence of Rognjeld before her.

The hall's peaked roof was visible above the fence. Once she'd thought it a large building, and grand in its size. But she had seen Aettarstað, and she had seen Skersstað, and she knew that neither of those places compared to Hvarlond or Svelsond, the home of the king. Rognjeld was nothing. A piddling little holding, so insignificant that the mere knowledge of its name had been enough to condemn her as one of its own.

Through the open gate she saw a woman go to the door of the hall, a water-jug braced against her hip. Even at this distance, even after months of absence, Hervor recognised Isrun. Her lip curled in an instinctive sneer.

A piddling little holding, with piddling little people. Hervor had seen more of the world than they dreamt of.

The thought was a spark of fire, warming her cold flesh. She tossed her hair out of her face and straightened up. Yes, she was being brought back in chains, following behind a warrior's horse like a disobedient dog. Yes, they probably planned to kill her, or worse. But she remembered Rannvar's words, the night Saeunn freed her. Nothing any of them had done to her before had broken her pride. She would not let them break it now.

Head held high, she passed through the gates of Rognjeld.

17

FREEDOM

Their arrival caused an uproar. Orvar dismounted from his horse while bonders ran shouting in every direction; by the time he was on the ground and had unlooped Hervor's rope from his saddle, quite a crowd had gathered. Hervor saw familiar faces all around, sprinkled with a few she didn't know. She met individual gazes, keeping her expression as cold as it would go. Hrodis flinched, and Hervor smiled thinly. Let them remember what she was. A bondsmaid, yes, but also breech-born, ill-omened, a berserker. Let them fear her.

One person's eyes she avoided. Rannvar towered over the crowd, and he stared at her along with the rest. But she wouldn't glare at him – not *him* – and she couldn't show him any other face, not with everyone watching.

One person she looked for... but Saeunn was nowhere to be found.

Anfinna appeared, clearly knowing only that some guest had arrived and needed hospitality. When she saw Hervor, she shrieked and crumpled to the ground. Everybody else was so busy whispering that it took a moment before anyone moved to tend Anfinna, which was fine by Hervor. Let her lie on the hard ground for a while. But where was her nurse?

A deep voice boomed out, and Feigald pushed his way through the throng.

Orvar bowed, hand still on Hervor's rope. "Feigald Feigundsson. I am Orvar Grimsson; I enjoyed your hospitality when Storleik brought his daughter here to be wed. Storleik told us of your escaped bondsmaid, and that you wished to reclaim her. I found her posing as a freeborn man in Skersstað. Here she is."

Feigald paled. Hervor took vicious pleasure in that. By his expression, he'd half been hoping that she was gone for good, that he would never have to deal with the problem she represented.

The jarl swallowed convulsively and dragged his eyes back to Orvar. "You've done me a noble service. I... ah—"

"The service is to Storleik, not you. But I'll offer this one bit of advice." Orvar's bored tone was more frightening than anger would have been. "I don't know why you wanted her brought back here instead of killed for her crimes, but it was a mistake.

You can't risk beating her, so she'll never be broken to the bit; you'll get no use out of her. I'd advise you to put her down, as you would any rabid dog."

Silence descended in the aftermath of his words, as if everyone were holding their breath. Feigald's eyes slid back to Hervor, and the look in them hit her like a blow. He wanted to do it. He was *going* to do it. He was afraid of her, and this man had just told him the sensible thing to do was listen to his fear.

In that moment of silence, Gannveig pushed her way through the crowd to the open space around the newcomers. She took one look at her husband's expression, and read it as clearly as Hervor did.

"No!" Gannveig threw herself at Feigald and whispered furiously in his ear. Hervor would have given her left arm to hear what the woman was saying. Feigald paled again, then darkened, and he shook his head. After a moment he started muttering back, only snatches of it audible – "advised me", "not safe", "old mother-tales". Hervor wasn't the only one straining to hear. Orvar alone seemed not to care; after all, it was no skin off his nose if Feigald decided to keep Hervor and got killed for his pains. Only that didn't seem to be quite what Gannveig was arguing for.

"Enough." Feigald cut his wife off with a chop of his hand. "This is not something to be decided out here in the garth. Orvar Grimsson, I thank you for returning my property to me." Property, as if she were a thrall. Hervor snarled again. "We hope you will stay with us tonight, and join us at our table. I will decide what to do with her tomorrow. For now, she can be chained up."

Chains. Again. But there was a glimmer of a chance she might not be killed, and so Hervor discarded her half-formed plan of attacking everyone in sight in the hopes of being driven berserk by someone not as smart as Orvar. There would always be time for that later. Right now, there might be a chance at something better.

No one brought Hervor food. She sat in her chains, back in the corner of the garth where they'd locked her up last time, and watched sardonically as everyone tried once again to pretend she wasn't there. They still failed. Only Rannvar didn't pretend; his eyes were on her whenever he walked through the garth. Hervor wished he would come close enough to speak to, but she couldn't blame him for staying away.

Night fell; everyone went inside. Hervor smelled roasted meat and knew they were giving Orvar a feast. She hoped he choked on a bone.

After the feast ended, the light streaming from the hall died down. The night was bitterly cold, and nobody had bothered to give her a blanket – not even Orvar, who'd provided one on the trip here. She supposed she wasn't his responsibility any more. Hervor closed her eyes, tried to ignore the ghosts, and drifted off to sleep.

But when she heard a foot scuff against the ground, she came instantly awake.

It was a measure of her desperation that her immediate

hope was that Saeunn had shown up at last. But when she rolled over, she saw that the shadowy figure, just barely visible in the night, was much too tall to be the old witch.

"Rannvar," Hervor whispered, and climbed to her feet.

"Hervor," he said, awkwardly. Then silence.

She managed to smile, despite it all. "I hope you won't be angry if I say I hoped I'd never see you again."

That startled a short laugh from him. It felt shockingly loud in the quiet, frosted night, and he flinched at his own noise. When he answered, it was much softer. "Me too. That is, I hoped *I* wouldn't see *you* again. I mean…"

"It's all right."

"You'd gotten out of here." Rannvar looked at the ground. "You actually managed it. And I thought, *someone* deserves to."

His dead tone made Hervor's throat close up. All this time she'd been sailing around, enjoying her life as a viking, as a houseman… sure, there had been bad parts, too. But for Rannvar there had been nothing but bad parts, trapped as a bondsman at Rognjeld.

"I'd run again if I could," she said, when her throat had loosened enough to speak.

"And I'd help you," he said bitterly, "if I had keys."

Keys. Hervor remembered. "What about Saeunn? Where is she? She stole keys before—"

Rannvar's head flew up at the name, and Hervor stopped mid-sentence.

"Saeunn?" the bondsman asked, his voice strangled.

Shite. "What happened to her?"

His hands rose, as if of their own will, to rub at his arms. Hervor doubted the night's chill was the cause.

"Tell me," she insisted.

"Valnarath's eyes – you, asking *me*?" Rannvar laughed again, bitterly. "You were the one to see her for what she was."

Hervor's heart sank. "A witch," she whispered.

"I don't know how they caught her at it, but they did. Anfinna started screaming and wouldn't stop; she was making herself ill. But even without that, I think Feigald would have had the old woman killed."

And with her, the last of Hervor's hope.

"She used blood magic," Rannvar said with revulsion. "Feigald had taken sick with fever. She bled him to bring the fever down, but then they caught her using the blood for some spell..."

He didn't finish the tale, but Hervor didn't need him to. "No keys, then. If you're caught trying to steal them, we'll both be killed." Her shoulders slumped. Was it worth asking Rannvar to beat her up in the hopes she might break her chains, or rip the post they were fastened to out of the ground? But although she remembered her fits now, she was a long way from controlling them, the way some berserkers supposedly could. And Hervor didn't want to face the risk that she might slaughter the first man who'd treated her with respect.

The last time she'd been in these chains, the thought of going berserk had scared her silly. Now she kept thinking of it as her only way out. Hervor laughed silently. When all you had was a hammer, everything looked like a nail.

Hammers.

Her gaze shot to the bondsman's broad shoulders, his large, capable hands. That strength ought to be good for something. "Rannvar," she whispered, fighting to keep her voice low. "What if you went into the smithy, got a hammer and a chisel?"

"Hammer and a—" He caught up with her thoughts slowly. "To break your chains?"

"No, to carve a toy horse with."

He was so nervous it took him a moment to recognise the sarcasm. "But what if they hear?"

"It's that, or wait for tomorrow and hope Feigald's feeling merciful. I don't want to wager my life on that." Hervor's body was thrumming with excitement, washing away the lingering aches from her bruises. "Will you help me?"

Rannvar shifted indecisively; Hervor sat on her urge to press him. He was running a risk, helping her. If they—

"Take me with you."

She stared at him in shock. "What?"

"I cut you free, and we go together."

"If they catch you with me, they'll kill you."

"Fine," Rannvar growled. "I don't care. I want a chance to get out of here. I'm going to be an old man before Feigald agrees I've earned off my bond. You can't run off again and leave me to that."

Hervor bit her lip and looked at him with new eyes. He was damned big, but not a warrior. And at this point she knew a hell of a lot more about living off the land than he did. What would he do, if he escaped with her? What skills did he have?

She hadn't had any skills, when she first ran off. But she'd learned.

Yes, and she'd starved, and been beaten, and suffered the loneliness of a rootless life. Could she really take him into that?

Could she really leave him here?

"Get the chisel," she said.

Rannvar jumped, as if he hadn't believed she would agree. But before Hervor could reconsider, he slipped off into the shadows. She rubbed some warmth into her limbs as she waited, trying to plan. The bondsman wouldn't slow her down; his legs were longer than hers, and he was used to walking the hills all day with the sheep. Keeping them both fed in the face of oncoming winter would be a struggle, though. And where would they go?

all go to hell
all but us

Footfalls on the hard ground. Rannvar appeared in the gloom, out of breath. In his hands were a hammer and a chisel.

He held them up triumphantly, grinning, and Hervor grinned back. "Let's get these chains off—"

no hell for us but the dark

So fast. Always so damn fast, as if he'd been fathered by lightning and not a mortal man. Hervor barely had time to see Orvar before he struck.

Rannvar's legs crumpled, and he crashed to the ground at Hervor's feet. In the darkness of night, the blood pouring from his back looked black.

The sight froze her with horror. Not the first dead man she'd seen, but – *Rannvar.*

No.

He was a bondsman. A herder. Not a warrior. He wasn't supposed to end like this, with his back cut open and his lungs making faint sucking noises as he died.

The hammer and chisel lay just inches from Hervor's toes.

If pure, unadulterated rage could have pushed her over the berserker edge, she would have torn the post from the ground and killed Orvar with her bare hands. But all she could do was scream at Rannvar's murderer with useless fury.

The sound brought people running. Hervor paid them no heed; she was jerking at her bonds, trying to rip loose so she could get at Orvar, standing there with his bloodstained sword hanging easily from one hand, watching as Rannvar died. The blood oozed across the cold ground. Blood-drunk, blood-mad, that was what they called berserkers, but for all her madness and all his blood she could do nothing.

By the time Feigald arrived, her energy had burned itself out. She sank to her knees, landing in Rannvar's congealing blood. The hammer and chisel lay right next to her, but there was no point in picking them up. Orvar had seen them; Orvar would take them away from her. As he had taken her axe. And Rannvar. And her every chance of freedom.

She sat numbly as Orvar told Feigald what had happened. The jarl was too scared to go near her, so Orvar retrieved the hammer and chisel. He stepped right up to her, unafraid; she stared at his scratched face and thought about drawing more of his blood. But the moment passed, and then he was gone, out of her reach.

Only at the end did she surface enough to hear their words. "I advise you again to kill her," Orvar said. "It's the proper blood-price for the man she killed; I cannot understand why you delay."

> *death should be the end*
> *downward the path to hell*
> *a path we cannot walk*

A long pause. Then – "Tomorrow," Feigald said wearily. "I said I'd decide tomorrow. She has no friends here – no other friends, I should say – she will not escape tonight."

"I would not leave her alone," Orvar said.

Hervor laughed. The sound was harsh even to her ears. "Alone? I'm never alone. I haven't fucking been alone since I was a child. Why don't I introduce you to my ghosts? I'm sure you'd get along great."

The warrior stared at her. Feigald explained in a low tone about her supposed madness. Angantyr and his sons moaned about weakness. "You and me both," Hervor muttered.

"I will keep watch over her," Orvar said at last. The crowd dispersed; two of the bondsmen dragged Rannvar's body away by the legs. She watched the man who had tried to free her scrape along the ground, leaving a trail of black blood, and couldn't even say farewell.

Maybe he'd come haunt her, too.

The garth quieted down slowly, until the only sound was the wind and the rasp of Hervor's own breathing. She huddled against the post, arms wrapped around her body, staring sightlessly at nothing. Orvar kept watch from some distance away, but she refused to look at him. She was too tired for rage.

The air was cold enough for her breath to form clouds of frost. She didn't notice right away that it was growing even colder. Not until she shifted, moving to keep warm, and her gaze fell on the sticky pool of Rannvar's blood.

It was shrinking.

The hard-packed ground wasn't soaking it up; the blood was simply *vanishing*. Hervor pressed herself against the post and stared in horror. She opened her mouth – but who was she going to yell for? Orvar?

That was delicious.

The voice carried something of the wind's moan, something of the creak of trees in a storm, and something that froze Hervor's blood in her veins. She scrambled backwards, around the post, tangling in her chains, staring at where the blood had been, looking frantically about the garth. There was no one but Orvar, who glanced at her, then turned away, clearly dismissing her sudden movement as a symptom of her madness.

Hervor was used to hearing dead men. But this wasn't one of her usual host.

"Who are you?" she whispered harshly, crouching like an animal ready to take flight. "Where are you?"

Where? A laugh like the crunching of old leaves. *Not Slavinn, that's for sure. I'd rather not find out what Eldaskrid has to say to me.*

The voice, distorted as it was, became recognisable. Hervor could barely get the name out. "Saeunn."

Clever girl, the witch said, her voice dripping with insincerity.

Hervor snarled. "You lied to me."

Lied? When did I lie?

"You fed me Berkel's blood!"

I never said I hadn't, Saeunn said calmly. *You didn't think to ask. Don't blame me for your stupidity. You wanted to be hidden from sight; I arranged it. You needed your strength back, and the blood of a berserker's victim—*

"I didn't ask for that!" Hervor's stomach twisted again at the memory of the taste.

Would you have preferred to stay here? Without that brew, you wouldn't have gotten far.

"And what about the danger? You never told me about that!"

A pause. *Danger?*

"Another witch told me. Berserkers are vulnerable to drauðr; it can go wrong and kill them."

I told you blood magic was dangerous, Saeunn hissed. *It can kill anyone – berserker or not.*

"Am I in *more* danger?"

Another pause, longer this time. Hervor risked one quick glance over to Orvar; he was watching her a little too closely. Best to keep him thinking she was just out of her head. Hervor twitched deliberately and began to bat at the air around her as if insects were swarming to bite.

What are *you doing?*

"Keeping him from asking who I think I'm talking to. You haven't answered my question."

It might be true, Saeunn admitted. *I know little about berserkers.*

Orvar turned away. Hervor gave up on her charade and shuffled back to the post to curl up once again, hugging herself for warmth. She said quietly, "So why the visit? You're dead. Why bother me? Don't you have someone better to haunt?"

You're the one responsible for me getting caught… so no, I don't. But I don't bear a grudge – well, not much. I'm talking to you because I wondered why you were stupid enough to get caught again, and because you so cleverly arranged for me to be provided with blood to drink.

Blood. Hervor's hands clenched into useless fists. Then she remembered Meltharkatla's words, and she went very still in fear. There had been nothing to close Rannvar's blood in. Were dead witches like dead berserkers? Could Saeunn drain Hervor's blood now?

Even with her mind numbed by Rannvar's death, Hervor wasn't stupid enough to ask. No sense giving Saeunn ideas.

Instead – "Is there anything you can do to help me?"

Saeunn growled. *I said I didn't bear much of a grudge. I didn't say I was your friend.*

Everybody had a price, even the dead. Meltharkatla had told her that, too. "What if I do something for you in return?"

Hervor could sense Saeunn considering it. *Perhaps,* the witch said at last.

She waited, but there was silence. "I need more than 'perhaps' to go on."

My current state rather limits me.

"Meaning…"

With blood, I can speak, I can hear you. With a body, I could do more.

Nauseated, Hervor thought first of Rannvar's corpse, soon to be dropped in an unmarked hole; no one built barrows for bondsmen. But there was a hint of dreadful eagerness in the air, and she realised, horrified, that Saeunn was suggesting something even worse. "No!"

Then they will kill you tomorrow.

"Maybe not."

You know they can't let you live.

"They didn't kill me before. I'm not letting you take over my fucking body! My ghosts have already tried that." A twisted smile made its way onto Hervor's face. "I've known *them* all my life. If I'm not going to let them have me, what makes you think I'd let you?"

You're desperate. Saeunn whispered it smugly. *Call them into your body, if you think you can; you hear them, but can you use them? They are distant, and weak. I am here, bound to this garth, and I am strong with blood. There is so much I can do now that I couldn't when I was alive; I'm far more than a simple witch now. I can take your body and free you. But without me, you will die.*

Bile rose in Hervor's throat. "No. If it's a choice between dying and letting you have my body, I'd rather die."

I can't take it forever, Saeunn said, and the annoyance in her voice lent truth to the words. *You'd have it back soon. And then you'd be free.*

"I told you, no. Now leave me the fuck alone and let me sleep."

Saeunn wouldn't leave without one last word. *This blood will keep me for quite some time. Ask yourself again, come morning, whether you really want to die. If not... I'll still be here.*

Then the ghost of the witch fell silent, leaving Hervor alone once more.

✦ ✦ ✦

Sunrise found her still awake, staring dry-eyed at the spot where Rannvar had died. Orvar vanished, replaced by three very nervous freeholders; Hervor ignored them all. The garth's usual activity was absent: a few bondsmaids scuttling back and forth fetching water, the smell of hot porridge from the hall, but that was it. Everyone, it seemed, was waiting.

Not for long. Soon Orvar returned, and this time he came straight to where Hervor crouched.

She could have stayed there, made him haul her to her feet, but she preferred to face her fate with dignity. So when Orvar approached, she forced herself to stand, swallowing a groan as muscles made stiff by the cold protested. Orvar watched this with a flat expression, as he might have looked at a sheep. He didn't care whether she was to die or not. He was just discharging a debt to Storleik.

He unlocked her chains, then led her to the hall.

Everyone was inside – every bonder on the holding, Feigald and his family, and a collection of freeholders who'd been at Rognjeld when she arrived. The hall was as full as if there were to be a feast, but the air was heavy and silent. Hervor followed Orvar to the front of the hall, where he released her and stationed himself at one end of the high table.

Hervor didn't need to glance around to know how far she

was from the door. Orvar was still more than close enough to catch her if she ran.

A whisper, meant for Hervor's ears alone, sounded from just inches away. *I can get you out.*

Fuck you, Hervor thought back at Saeunn.

Feigald cleared his throat uncomfortably. Gannveig was at his left hand, white and thin-lipped; Ungaut was on his right, patting Anfinna's arm. The girl looked like she was about to faint.

"Hervor," the jarl said at last. "The crimes on your head are many. You murdered a freeborn man. You ran away from me, who holds your rightful bond. You encouraged one of my bondsmen to help you escape again. And you're a berserker."

He fell silent for a moment, and Hervor felt a bitter, reckless smile touch her lips. "As storytellers go, you're not very good."

Feigald flushed, and Hervor thought with contempt of how poorly he compared to Bjarmar, even in the latter's worst moments. And Gannveig, next to him, was a sour mockery of Jordis. The gods had damned Hervor to the worst holding in the land: the first insult in a lifetime full of them.

"You'd do well to hold your tongue," Feigald snapped. "I'm willing to offer you mercy, if you give me a reason to, but much more of this and my patience will reach its end."

"*Mercy?*" Hervor snarled. "What, I'd get to stay here? How tempting. I can be your beast of burden again, insulted and whipped, with never a chance to earn out my bond."

"It's more than you deserve!" Gannveig cried. "For your crimes, you should be sold as a thrall. You lost your chance at freedom when you killed Berkel."

"What chance? You'd sooner stick a red-hot poker in your eye than let me go! I'm breech-born, I killed my mother coming into this world, my father was a pig-keeping thrall, and yet you're determined to wring every last drop of work out of my supposedly worthless hide!" Hervor's voice had risen to a shout. "I'm supposed to beg for the chance to go back to that? I've sailed the seas with Enjarik Enjakilsson and been a viking of the *Disir's Fury*. I've defeated Auðleif Torbrandsson in the circle to become a valued houseman of Bjarmar Bjarmundsson, the jarl of Aettarstað. I've driven a blood-witch from the lands around Skersstað with no more than my wits. That life I can be proud of. That life *is* a life. Chain myself to Rognjeld again? I'd rather die!"

"Then die you shall!" Feigald roared.

"Feigald, *no!*"

Gannveig's face had gone deathly white. Hervor stared at her. This wasn't just the woman's usual grasping need for control; there was real fear there. Saeunn had said they were afraid to kill her. But why?

The jarl's wife laid her hand on Feigald's arm. He shook her off, scowling. "What else am I supposed to do, Gannveig? We don't dare keep her here. We can't sell her bond; we can't even sell her as a thrall! No one would take her, not after what she's done. Do you want to just let her go?"

Even though she knew it was hopeless, for an instant Hervor's heart leapt. Gannveig's mouth twisted, and she shook her head. "No, but—"

"What 'but'? We free her, or we kill her."

"No!"

"Then you shouldn't have been so clever seventeen years ago," Feigald snarled, his face red with fury. "You and your lies, all because you wanted more hands and didn't want to pay for real bonders. I told you it would be trouble, keeping some stranger's child. If we'd done as *I* said, she would have died with Svafa!"

There was no clamour at Feigald's words, no shocked reaction. Why should there be? The name meant nothing to most of the people in that hall.

But Hervor heard it, and the last piece fell into place.

She began to laugh. No effort of will could have stopped it. She stared at the jarl and his wife, and she began to laugh; the sound rose, high and mad, and Hervor tilted her head back to let it free, laughing until her entire body shook and the rafters echoed with her bitter amusement, and everyone in the hall shrank from her.

"*Svafa*," she said at last, bringing her head down so she could look Feigald in the eye. "My mother was no bondsmaid on your cousin's holding; she was Svafa. *And my father was Angantyr.*"

That got a reaction; that name, people knew. There were whispers, and rustlings, and over them Hervor kept talking. "I am *freeborn*! My mother died here, and so you told Bjarmar

that I'd died as well. A free bondsmaid for your holding!" Her
entire body was shaking with fury, and she was distantly aware
of Orvar staring at her with an expression of absolute horror.
So much for his precious honour. "You sent him two corpses
and buried the truth in lies. You have *no right* to claim me!"

"You're still a criminal!" Feigald shouted, rising to his feet.
"You murdered Berkel—"

"And what of *your* crimes? The chains, the beatings – you
owe me a debt of blood for what I've suffered! I should make
you face me in the circle!"

She could see it in Feigald's face, the knowledge of his guilt.
He was ageing, weak; he couldn't stand against her in battle.
And if she took her case to a lawspeaker, asked for judgement—

"You don't deserve that honour," Feigald spat. "And you
won't get it. You will die – *now.*"

The words hit Hervor like a shock of cold water. Being
freeborn meant she had rights. He couldn't just have her killed.
Her eyes shot to Gannveig, deathly pale and too shocked to
speak; to Orvar, sick-faced and backed against a wall as if he
wanted to flee this disaster; to the bonders and holders, every
last one of them frozen by the confrontation.

To Feigald, who stood there with fear and death in his eyes.

"*Kill her,*" he snarled at his holders, and though some of
them hesitated, others began to move.

Hervor, tired, beaten, and unarmed, didn't stand a chance
against them. She could run, but they would catch her. In her

desperation, she reached with her whole being for the voices she was trying so hard to get rid of.

Berserkers, yes – but that wasn't why she heard them. They were her father, her brothers, dead these seventeen years. And for the first time in her life, Hervor thought of them with hope, as if they could somehow help her.

Saeunn answered in their place.

With a scream of victory, the witch's ghost surged into Hervor's body, filling it with cold fire. Hervor could feel her hideous, vengeful glee, that those who had killed her would suffer now. One of her hands rose: she tried to fight it down, but Saeunn had control of her body, and Hervor could do nothing. Her fingernails tore at her opposite forearm, gashing a rune-stave into her own flesh, and as the two leading holders came close Hervor's arm swung in a circle, spattering them with drops of blood. Saeunn's voice, speaking out of Hervor's mouth, shrieked unintelligible words, and suddenly the men were screaming, clawing at themselves where the blood burned into their skin like acid.

The men behind them halted in fear, but Saeunn advanced, driving Hervor's body forward, flinging more blood at them. The others ran for their lives. Then there was no one between Feigald and the horror that now faced him, the blood-witch in the body of a berserker.

Saeunn twisted Hervor's lips into a parody of a smile. "Do you remember being sick, Feigald?" she purred, malevolent satisfaction coating her voice. "Do you remember me bleeding you, to bring down your fever? I do."

In that instant, Hervor knew what Saeunn was about to do – but she was helpless to stop it.

"Die," Saeunn said calmly.

And Feigald did.

Not quickly. Not cleanly. His scream was worse than anything Hervor had ever heard, as if his blood were eating him from the inside. And Saeunn laughed over the sound of it, taking obscene pleasure in her revenge. The two sounds intertwined and went on and on, making Hervor wish with all her soul that she could flee the hall. But her body wasn't hers to control, and she didn't have the strength to throw the witch out—

strength

rage

WE WILL NOT BE WEAK AGAIN!

For a heartbeat she saw them: skeletons in a barrow, living men standing tall, her father and her twelve brothers. She heard their voices, felt their presence with her. Behind her. At her side. Reaching with her towards the roiling black cloud that was Saeunn, seizing hold of it by will and fury alone, and *hurling*—

Saeunn's shriek ripped into Hervor's ears, and the air around her exploded.

Hervor staggered from the force of it, caught her balance, realised her body was her own again. The witch was gone. And her expulsion had sent everything nearby flying – the bodies of the fallen holders, the ashes from the hearth, the flaming logs that gave heat and light to the hall. As Hervor looked around, coughing in the sudden smoke and dust, she saw that everything had turned to chaos; bonders and freeborn alike were screaming, and countless new fires blazed around the room, in furniture and in clothing.

At the front of the hall lay Feigald's body, decayed beyond recognition.

Hervor stared, sick to her soul, for one eternal instant.

Then her nerve broke and she bolted. Fought her way past those fleeing for the door, shot out into the open, ran for the gate as if all the monsters of Slavinn were chasing her.

18

TO SAMSEY

She ran for hours. Her eyes didn't see the ground ahead; she kept reliving that awful moment in the hall when she opened herself up and let Saeunn in.

Feigald. Dead. His freeholders – also dead. For the rest, who knew; at the very least the hall was ashes by now, and maybe some of them with it.

She hadn't wanted any of that.

But a nasty, insidious corner of her mind whispered, *didn't you? You wanted to get free. You would have done anything.*

No, Hervor answered. Not anything.

You hated Feigald. Wanted him dead.

Not like that.

She'd made a fatal mistake, letting down her barriers, giving Saeunn the opening she needed.

And she couldn't say for sure that it had been an accident.

She hadn't thought about doing it. Had never, at any point, decided to take the witch's offer of help. But unconsciously – in the depths of her mind, where all that mattered was escape, survival…

Hervor put her head down and kept running.

There was nowhere for her to go, no one who would take her in. Hervor was tougher and more resourceful than she'd once been, but the land was passing into winter, and it looked to be a hard one. She couldn't survive forever in the wilderness. Would she live on the edges of settlements, stealing, raiding, like a wolf cast out from her pack?

What was the *point* of living, if she had nothing more to her existence than that?

Her kin. They were her purpose, dead as they were – though she started in surprise when she realised Bjarmar was her grandfather. Her only living kin. She'd been that close to him and not known it. He wouldn't welcome her back, though, not after how she'd left. No, the only place for her now was Samsey… assuming she could get there.

And so, echoing the first time she'd fled Rognjeld, her steps carried her east.

She didn't strike the coast in the same spot as before, but Hervor recognised where she was. Hunching her shoulders against the cold – she'd stolen a cloak, but the wind kept trying to tear it away – she turned north, slogging through the wet sand, until she reached a familiar crevice in the rock.

Empty. Of course. And probably better that way.

She gathered firewood, seaweed, shellfish, just enough supplies to keep her alive while she waited – for what? For *Disir's Fury* to appear? At this time of year the vikings were much more likely to stay in southern waters, where the storms weren't as bad. And even if they did come back here, what then? The crew, she suspected, thought her dead, and Enjarik wouldn't thank her for proving him a liar.

But she needed a ship to reach Samsey, and she needed someone who might know where it was. Stealing a boat wouldn't do her much good if she had no clue where to point its prow.

"Tell me how to find you," she muttered at the ghosts, whose murmurs had been her only company on the run east. Somehow it was worse now that she knew who they were to her. Angantyr, her father. His twelve sons, her brothers – half-brothers, really. Hervor couldn't remember the name of Angantyr's first wife – she rarely came into the stories – but she knew Svafa had been his second. The mother she'd never known. And the bodies sent back to Bjarmar… what child now lay in the barrow-field south of Aettarstað?

Maybe the daughter of a pig-keeping thrall.

Hervor couldn't wait forever. Finally she set a deadline for herself: if the vikings hadn't appeared by the new moon, four days away, she would leave. It was as good as admitting that they weren't coming, but allowing herself the four days gave her time to accept that fact. And, in theory, to come up with some other plan.

Two days later, Hervor was sitting cross-legged by the cave wall, staring at the sand, when she heard voices.

She shot to her feet, not believing at first. Surely it was her imagination. No, the voices were real – fishermen, then. They had to be.

But the first familiar face appeared and stopped dead. Thurlang. He stared at her as if he'd seen a ghost, and she didn't blame him.

"What are you—" Arvind began, coming into the cave, but then the words died and he, too, stared.

One by one they appeared, each pushed forward a couple of reluctant steps by the press of men behind him, and every last one of them gaped in shock – except Heiðelt. Hervor, gaze flicking from face to face, saw that his expression was one of not very-hidden satisfaction.

And he alone didn't look afraid.

Then the voice she'd been awaiting came from behind the rest, demanding to know why they'd all stopped, and the men melted off to either side. Parting to let Enjarik through.

He, too, stared… but not with fear.

More than a few hands were creeping towards weapons; she had to do something before the fragile balance snapped. Hervor looked Enjarik in the eye and said, "I'm sorry. I wouldn't have come back, except I need your help."

A brittle silence followed her words, broken sharply by Enjarik's short laugh. "*Help.*"

"Yes," Hervor said, hoping she looked calmer than she felt.

"Help doing what?"

She glanced around at the other vikings. Heiðelt's relaxed posture was a lie; he felt the tension as well as she did. "Can I talk to you alone?"

"No."

Hervor wanted to argue, but it would have been like arguing with the tide. So she took a deep breath, squared her shoulders, and began to speak, not just to him but to everyone in the cave.

"There were things I lied about," she said. "And other things I didn't tell you. But I'm going to try honesty now – because I finally have real answers to give."

Silence. Hervor glanced at Enjarik, seeing the tension in his muscled shoulders, feeling the potential violence radiating off of him. One wrong word, and he really would kill her. She drew in another steadying breath before forging ahead.

"Seventeen years ago," she said, "Angantyr and his sons were killed in a duel and buried on the isle of Samsey. For as long as I can remember I've heard their voices in my head, but I've never known why. Now I do." Even saying it quietly, instead of shouting, brought back painful memories of the hall at Rognjeld. "I am the daughter of Angantyr, born to his second wife, Svafa."

The raiders shifted and muttered, their fear now mixed with confusion and surprise, but Enjarik might have been carved from stone.

"When I met you all, I was searching for a way to silence the ghosts. Now I have it. All I need is a ship." Hervor managed a small smile, tight with nervousness. "You see... I don't know where Samsey is."

All eyes went instinctively to Enjarik. Hervor knew she needed to convince the other men of her cause, or she'd be at risk of a knife in her back, but no one in the cave had any doubt that the final decision rested with him.

"Why should this matter to us?" he asked her.

"Because thirteen men are without peace," she replied steadily. "Because they were brave warriors, men whose deeds you respect, and they don't deserve to be caught between worlds the way they are. And because I sailed and fought at your side for three months. I got into fights, yes, but no worse than the others; the only thing I ever did that was worse was killing Vigmand, and he was trying to rape me."

Enjarik's mouth twisted. "You're a berserker. You can't deny that."

"I'm not trying to. And I can't help the fact that my father and brothers were berserkers before me; I come by it naturally,

I guess. But I won't go over the edge unless someone hurts me, the way Vigmand did."

"How do I know that's true?"

"You don't."

This time her answer was the curt one. Hervor could tell, though, that it had bought her progress with some of the men. If there was one thing she had learned about them in three months, it was that they valued honesty.

So she'd give it to them.

"I won't pretend I don't carry trouble," she said, forcing the words out. "I was an escaped bondsmaid before, or so I thought; now it turns out I'm freeborn. No one has the right to drag me back to my holding on that count. But in escaping—" She swallowed against the memory, tasting bile in her throat. "I got tangled with a blood-witch, with her ghost. Men... men died. I'm partly at fault for that, and if someone comes after me for that crime they'll be justified. In the meantime, though, I *will* put my kin to rest."

She'd run out of words. Now there was just waiting – for questions, for accusations, for decisions.

"Angantyr," Enjarik said. "He was your father."

Hervor nodded.

"And your mother was Svafa, the daughter of Bjarmar, jarl of Aettarstað."

Hervor nodded again.

"Does Bjarmar know about you?"

"He's met me. He doesn't know I'm his granddaughter – yet."

She knew that look. It was the same look Enjarik had worn when calculating the profit in offering the holy book of Alfrenvald to various buyers. But there was no risk of battle here; all Hervor wanted was passage. "You can bind me if you want," she said with forced carelessness. "And you're the best crew to sail the seas since An— since my father died. If you try to tell me you fear the season, I'll laugh."

"It's not the season," Enjarik said. "We don't put ashore at Samsey, and for good reason. The island is haunted – by your father and brothers."

A bitter, inappropriate laugh burst from Hervor. "They manage to haunt a whole island *and* me? What hard-working ghosts they are."

"Only their barrow," Enjarik said, "and only at night. But that's enough to have driven the people away. Samsey is abandoned, and even sailors don't touch its shore – not if they have any other choice."

Her heart was a stone in her chest. "So you won't help."

A touch of his usual wolfishness came back. "We can drop you over the side without touching the shore. But not for free. Ten eyrar." When Hervor gaped, he added, "I know you don't have the coin… but a jarl does."

Hervor knew she was stabbing herself in the foot, but she'd promised honesty. "I can't answer for Bjarmar's gratitude. His fortunes have fallen since his children died, and I've got no hold over him. He may not even believe me when I tell him I'm Svafa's child. I can't make him pay."

"If he doesn't," Enjarik said, "then you'll work off the debt."

He'd have shocked her less if he'd punched her. What he was suggesting was nothing short of a bond. Feigald had never truly held that authority over her; she'd been free all along, had she but known it. But if she took Enjarik's offer, and Bjarmar didn't pay...

She would be a bondsmaid in truth.

The question gleamed in his sea-coloured eyes, cold and sharp. How much was this worth to her? Was it worth her freedom?

Sanity against freedom – kin against freedom – honour against freedom. Choices she would have given her left arm to escape.

Hervor tried to tell herself that it wasn't anything she hadn't experienced before. Maybe she hadn't legally been a bondsmaid, but she'd believed herself one. She would still be the woman she'd always been. There was no shame in an honourable debt.

And there *was* shame in abandoning her kin.

"All right."

Enjarik unsheathed his sword in one smooth motion, and it was all Hervor could do not to leap backwards. But the viking wasn't attacking her. He held the blade upright in his hands and said, "Swear it."

The same way she'd sworn herself to Bjarmar – yet not the same at all. That time, she'd been taking service as an honoured houseman. Now she was selling herself into possible servitude.

But she'd agreed, and so Hervor made herself kneel, placing her hands on either edge of the blade.

Enjarik said nothing. She looked into his eyes and found them hard as stone. He was waiting.

Unlike Bjarmar, he was a traditionalist. Touching the blade would not be enough.

I've had too much blood in my life. But this wasn't drauðr – or if it was, it was a ritual worn so old and smooth, there was no risk in it any more. Hoping her apprehension didn't show, Hervor shifted her hands forward, so her wrists were against the edges, instead of her more vulnerable palms. Then she pressed in – carefully, so she wouldn't cut too deep. The pain wasn't bad; Enjarik cared for his sword well, and the edges were sharp and clean.

As her blood dripped to the sand, he spoke. "We will sail you to Samsey and back again. During the journey you will attack no one – not myself, not a member of my crew, not anyone we meet. If you disobey, or touch a blade during that time, I will kill you. In exchange for your passage, you will owe us ten silver eyrar. If you cannot get this money, or an equal value in kind, you will sail with us as my bondsmaid until you have worked off the debt. Do you agree to this?"

Her voice came out a rasp, her throat was so tight. "As Bolvereik is my witness, I do. May his sword strike me down if I break my oath."

She lowered her hands, blood slipping down to stripe her palms. Enjarik wiped the sword clean, then turned to face the vikings watching in tense silence. "Get moving," he said. "There's daylight left. We leave now."

Hervor wanted to do her share of the work, but it was clear that nobody would welcome it. Instead she stayed out of the way as the men edged around her, stepping the mast, rowing them out to open water, hoisting the sail. The oath, sealed with blood, had reassured them of their safety, but that didn't make any of them comfortable around her. When *Disir's Fury* was underway, they settled down as far from her as they could get.

Except for Heiðelt. Hervor jumped in surprise when the bald viking dropped onto the bench at her side.

"I knew you weren't dead," he said.

She looked into his weathered face and made a sudden connection. "*You* left the food for me."

"I helped knock you out," Heiðelt said. "When you were berserk. So I knew what kind of shape you were in. Wasn't much point in Enjarik leaving you alive if you were just going to die of starvation three days later."

The viking leader was at the stern of the ship, sitting alone, his face as unreadable as the winter sky. Hervor glanced at him, then back at Heiðelt. "How'd you know he *hadn't* killed me?"

"'Cause he's practical. Long as you weren't on the *Fury*, you weren't a threat to us. Oh, maybe you could have told someone about our movements, where we tend to land… but you wouldn't do that, and Enjarik's a good enough judge of people to know it. And for whatever reason, you got to him while you were with us. There was something about you he liked. He wouldn't kill you unless he had to."

Hervor thought about the misery of her journey. It had been the next worst thing to death, but she had survived.

She always survived. Her face twisted as she remembered Rognjeld.

Heiðelt asked, "Want to talk about it?"

"Fuck, no."

He shrugged. "Fair enough. We'll talk about something else."

And they did, as the *Fury* sliced through the water, heading south. It was a long sail to Samsey, days at sea, and if the raiders started to relax around her, Heiðelt was still the only one who'd keep her company. And to her acute embarrassment, Hervor had started puking again: with the choppiness of the sea in this season, her return to shipboard life wasn't going well. So much for looking tough.

But Heiðelt distracted her from that, telling her stories as the knife-edged winds of winter bore them across the sea. Mostly about Angantyr. Tales of his first wife Tofa, who bore him twelve strong sons; of Svafa, Heiðelt could tell her nothing she did not already know. Tales of Tyrfing: the Serpent's Tooth, the sword Angantyr bore, originally forged by the dvergar for King Sigrlami, who ruled long before the Blessed King came to the throne. Tales of Angantyr's exploits on land and sea, his twelve sons at his side, vikings of the famed ship *Troll's Fist*.

At one point Hervor asked, "Was he a hero or a criminal?"

"Neither, I'd imagine," Heiðelt said with a shrug. "No more than any man is. Or any woman." He glanced around the ship. "We're all vikings, but there are jarls and farmers, herdsmen and bonders, with less honour – and some with more. We make our living from theft, but in our own way we're honest about it. I never heard a tale of Angantyr betraying a man, or his sworn word, either. He was a brave warrior, true in battle, and loyal to his kin. There were better men, and there were worse."

"But the gods turned their faces from him."

"The stories say so. Maybe it was ill luck, as any man can have. They say Tyrfing was cursed, ages ago; maybe that caught up with him." Heiðelt shrugged again. "I wouldn't let stories stop you. He's your kin. You do what you must to help him. And to help yourself."

But the price had already risen so high. Hervor wondered how much more she'd have to pay – how much more others would pay – before she and Angantyr got peace.

Finally, late the next afternoon, as the winter sun was already nearing the horizon, a dark blot appeared amid the grey waves. Enjarik stood and spoke his first word to Hervor since he took her oath. "Samsey."

19

THE WAKING OF ANGANTYR

They put her overboard just offshore in a small bay. Heiðelt
gripped her shoulder as she left and tossed her a knife once she
was over the ship's wale, but otherwise no one said anything.
Hervor didn't look back as she splashed through the icy
shallows and onto the strand; she felt like crying, and she was
damned if she'd let them see that.

It was nearly sunset. Samsey wasn't a large island, but she
had no idea where Angantyr lay buried. As she crested a low
ridge separating the beach from the rest of the island, though,
she saw a mound in the middle of a rocky field, far too regular
in shape to be natural, and large enough to hold thirteen men.

A twisted smile touched Hervor's face. Finally. A small bit of luck.

She'd gathered most of what she needed on the way here, picking things up when the *Fury* beached to avoid storms. Heiðelt had given her a bag to put it all in, along with a bit of food. Hervor upended it on the ground in front of the barrow, and out tumbled bones, leather, and a cascade of gleaming white stones.

The only thing she lacked was blood. In the last of the daylight, she staked out a rabbit hole; when the animal emerged, lured by the apple she'd placed nearby, she threw a rock and stunned it. The rabbit struggled as she bundled it into the empty bag, making a nuisance of itself, but she needed it alive for now.

She'd had enough bad dreams about that encounter with Meltharkatla that remembering what to do wasn't hard. Hervor staked the square of leather to the ground with four bones, one at each corner. Then she placed the pebbles in a ring, taking care to ensure the line was solid. The witch had said this would hold them in, keep them from harming her. Would her kin really do that? Drain her blood? Hervor thought of Saeunn's malevolence after death – or had she always been like that? – and wondered what seventeen years of restless lingering would do to a man's mind.

Better to be safe.

She drew the knife Heiðelt had given her and stabbed it into the ground before her. With everything now in place, Hervor reached into the bag and pulled out the rabbit, which had been trying desperately to chew its way free.

The last sliver of sun vanished below the horizon. And in the peculiar light of dusk, the barrow opened up.

There were no doors. The ground did not shift. Hervor was looking straight ahead at the grass, and then suddenly she saw through it to the interior, where thirteen men sat cross-legged, their weapons leaning against their shoulders, chill blue flames dancing around them.

Their voices rose in her mind, so familiar.

blood
betrayal
MURDER
all alone
and they're beyond our reach…

They sat in two ranks, six in each section, and the thirteenth faced her from the depths of the mound, a sword at his side. The flames leapt higher around him, throwing his corpse-white face into hideous relief. His eyes glowed with the same blue light.

Hervor's heart pounded in her throat as she looked at him. Only the struggles of the rabbit in her arms broke her paralysis, reminding her of what she still had to do.

She pinned the flailing hindquarters of the rabbit between her knees, stretched its neck out, and slit its throat.

The blood fountained out, steaming in the cold air. Hervor dipped her finger in it and touched the leather, drawing the rune-stave Meltharkatla had shown her, praying she had the shape of it right. She had to dip her finger again and again to get enough, thirteen times before she was done, and as she finished the stones shone the same cold blue as the barrow's flames.

Then Hervor spoke to the ghosts, using names gleaned from her dreams, words she'd crafted over the long sail to Samsey, and the poetic rhythms of the songs that told of these men.

> *Wake thou, Angantyr – Hervor wakes you.*
> *Angantyr Arngrimsson; all know that name.*
> *Wake, sons of Angantyr – your sister wakes you.*
> *Rise from your howe; hear now my words.*

> *Hervard, Hjorvard, Hrani, Barri,*
> *kin of mine, I call you forth.*
> *Reifnir, Tind, Toki, Bofi.*
> *Before me I see you, in the barrow-mound laid.*

> *Bui, Hadding, Brami, Saeming!*
> *Feast on the blood brought here for you.*
> *"Warrior-ghosts, hear my words:*
> *from the barrow's hall I bid you come forth!"*

The thirteenth ghost stood.

Despite her determination, Hervor flinched. Even dead, Angantyr had a presence that threatened to overwhelm her, as if he were a hawk and she no more than the rabbit she'd just killed. It was hard to even look at him, much less believe that this ghost was her own father.

But his first words confirmed it. "*Why demand our rise, Hervor, daughter?*"

She almost laughed in disbelief. Seventeen years of haunting and he asked her *why*? Hervor swallowed the threatening hysteria and answered. "To lay you to rest. You've been in my dreams for so long, and now in my waking thoughts as well. What do I have to do to make you shut up?"

The answer came, not from her father, but from the ghosts of her twelve brothers.

"*Vengeance.*"

What else could betrayed men want? Still, the word landed on her like an iron weight, because it meant more wandering, more killing.

She had no other choice. "Tell me who killed you."

"*Two eagles flew against us,*" the ghost of Angantyr murmured. "*There was a battle in the sky. I will say no more.*"

Hervor dug her nails into her palms. They couldn't haunt her for so many years, demand vengeance, and then answer her only in riddles. But when had they ever spoken plainly? "The honour of this mighty line has turned to dust, if Angantyr and his sons fear to speak their slayers' names."

The other ghosts murmured, their words indistinguishable. One by one their heads turned to face her.

"*The eagles flew from Ingjald's hall,*" Angantyr said at last, his words echoing the cadences of song. "*His houseman Hjalmar, and Orvar the Wanderer. The first stood against me, and the second, my sons.*"

All the air left her lungs. "Orvar?"

"*Murderer,*" her brothers whispered.

It couldn't be. And yet – she'd heard Thjostan call him wanderer. And he'd spoken of killing berserkers.

And the look on his face in the hall at Rognjeld, when she named herself the daughter of Angantyr. Horror. She'd thought it caused by the revelation that she was freeborn, not a bondsmaid.

What if it was because he'd murdered her brothers?

As if he could hear her thoughts, Angantyr said, "*Behold how we fell.*"

The barrow vanished.

In its place she saw the island, but in daylight. Men stood about, next to a pile of shields – she recognised them. Faces last seen in spectral blue light. Her father, his sons at his side, and facing them were two others. One was unfamiliar, a man with unusually dark hair, but the other—

Orvar Grimsson, seventeen years younger.

Hervor snarled and tried to step forward, but nothing happened. This was only a memory. She was about to see her kin die.

Another man appeared, dressed more richly than anyone she'd ever seen, in sumptuous cloth covered with embroidery and pinned with jewels. A crown rested on his head, and she realised this must be the Blessed King, so favoured by the gods that he'd lived a normal man's lifespan many times over, without ageing a day.

He took their oaths, sealed with blood, then retreated offshore to one of the waiting ships. This was the formal duel of law, the holmganga or island-going, which only the king could oversee; the combatants must be alone. Hervor wondered what had led to it, and which men were the challengers.

The king called for the duel to begin.

Orvar and Hjalmar advanced, swords and shields at the ready, and Hervor's kin prepared to fight.

Then they staggered, struck by a crippling weakness. It was exactly like the weakness that followed after a berserker fit – but what could be causing it? They hadn't succumbed to the rage. Yet there it was, and no denying it; their limbs were weighted with lead, their weapons too heavy to lift.

They fought anyway. They were proud men; no sorcery or curse from the gods could convince them to surrender or run in fear. The brothers faced off against Orvar, but he moved as fast as ever, untouched by any weakness, and within moments Hervard had fallen. Hervor felt the killing wound as if it had been carved into her own flesh. Yet still they fought, snatching up replacement shields, closing ranks as their number dwindled... but the weakness only grew worse and Orvar only grew faster. Sick at heart, Hervor screamed in silent rage, wanting to do something, *anything* – but she could not touch the past.

Against Hjalmar stood Angantyr, alone and shieldless, Tyrfing in his hand, light shining from the blade. And though the weakness struck him the same, he refused to bow to it; he planted his feet in the sand of the shore and fought with all the stubborn force of his soul. If the strength of a berserker fit was denied to him, he yet had skill, and he used every bit of it against his enemy. Hjalmar's blows seemed not to cut him, while time and time again Angantyr scored small wounds on his foe, until the sand around them was spotted with crimson drops.

The outcome was inevitable, though, and had been from the moment the strength fled their flesh.

Bofi. Hjorvard. Hadding. And at the end, Reifnir, clever Reifnir, but his cleverness wasn't enough to save him. With his dying breath he cursed Orvar, beseeching the gods that his murderer might never find a home and never be happy in his wanderings, never know rest until the day a blade cut him down.

As the last of his sons died, Angantyr gave himself over to rage.

Not the fury of a berserker; that was lost to him. But he left his post at last, moving across the bloodstained sand, flinging his weakened body at Hjalmar in one final, desperate attack.

Four blows later, Tyrfing flew from his hand, and Angantyr fell dead to the ground.

Hervor screamed again. Then abruptly the scene was gone, replaced by the blue flames of the opened barrow.

"*Sorcery stood against us,*" her father said. "*By treachery were we taken.*"

Fury boiled in her veins as she realised how close she'd been. To have Orvar right there, within reach, and not to have killed him—

As if she could have. She'd attacked him enough times, and every single time he'd swatted her like a fly. She remembered his speed all too well. Even armed, she wouldn't stand a chance against him, and her axe had been lost to Auðleif. He'd killed Angantyr's twelve berserker sons, all by himself. And this other, Hjalmar – *he* had slain Angantyr, who the stories said was greater than his sons together.

What hope did she have of defeating them?

But she had no choice. If the ghosts weren't silenced, she would go mad. Honour demanded that she act – honour and pride. How could she go on her way, knowing that her father and brothers lay murdered and she'd done nothing to avenge them? The hell of Borguld awaited cowards who abandoned their kin.

She would probably die trying, but the wise said the time of her death was fixed by the gods. All she could do was choose the manner of it.

Hervor closed her eyes, summoning the courage to speak. When she opened them again, her gaze fell on her father's sword: Tyrfing, a blade as famous as the man who bore it.

A pointless gesture, maybe. But if she was doomed, she might as well do it right.

"Give me your sword," Hervor said, "and with it, I will avenge you."

Silence. No answering whisper, no call for blood.

Hervor raised her eyes to meet her father's, and found them as cold and forbidding as ice.

"*You ask for your doom,*" Angantyr said. "*Your sense deserts you, when you come to the barrow and call up the dead. Not for the living is this legend-wrought blade. Flee to your ship. Leave us in peace.*"

"You *have* no peace," Hervor cried. "Your unanswered murders have kept you lingering for seventeen years. And *I* have lingered with you, listening to your voices – but I will listen no more! Why should your blade rust in your barrow, when your foes walk free?"

She gestured wildly at the sword her father still held. "Had it been you alone, Hervard would have taken up your sword and avenged your death. If not Hervard, then Hjorvard, and if not him then one of your other ten sons, on down the line until it reached the last. But they're all dead, and I'm left. It's *my* duty now. I've made my way here, through a thousand challenges; I've been attacked and beaten and starved. I'm not afraid of hardship. I'm not afraid of danger. The only thing I'm afraid of is spending the rest of my life with your fucking voices whispering in my head, telling me how you were betrayed, and never letting me rest!"

She stopped for a moment, gasping for breath; her throat was raw with screaming. When she spoke again, her voice was quieter, but no less passionate. "One way or another, I will make you be silent. Either leave me be, or give me your sword. I'll give you peace."

The blade gleamed in Angantyr's hand. "*Listen, my daughter – hear my words out! Tyrfing, my blade, shall bring you no joy. Cursed it was, when first it killed. In my barrow let it lie, lest ruin it bring to all of your kin.*"

A harsh laugh broke free of her. "What kin? I have none. My father lies murdered; my brothers lie with him. My grandfather is wit-wandering in his grief. What have I to lose?" Hervor's hands clenched into fists, her nails cutting her skin.

"Sons," Angantyr replied. "*Disaster will this blade bring to the children you bear.*"

Hervor's breath died in her throat.

"*Hear thou, daughter, the nature of this blade.*"

Behind Angantyr, his sons rose and lifted their axes, standing in a solid line behind their father.

"*Deadly the edges; each carries poison. It shines as the sun when it is unsheathed – fierce is this light; it betrays you to foes. While it flies in your hands, fear not any blade. Tyrfing may never be drawn without the death of a man, and it may not be sheathed again unless blood lies warm upon it.*"

The tales told of this – but hearing it now, Hervor believed, for the first time, that it was true. The stories were not simply stories, and Tyrfing was not simply a sword. She opened her mouth to speak, but her father was not done.

"*This doom does it hold, from the dvergar who forged it: Tyrfing shall be the cause of three dishonourable deaths. In a barrow I sit, but still I see much; this doom will strike at you and your sons.*"

Horror welled up in Hervor's throat. Even when she'd thought herself the daughter of a bondsmaid and a thrall, she'd dreamt of release from the voices. Now she added to that the weight of kinship's bonds. But to avenge her father, her brothers – even her mother, hidden under Gannveig's lies – she would lay this stain on her future children.

"*Leave Tyrfing with me,*" Angantyr said. "*Take not this risk.*"

Yet what alternative did she have? Should she leave those murderers alive, men who would taint the sacred ritual of the holmganga with sorcery? No lawspeaker would listen to her, a berserker with no standing, and command a blood-price for their crimes. And if she went after them without Tyrfing, with nothing more than the scraps of her own skill… she would die.

But if she took the sword…

Either way she turned, she couldn't escape. No peace without vengeance; no vengeance without the sword; no sword without accepting its curse. The only question was which hell she wanted to wind up in after she died.

Fate. The stories often spoke of it, but how much did it really shape people's lives? Was it fate that Angantyr had died the way he did? Or was it just the choices of men?

Death and disaster, her father said: well, Hervor had met with plenty of that already. But she'd been careless. Hadn't thought. Rannvar had died because of it, and Feigald – and yes, even Vigmand. Was her father right, about the deaths from the curse falling to her? He wasn't a god; he was just a ghost, trapped in his barrow, seeing flashes of the world through his daughter's eyes. Maybe he didn't know everything.

Hervor stood.

She stepped over the leather square and the stones it contained, advancing until she reached the very edge of the flames that encircled the mound. They sank low at her approach. Angantyr stood before her, separated only by the veil of blue light.

"Let my sons fight for themselves," Hervor said quietly. "I have no dread of the doom you name. Not ghosts, nor gods, nor the flames of hell frighten me. Give me your sword; I will go after the warriors that slew you and your sons. My father and brothers will rest in their graves before I am done."

Behind Angantyr, the twelve brothers she'd never known stood arrayed, their axes in hand. In their dead eyes she saw pride, but in her father's she saw sorrow.

"Give Tyrfing to me," Hervor said. "I will find my own fate."

The cold blue fire grew until she had to close her eyes against its brilliance. When it faded, she found herself at the base of the grassy mound. Dawn warmed the eastern horizon; night had passed without her knowing.

The sun glinted off something at the top of the mound.

Tyrfing.

It took a moment for her legs to work; they were stiff with cold and tension. At last Hervor stepped forward, climbed to the top of the mound and picked up the sword. As she grasped the hilt, the blade began to shine with its own light, rivalling that of the sun.

She didn't know how to use a sword. She'd only just begun to learn the axe.

She'd have to learn.

Hervor looked down at the ground, imagining what lay beneath. The bones and rusting blades of her kin, and their spirits as well, waiting to be released.

"I will give you peace," she promised them.

peace, their voices whispered back.

Sword in hand, she turned and headed for the shore.

20

DIS

She walked without thinking, retracing her steps. Over the dead grass, up the ridge, to the shore—

There she stopped, because if she hadn't locked her knees, they would have given out.

Disir's Fury no longer rode at anchor, a little distance offshore. Its prow was knifed into the coarse sand of the beach, and even in the cold, thin light of morning, Hervor saw the men lined up along the wale.

She stood there, Tyrfing blazing in one hand, and tried to convince herself she wasn't hallucinating. *We don't put ashore at Samsey,* Enjarik had said… and yet here they were.

He was standing in the bow, one hand on the carved upsweep of the prow. He watched her, silent, until finally Hervor dragged herself back into motion and came close enough to see the expression in his eyes. She'd never seen anything like it in him before.

A kind of fear – but not of what danger she might pose. A fear that, if she didn't know better, she would have called *awe*.

"Why did you come ashore?" she asked, her voice cracking with weariness.

Enjarik cleared his throat. "We dropped anchor not far offshore to wait for you. And when night fell—"

"We heard you," someone said from behind him.

The viking leader was pale behind his beard. "We saw fires flaring up over the island, and we heard voices. A powerful voice, echoing and cold – and yours. Answering him. Challenging him."

The *Fury* and its men swam in Hervor's vision, and she swayed on her feet. Whatever Enjarik had to say, she wished he'd just get it over with so she could collapse. The sand wouldn't be very comfortable, but right now she'd lie on anything, so long as she could be flat.

"You *are* his daughter," Enjarik said.

Exhaustion made her curt. "I told you that already."

"And he was murdered. With sorcery."

"Him and his sons. My brothers. Are you going somewhere with this?"

Enjarik glanced back at his men. When he turned to face her once more, he'd drawn himself up, as if shouldering a burden – but not an unwelcome one. "We've always respected the memory of Angantyr," he said. "And the stories they tell, of the gods turning their faces from him... they never seemed right. Now you tell us they were killed by sorcery, and you're going to avenge them."

"Yes." Hervor gripped the hilt of Tyrfing tighter as if it could keep her upright.

"Even though you're his daughter. Not his son."

"*Look,*" Hervor said at last, losing patience with this uncharacteristic dithering. "The last few months of my life have been pretty shitty. The next few don't look like they're going to be much better. I just spent the entire night arguing with my dead father, and right now I would give my left arm for a warm fire and a bed. So whatever you have to say, *say* it, so I can start looking for things like fires and beds and a way to find the men I'm supposed to kill."

"We have neither fire nor bed aboard this ship," Enjarik said. "But we'll sail you wherever you need to go."

Tyrfing had to be magic. Otherwise Hervor would have dropped it in the sand.

"What?"

"This ship," Enjarik said, grip tightening on the carved prow, "is the *Disir's Fury*. Do you think we'd ignore an omen like this, when it falls into our laps?"

Hervor stared at him.

"I wondered about it months ago, when you first showed up. A woman, trying to be a warrior. You weren't much to note then, but now..." Enjarik shook his head, that awe still in his eyes. "There's more to it than just knowing how to fight. You've sworn to avenge your kin, and that's exactly the kind of thing the disir do."

She found her voice at last. "You think I'm a *dis?*"

Enjarik spread his hands. "You might be; you might not. But as I said: we'll sail you wherever you need to go."

Hervor had no clear memory of what happened after that. Just a confused recollection of babbling that yes, she'd like that very much, and then nearly falling over into the cold wet sand. Someone helped her onto the ship – probably Heiðelt, given that the others were treating her with superstitious reverence. The sword no doubt had something to do with that latter. Even Heiðelt avoided touching it. Tyrfing's light faded when she put it down on a bench, but it flared again every time she touched the hilt.

She awoke as they were beaching the ship again, this time on the mainland. By then it was nearly dusk; the shining of the sword was painfully obvious. She bundled a blanket around it and carried the whole thing with her as she went ashore, to the cave they'd be sleeping in that night.

"I still don't get why you're doing this," she admitted to Enjarik when he came to sit by her.

"Loyalty," the viking said. "You've shown it; you deserve to receive it. More than you got before. And like I said... I don't think you finding the *Fury* is coincidence. Not with who you are."

"And the rest of them agreed?" Hervor kept her voice low, but she gestured at the other men, scattered around the cave.

"You underestimate them, I think. I did. None of them ever much liked Vigmand – but they liked you, Hervard."

He'd clearly used the name without thinking, and it brought back a sudden, visceral memory of those stolen moments by the stream, before Vigmand attacked her. When she'd told him to think of her as Hervard. Enjarik's rueful laugh was the first awkward sound she'd ever heard him make. "Sorry. Habit."

"Habit with me, too," Hervor said, to smooth over the moment. "I'm still not used to the idea that Hervard is my brother. I hope it isn't bad luck for me to use his name." That brought back an uncomfortable memory of his pale, dead face, and one hand fell unconsciously to the hilt of the sword. Its light blazed through the cave, and for a moment all conversation died as everyone turned to stare.

Well, at least now she had something less personal to feel embarrassed about. "Sorry," she said as the men turned away and tried to pretend nothing had happened.

"That needs a sheath," Enjarik said. "We might be able to make shift for now." He went and conferred with Heiðelt, then returned and sat back down. "Now. Who are you after?"

Hervor grimaced. "Orvar Grimsson, and somebody called Hjalmar."

"Orvar? The Wanderer?"

"Unless my father lied to me." Heiðelt came back into the cave, carrying leather and some cord. He brought it to her, but refused to touch Tyrfing; she had to lay the sword on the leather for him so he could mark its outline. "Bolvereik's teeth, Heiðelt, it's not going to bite you."

He flashed her a quick grin. "Serpent's Tooth, isn't it? I'm not fool enough to mess with an enchanted sword. I'll leave that to the sons – sorry, daughters – of famous berserkers."

"Orvar's hard to find," Enjarik said, as Heiðelt began to cut the leather for the sheath. "He's not called the Wanderer as a joke."

"I know," Hervor said grimly. "I ran into him not long ago – well, that's an understatement. He dragged me back to Rognjeld by my hair. If I'd known who he was – that he'd killed my brothers—" She swallowed the rest of her words. Even an enchanted sword might not be enough against Orvar's speed. Angantyr had told her no blade could cut her while she held Tyrfing, but he'd died just the same; Hjalmar's sword had bruised and crushed where it could not cut, and in the end Angantyr, weakened and wounded, had been disarmed. She would fare far worse.

"Where's Rognjeld?" Enjarik asked, apparently assuming her silence was anger, not fear.

"Way inland," Hervor said. "And north of here. Just about due west of the cave where you found me. But I doubt he stayed there... hang on."

Even Heiðelt paused in his work, looking at her, waiting, as Hervor fought to remember. "At Skersstað. He said something about where he was going, that Rognjeld was on the way there. Shite, where was it?" Her mind had been on other things at the time. "Something... someplace-ast—"

"On the coast, then," Heiðelt said, sitting up in interest.

"From 'way inland'?" Enjarik said sceptically. "And going from Skersstað to Rognjeld – wait. Reiðast?"

"Yes!" Hervor exclaimed. "That's it. Where is it?"

"North," Enjarik said. "Far north of here, and on the *western* coast. Above the Ice Knives."

Heiðelt shook his head and began cutting holes in the leather. "Not a good place to be going at this time of year."

"But if I wait, I'll lose him," Hervor argued. "He'll be gone from Reiðast, and then how will I find him?"

"Track him," Heiðelt suggested, as if it would be that easy. "Ask where he went, and go from there. It'll take longer, sure, but you won't run the risk of drowning in the winter sea."

"I thought I was supposed to be a dis," Hervor said acidly. "Can I even drown?" She couldn't let herself delay. Not after waiting this long. She didn't have the patience, and she didn't have the nerve; if she held off, she'd just have that much more time to convince herself this was a stupid idea.

But also more time to train.

She shook the thought away with a scowl. Orvar knew who she was; his look of horror and fear had made that clear enough. If given a chance, he might go to ground. She had to follow him *now*.

It might get her killed. But dying against Orvar – or drowning in the winter sea on her way to him – was better than rotting in Borguld with the cowards.

She turned to Enjarik. "You said you'd take me wherever I needed to go. I need to go to Reiðast. And if there's a man alive who could get me there, even in the winter, it's you."

Enjarik met her eyes for a long moment, then nodded. "All right."

Heiðelt muttered under his breath, but kept it quiet enough that Hervor couldn't make the words out.

He finished his work a moment later, lacing the edges of the leather together with cord. The result was more a bag than a sheath, but it was better than nothing, and Hervor slipped Tyrfing into it. The light was dimmed by the leather wrap; when she released the hilt, it went out entirely.

Hervor smiled at Heiðelt and laid the sword on the ground. "Thanks."

A sudden burst of light blinded them all.

When she could see again, Hervor picked up a charred fragment of leather and stared at it. Her father's words came back to her: *It may not be sheathed again unless blood lies warm upon it.*

"Shite."

"What is it?" Heiðelt asked. He was a good two paces away now, staring at Tyrfing as if the blade were a wild animal in a bad mood.

"I'm a fool." Hervor steeled herself. She really didn't want to do this, but she could hardly ask someone else to do it for her. She picked up the blade, squinted against the light, held it over her forearm—

And stopped. Her father had mentioned poison, too. And that would be a damned embarrassing end to her vengeance, if she got killed by her own blade.

The others were staring at her in confusion. Hervor put the sword down again, drew her knife, and before anyone could stop her, cut a shallow slash in her forearm. The blood dripped onto the steel, and then she realised her other mistake. "Fuck. Heiðelt, make another sheath – fast."

Even working at his fastest, the viking took a while to finish a second one. By the time he was done, Hervor was forced to admit that her blood was now quite cool. She didn't know if Angantyr's words were *completely* literal, but she glanced around the cave at the other men and judged they weren't up to repeated experimentation; many more outbreaks of weirdness and they might bolt. Courage in battle was one thing, but courage in the face of sorcery was another. Sighing, she cut her arm again, and then grabbed the new sheath from Heiðelt.

"It's temperamental," she explained to him and Enjarik. "My father told me—"

A second explosion of light blazed out.

Hervor picked herself up off the ground and glared furiously at the sword. Did it have to be *completely* covered in blood? No way in any hell was she donating that much; they'd have to find a sheep for her to stab. She'd—

Her thoughts stuttered to a halt.

"Oh, *shite*."

"What this time?" Heiðelt asked wearily.

Hervor sighed and dropped her head into her hands. "I really am an idiot."

Tyrfing may never be drawn without the death of a man.

She'd thought that meant she'd be victorious whenever she unsheathed it. But Angantyr hadn't been, had he? And he'd fallen without killing anyone.

Which meant that Tyrfing wouldn't accept a sheath until someone had died.

She lifted her head from her hands and found that every single man in the cave was staring at her.

"Give it up for now, Heiðelt," she said wearily. "I've… I've got some things to do, apparently, before I can sheathe the blade. Things that won't happen tonight."

Like killing Orvar. She tried to hug that thought to her as she went to sleep, but it just left her cold.

She dreamt of her father's words: strange, confused dreams that wandered again and again through that hideous vision of the death of her kin. When she awoke in the morning, the echoes were still there, leaping into sharp, horrifying focus.

Disaster will this blade bring to the children you bear…

Her stomach rebelled. Hervor leapt to her feet and bolted for the cave's exit, barely making it to the water's edge before she spewed up everything she'd eaten the previous night. And there, on her knees in the sand, the waves washing cold around her fingers, she suddenly understood.

How long had it been?

She hadn't even thought of it. She'd been dressing like a man, and acting like a man, and sometimes even *thinking* of herself as a man, and half the time she'd been underfed and overworked, anyway, so she hadn't even fucking noticed that she hadn't bled.

Not this past moon. And not the one before, either.

Not since—

Her stomach heaved again, even though there was nothing left.

Not since that strange, hurried coupling with Enjarik, just before Vigmand tried to rape her.

"Hervard?"

The name brought her surging to her feet, but she didn't turn around. Couldn't make herself. Enjarik was the one man she couldn't face right now.

"Sorry," he said, coming closer. "Hervor. I'll get it right – someday. Are you all right?"

"Sure," Hervor said. Her voice sounded strangled. "Just –

the ghosts. My father. My brothers. Sometimes hearing them makes me sick."

"I remember. It always seemed strange to me that you spewed so often, when you were such a good sailor otherwise."

The first time she'd been on the *Fury*, it had been because of the voices. But not the second time. Not on the way to Samsey.

Hervor tried to think of something to say, but the only words that came to mind were curses.

"The tide will change soon," Enjarik said. "If you're up to it, we can leave then."

She wasn't up to anything of the sort. He might think she was a dis, but the reality was that she was young, inexperienced, and apparently gods-damned *pregnant*. She had the urge to grab him by the shoulders and shriek that she'd changed her mind, she didn't want to go to Reiðast after all. Not now. Not like this.

Enjarik misread her hesitation. "Hervard – Hervor – I release you from the debt you swore to pay. You've got enough to worry about."

Her stomach lurched again, this time in surprise. Hervor turned to stare at him. "What?"

"The ten eyrar." Enjarik managed a smile. "I can't call you a dis, then turn around and have you as my bondsmaid. The debt is cancelled."

She nodded weakly. She just wanted him to go away, so she could panic in private. "Good. Thanks. We should leave as soon as the tide turns." If she wasn't going to turn tail and run, then better to hurry. Three months: she'd be showing soon, and eventually it would begin to interfere with her movement. If she didn't find and kill Orvar now, she'd have to wait until she gave birth, until her son — and of course it would be a son, hadn't her father said so? — was weaned, or until she could find a wet nurse. *Fuck*. She was not prepared for this.

Enjarik nodded and walked away. Hervor listened to his retreating footsteps and closed her eyes, shuddering. She had to tell him. But not yet.

Bolvereik's blood, not yet.

21

BY ORDER OF THE KING

Heiðelt hadn't exaggerated the difficulty of the trip.

Hervor threw herself into the tasks of shipboard life: to keep herself warm, to keep herself from being underfoot, but most of all to keep herself distracted. When she was on the rowing bench, her hands frozen into blocks of ice and her back screaming with fire, straining with the rest to propel the *Fury* against the winds of winter, she wasn't thinking. She wasn't worrying about how to find Orvar, or how to kill him, or what the hell she was going to do about the child she carried. Oblivion was a blessing.

The tasks of crewing a longship weren't the only distraction she had, either. They put to shore one afternoon to avoid a storm and discovered that the locals were less than pleased to see them. They had to flee into the teeth of the storm to avoid a battle. Nor was that the only time they ran into trouble; coastal towns were keeping a sharper eye out than usual for vikings. Enjarik had to exercise all his cleverness to find safe harbours, especially as they sailed out of waters he was familiar with and up the western shore.

The Ice Knives loomed on the horizon, when they weren't obscured by clouds. Hervor stared at them and shuddered to think how cold their snow-capped heights must be. Reiðast, so far north, wouldn't be much better. But Heiðelt, after waffling back and forth between treating her like a spirit and treating her like a friend, finally settled on the latter and began teaching her more about winter survival. Hervor found it hard to concentrate, but she far preferred the lessons to awe.

Enjarik gave her survival lessons of a different kind. They weren't far into the journey when he came to her one evening. "Do you have any idea how to use that thing?"

Hervor glanced at where Tyrfing lay, swaddled in a blanket. Why the sword accepted being wrapped up like that, but not a makeshift sheath, she had no idea. "You know I don't. I'd only just gotten competent with an axe when I left."

"It's nothing like using an axe," Enjarik said. "So if you're planning on wielding that sword to get your revenge, you need to learn how."

The next time they put to shore, he led her off from the rest. After a bit of scouting, they found a flat area, well-shielded by trees, and Hervor unwrapped Tyrfing. The blade, of course, burst into light the moment she touched the hilt, but she tried to ignore it and pay attention to Enjarik.

He taught her how to stand, how to cover herself with a shield if she had one, and how to keep herself protected if she didn't. He taught her basic cuts.

He never touched her.

There were a lot of reasons he might avoid it; Hervor wondered which one it was, or if it was all of them together. The hint of awe with which he still treated her? The enchanted blade she held? The memory of that coupling by the stream?

She turned her thoughts very firmly away from that subject. Learning to use a sword was hard enough.

The second time Enjarik took her aside for a lesson, he tried something new. "Attack me."

Hervor stared at him. "What?"

"You don't learn to fight by swinging at empty air."

"No way in *any* hell. Were you listening to Angantyr that night, or not? This thing is *poisoned*." Yet it hadn't killed Hjalmar. But she couldn't assume that Enjarik would survive, too.

Enjarik seemed to be weighing his skill against the risk of getting cut. Finally he sighed. "I'd forgotten that. Damn – I wish one of my men had a sword. Sticks don't have the weight of swords; they won't teach you as much."

"Better that than learning by killing you," Hervor said.

So they sparred with sticks, and did drills with blades, side by side in the cold air of winter. A few times they sparred with real weapons, Enjarik using an axe and Hervor using his sword in place of Tyrfing, but that was only so much help; Orvar was a swordsman, not an axeman, and the difference mattered.

Hervor liked the drills best, partly because sparring made her think ahead to Orvar's incredible speed. And there was something clean about the drills, the precise, patterned moves, flowing naturally, each one to the next...

Tyrfing began to hum in her hand.

Enjarik was mirroring her, turning left when she turned right; the drill now turned them to face each other. And Hervor swung without thinking.

His reflexes swatted her blade out of the way instantly – but it came *far* too close, and Enjarik leapt back with a wary, closed expression. Hervor dropped Tyrfing to the ground and stared at it, shaking.

Tyrfing, seventeen years without a kill, did not seem to be patient.

She heard Enjarik's feet shift, a rare sign of nervousness. "What the fuck just happened?"

"Tyrfing." Hervor wrenched her gaze off the sword and looked at him. Her arms hugged her body, trying to banish the chill inside. "You know the stories about it?" He nodded. "They're not just stories. The sword really is enchanted – you've seen the light, and what it does to sheaths."

"You tried to kill me."

"The sword did." Lying there in the dirt, it didn't look special. The blade was well-forged, of course, with the rippling patterns of good steel, but the hilt was plain wire-wrapped leather, a plain block of metal for the pommel. No gems, no fancy work. Of course, the fact that the leather had survived seventeen years in the ground, and there wasn't a spot of rust anywhere on the blade, said that Tyrfing wasn't quite ordinary.

Hervor sighed and faced Enjarik once more. "Any time it's drawn, it kills someone. My father died without managing that, though, so it's still waiting. Can't go back into a sheath until someone's died. It… decided you were a good target."

Enjarik, to his credit, only paled a little and stared at the blade. "I see."

"I'm not using it around you again," Hervor said. "If that happens a second time—"

He managed a grin. "Who cares. I can still take you down with one hand tied behind my back."

"Do you really want to gamble your life on me being shite with a blade?"

Enjarik's jaw tightened, and shook his head. "No."

After that, Hervor practised her drills alone.

The land flattened out abruptly.

Hervor stared at the distant shoreline with her jaw set. The day was sunny for once, though bitingly cold; she could see the tail end of the Ice Knives not far away.

"We'll land just before sunset," Enjarik said from behind her shoulder. "Unless you want to wait."

Oh, she wanted to wait. Though her sword lessons had progressed, Enjarik could still beat her handily, and he wasn't nearly as fast as Orvar. But under her thick layers of clothing she was beginning to detect a swelling in her stomach, and the longer she delayed, the more likely it was that someone would notice.

And the more likely it was that Orvar would move on.

"We might as well land," she said. "I can go into Reiðast and ask after him. If he's there..." She clenched her jaw to keep from showing the stab of fear. "Then I'll do what I have to. If not, I'll plan my next move."

The sky began to darken as they came in towards the shore, threatening snow. Once four of the men had leapt over the wale and dragged the ship aground, Enjarik pointed at a low hill, barely visible in the dwindling light. "Reiðast is just past there, in a shallow bay," he said. "I've been there all of once, years ago, so I can't tell you what to expect. It was a small place when I was there, no guards on the gates – but it may have changed."

"From what I've heard, it has." Heiðelt joined them and squinted into the distance. "New jarl took over a few years back, and he's toughened the place up. Probably has more housemen around him than the old one did—"

"He does."

Enjarik's quiet voice held that edge of calm he only used when anyone else would be shouting.

Hervor turned to follow his gaze and swore.

Men had appeared over the ridge of the hill and were coming towards them at a purposeful trot. At least three dozen, probably more. Which meant they outnumbered the vikings. And these weren't the townspeople they'd fleeced over Alfrenvald's holy book; these were warriors, and well-armed.

Enjarik vaulted over the wale to the rocks below, and Hervor and Heiðelt followed.

Nobody attacked immediately. Enjarik walked to the front of his men and stood, arms crossed, while one of the newcomers slowed to a halt and addressed him. Fat flakes of snow began to drift down as the man spoke. "Who are you, landing here in secret?"

"Not in secret," Enjarik said, still with that edge of dangerous calm. "Our business just isn't in Reiðast, so we chose not to land closer to town."

The man scowled. "I asked for your name. And where does your business lie, if not in town?"

"Our business isn't with your jarl, either, which means it's not *your* business. If you'll just go your way, we won't bother you."

After all the trouble they'd had further south, Hervor couldn't blame Enjarik for not wanting to announce their identity. But it was a lost cause; one of the men had seen the ship's stern. "It's the *Disir's Fury!*"

There was a sudden and general creep of hands towards weapons.

The man's scowl deepened. "Then you are Enjarik Enjakilsson, the infamous viking."

Hedging wasn't an option any more, so Enjarik went for boldness. "I am. But I'm not here to raid your town."

The man didn't pause to listen; he went on talking. "And if you are that man, and this is the *Disir's Fury*, then *you*" – and suddenly there was a finger pointing at Hervor – "must be that daughter of Angantyr, escaped from Rognjeld."

All eyes snapped to Hervor.

She stood on the rocks, furs wrapped around herself, and tried to find something to say. How did this man know her? He was *looking* for her, and knew to find her on the *Fury*—

She found words then, every last one of them profane, as she remembered the defiant claims she'd flung out in the hall at Rognjeld. Boasting of her deeds, her time as a viking, and Orvar listening the whole time. Of course he'd spread the word; in his place, she would have done the same. Tell everyone there was a berserker woman running around, a viking and a murderer, and let someone else get rid of her for him. Save himself the trouble.

Hervor let the topmost fur fall to the rocks and strode forward. "I am," she admitted. "And if you know that of me, then you should also know I'm freeborn, with all the rights that gives me. Orvar Grimsson murdered my father; I'm here to find him and take revenge. Whatever orders your jarl has given you, he doesn't have the right to stop me."

The man smiled. Hervor had a sinking feeling there was something she'd missed.

"The *king* has the right," he said.

"The—" She stared at him. "The *king*? The Blessed King?"

"He's sent orders out, all across the land. Every town, down to the meanest village, is to keep an eye out for you. And when we find you, we're to take you south, to Svelsond."

Away from Orvar. "I'm not going."

"You don't have a choice."

"I have to find Orvar Grimsson—"

"We've heard stories of you," the man said coldly. "Of attacks no warrior can face. Orvar Grimsson has fled into the Ice Knives, fearing for his life. No one in this land will sleep safe until the Blessed King has made sure you're in chains."

Hervor barely heard his last words. Orvar – gone. Into the Ice Knives.

"You're not taking me," she snarled. "Try, and you'll regret it."

The man's eyes flicked to Enjarik. "Help us with her, viking, and we'll let you go free."

Enjarik replied with that same deadly calm. "We are the men of the *Disir's Fury*," he said, drawing his sword, "and you will not take her from us."

Everyone exploded into motion.

Hervor threw herself desperately out of the way, slipping through the line of vikings just a heartbeat before the local warriors crashed into them. As steel crashed in the cold winter air, she ran like hell for the ship – and what she'd left there.

Light blazed forth as she tore the blanket from Tyrfing, and Hervor turned back to the battle below, a fierce smile on her lips. The sword wanted to kill? It would get its chance.

But looking at the beach through the rapidly thickening snow, she saw with horror that the battle was going ill for the vikings. They were well-trained men, but so were their attackers, and the jarl's housemen had a substantial advantage in numbers. Already there were bodies on the ground, too many of them raiders.

Hervor flung herself back over the ship's wale and into the battle, Tyrfing in her hands, the blade singing for blood. Everything Enjarik had taught her crystallised, and what she lacked in skill she made up for in unshrinking courage. It was as if the men around her were mere dolls, carved out of wood for some child to play with, and she came fearlessly within reach of their blades in order to strike them down.

Fearlessly – but not safely. Though Tyrfing kept the blades that struck from cutting skin, they hurt all the same.

And the pain and the rage and the humming of the sword came together, burning in her stomach, then curling up her spine to fill her body with heat. A red haze came over her vision, and then she knew nothing but fire and steel.

She awoke to the strange silence of snow, broken only by the rushing waves.

Her entire body was frozen stiff, and hideously weak. The moment she felt that, Hervor realised with horror what had happened.

She'd gone berserk.

The knowledge made her struggle even harder to rise. There was snow all over her, and the sky was dark; how long had she been lying there? If the men of the *Fury* had won the battle, surely one of them would have had enough sympathy to move her from where she lay sprawled. And if they'd lost...

The thought choked her for a moment before she forced herself on. If they'd lost, then the jarl's housemen would have dragged her off. So why was she still here?

She finally made it to a kneeling position and looked around in the near-total darkness.

It took her brain a moment to understand what she saw.

The snow blanketed shapes all over the ground. Bodies.

Dozens of them.

Hervor rose to her feet, swaying with weakness, unable to resist the terrible impulse to look. From where she stood, she could see the entire beach. But everything was still, aside from the crashing of the waves.

She stumbled through the snow, trying to make sense of it and failing. Her mind refused to touch the memory, to accept what she saw now. So many bodies. Men she didn't recognise... and men she did.

The vikings.

Everyone was dead.

Everyone.

One face drew her, a body sprawled prone on the ground. Three times she convinced herself it wasn't him, but every time her heart said that yes, it was. She reached out to touch him – as if it would stop being Enjarik, if she just looked closer – and found her hands were covered in frozen blood, like she'd torn something apart with her fingernails. And the bloody gouges covering Enjarik's face and neck, rendering him almost unrecognisable, said what her target had been.

"No," Hervor whispered, through lips cracked by the cold.

Like an avalanche, the truth crashed over her. Here – where the battle had begun. Here – where it had progressed down the shoreline.

Here – where the last of the jarl's men had died.

And here—

Hervor's mouth opened in a silent scream.

A blade stood upright in a body, a grim sentinel in the snow.

Pain shot up her legs as she fell to her knees on the stones of the beach. One blood-covered hand reached out, shaking, stopping just short of Heiðelt's body. And the hilt of Tyrfing.

The scream escaped at last, shredding the night. In that moment, Hervor would have given *anything* to make it all not true. To make it so that she hadn't gone berserk, hadn't killed the jarl's men, hadn't turned on the vikings once her madness ran out of other targets, fighting them with her bare hands after the blade trapped itself in Heiðelt's body.

Snow began falling again as she wept next to her dead friend, dusting her body with white, adding another layer to hide the carnage. Its cold had sunk in deep before she ran out of tears and turned her mind dully to the question of what to do now.

What did it matter? She'd just murdered the men who'd chosen to help her.

> blood everywhere
> blood on bright steel
> and then the ravens come

The voices burned in her mind with cold fire. Maybe they were afraid she would forget her oath to avenge them – or the price she'd paid for it.

Hervor lurched to her feet and wrapped one hand around Tyrfing. After so much time straining her eyes in the darkness, the light blinded her; she closed her eyes and dragged at the hilt. The blade refused to come free of Heiðelt's body. She yanked harder, panting, new tears spilling down her cheeks, and finally had to put one foot against his ribs to pull the sword out. When it came, she staggered and nearly fell again.

She opened her eyes and glared in hatred at the shining blade. For a moment she hesitated, on the verge of flinging it into the sea.

But she couldn't do that. It was her father's sword. And it was the only thing that could keep Orvar from cutting her to pieces.

The blade's light cast ghastly shadows across the faces of the dead, worse than the ghosts of her brothers in their barrow. *Three* dishonourable deaths? The blood of dozens was on that steel now. On her hands. She couldn't even bury or burn them, not on this frozen, treeless shore. All she could do was gather stones, one for each man, viking and houseman alike, rolling their stiff corpses onto their backs and setting the rocks upon their chests in a token cairn. If it wasn't enough – if their ghosts haunted her, too, whispering of how she'd murdered them – that would only be fair.

At least, she thought bitterly, Tyrfing had drunk its fill of blood. Now she could finally put it in a sheath. Except that Heiðelt, who'd made two for her, was dead, and the thought of making a third one herself, the way she'd seen him do—

Another possibility came to her, and she did it before she could reconsider.

Enjarik's stiff body resisted as she struggled to unstrap the sheath from his waist. She was trembling with exhaustion by the time it came loose. She held it against Tyrfing's blade to judge size; no way she was putting the fucking thing in a sheath until she was sure it would fit. But for once, in a tiny way, luck was on her side: her father's sword was only a little different from Enjarik's, and narrower.

Hervor nicked herself with a knife, smeared blood on the blade, and slipped Tyrfing into the sheath. Then she knelt and placed the final stone atop Enjarik's unmoving chest.

"I'm sorry," she whispered, her voice raw. "You thought I was a dis, that I would bring glory to you. All I bring is death. You deserved better than that." Her eyes burned with tears as she looked around one last time at the scattered bodies. "You all did."

Then, a bundle of food from the *Fury* on her back, Tyrfing strapped to her hip, she began walking inland.

22

THE ICE KNIVES

It was a familiar misery: plodding onwards, one foot after the other, with only her ghosts for company. This time she had the added threat of the cold, and it only got worse as she went on, for she was walking into the Ice Knives.

There was nothing else she could do. She couldn't go into Reiðast; more than two dozen of their men had just died. She couldn't sail away; no hope she could manage the *Fury* on her own. All she could do was go onwards.

She couldn't even sink so far into mindlessness that she forgot about the dead. She remembered Heiðelt every time she scrounged to stretch out her meagre supplies, knowing she would be starving by now were it not for his teaching. She remembered Enjarik every time her growing stomach twisted with hunger, reminding her that she was eating for more than just herself. Bolvereik's blood – she was pregnant, alone, and lost, and somehow she thought she could find one man in the trackless Ice Knives. And kill him when she did.

She would die here, and no one but the ghosts would ever know.

Hervor accepted this, and hiked grimly on.

Even the keenest bloodhound couldn't have tracked Orvar. Gods only knew how long it had been since he went into the mountains and which path he'd taken; now, with the snowfall beginning in earnest, any trace he'd left was long gone. She would find a snow-cat or a troll before she ever found him – or they would find her. Hervor knew she was easy prey. And Tyrfing wouldn't do a damn thing to protect her from their fangs.

So when the hairs on the back of her neck rose, she wasn't surprised.

Nothing attacked, but the feeling stayed with her all through the short afternoon, then vanished shortly before the sun set. She curled up beneath a rocky overhang that gave her a scrap of shelter and wondered dully what the watcher had been, where it had gone. Was it just waiting for her to weaken further? But even the knowledge that she might wake up in a troll's stomach wasn't enough to keep her from falling asleep.

She opened her eyes to find it was morning and she was still alive, so she got up and moved on.

All through the day the feeling came and went, until Hervor was convinced she was imagining it. After everything she'd endured, what a fine joke that would be, to truly go mad. The idea was oddly appealing: maybe then she could forget about the dead men on the shore, forget about Feigald, forget about Rannvar.

A second night, a second waking, and still she was alive.

The sun had just reached its zenith – barely a handspan above the horizon – when her patience snapped.

"Do it already!" she screamed at the surrounding peaks. Her voice echoed off stone and was quickly muffled by the snow. "Stop following me and kill me, if that's what you're here to do! Do it! I'm ready! I'm vulnerable! Stop fucking *playing* with me!"

Silence, for an eternity.

Then a laugh.

The sound was far more melodious than Hervor would have expected from a troll, and snow-cats didn't laugh. Nor did they speak: "Little lost girl, wandering in the cold."

Hervor's skin crawled, and her hand crept towards the hilt of Tyrfing. If she drew the blade, it wasn't going back in until she killed someone, but that might happen pretty damn soon.

"Little lost *liar*," the voice said, but although it stressed the last word, it sounded more amused than angry. "Not nice to mislead, to aim wrong, to say it's here that isn't."

The voice was distorted by the wind and stone and snow, but Hervor, listening through all that, realised it belonged to a woman. She'd thought she was the only woman mad enough to wander around the Ice Knives.

Mad.

"Oh, fuck," Hervor said before she could stop herself.

Again the laugh, and then movement. A figure emerged from behind a tall pine tree and came towards Hervor, barefoot in the snow.

"You said it lived here," Meltharkatla reminded her, heedless of the vicious cold. Just the sight of her, half-scalped, clothed in nothing but shredded rags, was enough to make Hervor long for the warmth of a fire. "What drinks the life and does not die. The Ice Knives, you said – but it isn't here."

"My mistake," Hervor said through her teeth. The weight of Tyrfing dragged at her hip. She still wasn't sure she wouldn't have to use it.

The witch looked directly at her then, turning on Hervor the full force of her midnight blue eyes. "But we are alike. You seek something here, too."

Hervor opened her mouth to ask how the woman knew, then gave it up as a lost cause. Hells, maybe it was just common sense; why else would Hervor be here, if not because she was looking for something? "Yeah. And if you don't mind, I should get on with that—"

"Wrong way," Meltharkatla said calmly as Hervor began walking.

Her feet stuttered to a halt. "What?"

"He's not that way."

"How the fuck do you know?"

The witch smiled, baring her uneven teeth. "Not the fool you are. I know what's here and what isn't, even if you don't."

Was this more blood magic? Hervor had had enough of that for a lifetime – but she couldn't bring herself to pass up this chance. Even if Meltharkatla proved completely wrong about where Orvar was, it couldn't be any worse than Hervor wandering on at random. At worst, she'd be going in a new wrong direction.

"Tell me," she said.

A scowl. "Right answers for wrong, is that it?"

"Look, I'm sorry I sent you the wrong way. It was an honest mistake. I must not have understood what you were looking for." Hervor took a deep breath to steady herself. This unexpected encounter with another human – even as twisted an excuse for one as Meltharkatla – was destroying the barriers she'd put up to keep away all thought. Tears were threatening to spill again, and she couldn't bear the thought of crying in front of this woman. "But if you don't help me, I'm going to die up here. *Please* tell me where he is."

"No," Meltharkatla said, and Hervor's heart turned to lead. Then the witch smiled again. "You'd just get lost. I'll show you."

◆ ◆ ◆

Sometimes they walked in silence, the only sound the crunch of their feet through the snow. Sometimes Meltharkatla raved, and then Hervor wished longingly for the silence.

Sometimes, Meltharkatla spoke sense.

"He's strong," she said out of the blue one morning. Hervor had lost count of the days by then. "Strong, and very fast. Not easy to kill."

"Thanks for the encouragement," Hervor said sourly.

"What will you do, warrior? Sting him with your serpent's tooth?"

Hervor was past being surprised at any knowledge Meltharkatla showed. She touched Tyrfing's sheath with one hand. "It beats glaring him to death."

Meltharkatla cast a sly glance over her shoulder. "A warrior could use help."

"You offering?"

"Perhaps." The witch continued on through the snow without speaking for so long that Hervor wondered if the conversation was over, or if they'd be back to raving when Meltharkatla opened her mouth again. But her next words were still coherent – mostly. "I smell blood on your hands."

The stain was long gone, scrubbed away by handfuls of snow, but Hervor wouldn't expect that to stop Meltharkatla anyway. "Men have died," she said, through clenched teeth.

"Not all of them." The witch turned so abruptly that Hervor shied back. Meltharkatla caught one of her hands and sniffed it through the thick, fur-lined glove Hervor wore. "*His* blood is here."

Orvar's? Hervor remembered attacking him outside Rognjeld, scratching at his face with her nails. The only wound she'd managed to inflict on him. "I guess. It was, anyway. But that was ages ago."

"It might yet be enough."

Hervor snatched her hand back. "For what?"

The witch gave her a patronising look, as if she were a very small child. "For help."

"I don't want your fucking help."

"Taking it already, aren't you?" Meltharkatla smirked.

"You know what I mean. No more magic. No more spells." Hervor shuddered at the memory of Saeunn. "I've had more than enough of that."

"Death stands before you," Meltharkatla said, sounding amused.

As if Hervor needed reminding. She curled her hands into fists, thinking of the offer. But – no. She couldn't do it. She couldn't get revenge by using drauðr; that was no way to honour her kin. And the cost was too high.

"So I'm doomed," she growled instead. "I'm aware of that. Thank you very much for pointing it out. Could we move on, please? I'm freezing to death, standing here."

Meltharkatla held her eyes for a long moment, until Hervor's skin crawled. There was something in the witch's look she couldn't read at all, and didn't want to.

Then she moved on, and Hervor followed, and there was no more talk of blood magic.

Without the witch, Hervor would have starved. But Meltharkatla, in addition to being immune to the cold, had an uncanny knack for finding food and shelter. One night she led them under a pine tree so huge and thickly grown that the ground beneath it was clear of snow, and well-protected against the wind. Hervor built a tiny fire to roast the fish the witch brought her, then curled up and slept soundly for quite some time.

She awoke in silence; the wind had died down. When Hervor stuck her head out from under the tree, she discovered it was well past dawn. How long had she slept?

For once she felt well-rested. Hervor retreated into the deep shadows of the tree to await Meltharkatla's return, wondering where she'd gone.

But the witch didn't come back.

Hervor pushed her way out into the air and stood blinking against the dazzle of sun off the snow. She looked around for tracks, but couldn't find any apart from her own. No new snow had fallen to cover them; they just weren't *there*.

There was no sensation of being watched. Meltharkatla seemed to have vanished.

"Shite," Hervor muttered, and wondered what to do. Wait for the witch to come back? But for all she knew, the woman's senses had decided to leave her again; Meltharkatla might be walking in circles or chasing imaginary butterflies through the snow. There was no reason to believe she *was* coming back.

Without her, though, Hervor had lost her guide.

She hadn't realised how dependent she'd gotten on the witch – not just for food and shelter, but for direction. For company, twisted as it was. She'd sunk pretty damn low if a raving blood-witch seemed like a good companion, but there it was: the thought of slogging on alone wearied Hervor. She'd lost the dazed stupor in which she'd left the shore, and she didn't think she could get it back.

If she waited here, though, she ran the risk of starving. In the end, the growl of her stomach decided her. She was eating for two; there was no food anywhere nearby; therefore, she had to move on.

Hervor settled Tyrfing's sheath on her hip, wrapped her furs more closely around her, set off in the direction she'd been headed the previous day – and stopped in shock.

She'd come to a ledge that overlooked a small valley below. And in that valley was a wisp of smoke.

Hervor flattened herself instinctively in the snow. She didn't think trolls built fires, but that didn't mean a human would be glad to see her.

She made her way down from the ledge slowly, carefully, grateful that the fur she'd been lent on the *Fury* was a mottled grey and white that blended well with the snow-covered trees. Soon she gained the valley floor and lost sight of the smoke, but her nose led her onwards to the bank of a small, frozen stream. Across the way, at the far side of a clearing, was a lean-to Hervor would have called ramshackle in the days before she found herself grateful for a pine tree's shelter.

Few people lived in the Ice Knives, and those who did generally weren't looking for company. But Hervor could see the fire built in front of the lean-to, and she could see the meat on a spit over it – and, more to the point, she could *smell* it. Her stomach growled audibly.

Orvar crawled out of the lean-to, and her heart just about stopped.

Meltharkatla had taken Hervor as far as she needed to go. For one desperate, irrational moment, Hervor wished she could take back her refusal of help.

Then the voices crashed in on her.

MURDERER
sorcerer
cursed us with weakness
cast us into death
WE WILL HAVE HIS BLOOD

Their voices thundered in her head, and Hervor cried out. And Orvar, of course, heard her. His sword flashed into his hand.

So much for any hope of surprise. Hervor damned her brothers for costing her that.

"Who's there?" Orvar called out.

Hervor wanted to sneak away and come back later, when he wasn't on his guard. But a sudden jerk of her muscles brought her to her feet, out of the cover that had hidden her.

"Stop fucking doing that," she snarled to the ghosts who were determined to control her body, but it was too late; Orvar had seen her.

"Who the hell are—" he began, but his voice died. Hervor had the satisfaction of seeing him recoil as he realised who she was.

"Hervor," she said, coming forward one slow step at a time until she stood at the edge of the stream. "Daughter of Angantyr." Her lips skinned back in a mockery of a smile. "I think you remember me."

"*Witch*," he spat.

"No. Stupid, maybe. I let my guard down, and a blood-witch Feigald had killed took me over. I never asked her to do that, though. I wanted him dead, but I would have done it with a blade. Not by magic." The ghosts were snarling steadily in the back of her mind, reminding her of why she was here. Anger helped stop the nervous shaking of her limbs. "Besides, who the fuck are you to lecture me on killing people with magic?"

If his accusation had struck her where it hurt, so did hers. Orvar's mouth twisted. "I fought them. Honourably."

"Honourably?" Hervor laughed, hearing in it a tinge of the madness she'd felt at Rognjeld. "You drained the strength from their bodies because you knew they'd kill you otherwise. How was that honourable?"

"I used no magic!"

His desperate cry carried guilt, though. "No?" Hervor asked. "Then maybe you just *made use* of it. How's that? Have I found the right words to pin you down yet? You asked someone to cast a spell—"

"I didn't!"

"Your friend did, then."

"Hjalmar Modfinsson is an honourable warrior."

"Fuck you and your 'honour'," Hervor spat. "You dragged me back to Rognjeld to be killed, then did nothing to save me when you found out I was freeborn. You spread lies about me after I fled, tried to get other people to do your dirty work, to kill off the last of Angantyr's children. If you didn't use magic against my kin, then you had someone else do it for you and reaped the reward. Who in all eight hells are you to talk about honour?"

She pulled her gloves off and drew Tyrfing, very slowly. Orvar's eyes slitted halfway shut as the light blazed out, but she still saw fear in them. "Recognise this, don't you?" Hervor asked, grinning like a wolf. "Were you the one who made sure they got a decent burial? Because of that, my father was able to give me this. Oh, yes – I went to his barrow and got his sword. He told me of its powers, and sent me after you."

Orvar was an experienced warrior. To be hunted by the sister of the men he'd killed had unsettled him, but it wasn't enough to break his nerve. He hardened his jaw and lifted his blade. "Come, then, daughter of Angantyr. I've killed berserkers before. I'm not afraid of you."

"Killed them when they were weak. If you're telling the truth, though, and you didn't work the spell, then I guess you're out of luck this time. *I'm* a berserker, too, and I'm at my full strength." Hervor made the words sound as threatening as she could, but her guts had frozen into a ball of ice. Her one hope of killing Orvar lay in the power of a berserker rage, but how could she risk giving in to it? In that state, she had no control over herself. Once it began, there was no stopping it – not until her energy ran out or someone knocked her cold, and she'd seen on the shore what happened when she let it loose—

Orvar hadn't answered, and in that gap Hervor heard the rushing of the wind through the trees.

That, and nothing else.

It finally struck her: *they were alone.*

Meltharkatla was gone, and even if she wasn't, Hervor bet the witch could take care of herself. No one else was around. The only targets for her fury were the beasts of the mountains... and Orvar.

No one to kill, no more dishonourable deaths to add to the toll from the shore of Reiðast. The worst she had to fear was dying of exposure after the fit left her. And that was a risk she was more than willing to run.

"I am Hervor," she said, stepping over the stream with Tyrfing outstretched. "Daughter to Angantyr, sister to his twelve sons, and I am here to avenge them. May Bolvereik grant me victory." The name produced a stir in her blood; she went on, chasing that flicker. "His hand has given me strength, has taken away my fear of pain. I am his chosen, touched by the fire of battle." The feeling grew stronger, like a warm rush of heat running down her limbs, loosening their tension, leaving them limber and ready to move. "You will die by my hand. Your blood will fall to the snow and be lost in the thaw. Your deeds will be forgotten, your name reviled. You will rot in the hell of Losfja as a traitor. I have no dread of you." The warmth was building to an electric edge, producing a humming in her ears, a ready eagerness, and Orvar was retreating.

"Stand and fight me," Hervor said, pausing her advance, "or run like a coward. It will make no difference. I am Bolvereik's sword, and you..." The fire was beating at her vision now, flooding her body, and she welcomed it in, surrendered herself to its power, free, for once, of fear. "You are a dead man."

Orvar struck then, and as he did so Hervor wondered idly why he was so slow, this man who used to be so agile. She had all the time in the world to decide how to parry and counter-attack, and Tyrfing sang in her hands as she moved.

Then the full force of the rage burst over her, and everything became crystal-clear and lightning-quick.

The world was a frozen stillness around them, ice and wood and the brittle cold of the sky above. Through this stillness they moved, trading blows with furious strength. Orvar was the better swordsman, with years of experience behind him, but Hervor had the power of Bolvereik in her, and if Enjarik and his men had been in the valley to see this battle they would have fallen to their knees and called her a dis in truth.

Orvar struck her, of course. The god of war gave her strength, but not skill. Tyrfing's magic protected her from the cuts, though, and the bruises were nowhere near enough to stop her. She pressed her advantage mercilessly, stepping into his attacks, welcoming the hits because they brought her inside his guard. Orvar, unused to that tactic, couldn't adapt in time. Before long Hervor managed to slash his leg, and he screamed in pain.

They broke apart, and Hervor, gasping in the bitter winter air, saw the knowledge in Orvar's eyes. Poison. Whatever had made Hjalmar immune, Orvar didn't have it.

Hervor bared her teeth and flung herself at him again.

Orvar fled into the trees, trying to create distance. Hervor drove him back out into the open and came at him once more. But as she lunged eagerly, she made her first mistake. His foot lashed out and struck the side of her knee.

Her leg buckled briefly, but she straightened it and laughed. What was pain to her? She stepped as surely as ever. Tyrfing leapt for Orvar's heart and he barely avoided it, stumbling, his face twisted and slick with sweat. The two of them fought their way across the clearing, reached another stand of trees, began to move among them—

Orvar tripped on some obstacle hidden beneath the snow, and he fell.

Hervor was on him in an instant, stabbing downward with all her might. Her sword sank deep into the earth as he rolled aside. In the brief moment when she turned her attention to pulling Tyrfing from the ground, he threw his arms around her legs and brought her crashing down.

They wrestled on the ground, both of them disarmed, each striking at any vulnerable spot they could reach. Then, just as they had once before, Orvar's hands found her throat and began to squeeze.

Hervor flailed, but his arms were longer; she couldn't hit him anywhere that would really hurt. Her lungs howled for air. She struck at his arms, glancing off the thick protection of his coat, and then her hands dropped lower—

She seized one of his fingers and twisted with her new-found strength.

The bone broke with a sickening crack. Orvar screamed. His grip loosened, but his hands were still there, and so she snapped another finger. As she was reaching for the third he pulled back, trying to grab his sword; she lunged up and slammed her fist into his throat. He fell to the snow, choking. But like a true warrior, he kept struggling. His maimed hand reached the hilt of his sword, and he swung it around at her.

The blow was weak, and her furs blunted most of it. But this time, Hervor didn't have Tyrfing in her hand. Orvar had cut in. Blood began slicking her skin beneath the furs. Still, she laughed the pain away and struck at the choking warrior, shattering his wrist with her fist.

Orvar couldn't even scream: her previous blow had crushed his throat.

Hervor rolled through the snow and took hold of Tyrfing once more. In its radiant light, she stood and turned to face her enemy.

Lying there on the ground, tangled in his thick winter clothes, struggling for breath that would never come, he didn't look as imposing as he once had. His ruined hand and wrist he'd tucked in against his chest; his left hand was groping for his sword, but it was out of reach, and he lacked the strength to move. Blood from his poisoned leg soaked the snow.

Hervor looked down on him without pity. He'd murdered her brothers, the sword in her hand awaited its kill, and the fiery rage of Bolvereik burned in her veins. She wanted his blood, and she would have it.

"For the sons of Angantyr," she said, and struck his head from his neck.

23

THE JARL OF AETTARSTAÐ

Had it not been for Orvar, she would have died that night: an irony that didn't escape her. While the berserker rage lasted Hervor screamed her victory to the mountaintops, but when it drained out of her – the first time she'd ever been conscious for the change – she realised just how badly he'd hurt her. Checking the cut he'd made along her ribs was impossible without stripping, but it blazed with pain; her throat ached where he'd choked her, and her knee almost wouldn't support her weight.

A snowstorm howled through the mountains that night, and only the shelter Orvar had built kept her from freezing to death. By the time it struck she lacked the strength to stand, let alone walk. There was a small store of grain and dried fruit in the lean-to, which she was nearly too tired to eat; she choken it down raw and then fell into an exhausted sleep.

She awoke the next day feeling only faintly better. But time was against her now: the longer she stayed in the mountains, the lower her chances of making it out alive. Hervor made herself get up, rigged a makeshift splint for her knee and a crutch to support her weight, then went to look at Orvar.

His body was thickly coated with snow. She stood over it and thought of how someone had given her father and brothers decent burial. Not a token stone atop their chests, but a proper barrow, such as honoured warriors received. But she was no more capable of building that for Orvar than she'd been for the men of *Disir's Fury*.

The previous day it hadn't mattered to her. The previous day, she'd been berserk. Now that she was herself again, she felt he should have something. Not to keep him from haunting her, but because nobody's spirit deserved to be abandoned like that. Any further judgement for his crimes would come to him when he faced Eldaskrid in Slavinn.

Hervor dug under the snow until she found a rock, far heavier than the pebbles from the beach. Lifting it made her knee scream, but she staggered over until she could place it atop Orvar's chest.

"One down," she said, the words a cloud of frost in the air. "One to go."

✦ ✦ ✦

Hervor knew exactly how strange a sight she made: a pregnant woman, wrapped in bloodstained furs, a sword across her back, walking the winter roads alone. She didn't blame the people she encountered for making signs against evil and backing away.

She still cursed them for doing it, though.

One farmer was kind enough to let her shelter for a night in the low hut he'd built for his sheep. The price was listening to his dire predictions of famine to come: winter had the land fully in its grip, and cold that struck so early and so hard rarely let go until well into spring. It was as much to stop his foretelling of doom that Hervor started questioning him about her own quarry. Unsurprisingly, he'd never heard of Hjalmar, but at least he was able to tell her where she was.

"South about a day'll take you to Thessurjeld," the farmer said, nodding in that direction, "and if you go east another two days from there you'll be at Aettarstað, who we're all beholden to."

Hervor stared at him. "Aettarstað?"

"You've never heard of it?"

Her laugh sounded a bit hysterical even to her own ears. He gave her a suspicious look and soon left, probably thinking that letting her sleep among his sheep wasn't such a good idea. Hervor didn't care; she pushed her way between the ewes and considered what he'd just told her.

Aettarstað.

She hadn't thought about going back there. Not until her vengeance was won, anyway; that came first. Besides, she cherished the image of walking into Bjarmar's hall, proud and tall, to announce her real identity and tell everyone how she'd laid the ghosts of Angantyr and his sons to rest.

She wouldn't make such a grand sight now.

But she might have no choice. The farmer had given her shelter, but no food. She needed supplies, and as much as it galled her to admit it, she needed rest. Her knee was solid enough to let her walk, but the constant movement and cold had kept it from getting any better than that.

To go back, after the way she'd left…

Hervor told herself she would consider it more in the morning, and went to sleep.

Five days later – the farmer's estimates had left out the weather and her aching knee – Hervor spotted Aettarstað on the horizon.

She could just walk on by. No one would ever know.

Instead she passed through the gates.

The town was disturbingly silent. Hervor saw people around, and they gave her the usual crossways looks, but the streets were far emptier than she remembered. She wondered what was going on.

The hall and its garth looked the same as before, under their layer of snow. The sight made her stomach twist. This time there were no visions from her dead kin; the memories were all her own. Here was where she'd been when the

messenger from Skersstað arrived; over there she'd fought
Auðleif and received his axe from Bjarmar.

The axe he'd demanded back when he found out she was a
bondsmaid and a murderer.

She might be freeborn after all, but she was still a murderer.
And there was no reason to assume anybody here would be
glad to see her back.

But she'd come this far, and the thought of being warm was
enough to make her face whatever lack of welcome she'd find
here. Jordis would at least let her have a night among the sheep.

Hervor walked across the garth, pulled open the door to the
hall, and went in.

The interior was deserted – not a warrior or servant in sight.
More ominously, no fire burned in the hearth; the hall was almost
as cold as the open air. Hervor saw a discarded bone, picked bare
of flesh, but no other sign that anyone had been here in days.

"What in hell…?" she murmured to herself, hearing it echo
off the rafters.

"Hey, you! What do you think you're doing in here?"

Hervor spun and found herself blinded by the glare of the
sun off the snow outside; she could make out nothing of the
speaker except his silhouette. She raised one hand to shield her
eyes, squinting, and saw the man was shorter than her and bull-
necked. At the sight of that familiar outline, the bottom
dropped out of her stomach.

"Auðleif," she said.

"What makes you think you can just—" Auðleif's voice started off challenging and ended in strangled silence. Hervor waited, frozen, and wished like hell she could see his expression.

"Hervor," he whispered at last.

She dropped her hand and then didn't know what to do with it. Crossing her arms seemed too belligerent. She smiled weakly at him. "Bet you didn't expect to see me back here. Not after what happened in Skersstað. But I have to talk to Bjarmar; that's why I came back. Just let me do that, and I'll be on my way."

Auðleif went very still. Then he finally moved, coming a few steps closer and moving to the side, so she could see his face. "You can't. I'm sorry."

Frustration twisted Hervor's gut. "You have to let me. I know what Orvar said, but I'm not a bondsmaid, I swear it—"

"Bjarmar's dead."

What little energy she had left drained right out of her body. She swayed on her feet as she stared at Auðleif. "Dead?"

"He…" The warrior's face was hard with grief. "After Skersstað, his mind just… went. He didn't see any of us any more, just raved about Bjarrik and Svafa. For a while we hoped he'd get better, but then he started to sicken, and even Jordis knew it would be over soon. He died three days ago."

Hervor turned away, not wanting him to see her expression. She hadn't realised how much she was clinging to the image of meeting Bjarmar again, of telling him that his kin were not all dead, that he still had a granddaughter.

That *her* kin were not all dead.

She sat down abruptly on a bench.

"Three days," she whispered, barely getting the words out. "If I'd moved faster – gotten here sooner – I was going to tell him—"

"He knew."

Auðleif's voice was so quiet, she didn't immediately catch what he'd said. When she did, her head shot up. "Knew what?"

The houseman came a few steps closer, stopping just out of reach, his hands hanging uselessly at his sides. "That you were – are – Svafa's daughter."

Hervor stared at him, unable to speak.

"At least, I hope he knew," Auðleif said. "I told him, a dozen times. But I don't know if he ever heard me."

"*You...?*"

"I figured it out after Skersstað. Not soon enough; the messenger got to Rognjeld just in time to find out what happened there. But it all fit. A northern jarl, and Holmstein recognised the name when I asked him – and you were the right age." Auðleif shook his head; he couldn't take his eyes off her. "We were all blind to it. We knew you looked a bit like Bjarrik – told you so, more than once – but that was because we thought you were a man. If we'd known, we would have said you looked like Svafa."

They were still staring at each other when footsteps crunched in the snow outside. "What is this door doing open—"

Another silhouette froze in the doorway, looking at the two of them. This one wore skirts, and Hervor knew immediately who it was. Only one woman would be so concerned with a door left carelessly open, and authoritative enough to chastise the guilty party.

"Jordis," Hervor said, making herself stand.

Bjarmar's wife came towards her, slowly, reaching out as if to touch her and make sure she was real. "You," she whispered, and to Hervor's shock she saw tears spill down the older woman's cheeks. "Oh, child, welcome home."

They held a dual feast that night. It was the end of the third day of mourning for Bjarmar, and a celebration of Hervor's return. If anyone had asked Hervor, she would have told them she didn't want a feast in her honour, but nobody asked. So she was forced to sit at the high table with Jordis and oversee the subdued revelry.

People were happy to see her – happier than she had any right to expect, given the stories about her – but it was clear that Aettarstað had decayed even further in her absence. The food served that night wouldn't have graced the feast tables of Rognjeld. But Hervor had stolen food out of pig troughs to survive on her way here; she ate every scrap she could.

When her stomach was full enough to allow words between bites, she turned to Auðleif. He'd objected to sitting at her side, but Hervor was damned if she'd be up there with just Jordis. Nothing against the older woman, but Hervor felt horribly exposed. Having more company helped.

Now that she had a chance to speak to him, though, the words came hard. "Auðleif... I have to say, I didn't expect this kind of a welcome."

"Because of the things we've heard?" Auðleif tore off a hunk of coarse bread. "You forget, we knew you before that – even though we thought it was Hervard we knew. There was no chance you'd get involved in blood magic, and as for murdering people... well, you'd been falsely held as a bondsmaid for seventeen years. That's a crime right there."

Hervor hoped no one was looking her way when she flinched. She would have to tell him eventually, of course, admit the truth about Saeunn – and Meltharkatla – but not tonight. "Fine, that explains everybody else. But you..."

Auðleif cocked an eyebrow when she fell silent. "What about me?"

"You made me give back your axe." Hervor tried and failed to keep the bitterness out of her voice.

Now he looked truly surprised. "And?"

Jordis excused herself and left the hall. Hervor waited until she was out of earshot, grateful they wouldn't be overheard. "You *humiliated* me."

"I what?"

Auðleif wasn't faking the confused shock in his voice. Hervor dug her fingers into her own bread and refused to look at him. "If you had to have it back, why not ask Orvar later? Or let him be the one to give it to you? Why make me do it?"

His silence stretched out long enough that she had to glance up at last. What she saw made no sense; Auðleif was staring at her as if she'd just told him she was actually a talking pig.

"You got the axe from Bjarmar," he finally said.

"I got it from *you*."

"You won it off me, yeah, but you accepted it from Bjarmar's own hands. Don't you realise what that meant?" Apparently her expression made it very clear she didn't, because Auðleif went on. "Receiving a weapon from someone – and I'm not talking about your friend saying, 'Here, hold this for a moment'; I mean receiving it to keep – that's a sign of respect. It's why housemen always accept their weapons from their lords, even if they had them already; they give them to the jarls and the jarls give them back. It puts you in the giver's debt, and shows your respect for them."

Hervor felt like she'd drunk a vast quantity of mead in the last few minutes. "That was supposed to be a compliment? You'd just found out I was a bondsmaid, a berserker, and a murderer, and you wanted to show your *respect*?"

"Yes," Auðleif said steadily, meeting her gaze. "I did."

"Didn't sound like it to me!"

"Well, I couldn't exactly announce it to the world, now could I? Not with things the way they were. I didn't dare do anything that would cause Bjarmar more trouble. Orvar probably thought like you did; otherwise he wouldn't have let you do it. But—" Auðleif glanced down at his bread and noticed for the first time that he was shredding it into little pieces. He put it down hastily.

"I figured that, whoever Orvar said you were, you'd been a good companion, and loyal to Bjarmar. You'd bested me in the circle, so I knew you were strong, too. And I decided that mattered more to me than what Orvar had said. I respected you. But since there wasn't a damn thing I could do to get you out of there, all I could do was take my axe back from you, and carry it in your honour."

Then he faced her again, pride shining in his eyes. "And now that I know who you are – Bjarmar's rightful heir – I'm even more glad I did. If you'll let me, I'll be the first to swear into your service."

"What in hell is this business of me taking Bjarmar's place?"

Jordis looked very startled when Hervor grabbed her at the hall's door and dragged her and Auðleif out into the snowy night again, but she regained her composure quickly. "None of his children are still living, and you're the only grandchild."

"He has other kin!"

"Distant ones," Jordis said, as if they ranked just above sheep.

"You think we're going to let one of Thjostan's bastards ride in and rule here?" Auðleif demanded.

No, not after the stories she'd heard on the way to Skersstað. But that didn't make Hervor ruling Aettarstað any less stupid an idea. "Jordis."

The older woman didn't pretend not to know what Hervor meant. "I was his wife. Not blood-kin. Any lawspeaker would tell you I can't inherit."

"You've been running Aettarstað for years, and we all know it. Better than I ever could!"

"I'll be more than happy to assist you."

Hervor felt like tearing at her hair. "I can't be jarl – or whatever the hell you'd call a female jarl. I don't even know how to *read*."

"That's a problem," Jordis admitted, "but you can learn."

"Did you forget that I'm a berserker and a murderer?"

Auðleif seemed to think her protests were funny. "I already told you," he said. "We don't care about that. Svafa married a berserker, remember?"

"And what about the blood magic?" She hated to bring that up, but by all the gods, she had to convince them this was a bad idea. "It's nice of you to assume I'm innocent, Auðleif, but I'm not."

That finally got their attention. Jordis and Auðleif lost their grins.

"There was a blood-witch at Rognjeld," Hervor said mercilessly. "She helped me escape the first time – I didn't know what she was doing for her spells, draining Berkel's corpse, but that's no excuse. I knew it was drauðr. And then when I went back, she'd been killed, but her ghost possessed my body and used me to kill Feigald."

Jordis backed up a step, one hand rising to her throat.

"You want *that* for your jarl?" Hervor asked.

"Did you…" Auðleif's voice came out strangled; he had to stop and try again. "Did you ask her to kill Feigald?"

"No. But I let my guard slip—"

"So she took you, against your will."

"If I hadn't gotten careless—"

"You didn't do it on purpose."

"No!" Hervor shouted, not caring whether anyone else overheard them. "It's never fucking on purpose. People just die by *accident*, like that's so much better. I didn't mean to get Rannvar killed; I didn't mean to go berserk and slaughter Enjarik and everybody else; hells, I didn't even mean to kill Vigmand. Orvar's the only one I decided to kill. But how is that better? I'm a walking disaster, and there doesn't seem to be a gods-damned thing I can do about it. That's why I shouldn't be your jarl: my father carried ill luck, and apparently I do, too. At the rate I'm going, Aettarstað will burn to the ground inside a month, and all of you will be dead."

Breath frosting in the cold air, she stopped. She'd run out of words.

The silence lasted long enough for Hervor to notice the quiet inside the hall – people had *definitely* overheard – and then Jordis spoke.

"Sometimes," the older woman said, "the gods make things this way. And we don't know why."

"So you should—"

"But," Jordis continued, cutting her off, "the best anyone can do, in the face of such problems, is live according to what's right." She gestured around Aettarstað. "This land was Bjarmar's; now he is dead. It must pass to his kin, and that means it should pass to you. You, and the child you carry."

"But I told you, I'm—"

"You're a woman who's done her best, under terrible circumstances. You said so yourself: you didn't mean to kill those men. If the gods decreed that it should be so, however, what can you do to change it?"

Fucking fate. The gods never seemed to interfere to anyone's benefit, apart from blessing the king. Maybe they used up all their goodwill on him, and left everybody else with the bad. Hervor said, "Oh, no. I'm not falling into that trap. If I go around saying, *well, the gods meant things to be this way and I can't do anything about it*, then I'm dodging responsibility for what I've done. I *am* responsible. I have to accept that."

"And that's why you should be jarl," Auðleif said quietly. "Not just because you're blood-kin, and damn near all that's left, though that matters, too. Because you do take responsibility for what you do. Maybe the gods have decided you should have a shitty life, but you're going to go on trying to make it better. Aren't you?" He paused, searching her face. "Or did I misjudge you, back when you were Hervard?"

Hervor felt like they'd backed her into a corner, and she couldn't even see how it had happened. "Pretty words," she said. "But you're the ones who will suffer, when I fail to stop this kind of shite from happening."

"We owe you what help we can offer," Auðleif said.

The words reminded her of Enjarik. Hervor looked up at the sky, not wanting these two to see the tears that threatened. The stars shimmered and swam in her vision. Enjarik and his men had decided they owed her loyalty, because of what she was, and they'd all died for it. How could she let somebody else do the same? What if that happened again?

Then maybe the gods meant for it to be that way, a voice in her mind said.

Fuck the gods, another voice said.

Exactly, said a third. Fuck their plans. Overturn them. Keep your people safe.

Your people?

Hervor recognised the shift she'd just made, and almost swore out loud.

Aettarstaд was the one place she'd ever thought might become a home. Jordis had shown her what a home could look like, even when it was withering. And the men here – Auдleif, Isbjorn, Holmstein, spindly Kjarvald and all the rest – they were her companions. Auдleif had already said he wanted to swear into her service.

And she owed Bjarmar this much, to take care of what he had left behind. She would be shamed forever if she avenged some kin, but left the legacy of others to rot.

"I've made a promise," she said heavily, facing them once more. "To my father and my brothers. Their deaths were caused by sorcery, and so I've sworn to avenge them. Orvar

Grimsson is dead, but the other one... I have no idea how to find him. I've got to do that first."

At the word "first", a grin split Auðleif's face.

"No," Jordis said.

Hervor felt like shaking her. "I just said—"

The older woman held up her hands. "I'm sorry. What I meant was, it might help you achieve your goals to do one or two other things first."

"Like what?" Hervor asked suspiciously.

"Jarls have many rights and privileges that ordinary freeborn lack. Moreover, the Blessed King has sent the word out, all across the land, that you are to be brought to Svelsond."

Like the men outside Reiðast had said. "You can't be serious."

"If you go to Svelsond to be recognised as jarl, you can clear matters up with the king. Then you won't have to worry about being captured as you search for this second man."

"And what if he decides to throw me in chains?"

Jordis nodded calmly, as if this were a discussion of the spring shearing. "That's a risk. But if you come to him of your own free will, I think it will be a small one. If, on the other hand, you have to be dragged back..."

"Besides," Auðleif said, "the Blessed King was there for the duel, wasn't he? He might know where that other man went."

Hervor buried her hands in her hair and wished the two of them weren't making such persuasive sense. She didn't want to go to Svelsond. She wanted to hunt down Hjalmar and kill him, and maybe get killed herself so she wouldn't have to face the idea of running Aettarstað. But Auðleif was right. If the king did know Hjalmar, he could save her months of searching.

Assuming he didn't throw her in chains.

But that was where Jordis was right: a measured risk might be the best choice.

Hervor paused for a moment and listened, but the ghosts were quiet. At the very least, they weren't rising up in fury at the thought of her taking a detour.

"All right," she muttered, striding past the two of them before they could make any more helpful suggestions. She reached the door to the hall and threw it wide open. Sure enough, every head inside was turned that way, listening with bated breath to the conversation outside.

"Looks like I'll be the new jarl," Hervor said to them with a self-mocking smile. "Gods help us all."

Of course, they couldn't leave for Svelsond the next day. This was supposed to be a new beginning for Aettarstað; they hoped to make it a good one, and that meant making everybody involved *look* good. So everyone dug out what finery the town had to offer, as well as gifts for the Blessed King.

Hervor and Jordis got into fights immediately, starting with Jordis's attempts to loan Hervor her clothing. "Over my dead body," Hervor said. "I'm not going to go in and announce that I'm sworn to vengeance while wearing a *dress*. Besides, you'd have to chop me off at the knees to make that fit." Jordis conceded the point, grudgingly, and then the hunt was on to find clothing – men's clothing – that would fit her. Between the twin needs to fit her new status and her expanding stomach, they had a hard time of it.

Then there was the issue of how they would get to Svelsond. Hervor ought to show up in style, and that meant on a horse; Auðleif looked dumbstruck when she told him she'd never ridden one in her life. And again her pregnancy caused problems, because the journey to Svelsond wasn't short, and she wasn't getting any smaller. Jordis was appalled at the very notion of Hervor riding while she was with child. Once more they were forced to compromise: Hervor would learn to ride as well as she could on the way to Svelsond, fleeing to a sledge when her body protested, and then if she was in good enough shape on arrival she'd go through the gates mounted.

"Life would be easier if I weren't pregnant," Hervor grumbled once, early on. She learned not to say it after that. No one asked her anything – least of all who the father was – but she saw the sidelong looks, from Jordis, from Auðleif, from everybody. Kjarvald didn't even manage to be sidelong; he stared openly, until she caught his gaze and raised one meaning eyebrow. Then he flushed and looked away. Since Hervor didn't feel like explaining, she kept her mouth shut, and everyone went on trying to pretend she wasn't unmarried and carrying a child.

The weight of the unasked questions grew heavy enough that by the time they were ready to leave for Svelsond, she was actually looking forward to the trip. Before they could go, however, there was one last thing she had to do.

She'd avoided it for as long as she could; she'd had enough contact with the dead to last her a lifetime. But Hervor could feel the disapproval growing with every day she put it off, until finally she had no choice but to visit Bjarmar's barrow.

They'd laid him inside just before she arrived in Aettarstað, on the third day after his death, but she didn't go near it until the day before they left. To be honest – and she could be honest with herself, at least, if no one else – she was afraid of what might happen. True, Angantyr and the others had spoken without her ever going near their barrow, but that didn't mean she should tempt fate by visiting Bjarmar. Jordis's expression grew stiffer with every passing day, though, so eventually Hervor yielded. Taking the horse Auðleif had been trying to teach her to ride, she went to the hills south of town, where her ancestors lay buried.

No voices rose up in her mind as she went – no new ones, anyway. Her father and brothers were there, but they stayed too quiet to understand, and in a strange way it was comforting. Hervor rode between the snow-covered mounds and realised that those who lay within were her blood-relatives, generations of them, reaching back into a history only skalds remembered. The thought was an odd one, like the new clothing Jordis was making for her: it fit, but she had to remind herself that it was hers.

She wondered which one held Svafa, and the unknown girl passed off in Hervor's place.

After she dismounted at the foot of Bjarmar's barrow, she had no idea what to say. This wasn't like her confrontation with her father; she had nothing to demand of him. Except maybe an explanation for why he couldn't have hung on a little while longer, until she came home.

"Grandfather," she said, tasting the word. "I… I'm sorry."

The wind blew over the snow-covered mounds, a thin and lonely sound.

"I should have come back sooner. I should have admitted the truth sooner; maybe then we would have figured it out before Skersstað, and Orvar never would have dragged me back to Rognjeld. I should have—" Her breath caught in her throat; an extra edge to the wind stung her face and told her she was crying. Pregnancy was throwing her feelings utterly out of balance. "I'm sorry."

No answer from Bjarmar, and even her father was silent.

"I'll redeem the family's honour," she said, touching Tyrfing's hilt. "I swear it. And I don't care what the damned curse says – I'll make sure my son doesn't suffer for it." An uneven laugh bubbled up out of her. "Pointless to be thinking about him having honour when his father was a viking and his mother was an infamous murderer, maybe… but I can't just give up."

Hervor swallowed the lump in her throat and went on. "I hope you're well, grandfather. I hope that Eldaskrid has judged your worth truly. You suffered, but did the best you could in the face of it, even though you had so little hope. No god could ask more."

Then she stood, brushing the snow off her knees, and prepared to go. "I'll try to be worthy of you, grandfather," she said, and then she retrieved her horse and rode away.

Four days into their journey, Auðleif's patience cracked.

"So who was he?" the warrior demanded.

"Who was who?" Hervor shifted uncomfortably in her saddle. Short rides around Aettarstað and the longer one out to the barrow-field had done nothing to prepare her for a true journey on horseback. She'd be back on the sledge soon; only the desire to look something like a jarl was keeping her mounted for now.

"The father."

She'd known it was coming, sooner or later. If she was Bjarmar's heir, the contents of her belly were hers. Of course they would want to know. "None of your business."

"Can't be one of us, can it? Anybody of Aettarstað. You're too far along." He eyed her as if she were a mare whose health he was evaluating.

"Do you mind?" Hervor asked mildly. "I'm not livestock. And no, the father isn't anybody you know, so you can stop trying to guess."

"Was it one of the vikings? Enjarik himself?"

"Push off, Auðleif. You're worse than an old granny."

He grinned and didn't take offence. "What will you name him? Assuming it's a him, of course." That last was added hastily; Auðleif was still having trouble remembering she was a woman, and might not look on a daughter as a terrible disappointment.

"I think it will be," Hervor said, remembering what her father had said. Doom, for herself and her sons. She tried to take comfort from the prospect of living long enough to have more than one, and failed. "But I haven't thought about names yet."

"Bjarmar's too newly dead to be a safe choice, but you could name him after your father or brothers, couldn't you? Angantyr would be appropriate; after all, you're trying to avenge him. Or Hervard. That would be kind of funny, since you were calling yourself that for so long."

It was true that naming a child after newly-dead kin was considered dangerous, and also true that men seventeen years dead ought to be safe... but Auðleif hadn't been living with their voices for those seventeen years. Hervor wasn't minded to give them any more excuses for wakefulness. "No. Not Angantyr, nor Hervard, neither."

Her tone was clipped enough to startle Auðleif, but he recovered quickly. "All right, then. Just the tried-and-true practice of taking elements from their names, I guess. Angan-something. Anganvald? Anganolf?"

"Will you quit, already?"

"Just ask a skald before you decide. You want to be sure you know what the name means, before you stick the poor kid with it."

That, Hervor reflected, was the first decent suggestion Auðleif had made.

Fortunately for her sanity, he didn't have a lot of chance to chatter at her. Travelling in winter was far from easy. The sledges worked well in the snow when the ground was flat or sloping downhill, or when they could follow the frozen surface of a river, but on upslopes they often had to unpack everything and carry it to the top. Or rather, others had to carry; Jordis wasn't with them, but she'd given strict orders that Hervor wasn't to be allowed to lift anything heavier than a bedroll. After seventeen years as a bondsmaid and several months as a longship's bilge-boy, Hervor felt uncomfortable standing around while other people worked. But it turned out they were all more afraid of Jordis than they were of her, and so her hands remained empty.

But if she was often cold, at least there was a fire at the end of the day to warm her; if the food was plain, at least there *was* food; and for once she had more company than the voices in her head.

She'd had worse journeys.

The only bad part of this one was that it ended at Svelsond, and the end came far too quickly.

24

THE BLESSED KING

Svelsond took her breath away. Hervor didn't know what she'd been expecting – Skersstað, she supposed, only bigger.

That was like calling the Ice Knives hills, only bigger.

Svelsond had the same things a lesser town had: walls, gates, workshops and temples and homes. But there were more of them – hundreds more – packed in so closely Hervor couldn't imagine how anybody lived there. While some were little and squalid, like the pig-shed on a holding, others put Thjostan's hall to shame. At the centre of Svelsond was an enormous, rocky hill, rearing up out of the surrounding land like the head of some petrified beast, and atop that hill sat the hall of the Blessed King.

It shone even from a distance, despite the weak winter light. Auðleif had told her it was covered in gold, but she hadn't believed him; who would have enough gold to cover a *building*?

A king who had lived for centuries under the blessing of the gods.

did the gods truly forsake us?
or was our own weakness to blame?

"Now you see why you need to ride," Auðleif said, his grin not quite masking his own nervousness.

Hervor did see. This place made her feel little and grubby; hells, compared to that shining beacon on the hill, she *was* little and grubby. But she still had her pride, and riding helped her keep it. Hard to look impressive when sitting on a sledge.

So she rode into Svelsond on the back of a horse, head held high, pretending that her growing belly wasn't making this awkward, while townspeople pointed and whispered at them all.

The hall was even more dazzling up close. It wasn't quite true to say that it was plated in gold; artisans had sculpted and etched the metal into thousands of intricate decorations dense enough to look solid from a distance. The effect was even more dazzling, though, the craftsmanship reminding Hervor very forcibly of just how powerful the king was.

The bold posture of her men faltered as they approached, but when they reached the space before the hall, Kjarvald shook himself out of his reverie. The youth had begged for the chance to serve as Hervor's herald; now he tugged his clothing straight, touched his axe for reassurance, and strode forward.

It was a formality, of course. Word had reached Svelsond that she was on her way. But proper behaviour would be observed all the same.

"Who comes to the hall of the Blessed King?"

The challenge was delivered by a warrior in his prime, tall and muscled, in decorated armour that would have been stunning if he hadn't been standing in front of a building covered in gold. Kjarvald planted his feet widely – probably to keep from falling over out of nerves – and answered in the most ringing tone he could manage. "Hervor, whose father was Angantyr, son of Arngrim, and whose mother was Svafa, daughter of Bjarmar, the late jarl of Aettarstað."

He'd pleaded day and night to be allowed to list her deeds, but Hervor had refused. No sense reminding everyone of her stint as a viking, nor that she had any association with a blood-witch.

The warrior at the door nodded. "That name is known to us. From where do you come?"

"Through snow and wind we have come from Aettarstað, long the home of Hervor's kin."

"So noted. For what purpose do you come?"

"Hervor, daughter of Angantyr, granddaughter of Bjarmar, comes to the Blessed King to seek his recognition of her claim to Aettarstað, and to give him a true account of the deeds which have been attached to her name."

That got the first visible reaction from the door-guard, whose eyebrows rose slightly. "Very well," he said. "The Blessed King is open to such petitioners. Leave your weapons here, and you may pass within to present your case."

Hervor's housemen disarmed themselves. She herself stood motionless.

The guard noticed, of course. "Do you refuse to lay your sword aside?"

"With all respect to you and the Blessed King," Hervor said, "the sword I carry isn't normal. This is Tyrfing, forged by the dvergar for King Sigrlami, and it's… temperamental. I don't want to leave it in the hands of strangers. Besides which, it has a bearing on my petition; I think the king might want to see it."

Her conversational tone cut through all the ritualised patterns. The guard looked momentarily disoriented, unsure how to cope. Finally he summoned a servant and sent the other man within to ask.

Hervor waited, trying to look as if this weren't scaring her juiceless. Her mouth was so dry she could barely speak.

it was not fear that stole our strength

So nice for you, she thought sourly at the ghosts, clenching her teeth.

The servant came back out at a run, face very pale, and whispered to the guard.

Who looked startled, then set his jaw. "The Blessed King has heard your words, and he grants you this privilege. You will be permitted to bear your sword inside. But if you draw it in the presence of the king, your life will immediately be forfeit."

As if anybody could draw a sword that long when it was strapped across their back. That was why Hervor had put it there, so it wouldn't look like a threat, and so her ghosts couldn't make her do anything stupid. But she didn't blame the guard for telling her anyway.

Two servants grasped the handles of the hall's great doors and swung them wide to admit the new arrivals.

The interior made all the grime and dirt and decay of the outside world, the hostile, unpredictable weather, and the hand-to-mouth existence of life in places like Rognjeld, seem like a bad dream. Tapestries embroidered with jewel-coloured thread lined the walls; goldwork, more delicate than that outside, decorated every surface not covered by a tapestry. The light of the lamps reflected back a thousand times, creating a dizzying, glittering tunnel down the middle of the hall, through which Hervor and her men had to walk, while all the people in the hall – and there were a *lot* of them – stared in complete and utter silence.

Footsteps on a wood floor had never sounded so loud.

And at the far end, upon a dais, waited the Blessed King himself.

Somehow, despite knowing he was immortal, she expected him to have aged. But the face was exactly the one she'd seen when Angantyr showed her the holmganga: not young, but not old, either. His hair was a rich golden blond untouched by grey, and his face was virtually unlined; the only hint of his tremendous age was in his eyes, which were the pale, cold blue of a winter's sky, and which studied her with an expression she couldn't begin to interpret.

"You are the daughter of Angantyr," he said.

Hervor swallowed and prayed to any god who might be listening that her voice would not shake. "I am."

"I saw your father die."

"As did I, high one. He showed it to me in a vision."

A quiet murmur washed down the hall at her words.

The Blessed King's eyes became even colder. "Is that so."

"High one, I came here today to explain what I've done, and why people have been... telling certain stories about me." Hervor paused. He didn't tell her to stop, so she forged ahead. "The spirits of my father and brothers have haunted me for as long as I can remember – though I didn't know that's who they were, not at first. From an early age, my main desire in life was to silence them. To lay them to rest."

For a moment she was seized by an irrational desire to drop something on the smooth wooden panels of the floor, just to hear it clunk; the sound would have been like a bolt of lightning in the silence of the hall. Even her ghosts said nothing.

"Everything I have done," Hervor said, "has been a result of that quest. I'm not proud of all of it. Some of it, I would undo if I could, and would have prevented if I'd known it was going to happen. But I didn't, and I can't. So I'm here to ask for your mercy. It's true that I've been a viking, raiding towns along the coast." She clenched her hands into fists. "It's also true that I've been involved with blood magic. I asked several witches for advice, because only they could tell me how to speak to the dead."

"And what," the Blessed King asked in a dangerously quiet voice, "did the dead tell you?"

Hervor lifted her chin and pitched her voice for everyone to hear. "That they were betrayed."

This time the wash of sound was louder.

"They told me," Hervor said, "that the holmganga was corrupted. They were weakened by some kind of sorcery. How else could two men defeat thirteen berserkers? Some spell robbed my father and brothers of their strength – not just the power Bolvereik lends those he touches, but the natural strength of their bodies." The murmurs had died down; Hervor spoke into dead silence again. "They charged me with vengeance."

Then, moving very slowly, so that no one could mistake her intentions, she unbuckled the strap that held Tyrfing to her back and held the sheathed sword out where everyone could see it. "This is Tyrfing, the sword my father bore. He gave it to me, from out of his barrow, so that I could avenge his unnatural death. I'm halfway there. Orvar Grimsson is dead by my hand."

The response now was not an indistinct wash; she heard several distinct oaths from among the crowd.

The Blessed King eyed her as if she were a wolf, possibly rabid, possibly in need of being shot down before it could hurt someone. "Sorcery, you say."

"Yes, high one. Orvar denied it before he died, so I suppose either he was lying, or it was the work of Hjalmar Modfinsson, the man who killed my father."

For the first time, an expression touched the Blessed King's face that didn't make Hervor feel like her life hung by a thread. It was almost a smile. And then he looked up, past where she stood, to the gathered people watching them both. "What say you to that, Hjalmar?"

All the blood drained out of Hervor's face. He couldn't be serious.

But there were mutters from behind her, and when she turned, her joints creaking with tension, she found that a man had risen to his feet, his face as pale as hers.

He had aged, like Orvar, unlike the king. His dark hair was shot with grey, and the weather had carved deep lines into his face. She still recognised him, though.

"You," she snarled.

Hjalmar set his jaw and came forward, walking stiffly as if some unseen force was driving him. "I am Hjalmar Modfinsson," he declared, but she could sense the fear behind his bravado. "The slayer of Angantyr."

Hervor waited for a response from inside her head. The ghosts had always renewed their fury in Orvar's presence. This time, though, there was only silence.

But this was the man she was looking for. He'd admitted it.

She spun back to face the king. "High one, I'm a freeborn woman, and the only surviving child of a murdered man. I have the right to claim vengeance. Please – give me your leave to challenge this man."

"High one—" Hjalmar's words landed on top of hers. "This woman is a confessed criminal! Like her father, she has sailed the seas to prey on innocent people, and she's admitted to consorting with witches. Granting her the right of challenge would make a mockery of that ancient practice."

"Afraid?" Hervor spat at him. "You know I killed Orvar; you know I'll do the same to you."

"You're barely grown, girl," Hjalmar said with contempt. "I don't fear you."

"Then face me in a duel!"

"And stain my sword with more of your tainted blood?"

"*Enough*," the Blessed King said. His voice was quiet, but it cut through their rising shouts like a knife.

They both clamped their jaws shut and turned towards the king.

"You each stand accused of evil deeds," he said. "What say you to that?"

He looked first to Hervor. "My deeds have had evil consequences," she said, trying to sound confident, "but my intentions were good. I spoke to witches only so that I might lay the dead to rest. What happened at Rognjeld... that was possession, against my will."

"But you still benefited from it," Hjalmar growled.

The king stopped him with a raised hand. "What say you?"

"To her accusation? I worked no sorcery. No magic of any kind. It was just as you told me before the duel, high one: the gods decided the victors."

The Blessed King smiled thinly. "Very well. Since you place such faith in the judgement of the gods, Hjalmar, we will put this in their hands."

Hervor's hands tightened on Tyrfing's sheath.

"A holmganga," the Blessed King said. The word echoed through the hall. "Such a duel began this tale; let a second end it. Were it not winter, we might even journey to Samsey, to bring it all full circle. But there is an island closer to hand, in the Arinvar River. It has been host to countless duels before. You two will face each other there, and let the gods decide whose claims are true."

No one made a sound. Hervor had to try three times before she could ask the question beating at her. "When?"

"Now," Hjalmar snapped.

"No!" Auðleif leapt forward. "High one, he's claiming an unfair advantage. We've been travelling a hard road; to make her fight now—"

"This is in the hands of the gods, isn't it?" Hjalmar said mockingly, throwing a contemptuous look over his shoulder. "If she's as virtuous as she claims to be, then she'll win no matter what. But I think the state of her virtue is *quite* clear." He sneered at Hervor's expanded girth.

The scuffling noises from behind them indicated that someone, probably Kjarvald, had tried to throw himself at Hjalmar. Hervor's eyes were on the Blessed King, though. If he agreed with Hjalmar—

Fuck it all, she hadn't expected to find the man here. She had thought she'd have more time. Time spent in Svelsond, smoothing matters over, and then the roads would be impassable, and she'd give birth while waiting for them to clear. Then, once she was ready again, she'd set off in search of her father's killer. She hadn't expected to face this *now*.

"No," the Blessed King said, and her heart leapt in her chest. "Not now, nor today, nor tomorrow."

Relief weakened Hervor's knees.

"But the day after," the king went on, "at sundown, you will fight."

Her nerveless hands almost dropped Tyrfing.

"High one—" she began, her mouth dry with horror.

He didn't even look at her. "In the interim, I will recognise Hervor, granddaughter of Bjarmar, as the jarl of Aettarstað, so that she may duel Hjalmar Modfinsson with the proper honour."

"She's six months pregnant!" Kjarvald yelled.

The king nodded. "Yes. But matters of vengeance cannot wait. To delay would be an insult to the dead."

They've waited long enough, Hervor wanted to say; what's a few months more? Me dying will be a bigger insult! Next to her, Hjalmar was grinning in anticipation of victory. Hervor tried to tell herself that if this was her time to die, then so be it, but the thought brought little comfort.

And still the ghosts were silent.

"I have spoken," the Blessed King said, his voice carrying such a weight of authority that it stifled all hope of protest. "Two days from now, we will go to the island of Talfey, and there observe the truth of this matter. Prepare yourselves."

25

HOLMGANGA

Hervor suspected the only reason she slept that night was because one of the serving-women dosed her with something. True, she was exhausted from travelling, but shrieking terror of her impending death should have kept her awake.

She rose late the next morning and sleepwalked through the day. Not until Auðleif came to see her did she really wake up – and then it was because of bad news.

"Hjalmar's one of his housemen," Auðleif said without preamble.

She stared at him, not understanding. "Whose?"

"The Blessed King's."

"What?" Hervor shook her head. "No. To one of his jarls, maybe—"

"To *him*. Has been for years. Orvar used to be, too, but after the duel with Angantyr he got restless and left."

Hervor remembered the vision of the holmganga, the Blessed King standing with the men on Samsey. He was the only one who could legally oversee such a duel – but why had he given leave for a holmganga in the first place? Simple: because one of his men was involved.

She sank down onto her bed, knees no longer able to hold her up. "Oh, fuck."

Her father's words were burned into her memory, but she'd focused on what he'd said about Tyrfing, not the rest of it. Now another detail came to mind.

The eagles flew from Ingjald's hall.

"Auðleif," she said, her voice unsteady, "you served the king once, right?"

"Not directly."

"Do you know his name? I mean, he's got to have one, right?"

Auðleif nodded. "People don't often use it – I mean, it's not like he's just another man – but his name is Ingjald."

Hervor took a long, wavering breath. "Great. So I've killed one of his old housemen, and now I'm trying to kill another one. Why in hell did he suggest a holmganga? He could tell me to fuck off and leave his man alone. He's the *Blessed King*."

Auðleif shrugged. "Maybe he prefers to leave things to the gods. People have been talking about the last duel. They were at a holding on the coast, dealing with a jarl who'd tried to rebel, and Angantyr and his sons got into an argument with Orvar and Hjalmar. The king stepped in and suggested they settle it by holmganga. Said the gods should judge the matter."

She gave a short, bitter laugh. "And that went so well for my family. I guess he's counting on the same thing happening again."

"I doubt it," Auðleif said. "I mean, look at how he's treating you."

Hervor glanced up. "What do you mean?"

He gestured at her bed, strewn with pieces of clothing servants had been bringing all day. "Why do you think he's giving you these things?"

"I look like a jumped-up farmer, and he's trying to make sure I don't embarrass myself by showing up in shoddy clothing."

"Exactly! Well, not exactly; you don't look that bad. But he's giving you gifts, don't you see?"

"So?" Hervor stared at the clothing. It was all finely made, better even than Jordis's dresses, with rich dyes and wool as soft as fog. If she hadn't been sure of her death tomorrow, a part of her would have been torn between glee and laughter at the thought of wearing it.

"So he's showing you favour," Auðleif said, with exaggerated patience. "Melsafny's tits, don't you ever listen to stories? Kings don't give fancy clothes to people they expect will die in shame the next day."

"So I'll die in glory instead. Big improvement."

"Or he doesn't think you'll die at all."

"Right." Hervor flopped backwards onto her bed and noted morosely that her belly seemed to have gotten even larger overnight. "Because he doesn't know how incompetent I am."

"You beat me, didn't you?"

"With an axe. And only because my brothers tried to possess me and fight you in my stead."

The shocked silence lasted long enough that Hervor sat up. Auðleif was staring at her, his face pale. "Shite," she said. "Guess I never told you about that."

He shook his head, still wordless.

Hervor scowled. "Don't look at me like that; I'm not about to go berserk or get possessed or do anything that deserves you soiling yourself. I'm just trying to reconcile myself to dying, is all."

A knock at the door saved them both. He opened it and accepted a gift of gloves from one of the Blessed King's servants, and soon it was time to go back to the hall for the feast in her honour. Auðleif kept his distance from Hervor as they walked, and she sighed to herself. Another friend scared off.

The food tasted like ashes; the mead might as well have been sea water. Hervor forced herself to eat and drink anyway, but not too far into the feast she had to excuse herself to go outside and throw up. Wiping her mouth, she tried to blame it on the pregnancy, but she didn't believe it. Her nerves were wound so tight, she was afraid she would snap.

The last thing she wanted was to go back into the hall, where Hjalmar and the king and Auðleif and everyone else was watching her. Out here, though, the voices whispered to her non-stop, blood and ravens and Hjalmar's sins, and if she didn't know why they were quiet inside, she also didn't care.

But she couldn't hide out here forever. She forced herself back inside, and soon the time came for the ceremony that made her a jarl. Fortunately it was short. The king established her identity — a mere formality; the appearance of the daughter of Angantyr had fascinated everyone enough that they'd swallow it even if it were a lie, just for the sake of the gossip — and then she expressed her intention of ruling Aettarstað well — not that she had the first clue how to do that. Then the king took her blood-oath. The cuts were supposed to be made on both of her wrists, but she would be fighting a duel the next day; instead he cut her shoulders, and made the wounds small.

As he pronounced the words binding her to her duty, Hervor's stomach gave a terrible lurch. She thanked the gods silently that there was nothing left inside her to spew. If she was going to die, at least she could leave a dignified memory behind.

When the feasting was over and Hervor was finally allowed to retire, she found she couldn't sleep.

No amount of telling herself that tomorrow would go even worse if she was tired could compel her to relax. In the end she left the house she'd been put in and walked through the quiet, snowy streets to the temple of Bolvereik.

Aettarstað's temple was a single large hall that played home to all the deities. Here in Svelsond, every god got their own house. In shape Bolvereik's was like the king's, with pillars as big around as Hervor was – stomach and all – but where the king's hall was gilt and carved and draped with tapestries, Bolvereik's temple was harsh and austere. This place wasn't meant to dazzle; it was meant to intimidate. Hervor felt very, very small as she entered.

There were no guards. None were needed. Skalds told enough stories of what happened to people who tried to steal from Bolvereik.

Besides, there wasn't much to steal – no gold, no jewels. Just a bare wood floor, the heavy posts holding torches, and at the far end, hanging point-down from a slender rope, a bloodstained sword.

Hervor stopped a few feet away. The torchlight shone dully off the clean parts of the blade, and wetly off the blood. If the stories were true, the blood had been there for as long as anyone could remember, and it had yet to dry. They said it wouldn't until the day the land was at peace, and that would be after the end of the world. The cynic in Hervor's mind said it was more likely the priests regularly touched the blade up with pig's blood... but standing here at night, in the presence of the sword, it was hard to be a cynic.

She'd been cut already that day, but Hervor drew her dagger anyway. With it she made a shallow slice on one forearm, flicking one red droplet off the tip of the blade and into the basin that sat before the hanging sword.

"I am Hervor," she whispered, hearing the words echo in the icy silence of the temple. "Daughter of Angantyr. Daughter of Bolvereik. I am a berserker. Four times I have been overtaken with the fury of the god. Months I fought against it, but the fourth time I surrendered, giving myself over to Bolvereik's power. I dedicate the death of Orvar to you, Bloody One, in the memory of my murdered brothers."

The sword hung perfectly still. The flickering torchlight glinted off the blood.

"Tomorrow I face my father's killer, on the island of Talfey, in the sacred holmganga. When my father stood in my place, his strength was taken from him, by a sorcerer or by the gods." The shining wetness of the blood was mesmerising. Hervor swallowed. "If it truly was by the will of the gods that my father fell, then so be it; deny me my vengeance. But if he died by treachery, then I pray you will give me the strength I need."

She hesitated for several heartbeats, then added the rest. "And the skill. Because you of all people know, Bolvereik, that I need it."

If she had expected a response, she didn't get one. In silence she left the temple and the hanging, bloodstained sword.

◆ ◆ ◆

Then, as if the world had blinked, it was dawn.

Auðleif armed Hervor, not that there was much to do; for the holmganga, they would wear no armour apart from their shields. She stood mutely as he did it, as if she were a bride being prepared for a wedding. Or a corpse, being prepared for burial.

The winter sun strained towards its peak as they all walked through the streets, watched by crowds of uneasy townspeople, and out the gates to the Arinvar River. The ice was thick enough to support their weight, so Hervor and Hjalmar and the Blessed King simply walked across to Talfey and stood on the island's shore to give their oaths.

Like her oath to Enjarik, this was done with full formality. Hjalmar, as the challenged, went first. After the sword the king held made shallow cuts in his wrists, he said, "I come here today of my own free will to submit to the judgement of the gods. May my blood flow like water, if they find me guilty."

Then it was Hervor's turn. She repeated the same words, and was proud that her voice didn't shake.

The Blessed King laid his hands over their wrists, pressing to staunch the thin trickle of blood. "The gods watch all that we do. Conduct yourselves with honour, and living or dead, you will not be found wanting."

He bandaged their wounds himself, his hands surprisingly warm in the cold air. Then he said, "I retreat now from the island, so that you may be free to duel as you will. This island is your battle-ground: no part of your fight will pass its shores."

He walked back across the ice to the river's far shore, and Hervor was left alone with Hjalmar.

death upon us all, her father whispered. He sounded eager.

Hjalmar drew his sword and swung it a few times, loosening up his shoulder. The two replacement shields he was permitted for the duel lay at his feet. "I am innocent, bitch, and I'll prove it on your body."

Hervor reached for Tyrfing, her eyes slitting automatically against its light. "We'll see how you do against this."

But Hjalmar only laughed. "What, its poison? You didn't think the Blessed King would allow a trick like that in the holmganga, did you?"

"What do you mean?" Hervor asked, her blood curdling.

"The poison won't touch me," Hjalmar announced. "No more than it did seventeen years ago. He gave me medicine to protect against it. This will be about you and me, not that piece of steel."

Hervor fought to keep her face calm. She'd expected the poison to level the field, the way it had against Orvar. Without that…

She still had some advantages, like the protection Tyrfing gave her against cuts. But now her lack of skill weighed much heavier.

Hervor picked up the first of her shields, trying to keep herself from panicking. "Tell me," she said, buying time, "what was it that you duelled over in the first place?"

"The death of my cousin," Hjalmar said stiffly. "Ingmar Hjaldorsson."

"How did he die?"

"Your brother Hjorvard killed him. In a drunken brawl."

The shield dangled loose from her hand. "Wait. You're telling me it was a stupid, ale-fuelled mistake... and for that you killed *my entire family?*"

"They wouldn't stand aside and let me take the blood-price from your brother," Hjalmar growled. "And the king said it should be settled by island-going. I do not question the king."

Hervor could feel the eyes on them from the river's shore. She didn't dare stall any longer, lest she look a coward. "Well," she said, forcing the words past the sick tightness in her throat, "he's said it again. So let's get on with it."

She lifted Tyrfing, settled her feet – and suddenly it was all so familiar. Like that first rush of memory on the *Disir's Fury*, like the flashes of knowledge in her duel against Auðleif. She *knew* this, bone-deep.

No. Not her. Her father.

Her heart lurched – and in that moment of unease, Hjalmar attacked.

His first blow shattered her shield. Hervor leapt back, gasping. Hjalmar retreated a few steps and waited while she shook off the remains of the shield and reached for another one. When it was securely on her arm, she advanced at him, more wary now. Of him... and of her father's influence.

It was as if she fought someone for control of a ship's rudder. One block was smooth as water; the next barely rose in time to meet Hjalmar's blade. Hervor sweated with effort. He was a good swordsman, as good as Orvar, maybe better—

Her father had been better.

She would *not* let him take her over!

They came together again, back and forth in the snow. The tip of Hjalmar's blade caught against her thick sleeve, slicing through it but leaving her skin intact. A moment later, he cut her second shield apart.

Hervor picked up the third shield, hands shaking almost too badly to grasp it. She hadn't had time to work herself up into the fury of a berserker, and Hjalmar wasn't going to give it to her. Without that fury, though, and the benefits it gave her – the strength, the speed, the disregard for pain—

She could *let* him hit her. Pray that taking a few wounds was enough to bring on the rage, without weakening her to the point where she'd die even with the fury to keep her going. But that would be a stupid fucking gamble.

Or... let her father do as he wished.

Rognjeld rose up in her mind's eye, and Feigald's screams echoed in her ears. *No.* She wouldn't let innocents die again.

Hjalmar was waiting. He had enough honour not to strike before she had the shield settled on her arm, but the longer she fumbled with it, the more of a coward and a weakling she looked. Was this how she wanted to die? Fighting her own father instead of Hjalmar?

death brings no rest

It certainly hadn't made Angantyr shut up; he was awake as ever, and ready to fight for her if she let him. If she dared. If she was desperate enough to risk him killing others.

But this was the holmganga. The Blessed King had said it himself: no part of their fight would pass the island's shores. Could she trust that to keep her father contained?

trust is death

So was lack of skill, and Hjalmar stood ready to gut her like a fish.

Hervor prayed to Bolvereik, that he might get her out of this alive, that he would stay his hand so that she wouldn't kill anyone else… and she opened herself to her father's ghost.

It was the fire of a berserker's fury, but contained, directed, like a blacksmith's forge. In one swift move, she flung her last shield aside and gripped the hilt in both hands, stance shifting to match. Tyrfing came alive in her hands, no longer a thing of legend, powerful and feared, but a familiar friend. She knew its weight and speed, the uses of the cross-guard and pommel, how to angle its light to blind her enemy. She found her footing in the snow and met Hjalmar's rush without flinching. It was simple, even trivial. From an overhand strike, his next move would be to swing low. A blow repeated was a prelude to a sudden change. All she had to do was watch for the warning signs, take her opportunities where they came, then start shaping the battle to her will.

Hjalmar felt the change, though she doubted he knew why. And his expression chilled: first to grudging respect, and then, when his first shield broke, to fear.

Hervor had overwhelmed Orvar with the speed and fury of her attacks and slowed him with the poison. Hjalmar faced a different foe. This was what had made her father a legend while he still lived: he had the power of a berserker, but that wasn't all. Like Enjarik, he had cunning, experience, skill. All of them were tools to his hand. And Hervor knew, instinctively, that this was something none of his sons had inherited. Blinded by the infamous glory of being berserkers, none had ever managed to look beyond, to the strengths not given by Bolvereik.

This was why Angantyr, alone, had held his own against Hjalmar, while his sons fell to Orvar's blade.

The duel stretched out in the cold winter air, through Hjalmar's second and third shields, until he had none left. Even with Angantyr's aid, Hervor began to tire. Hjalmar was suffering, too, but not as much; after all, he was a warrior in constant training, and *he* wasn't pregnant. But if he landed blows more often than she did, hers cut, whereas his didn't. They were evenly matched.

At last there came a pause, the two of them standing just out of range, breath steaming the air.

"Doesn't look like the gods are favouring you, bitch," Hjalmar said between gasps.

"You, either," Hervor said, glad to find she had control of her own tongue. "Or are you so weak that even with the gods' help, you can't take down one pregnant woman?"

He snarled and charged, but they only fought briefly before breaking apart again. Neither had the energy to keep up the attack. At this point a single mistake could end it all. Hervor just prayed Hjalmar would be the one to make it.

He shifted his footing, flexing his left leg before settling his weight back down. Angantyr's attention focused on that like a wolf scenting blood. "I used no sorcery," Hjalmar insisted. "The only magic was the king's, binding us to the duel. He knew – we all knew – that Orvar and I were in the right. You've murdered a brave warrior, just because you can't admit the gods turned their faces from your kin."

"Murder?" Hervor said absently. Her attention – her father's attention – was still on that leg. On that brief flex, as if to ease a particular weariness or stiffness. "I faced him in a fair fight."

"You probably cut his throat in his sleep!"

Fury surged through Hervor. Not berserker madness; just plain old anger. "I faced him in broad daylight, with both of us armed, and me half-starved besides. If anybody had the advantage, it was him."

"You're a berserker."

"It's not cheating to be favoured by Bolvereik." This time

Angantyr didn't wait for Hjalmar to attack; he sent Hervor's body forward, swinging Tyrfing in a quick feint before slicing at the warrior's knees. The blow didn't connect, but Angantyr hadn't expected it to. The point was to see how Hjalmar moved.

He leapt out of the way, but the motion confirmed it: his left leg *was* stiff, from the cold and the strain.

And Angantyr, left in his barrow for seventeen years with nothing to think about except his final battle, remembered inflicting a wound on that knee, a wound that had been almost enough to bring Hjalmar down. Now, years later, it had healed, but not perfectly.

weakness is death, Angantyr growled in her mind.

For once, Hervor agreed with him.

Then there were no more thoughts, no more words, just the last of her strength – their strength – flung against Hjalmar. They pressed him backwards, giving him no chance to rest, constantly forcing him into a pattern of movement reliant on that left leg, that stiffened knee. Hjalmar's face twisted with effort as he kept himself upright and strove desperately to turn their attacks to his stronger side, but Angantyr had been a brilliant swordsman. Even hampered by his daughter's ungainly body, he knew exactly what responses to make.

They swung Tyrfing down, an arc of bright steel in the dying winter light, and the natural defence was to turn out of its path. Hjalmar turned – and his knee gave out.

He fell to the snow with a cry of pain.

They kicked the sword out of his hand, trusting Tyrfing to protect them from its edge, and then stood over him with their own blade at his throat. Hjalmar glared up at them with hate-filled eyes.

Hervor opened her mouth to speak, and Angantyr's voice came out.

"Betrayer."

Fear overtook the hate. "You," he whispered.

"You murdered me, you murdered my sons – but my line has lived on."

"I'm not a murderer," Hjalmar snarled. "The king and the gods favoured *me*!"

"And now they favour my daughter," Angantyr said. "Your crimes have been proved."

Hjalmar floundered in the snow, rising to one knee, left leg twisted to avoid taking his weight. "I am innocent of treachery," he said, flinging his tangled hair out of his face to meet Hervor's gaze squarely. "By the gods, I swear it."

"Eldaskrid will judge the truth of that," Angantyr said, and then his hand rose – Hervor's hand – and together they cut him down.

26

NAMING THE LIVING

For a long moment Hervor stood, looking down at the body of the man who'd killed her father.

Angantyr looked with her, and she could feel his satisfaction. Not Saeunn's obscene glee at destroying Feigald; this was cleaner, and didn't leave Hervor feeling tainted. But satisfaction, nonetheless. After seventeen years, it was done.

Tyrfing hung loosely from her hand. It needed to be sheathed while the blood was still warm – a terrible idea for a normal blade, but this one wasn't normal – and so her father slid it home.

The holmganga was done, yet Angantyr was still with her. Hervor wondered if she could trust him. Angantyr wasn't deranged like Saeunn... but who was to say what a ghost seventeen years dead might do, now that he had a body?

She made her way towards the shore of the island, stepped onto the ice. Angantyr was still present as she crossed the boundary, not a controlling force, but far more than a murmuring voice. She walked slowly and carefully across the ice, as much to keep watch on the ghost in her mind as to keep her weary feet from slipping. As she neared the Blessed King she prayed that his words were true, that her battle would not pass the boundaries of the holmganga.

As she stepped onto the riverbank, Angantyr's presence melted away like snow in the sun, leaving her alone and exhausted.

"The gods have judged you both," the king said formally, "and they have struck Hjalmar Modfinsson down."

Hervor wondered if the gods really had anything to do with it. She hadn't felt any of them watching during the duel; only her father. Then again, the priests said the gods didn't usually interfere directly in the affairs of men. They saved that for moments of great import – and the age for those was long past.

"He was a warrior and a noble man, despite his crimes," the king went on. "We will bury him as such. For now, let his comrades take his body to the temple of Eldaskrid."

Four men went across the river to retrieve Hjalmar's body; one glared at Hervor as he passed, but the others were stony-faced. She stood by awkwardly as they carried their dead friend away, through the fading afternoon, towards Svelsond.

The Blessed King watched them go, then turned back to Hervor. "For you, this must be a time of celebration. Your kin are avenged at last. There is a feast prepared—"

"High one." Interrupting him was rude, but Hervor didn't care. "I just want to rest."

He eyed her for a moment, then nodded. "So be it. After seventeen years, you too have earned your rest."

The feast came the next day instead, which Hervor sleepwalked through. Then more feasts after that, for a variety of reasons. Apparently the life of the king centred around feasting to honour his various followers. She went to some but avoided others; the strain of her quest had taken a great deal out of her, and she wasn't getting any less pregnant.

The king offered the best of his midwives to attend her, and Hervor told him she'd be glad of it when the time came, but she didn't want them poking at her before then. Those women wanted to coo over and cosset her, which was more unnerving than the sidelong looks she got for being a berserker and a viking, or the respect she got as a jarl. Besides, what could they do for her now other than offer a lot of superstitions that, from what Hervor had seen at Rognjeld, made very little difference to the outcome? She went to the temple of Melsafny to pray for an easy birth; apart from that, she could do nothing but wait.

She didn't feel like she'd accomplished anything. All she had to show for her effort was two dead men, and ghosts that still whispered in her mind. Angantyr had to know that Hjalmar was dead – he'd been there for it – but was he aware of Orvar? The ghosts had only been able to hear her on Samsey, after she fed them with the rabbit's blood. Hervor had the unpleasant suspicion she'd have to go back there and repeat the ritual before her kin would rest at last.

Not until spring, though. Storms raked the land and sea; attempting to sail there now would be a near-certain way of killing herself. Nobody would even let her travel back to Aettarstað, not while she was still bearing.

Out of a vague hope that it would hurry childbirth along, she spent an afternoon with Valarin, one of the king's skalds, talking about names for her son. She questioned him on the meaning of a great many name elements; her pregnancy was a topic of much gossip around Svelsond, and she didn't want anyone trying to spot patterns in the names she was considering. But she learned that Angantyr came from the ancient words for "swift" and "serpent", and Enjarik from the ones for "proud" and "warrior", and she kept her mouth firmly shut when Valarin asked her what name she favoured for her son.

"Who says it's going to be a son?" she said, hoping to turn him from his prying.

"You haven't asked me about women's names," he pointed out.

The first elements were the same as those for men, and Hervor knew the meanings of many of the second ones, but his comment reminded her of something she'd forgotten. "What does 'thar' mean?"

"Thar?" The skald looked confused. "You mean, as part of a name?"

"Yes."

"It's not used in names."

"Never?" Hervor supposed it made sense, in a twisted, Meltharkatla kind of way; someone with that many wits missing probably had trouble remembering what belonged in a name and what didn't.

"Well, almost never."

Hervor's curiosity was piqued. "What do you mean?"

Valarin sighed and laced his fingers together in a way that meant he was about to start expounding on something. "It comes from *tharenja*, an old word meaning 'to devour'. The only place it's ever used is in poetic epithets for a few gods. Bolvereik, for example, is also called Hralthareng, the Ever-Devouring One, and Eldaskrid is sometimes referred to as Meltharkatla, the Dark Devouring Spiral."

He came back from wherever his mind went when he started lecturing and looked at Hervor in concern. "Are you all right?"

She flapped one hand at him, trying to force a smile onto her face. She was fine. No problem. She'd had two brushes with a witch brazen enough to borrow a goddess's name, that was all.

The other possible explanation was *so much worse*.

"At any rate," the skald said, still eyeing her uncertainly,

"I wouldn't suggest using 'thar' in the name of a son *or* a daughter."

"No," Hervor said, her voice wild with the disbelieving laughter she was barely holding in. "I don't intend to."

She'd gone to the temple of Eldaskrid briefly after the holmganga, to say her farewells to Hjalmar; she hadn't much wanted to, but it was expected. Her interaction with the priests there had been minimal at best.

She would've preferred to keep it that way, but the skald's words battered at her incessantly, making it impossible to sleep. She had to ask. And so she heaved her ungainly body out of bed one morning and made her careful way through the icy streets to the temple.

Compared with the houses of the other gods, the interior of this one was cramped and dark. Eldaskrid wasn't the kind of goddess who got lots of expensive donations. Her favour couldn't be bought with gold; it could only be bought with your actions in life. She wouldn't postpone your death, and once it happened, she would judge you for what you had done, regardless of gold. So Melsafny's temple was a work of art, and Eldaskrid's was merely enough to serve its purpose.

Hervor didn't want to be overheard if someone wandered into the temple. When she found a priest, she convinced him to speak with her in the small enclosure where they kept animals for their sacrifices.

"Meltharkatla?" The priest, a wizened old man who barely came up to her collarbone, squinted in thought. "What do you want to know about her?"

"I heard that's an epithet for Eldaskrid."

"Yes, yes, so it is. Whoever told you that was very well-educated. She doesn't get called that very often." The priest winked at Hervor; he was surprisingly good-natured for someone with his job. She'd expected Eldaskrid's servants to be grim and terse.

"Why not?" Hervor asked, tucking her hands into her armpits for warmth. Her circulation hadn't been the best lately. Maybe she'd stop at Melsafny's temple on the way back and pray again to pop the child out already.

The priest shrugged. "Well, the gods have their epithets for a reason; each one tells a story, or refers to the god in a specific... mood, if you will. Meltharkatla is a very specific name for Eldaskrid – one linked with drauðr."

Hervor would cheerfully have gone the rest of her life without that knowledge. Even the priest's friendly voice had gone darker and quieter. Drauðr was not something to be talked of lightly, even when you were a priest of the goddess of death.

"What happens," Hervor asked in a carefully level tone, "if a human decides to borrow a god's epithet?"

"Borrow?" The priest's eyes went very wide. "You mean, call himself by that name? Or rather herself, as I assume you're referring to Meltharkatla."

"Yeah. What if a woman tried to call herself Meltharkatla?"

The priest looked baffled. "I honestly don't know. No one's ever tried it, so far as I've ever heard."

"So the gods wouldn't, oh, drop a lightning bolt on the person's head?"

"Eldaskrid is unlikely to use lightning bolts... but I can't imagine she'd be pleased. Of course, these days the gods don't often interfere directly in human matters; she wouldn't manifest and kill the offender herself. But she might arrange for the woman's death to be a painful one, when her time came. Certainly the woman would regret that choice when her spirit reached Slavinn."

Hervor thought of the witch she'd encountered twice, once outside Skersstað, once in the Ice Knives. "What does she look like?"

"Eldaskrid? Or Meltharkatla? Well, I don't know that they look any different, to be honest, and she doesn't get depicted much under either name; artists prefer other subjects. She's not attractive, not any more. I'm sure you've heard the tale of how Melsafny got jealous and stole her beauty. Sometimes she looks like an old hag, and sometimes like a madwoman, but in any appearance she's supposed to be quite ugly." The priest paused, looking thoughtful. "Except for her voice. That was the one thing Melsafny couldn't take from her. Eldaskrid's voice is still beautiful."

The witch's melodious voice echoed in Hervor's ears. Oh, yes, you could call it beautiful, and as for the rest... the dirt, the starvation, the badly shaved scalp. Meltharkatla looked more like what people expected of a madwoman than Hervor ever had.

The priest peered up at her in concern. "Did I tell you what you wanted to know? I'm afraid I can't be more helpful. I've served Eldaskrid for many years, but of course I've never had the honour of seeing her. It has been a long time since the gods granted us such favour."

Favour. Hervor's face twisted in a smile, because the alternative was to run screaming. Such favour. Meltharkatla had almost killed her, once.

But the second time, the witch – the *goddess*, if Hervor could bring herself to believe it – had led her to Orvar.

Hervor didn't have the first clue why a goddess would do that. But the next time someone said the gods didn't meddle directly in people's lives, she was going to *laugh*.

She forgot to visit Melsafny's temple on the way back, but it didn't matter. Soon after her trip into town, and nearly a month before she was supposed to, Hervor went into labour.

The pangs woke her in the middle of a nightmare. By the time Hervor roused enough to separate dream from reality and call for help, it was too late to go to the temple, even by sledge. There was an ice storm raging outside; they didn't dare move her.

So the Blessed King's people did the best they could. Servants brought lamps and everybody who knew anything about birthing, while an agile young boy with no fear of ice braved the streets to bring midwives from the temple. As

Hervor sweated and strained amid her tangled sheets, dozens of people scurried around, boiling water, making teas for her to drink, and generally getting in the way.

The head midwife, when she showed up, was not amused. "Out!"

As if by magic, most of the people vanished. The midwife took command of those who stayed, and soon Hervor was arranged more comfortably, with an unsheathed sword on either side of her. Back at Rognjeld, where swords were rare, they'd just used knives, but the principle was the same: the blades would keep evil spirits at bay, so they couldn't possess her newborn child. Hervor had thought the custom sensible until she was the one flailing around next to sharp objects, but she wasn't about to argue with a woman educated in Melsafny's lore. The midwife looked like she'd smack anyone who didn't do exactly what she said, when she said. So when the midwife said push, Hervor pushed.

The hours dragged by – or was it only minutes? Hervor lost all sense of time. Men were barred from the birthing room, but they were with her anyway; her father and her brothers spoke in her mind, their voices interweaving with those of the midwife and her assistants until Hervor couldn't tell what was real and what wasn't. She floated in a delirium of sweat and pain, and a corner of her mind wondered in confusion why she hadn't gone berserk already. It certainly hurt enough. But apparently Melsafny wasn't about to put up with that kind of meddling from Bolvereik, because Hervor's body remained in the grip of labour, not the fury of battle.

And if this was a fight, she feared she was losing.

The rags and sheets they kept taking away were soaked with blood. The midwife muttered in a corner with another woman, who ran out and came back with something foul they poured down Hervor's throat, half of which she coughed back up. Her throat was raw with screaming. She barely even heard another voice joining hers, the cry of an infant forced out into the world, because the pain didn't stop; more contractions, more blood.

She reached the end of her strength and yet had to keep going; there was no way to make it end except to endure. Memories flickered through her mind, all the times she'd been tired to the bone from slogging endlessly across the land. Except that for once she was unbearably hot, instead of freezing her toes off. She would have given anything for the touch of the winter wind, just to cool her burning body. She tried to ask for someone to arrange that – maybe they could carry her outside – but nobody would listen. Hervor swore at them and tried to strike out, but she was tired, too tired, all the energy sapped from her body, and why in all eight hells wasn't this *over yet*?

She gave one last, tremendous push, howling with the effort – and then there was nothing more.

She slept and woke and slept and woke and had a hard time telling the two apart; she'd lost a lot of blood, and the birthing had left her with a fever. The swords stayed on either side of the bed, and she gathered this was because everyone feared she herself might be vulnerable to evil spirits, in her weakened state. Food wouldn't stay down, even when it was nothing more than meat broth, but she drank anything they gave her, because she was starving.

When she surfaced to something like awareness, she found three women in the room. Two girls, really, and an older woman she thought for a moment was Jordis.

The woman came forward after Hervor croaked a request and gave her cool water to drink. Hervor gulped at it gratefully, then waited, but the water stayed where it belonged. A tiny victory.

When Hervor tried to sit up, the woman pushed her back down, and Hervor was ashamed to find she couldn't even fight back. "Rest," the woman said. "You've had a hard battle."

Battle indeed. Why was gentle Melsafny the goddess of childbirth, when it felt more like Bolvereik's domain? "Where…" Despite the water, Hervor's voice was still a rasp, as if she'd been screaming even more than she remembered. She licked her lips and tried again. "Where's my son? Or was it a daughter?"

The woman smiled at her, genuine pleasure in the expression. "A son, all right, or rather two."

Her words didn't make sense. "Two?"

The midwife nodded. "Two. If you'd let me see to you before the labour, I likely could have warned you. Two healthy, strong sons."

The room went white for a few moments. When Hervor came back to herself, her first thought was: no wonder it took so damn long. *Two* sons.

"Where are they?"

"Safe," the midwife said. "At the temple. There's a wet nurse there looking after them."

This doom will strike at you and your sons. Her father's words, when she demanded Tyrfing from him. Would they be safer if she stayed away from them? Hervor didn't know how to be a mother, anyway. But at the same time, they were *hers*, born of her own blood. How could she set out to avenge her father and brothers, then turn her back on her sons?

The haze of fever still lay heavy on her mind. The midwife had asked her something, and she hadn't even heard it. The question came again, and Hervor lay back in her pillows and tried to think. She hadn't planned on two. But to her surprise, she found the decision wasn't at all hard to make.

"Enjarað," she said, "and Heiðrek."

The midwife cocked her head to one side. "Are you sure?"

"Whichever one came first is Enjarað. Whichever came second is Heiðrek."

"But—" The midwife still looked nonplussed. "Your father's name was Angantyr."

The croak of Hervor's laugh sounded as if it belonged to someone else. "I've been haunted by my father for seventeen years, and he still hasn't shut up even though I've killed his enemies. No way in any hell am I giving a kid even part of his name. Enjarað, and Heiðrek. To honour two men—" Her throat closed up for a moment before she could go on. "To honour two men who got me here. Without them, I would have died a dozen times over, or never gotten my vengeance. I owe them a debt of blood." A tear trickled down her cheek, but she was too tired to care. "This doesn't repay it. Nothing can repay it. But it's the least I can do."

The midwife was still staring at her, so Hervor turned onto her right side, putting her back to the woman. It felt strange, now that her belly was sagging empty. "Tell the king," Hervor said, and lay there, staring at the lamplight winking off the sword at her side, until the woman went away.

She told anybody who came near her that her sons were called Enjarað and Heiðrek, and that they should tell the king, because she kept forgetting it had already been taken care of. The fever, having gotten hold of her, didn't want to let go.

Hervor drifted in and out of fever-dreams, never quite sure what was real and what wasn't. Sometimes she even thought she was imagining the ghosts. Shouldn't they be quiet by now? She'd avenged them, for the love of all the gods. What more did they want from her?

But they never listened when she told them to go away.

Sometimes she thought she was back at Rognjeld, sleeping on the floor of the hall, dreaming of escape to the world outside the fence. Sometimes she was on the *Disir's Fury*, being rocked to sleep by the waves. Sometimes she saw Orvar or Hjalmar, and they screamed at her while blood ran down to cover their faces like a mask.

Sometimes she was back on Samsey, in front of her father's barrow, listening to his cold, dead voice.

Tyrfing shall be the cause of three dishonourable deaths…

Memory came back in flashes of fire, and she saw again the coast of Reiðast, where the men of the *Fury* fought and died.

I don't want to remember, she whimpered in the depths of her mind.

Fighting. Men dying. The warriors of Reiðast fell before her, fair deaths, honourable battle.

Then they were gone, and there was no one left but the last of the vikings, and still Hervor fought on, caught in the grip of Bolvereik's fury.

Heiðelt fell, cut down by Tyrfing, and the blade stuck in his body.

So she took up an axe and fought more and more, until the axe, too, was gone and she fought with her bare hands, but that one image was seared into her mind: Heiðelt and Tyrfing.

He was the only friend she'd killed with the sword.

…three dishonourable deaths…

Heiðelt was only one. The berserker fury killed the others.

Orvar's and Hjalmar's deaths were vengeance; there was no dishonour in them. Who else had she killed, with Tyrfing, whose death could be called dishonourable?

No one. Yet.

Hervor thrashed, half-aware. Hands pressed her back down to the bed, and a cloth was laid across her forehead, icy cold against her burning skin.

This doom will strike at you and your sons.

Sons. Plural. She should have known it was coming, should have known *they* were coming. Enjarað and Heiðrek. She'd decided on the names; she ought to let someone know.

But how had Tyrfing caused them trouble? It was just a sword, and she was done with it. She would return it to the barrow, then go back to Aettarstað and try to be a good jarl.

This doom will strike at you and your sons.

She'd throw the sword in the sea, if that was what it took. Let it and its curse sink beneath the waves, and never trouble anyone again.

Orvar and Hjalmar screamed in her mind. They had not used sorcery.

And yet her father and brothers had died.

The king and the gods favoured me, Hjalmar insisted again. But they hadn't favoured him this time, had they?

Tyrfing shall be the cause of three dishonourable deaths...

Shut up, Hervor screamed at her father, but she couldn't find her voice.

If Orvar hadn't used magic, and Hjalmar hadn't... then who had?

Fear clutched at her throat, jarring her into wakefulness. The room was almost completely dark – it had never been dark before – there had always been lamps—

A foot scuffed against the floor, the sound shocking in the quiet and the dark.

Hervor's mind snapped into crystal-clear focus. Someone was in the room with her, and her fever-dream still echoed in her mind. Orvar and Hjalmar had been the slayers of her kin, yes, but they hadn't used magic. Someone else had.

She had another enemy.

Her right hand crept outwards, slowly, until it felt the cold steel of a blade at her side.

The footsteps came closer, and then a shadowy figure bent over her, one hand reaching for her face.

Hervor screamed, and with all of her strength she surged upward and struck her attacker with the sword.

Light blinded her, but the shock ran up her arm; she had struck true. A sickening crunch as steel sliced into meat and bone. Her attacker made the wet, choking sounds of someone whose lungs were filling with blood. He fell backwards, and Hervor lacked the strength to hold on to the blade; the hilt slipped from her hand.

Darkness fell again.

Footsteps pounded along the hall outside, and then the door slammed open. Light flooded the room, blinding her a second time; she shut her eyes and threw her hands up against it, and then as people began to pour in shouting, she squinted to see who her enemy was.

Auðleif stared at her from where he knelt in a pool of his own blood.

No.

Hervor gaped in numb, uncomprehending shock. It wasn't possible. Not Auðleif. He couldn't be her betrayer, the betrayer of her kin. He'd been a mere boy when Angantyr died.

The midwife was at the foot of the bed, hysterical, shrieking, "He'd been so worried for you, my lady, he wanted to see you, I told him he could come see if your fever had broken—"

Men rushed forward to take hold of Auðleif as he swayed on his knees. Their bodies blocked him from her sight. Hervor lurched halfway out of bed, pushing at them, trying to get through to him. It *couldn't* be true that she had just killed Auðleif, when he was not an enemy but a friend.

The bodies gave way suddenly, and she fell into a heap on the floor next to Auðleif. They had him half propped up, uselessly; they could do nothing to help him. She'd seen enough wounds to know that. And now, this close to him, she saw all too clearly what she had done, and she knew what the light had been.

Tyrfing's familiar, hateful hilt stood out from his ribs.

One of Hervor's hands reached for it, shaking. Someone grabbed her wrist and said, "We can't draw it out. That'll kill him."

"He's dead anyway," someone else said in a low voice.

Auðleif opened his mouth to speak, but nothing came out save a wet, bubbling noise.

Three dishonourable deaths.

Who the fuck had done it? Who had put *Tyrfing* in her bed? The sword was fucking cursed; it couldn't protect her from evil spirits! But someone had unsheathed the blade and laid it at her side, and it could not go back in its sheath until someone had died. So it began to look for a target.

Hervor, in her fevered paranoia, had given it one.

Auðleif's bloodied hand rose to grip her fingers.

"I'm sorry," she whispered, knowing it was completely inadequate, that no words would undo the last few moments. But what else could she say? I'm sorry I accepted a cursed sword so I could win my vengeance? I'm sorry I mistook you for an enemy?

I'm sorry you became my friend, because all my friends die.

She held on to his hand for as long as she could, but there was no strength in her own fingers. When his arm went limp, she lost her grip and let his hand fall.

An uncomfortable silence filled the room, save for the midwife's weeping.

Finally people began to move. Someone picked Hervor up and carried her away from Auðleif, back to the bed; she would have protested, but her body felt drained of its own life. She should have died back at Rognjeld. Then Rannvar would be alive, and Enjarik, Heiðelt, Thurlang, Arvind, all the rest of them. Auðleif, who'd never done anything to earn this end except show loyalty to a woman who didn't deserve it.

His body was removed. She was already thinking of it as a body, not her friend. That limp, bloodstained shell wasn't the man she'd bested in the circle, who'd risen above his resentment towards her to help Bjarmar. Not the first man to swear into her service, when she returned to Aettarstað as Angantyr's daughter.

That man was gone. By her own hand.

Movement, noise, low voices. She ignored it all until she heard someone say, "What do we do with the sword?"

Then she roused and held out one hand. "Give it to me."

The two men discussing the matter exchanged uncertain looks; Hervor had to summon the last of her energy to strengthen her voice. "I said, *give* it to me. And go find the sheath."

The man holding Tyrfing came to her side, while the other vanished to find the sheath.

It was as she'd feared. Not a speck of blood remained on the steel. Someone had cleaned it. Nobody knew the first thing about Tyrfing; they thought it was just another sword, famous, glowing, but otherwise ordinary. She should have told them. Warned them.

The second man came back with the sheath, and reached as if to take the sword from her.

He flinched back when Hervor snarled at him. "The sheath. And your knife."

This time he obeyed without hesitation. Hervor laid the sheath in her lap, then gritted her teeth. Had to do it fast, or they'd stop her. With good reason; this was a shitty idea. But she owed it to Auðleif. She'd make the third dishonourable death her own, before she let this sword kill anyone else.

She slashed the knife across her forearm, smeared the blood on the sword, then rammed Tyrfing into its sheath before the men, who cried out in shock, could snatch it from her.

"Nobody fucking touches it," Hervor said, very calmly. "Nobody draws it, nobody does *anything* with it unless I tell them to. You people don't know how dangerous it is."

She had more to say, but instead she fell over in a dead faint.

27

CURSED

She'd cut deeper into her arm than she'd meant to; her anger and grief had given her more strength than she thought. The resulting blood loss kept Hervor bedridden for several more days, and when she finally rose, her legs would barely support her weight.

But now that she was up, it was possible at last for her to see her sons.

Hervor expected the sight to be painful. After all, the two infants would remind her of how many had died. Their namesakes, the other men of the *Fury*, and now Auðleif – all for the sake of vengeance. Nor had she forgotten that Auðleif's death was only the second of three.

In truth, the sight of her sons was a balm to her wounded heart. Hervor took the chair she was offered and sat there, one infant in each arm, smiling down at them, her first smile since going into labour. They were even uglier than most newborn babies, their skin as wrinkled as cloth, which the midwife told her was common for births that came early – but they were *her* ugly babies.

Hervor bristled when the midwife added, in an ominous tone, that the second one – Heiðrek – had been born breech. "Who cares?" she demanded. "I've avenged their kin. They won't be haunted like I am." And the midwife flinched away.

She tried to nurse them, but it went badly. Born so soon, they had even smaller mouths than most babies, which made it hard to latch on, and the breech birth had left Heiðrek's jaw notably tight. It was with mingled relief and anger that Hervor let an experienced wet nurse take over. She hardly knew what to do with these two fragile lives – could hardly even think of herself as a *mother*. Nor, it seemed, was she the only one. There were precedents, barely, for a viga-kona, for a woman ruling as jarl... but squaring such masculine roles with motherhood left everybody confused.

Jarl and viking. Mother and avenger. Ex-bondsmaid and hero. She didn't fit anywhere.

All she could do was follow the path in front of her. As always, it was steep and filled with threats: *This doom will strike at you and your sons.* And if Heiðelt was the first dishonourable death, Auðleif second...

Was there any way to avoid that fate?

Hervor didn't know.

So she would find someone who did.

Hervor slammed Tyrfing down on the table where Valarin sat carving a rune-stave, sending chips of wood flying. Clenching the abused muscles of her hips to keep herself steady, she said, "Tell me about this."

The skald looked at the sword as if it were a live serpent, then glanced up at her with much the same expression. "My lady?"

"Don't fucking 'my lady' me. I asked you a question."

"Ah, I'm afraid it wasn't exactly a—" Valarin flinched and quickly changed tack. "Yes. Ah. Tyrfing. The Serpent's Tooth. There are many stories about it; perhaps if you would give me some idea of what you—"

"How it got cursed. It was made for some king, I can't remember his name—"

"Sigrlami." Valarin began to relax as the territory of the conversation became more stable. "Though he was not yet king when the dvergar made it for him. I assure you, this is relevant!" he hastened to add, as Hervor snarled at him. "He was the son of a king, with his brother Svafrlami, who was the elder of the two. When their father the king died, Sigrlami slew his own brother with Tyrfing, and took the rule of the land for himself."

Kinslaying. Few things were more foul in the eyes of the gods; it damned the soul to Kjellar, the worst of the hells. Hervor could see why that would spark a curse. "Then what?"

She must have given some hint of the ache pulsing through her lower back, or maybe Valarin was just polite, because he hastily dragged over a stool for her to sit on, talking all the while. "The dvergar were the ones who placed the curse. They'd made Tyrfing under duress, you see; Sigrlami captured two of them, and spared their lives only when they promised to make him a blade. When he killed his brother, the dvergar said they had not made the sword to put a false king on the high seat, and so they cursed it."

"With three dishonourable deaths." Fury at those unknown dvergar gave her the first real energy she'd had in weeks. "What the hell kind of sense does that make? It already killed one person who didn't deserve it, so now we'll make sure it does that some more?"

Valarin managed a nervous smile. "I cannot say I understand the minds of the dvergar. But I believe the idea was that, as Sigrlami held the sword, the deaths would fall on those he held dear, and thus constitute a kind of revenge against him."

"But it didn't work."

"No. Sigrlami immediately gave Tyrfing to one of his housemen as a gift – at the time, no one else knew about the curse – then sent the man on a task that took him far away. Sigrlami himself died without ever seeing it again."

So she was the inheritor of somebody else's gods-damned curse. Hervor felt like screaming. She tightened her jaw until she was sure she wouldn't scream at Valarin, who didn't deserve it, then said through her teeth, "I don't suppose you have any idea how somebody might go about *removing* that curse?"

He eyed her carefully. "I suppose you could seek out the dvergar, and try to convince them to help, but I haven't a clue how you might find them."

If the old tales were true, it used to be all you had to do was wander into a forest or the mountains and you'd trip over one before you went half a league. But Hervor had been in forests and mountains alike, and hadn't seen so much as a whisker of a dverg. Her shoulders slumped in defeat. So that was it. Keep Tyrfing, and maybe kill some other friend, or foist it off on somebody else, like Sigrlami had.

"Why didn't they curse him instead?" she demanded, hands balled up into fists. If she *could* find a dverg, she might have punched him. "Why curse the fucking *sword?*"

"Because the magic of the dvergar was always linked to things, not to people. They *intended* the curse to be on Sigrlami; they said that the third death would be the downfall of the false king. But he found a way to escape that fate. When his time came, he died in an ordinary war, far from Tyrfing."

The sword itself still lay on the table, among Valarin's unfinished rune-sticks. Hervor wondered what would happen if she walked out of the room and left it there. Valarin would take it to the Blessed King, no doubt. Maybe he would lock it away, somewhere that nobody else could ever get at it. Put it in a chest, wrap the chest in chains, take the chest out to sea and banish it beneath the waves forever. She'd taken Tyrfing because it seemed to be her one chance at redeeming her family's honour, but in the process, she'd put a stain on her line that would never fade. So what if people called Auðleif's death a tragic accident? So what if no one knew about Heiðelt? *She* knew, and so did the gods. Unanswered murders were nothing next to that. She'd tried to improve things, and she'd made them worse instead.

She should have left Tyrfing in the barrow with her father and gone after Orvar by herself. Since she couldn't go back and change that, though, she could at least wash her hands of the blade now, before it did any more damage.

But somehow those selfsame hands reached out and picked it up before she left Valarin's workshop. Because she remembered when she'd stood outside the hall of Aettarstað with Auðleif and Jordis, talking about responsibility.

Making Tyrfing somebody else's problem was a coward's way out. And however far gone she might be, she wouldn't add cowardice to her sins.

The horror of Auðleif's death had pushed one thought to the back of her mind. But as Hervor's head cleared of the last of the fever, she remembered it again, all too well.

She had another enemy.

Angantyr didn't rest yet. Orvar and Hjalmar had insisted that they hadn't used sorcery. Someone else must have, and until she found that person, her vengeance wouldn't be complete. Fouling the ritual of the holmganga was a crime worthy of death.

But she had no idea who this enemy might be, nor where he might be found after all these years. Hells, the sorcerer might even be dead already. Then she might never finish her vengeance.

The thought that he might *not* be dead was even more unnerving. Svelsond didn't feel safe; she feared for the lives of her infant sons, so vulnerable to any attack. Aettarstað wasn't all that much safer, but Hervor knew she would sleep better if they were there, surrounded by loyal men and women, not these strangers. Except that winter was hanging on well into spring, and she didn't dare risk the twins in the cold. The bind she was in made her want to scream.

And Tyrfing stood in a rack in the corner, biding its time.

Hervor was on the edge of snapping when the Blessed King came to her. His arrival was a shock: people went to see *him*, not the other way around. But here he was, gesturing for his two guards to stay in the hall, then closing the door behind him.

"You are looking better, I see," he greeted her. His golden hair shone in the lamplight, and his presence filled the small room to overflowing. "I am relieved. I prayed to the gods for your recovery."

Hervor thought her own stubbornness had more to do with it than prayer, but you didn't say that to the Blessed King. "Thank you, high one. I don't feel completely well yet, but I'm getting there."

"If there is anything I can do to help you regain your strength, you have but to ask. I owe you a debt, for ridding me of Hjalmar. I never realised he would be treacherous enough to taint a duel with sorcery." The king shook his head sadly.

A laugh escaped her before she considered that it might

sound rude. "Sorry, high one, I don't mean to offend – I'm just uneasy. I thought killing Hjalmar would put my kin to rest at last, but it hasn't. I'm worried that…"

She hesitated, trying to decide how to put it, but the king spoke before she could find words. "That your own crimes keep them unquiet?"

It jolted her. "High one?"

He nodded towards the corner, where Tyrfing's hilt gleamed in the dim, smoky light of the tallow dips. "Yours was not an act of grave robbery; if you have told the tale true, then your father gave you the sword of his own free will. Still, I imagine he will not rest properly until it is returned to him." The Blessed King gave her a shrewd look. "Nor will you."

All she could think was that she had to be polite. "High one?" she repeated, weakly.

"Valarin has spoken to me." The king held up one hand as apologies and explanations tried to rush from her mouth. "It's quite all right. But he told me of your concerns regarding the sword. Tell me—" He shook his head, apparently at himself. "I am sorry. I hate to ask such a painful question. But I know of the curse on the sword, and I suspect it has found one of its three dishonourable deaths in your houseman Auðleif. I know of no other such prior to his; are you aware of any?"

Hervor's tongue dried up in her mouth. Her voice was hardly more than a whisper as she said, "Yes, high one. There was… another companion of mine…"

For a moment his eyes looked as cold as the winter wind that still howled outside. Hervor's stomach lurched, imagining what he must think of her. Then his expression softened. "I am sorry," he repeated. "I hate to make you relive such things. But I think it would be best if you returned the sword to your father. It can wreak no further harm if it rests with the dead."

Could he be right? Were her ghosts unquiet merely because she hadn't returned the sword? Maybe there was no other enemy. Orvar or Hjalmar could have been lying about not using sorcery. Tyrfing had already brought disaster to Hervor and her sons, by driving her to kill her own houseman; maybe her time with it was done.

She walked over to the sword-stand and picked up the blade, wondering. Tyrfing seemed to throb in her hands, thirsting for blood.

The ghosts were silent in her mind. Not even a whisper.

That had happened two other times, long before she came to Svelsond: when she held the holy book of Alfrenvald, and when she entered Meltharkatla's forest. But not because a goddess was present; the voices had returned as soon as Meltharkatla drew back her spells.

Blood magic.

The third death, Valarin said in her mind, a memory instead of a ghost, *would be the downfall of the false king.*

Why was the Blessed King so eager for her to give Tyrfing up?

Neither Orvar nor Hjalmar had used magic. But *someone* had. And the Blessed King had been uncommonly eager for the argument to be settled by holmganga: a ritual that involved blood.

The ghosts were always gone, when she stood in his presence. Even if Hjalmar was there.

That cold, calculating look in his eyes, when he heard two deaths were wrought already.

Had Sigrlami truly been the false king of the dvergar's curse?

Hervor came back to herself and realised she was still standing there, Tyrfing in hand. But she'd turned to face the king, and as she looked into his eyes, she saw the answer to that question.

Instinct moved faster than caution, her hand flying to Tyrfing's hilt. But as quick as she moved, the Blessed King was quicker. He flung one hand out, and she froze.

"You should have come in summer," he said calmly. Quietly. No hint of distress that might bring the guards inside. "If you'd come in summer, you could have left after the duel, and then perhaps your thoughts would not have taken you so far down this path. You could have returned the sword to your father and been at peace."

Hervor tried to scream, but it was like being back in Meltharkatla's forest. Drauðr held her paralysed. He'd taken her blood more than once, for the holmganga, for her oath to him; oh, she'd given him all the opportunity he needed and more.

"I knew when Tyrfing appeared at Angantyr's side that it would be trouble. But Sigrlami avoided becoming its victim, and I see no reason why I should not do the same. After all, I have cheated every other form of death for many, many years."

Hervor strained madly to break the spell as he approached her, to draw Tyrfing and let it have its third dishonourable death, the murder of a king. Sweat poured down her body, but she couldn't move.

"Berserkers are so very useful to me," he mused, studying her as if she were a curiosity at a fair-day. "So much strength for me to take. Much more than I can take from ordinary people, and they don't die of it. You present a much greater problem than your father and brothers did, though. I'm not foolish enough to kill you; I've been alive long enough to know that some stories are not just stories, and I have no wish to compound my problems by turning you into a dis. But neither can I leave you alive. Blood magic is very good at controlling the body, much poorer at controlling the mind."

His gaze fell to Tyrfing, and a faint, cold smile touched his lips. "But perhaps I can make that damnable blade serve my purpose after all. Yes, that will do quite well. And it will make the legend of the Blessed King even greater."

Hervor screamed with all her soul for the ghosts of her kin to come to her, to help her as they had at Rognjeld. But the king was so much more powerful than Saeunn; his magic was an impenetrable wall, holding them back.

"If it is any comfort," he said, in a voice that held no comfort at all, "I'm sure you, too, will pass into legend."

Then his hand touched her forehead, and ice invaded her body, freezing her blood and her heart and her mind, until she saw nothing but the cold, blue flames of death.

28

HERVARARSON

betrayal
murder
blood as ice in the veins

Blackness, darkness, shadows without end, a night that went on forever, gaining life of its own, night as a palpable thing, pressing down with the crushing weight of eternity, inescapable, inevitable.

blood is the weakness
blood is the doom
BETRAYED

by one who should have been true

Familiar words, familiar rage, echoing through her mind…
but this time the voice was her own.

can't get out
body a trap
earth a trap
TRUST a trap

There was no time, no space, nothing but darkness and
weight and her own voice screaming, no one to hear but herself,
and she was nothing. No anchor, no point of stability, just an
endlessly circling loop, the same words, the same rage, never
fading, never ending, never answered.

betrayed by the king
and Bolvereik
and Eldaskrid
CURSE the gods
to honour one such as him
while the rest of us ROT
WHERE IS JUSTICE?
where is freedom
damn them all
let me OUT

give me blood
SET ME FREE!

In the darkness of the barrow, a light arose. Cold blue flames
breathed up from the soil and began to dance, illuminating the
figure lying in solitary glory on a flat stone slab.

The light frosted the edges of the figure, gleaming like ice along
the rings of chain mail, gilding the helm, and most of all shining
along the hilt of the sword clasped in the figure's cold, still hands.

And then, in the midst of the flames, standing before the
bier, there was someone else. She stood for a moment, looking
at the figure on the slab – and then she smiled.

Awareness.

Pain.

A rasp along her skin, like sand, like a metal file, too much
sensation at once. She opened her mouth to scream and choked
on air her lungs didn't know how to use. Light turned everything
to blue flame for an instant that lasted an eternity – and then she
was back to herself, back in a *body*, and dizzy at the change. For
a few heartbeats she felt it all: the solidity of bone, the tension of
muscle, the pulsing fluidity of blood, all contained in skin.

Such awareness couldn't last. As it faded, Hervor was
herself once more.

Her body was as stiff as wood, but not tired. She was lying
on her back, hands clasped on her chest, and after a moment

realised the weight she felt came from the armour she wore. Mail draped her torso and arms, for the first time in her life.

She sat up and noticed two more things at once: Tyrfing was in her hands, and someone stood not far away, watching her.

"So that's what I get for my help. Curses."

The sight of Meltharkatla should have scared Hervor. Looking at the woman now, Hervor wondered how she could have ever mistaken the goddess for a mortal woman. But after that eternity of being trapped in the nothingness of her own body, she couldn't really muster the conviction to be scared of anything. Compared to that, this was perfectly acceptable. Goddesses walking around. Why not?

She bent her mind to what Meltharkatla had said. Something about curses.

Her soundless screams still echoed in her mind, blasphemous words flung at Bolvereik, at Eldaskrid.

"Sorry," she said, her voice rusty, stiff, and a shock to her own ears.

"Sorry." Meltharkatla repeated the word, mocking, baring her teeth at Hervor in a snarl of a smile. "After all my help. Three times I helped, and you curse me for it. But you're *sorry*."

Hervor bit back new curses. "I don't know what else to say."

"Of course not. You're a fool." Meltharkatla's eyes reflected the blue flames dancing along the earth. Where *were* they? Hervor looked around and found very little to help her. They were in some kind of earthen cave, nothing in it except the slab she was sitting on, and wooden beams propping up the walls. She couldn't even see a tunnel or a door. What kind of cave had no entrance?

One that wasn't a cave at all.

She was in a barrow.

Hervor was off the bier in one convulsive move, only keeping hold of Tyrfing because she knew better than to drop a sword. That feeling of weight on her, of darkness, the earth pressing down – the king had enspelled her and then *buried her alive*.

The horror of that made her voice sharp. "How the hell was I supposed to know he was a fucking sorcerer? He's the *Blessed King*. I assumed he must be a good man, since he's still alive. How was I supposed to know I was wrong? If you're Eldaskrid, then why in all eight hells haven't you claimed him?"

The goddess's eyes went cold as frost. It occurred to Hervor, too late, that mouthing off to her – right after cursing her name – might not be the best of ideas.

But when Meltharkatla spoke, her words weren't an attack. They were an echo.

"What drinks the life and does not die?"

It was the riddle she'd asked in the forest – only she'd said, hadn't she, that it wasn't a riddle. It was her reason for being here.

What does not die? The Blessed King, Ingjald, immortal and unageing. And he'd spoken of draining people. Hervor thought of the crippling weakness that had struck her father and brothers – as if nearly all the life had been leached out of them. They'd been left with just enough to fight Orvar and Hjalmar… but not enough to win.

"You—" Hervor found the words surprisingly hard to get out. Somehow it was easier to mouth off to a goddess than to say something that would undermine one of the fundamental truths of the world. The Blessed King was *blessed*. Everybody knew that. "You're telling me, him still being alive's got nothing to do with you lot? With the gods?"

Meltharkatla laughed, a low, unnerving sound. "Melsafny's pitching fits."

He'd done it with drauðr. By *draining* people, the way he'd done to her kin. Stealing their life to extend his own, past what the gods had granted him.

Fury brought warmth back into Hervor's body at last, after so long lying on the cold stone. "Then why haven't you done anything? Can't you just strike him down? Why'd you let so many people die?"

The goddess licked her lips as if Hervor's rage was honey-sweet mead. "Such an angry little child you are, screaming for Mother and Father."

Hervor opened her mouth to snarl, but stopped. A flicker in Meltharkatla's eyes made her reconsider what she was about to say.

When she finally spoke, it was in the calmest tone she could manage. "There's a difference between wanting your parents to take care of everything for you, and asking for help when you need it."

Meltharkatla shrugged, as if the difference were trivial. "Every jarl is king, inside his own fence – and you have made your fences so very strong." She began to circle the barrow, bony fingers trailing along the beams. "These are not the times they were. You are not Holmdan, nor Torgrim—" A twisted grin split her face. "*Like* Torgrim, sleeping the days away... but he was of the other time. The time this isn't."

Hervor tried to sort through that. "You mean – this isn't the time of legends."

"What's a legend?" Meltharkatla dismissed the word with a wave of her hand. "Angantyr's a legend. Even *I* know of him, though he hasn't yet come to me."

"But you – all of you, all the gods – you used to interfere. Used to walk among men. You don't any more – the others don't, anyway, except for you." Hervor realised she was clutching Tyrfing to her chest, as if it were somehow comforting. It wasn't, and she put it down on the stone slab. "Why not?"

"The children grew up. Wanted to walk their own path, free from our bonds."

And made their fences very strong. It wasn't that the gods had grown distant from mortals; humans were the ones who'd stepped away. Closed them out. Hervor thought about her visit to Valarin, trying to find a way for her and her sons to avoid the last of Tyrfing's curse.

Maybe they couldn't have both: divine aid, *and* a life not bound by fate.

She wondered if things might have gone differently, had she not accepted Meltharkatla's help.

There was no taking it back, though, and some problems were beyond ordinary people. "But what about the Ble— about *Ingjald*?" Hervor refused to keep calling him by that title. "Clearly we need help against him, or we would have gotten rid of him long since. Yet you do nothing!"

"Back to cursing now, are we?"

Hervor hadn't cursed her, but she got the point anyway. What was Meltharkatla doing now, if not helping? "Couldn't you be a little more direct?"

The goddess simply turned and smiled at Hervor, the blue flames reflecting off her midnight eyes. Again, Hervor got the point. Eldaskrid was not and never had been direct.

She put her hands to her own eyes, wearily. "So you've helped. You told me how to speak to my father, you led me to Orvar, and you woke me from Ingjald's spell. I'm grateful for that. But what now?"

Meltharkatla's smile widened into something feral. Hervor had the sudden, sinking feeling she'd just walked into a trap.

"Now," the goddess of death said, "the child finishes what she started. Her thread is almost done."

Hervor opened her mouth to object, but the words turned into a scream as her body hurtled upward. She threw her arms over her head to protect it from the earthen ceiling—

The ceiling gave way as if it were water, and she found herself alone in the grass on top of the barrow.

The grass was her first clue that something was seriously wrong. When the king had come to her it was still full winter, the spring long delayed. Now the land seemed well into a very dry summer, as if there had been no rain since the thaw.

"How long did you leave me there?" Hervor muttered, but Meltharkatla wasn't around to answer.

From the vantage point of this rise, she could see a small stand of trees, and where there were trees there was a decent chance of finding water. When Hervor stood to head that way, her foot kicked against something in the grass.

Tyrfing had come with her.

She glared at the blade as if it were at fault for everything that had gone wrong. Certainly it was to blame for some of it.

But it was also a weapon against Ingjald. If she'd interpreted the curse right.

"Fucking hells," Hervor growled, but in the end she picked the sword up and took it with her.

The heat was brutal. By the time she reached the shade of the trees, she was drenched in sweat. The helm and mail she was still wearing didn't help. Once Hervor found a small stream, she wasted no time in stripping the armour off and dumping it, with Tyrfing, in the shadow of a bush.

She soaked her head in the stream and splashed its water over her arms, like she could wash away the horror of being buried alive. Hervor knew she needed to think, to plan – Where was she? What had happened to her sons? How was she going to get at the king? – but for these few beautiful moments, all she wanted to do was revel in the joy of her freedom.

Lost in that sensation, she didn't hear the hoofbeats until the rider was almost on her.

Hervor shot to her feet, but by then it was too late to run for cover. She was still standing there, like a rabbit frozen beneath a hawk's stoop, when the rider appeared around the edge of a clump of trees and reined his horse to a halt.

He looked familiar, though she couldn't place his face. He could have been any warrior – any *young* warrior, she amended; he didn't look much older than her. But he might have been any one of a dozen young men she'd seen since leaving Rognjeld.

Plainly he didn't recognise her, either. "Who are you? And what are you doing here?"

Hervor's hands flexed, wishing Tyrfing were in her hand instead of lying hidden under a bush. The warrior sounded less than pleased to find her there. "I'm sorry – I didn't mean to trespass. If I even am trespassing. I… I don't know where I am."

More hoofbeats brought her head up sharply. The young man didn't bother to turn around. A moment later a second rider appeared, from the same direction as the first; the young men were enough alike that they could only be brothers

"Who's this?" the second one asked cheerfully, looking on her with more kindliness than his brother had.

The first rider scowled. "Some wandering beggar. She doesn't know her name or where she is."

Hervor didn't bother correcting him as the second brother gave her a sympathetic smile. "Well, not much we can do for the first, I'm afraid. But for the second, you're about a half-day's ride south of Aettarstað. Does that spark anything?"

She almost put them off by laughing. Yes, that name was familiar.

"How did you get here?" the first rider demanded. "Which way did you come from?"

"Look," Hervor said, trying to keep the rising hope in her heart from getting out of hand. "If you could just take me to Aettarstað, I'd be more grateful than I can say."

The request only made him look at her suspiciously. "Why? What's there for you?"

"People I know."

"Oh yeah? Like who?"

Both brothers were reasonably well-dressed and mounted on horses. They might recognise the names of housemen and the like. Hervor couldn't decide if that was a good thing or a bad one. If word got back to Ingjald that she'd escaped his trap…

Hanged for a fleece, hanged for a sheep. "Jordis."

The first brother snorted. "Pull the other one."

"I'm serious," Hervor insisted. "Jordis, wife of Bjarmar, the old

jarl. Holmstein Vandingsson. Isbjorn Alfsteinsson. Auðleif—"
The name slipped partway out before she could stop herself.

The two brothers exchanged glances. "All those people are
dead," the second one said, in the tone of a man convinced he
was dealing with a madwoman.

Dead?

Hervor felt like she'd been slugged in the gut. What had the
king done, after he dealt with her?

"You must be mistaken," she said harshly.

The eyes of the first rider narrowed. "*We're* mistaken?"

"Do you even know these people? Who in hell are you two,
anyway?" Hervor heard the anger in her own voice and couldn't
stop it. Anger kept the grief at bay. How much disaster had she
brought down on her people?

Another exchange of glances. "She doesn't know," the first
brother said.

The second raised one eyebrow. "I thought we were infamous."

"Look, she doesn't even know her *own* name—"

"I know my name," Hervor snapped. "And stop talking
about me like I'm not here. Tell me who you are, and how you're
so sure those people are all dead."

The second rider swept her a mock-bow from his saddle.
"I'm Enjarað Hervararson, and this is my brother Heiðrek.
And since we're the jarls of Aettarstað, I think we know pretty
damn well who's dead and who isn't."

If the first revelation had been a punch to the gut, this one was an axe-handle to the head. Everything spun. When Hervor came back to herself, she was sitting on the ground, staring up at the two young men, who'd dismounted from their horses and come forward in concern – the two of them, so very alike.

"You can't be," she whispered up at their startled faces.

The second brother raised his eyebrow again. He couldn't be Enjarað. Surely some other young man out there had that name.

But he'd called himself Hervararson.

"I know it's unusual to have the title shared," he said, "but we *are* both jarls. And if the way you fell over is any proof, you recognise our names."

"Who doesn't?" his brother said bitterly. "It's a quick road to fame: just have a mother who tried to kill the Blessed King."

Hervor lurched to her feet, still staring. Still not believing. "You can't be. You're too old."

Enjarað grinned. "That's the first time I've heard eighteen called 'too old'."

She was having trouble breathing. *Eighteen?* It wasn't possible. There was no way these men – grown men – they couldn't be her sons—

They were close enough now for her to see their eyes, blue-green, the colour of the sea.

The words burst out of her, unstoppable as the tide. *"How long did she leave me in there?"*

Both men dismounted. Heiðrek reached out to grab her shoulder, probably to steady her; Hervor slapped his hand away and stumbled back a few steps. Hard enough to accept that an entire season had flashed by while she was trapped, but this – eighteen *years*—

"I think you'd better sit down," Enjarað said, concerned.

Jordis. Holmstein. Isbjorn. All dead. She couldn't swallow the change, eighteen years gone in an eyeblink. Friends had aged and died, these boys had grown from infants to men while she screamed for release. Hervor realised she was still stumbling backwards, still muttering denials, while the two young men who called themselves her sons were following her, hands out, trying to catch her before she could hurt herself.

Her back slammed into a tree and it knocked the words out of her, the ones she'd been trying not to say. "You *can't* be my sons!"

They stopped and stared at her, then at one another.

"Your sons?" Heiðrek said at last, dubiously.

Enjarað managed an uneasy laugh. "We'll have to agree with you there. You're no older than we are."

"Who was your grandfather?" Hervor asked in a whisper.

"Angantyr," Heiðrek answered grimly. "The legendary berserker. And his daughter, our mother, was Hervor, who died eighteen years ago when she tried to kill the Blessed King."

"He actually *told* people I tried to kill him?"

"That's the story," Enjarað said. He'd retreated a step, as if her strange behaviour were catching. "That the cursed sword Tyrfing drove her mad."

Bitter laughter flooded out of Hervor. Oh, it was a goo

tale. It fit so perfectly with everything, with all her actions leading up to that day and even her attempt to murder the king. She sidestepped Enjaraŏ – her laughter had put him off guard – and went to the bush where she'd dropped her belongings. Tyrfing's hilt glinted in the sunlight as she picked it up. "You mean this sword?"

Heiŏrek came forward a few steps, very carefully, and Hervor could tell it was as much to give Enjaraŏ room to move as it was to come near her. "Who says that's Tyrfing?"

It was true, the sword didn't look special. Hervor grasped the hilt, thinking to draw it and let the blazing light prove her point, but both brothers reached instantly for their axes, and she thought the better of it. Besides, if she drew it—

Someone would have to die, sooner or later, and right now, the only targets were her sons.

That was the final blow, the one that convinced her these *were* her sons. "Oh, no," she muttered, glaring at the blade. "You're not going to trick me that easily."

"Look," Heiŏrek said, even warier now that she was talking to a sword. "If you're our mother…" Doubt dripped off his words. "…Then tell us who we're named after."

Hervor closed her eyes as the grief surged up anew. "Yours is from a viking of the *Disir's Fury*," she said quietly. "Heiŏelt was a good friend of mine – one of my first friends – he taught me how to sail, how to use an axe, how to survive in winter. I…" She couldn't bring herself to say the rest. "Enjaraŏ's name is

from Enjarik Enjakilsson, who was the captain of the *Fury* –
and the father of you both."

Silence. She opened her eyes to find both young men open-
mouthed in shock.

"No one knows who we're named after," Enjarað managed
at last, his voice cracking. "No one knows who our father was."

She smiled sadly at them. "I had enough trouble at the time.
I didn't want to tell anyone my sons were sired by a viking." Their
eyes – Enjarik's eyes. And their faces… she'd seen ones very like
them, cold with death, staring out through a curtain of blue flame.
She'd probably see much the same if she owned a mirror to look in.

"You're a ghost," Enjarað whispered.

Heiðrek shook his head. "She's solid. I felt it." But his face
was very white.

"I'm alive," Hervor said. "At least, I think I am. I don't know
what I was before. Trapped. In a barrow." She shivered involuntarily,
one hand releasing Tyrfing to rub at the opposite arm. "The
king… he didn't kill me. Did something else. Some… blood magic."

Both brothers – both of her *sons* – flinched.

Hervor met their eyes, looking from one to the other, trying
to convince them of her sincerity. And her sanity. The second
one was harder; she still wasn't sure she believed in it herself.
"You've heard the king's story," she said. "Want to hear mine?"

◆　◆　◆

They sneaked her into Aettarstað late that night. There were people there who would remember the viga-kona who'd so briefly ruled them.

Like Kjarvald. Hervor wasn't sure she could handle seeing him fully grown, no longer the snot-nosed stripling she remembered.

Enjarað and Heiðrek agreed with the need for secrecy, even though they hadn't yet heard her side of the story. Hervor gathered that their lives had been made very difficult by the revelation that she'd tried to kill the king. They were the jarls of Aettarstað, but that didn't mean much; they were near-universally shunned. Too much bad blood in the family line. And Aettarstað had suffered for it: Hervor could see that, even in the darkness.

She'd once had such dreams of restoring it to glory.

They went to the house of a man whose daughter Heiðrek had an understanding with. There Enjarað bribed the man and his daughter to go somewhere else for the night, and alone in the house, Hervor and her sons talked.

"You'd been acting unstable," Enjarað said. He was the friendlier and more talkative of the two, unlike his namesake; Heiðrek had inherited more of Enjarik's commanding presence, and also his perceptive mind. The two of them complemented each other perfectly, working together as a yoked team, and Hervor understood this was why they'd managed to hold on to Aettarstað. That, and the sad truth that Aettarstað wasn't much worth taking. "Everybody agreed on that. And then the king came to speak to you, alone—"

"That was his doing," Hervor said. "Us being alone. He was

suspicious of me already, I think, and he didn't want witnesses."

"People don't much care about the reason. You were alone with him. And Tyrfing possessed you, made you try to kill him. But the gods struck you down – protecting the Blessed King, the way they always do." Enjaraŏ paused as Hervor's mouth curved in bitter amusement, but she gestured for him to go on. "The king had sympathy for you, because of everything you'd gone through, so he said you should be buried properly, and that we should be allowed to grow up and rule Aettarstaŏ. He even provided the armour and helm for you – a tribute to your courage, he said. And he sent men to build the barrow. But they did it way south of the usual barrow-field, because of your shame."

"Shame that's stuck to us ever since," Heiŏrek said bitterly.

"It's not her fault the sword's cursed," Enjaraŏ shot back. From the sound of it, they'd had this argument before.

They fell silent the moment Hervor held up her hands. Her sons kept swinging back and forth between treating her like a woman their own age, and remembering she was their long-dead mother. She couldn't blame them; they'd had even less chance to get used to *having* a mother than she'd had to having sons.

"It *is* cursed," she admitted, "but that's not what happened."

"So you didn't try to kill him?"

She smiled sourly at Enjaraŏ. "Oh, I did. But I had a fucking good reason."

Both of them recoiled. "He's the *Blessed King*," Heiŏrek breathed.

"No, he's *not*," Hervor growled. "King, yes – but far from blessed."

She told them the full story, starting all the way back with the curse placed on Tyrfing, and finishing at her confrontation with the king. "I would have killed him," she admitted fiercely. "I tried to draw Tyrfing and do it. But he froze me, then knocked me out – he must have put me into some kind of sleep, with drauðr, and told everybody I was dead."

Heiðrek had been listening with an air that reminded her of Enjarik, weighing her every word. Now he spoke. "Why not just kill you? Wouldn't that be easier?"

"He didn't dare," Hervor said. She hadn't thought about it since waking, but once she did, the piece clicked into place. She could almost hear Gannveig's fearful shrieks again. "He said that killing me would turn me into a dis."

If she had mead, she could get thoroughly cup-shot by drinking every time the brothers exchanged glances. "That would explain it," Enjaraðr said.

Heiðrek grimaced. "If you believe her. Either of them."

They seemed to read each other's minds, but Hervor wasn't as lucky. "Believe who?"

Enjaraðr held his brother's eyes a moment longer, then turned to face Hervor. "Our wet nurse used to tell us that the disir were the spirits of dead female berserkers. Of course, we didn't believe it, because you'd been a berserker, and you never showed up as a dis. We figured that either Bolvereik had decided you didn't deserve that, or – more likely – it was just a tale."

"Now we've got a third explanation," Heiðrek said. "You weren't really dead."

Hervor's entire body shuddered. She'd come that close to dying, both in Rognjeld and Svelsond. Saved only by Bolvereik's touch.

She couldn't decide whether that would have been better or worse than the fate she'd ended up with.

"So how'd you wake up?"

Enjarað's question brought her back to herself. "With help. There…" Hervor believed now, but would anyone else? "There was a blood-witch outside Skersstað – you've heard that story? – well, I met her again in the Ice Knives. Which seemed strange at the time, though not nearly so strange as it should have. But I got a possible explanation in Svelsond…" She was chasing around the edges, trying to avoid having to say it directly. Hervor made herself plunge in. "She's not a witch. She's a goddess."

That got *precisely* the sceptical silence she expected.

But perversely, their scepticism gave her confidence. "Meltharkatla," Hervor said firmly, meeting her sons' gazes. "It's one of the names of Eldaskrid. And if you don't believe me, explain to me how she showed up in the middle of a barrow with no entrance, woke me from an eighteen-year sleep, and shot me up into the open air without leaving any hole behind."

That habit of exchanging glances could get annoying very fast. "We believe you," Enjarað said slowly. "It's just…"

She sighed and dropped her head into her hands. "I know. I

didn't believe it myself, until I saw her again. But it's true."

"Eldaskrid isn't known for bringing people back to life," Heiðrek pointed out. "More the other way around. Why didn't she just claim you, make you really dead?"

"Because it's not my time," Hervor said wearily, through her hands. "And she wants him dead. The king."

Even though her sons had no love for the Blessed King, that suggestion shocked them. Hervor couldn't blame them. He was one of the foundations their world was built on, taken for granted as much as the presence of the Ice Knives. To talk about removing that foundation…

Enjarað got up to pace. He didn't have much room for it, and the constriction only made him more agitated. His voice grew wilder as he spoke. "If she's really a goddess, I don't see that we can argue with her, but – he's the *king*. We can't go against him; we're jarls sworn to obey him—"

"Look around you!" Hervor bellowed, stopping Enjarað in his tracks. "The gods so favoured Ingjald that they let him live forever, as a gift to the people of this land. That's the way the story goes. But does the land look like it's doing very well? Winter is colder and lasts longer every year. Spring brings storms that wreck everything, and then when summer hits there's no rain to be had for months. Crops fail, cattle die, and with every passing year things wear down just a little bit more."

In the back of her mind, she could hear Meltharkatla saying, *Melsafny's pitching fits.*

"We should have known ages ago that something was wrong," Hervor said, her voice lower, but no less intense. "If he truly were blessed, like the stories say, wouldn't Melsafny show it? We'd be up to our eyeballs in bounty. Instead the land withers, and we starve." For all she knew, the king was draining life from the world around him, too, even though it had no blood for him to take.

Enjarað and Heiðrek both stared at her, open-mouthed. They might be nearly her age, and formally educated, but neither of them had seen a tenth of what she had. In that moment, Hervor suddenly felt as if she were many times older than them.

Then Enjarað sat down again, slowly, breaking the spell her words had cast. "So what do we do?" he asked heavily.

Hervor blew out a heavy breath. "I don't know."

"He's got guards around him all the time," Heiðrek said. "Thanks to you."

"And there's no way he'd let either of us near him," Enjarað added.

Hervor smiled without humour. "Much less me. And if—" She cut that off as a thought occurred to her. "Shite. You said you're sworn to obey him. Please tell me you didn't mean that literally – you haven't taken the oath."

"We have," Enjarað said, and her heart sank. "Both of us. Why?"

"Fuck," Hervor growled, smacking one fist into the opposite palm. "That's the other problem here. Forget guards – well, don't *forget* them, but they're not our worst hurdle. Ingjald himself is. He knows drauðr. Once he's gotten hold of your blood, then he's got all the defences he needs. Look what he did to me."

"If we tried something in public—" Enjarað began.

But Heiðrek shook his head. "No way in any hell. People would swarm to defend him before we got two steps. He's the Blessed King, remember?" He snarled and clenched his fists in frustration. "But there's got to be a weakness there, somewhere."

Enjarað laughed sourly. "Why should there be? He hasn't survived this long for no reason."

"Everybody has a weakness," Heiðrek said. He added more after that, but Hervor didn't hear it, because a thought had come to her at last, cold and hard as the edge of a sword.

Her thread is almost done.

The third death would be the downfall of the false king.

She held up a hand for silence, but this time she didn't get it; they'd gone back to thinking of her as just another woman. "*Hey,*" she said sharply, and they finally stopped arguing.

The words came out of her as if dragged. "I've got one idea."

The hope that bloomed in them made speaking even harder. "Drauðr isn't all-powerful," Hervor said. "He told me so himself. It's good at controlling the body, but not so good at controlling the spirit."

"For all the good that does us," Heiðrek said. "Our spirits aren't much use without our bodies."

Hervor looked straight into his sea-coloured eyes and answered with the full, terrible knowledge of what she was proposing. "Mine is."

29

THE THREAD IS CUT

It took three days of argument, and eloquence Hervor didn't know she had.

Or maybe she just won through sheer stubbornness. Whatever the reason, three days later, Hervor stood with her sons on the sere grass at the crest of the barrow where her body had been laid.

She took a tall wooden stake and drove it into the ground with a small hammer. The parched soil resisted, but finally gave way. Runes carved along the stake's length spelled out Ingjald's name, or so Enjaraô said; Jordis had never gotten her chance to teach Hervor to read.

A burlap sack, stained with blood, lay on the ground next to her. Hervor took it by its corners and shook until its contents – the mutilated head of an old mare – rolled out into the dust.

Both her sons looked ill. "Are you sure you want to do this?" Enjarað asked her, for the seventh or eighth time.

"He'll find out about it," Heiðrek muttered.

Hervor merely shrugged. "What's he going to do about it? Kill me?"

"Or kill *us*," Heiðrek said.

"I won't let that happen. All you have to do is blame me. I'll take care of the rest." She took the bloody head in her hands and rammed it onto the top of the stake, then began to twist it slowly down as she spoke.

"Here on the ground of my forefathers, here upon the barrow built for me, I set up the stake of scorn against Ingjald, who calls himself the Blessed King." As she uttered his name, the mare's head trembled between her hands, then jumped slightly, coming to rest about an eighth of a turn along. Hervor released it as if it were a snake, and hoped her sons believed she'd known that would happen. In truth, she'd meant this to be symbolic; she was working from half-remembered stories. Hervor didn't know how to craft a stake of scorn for real.

But somebody – Meltharkatla? – seemed to be lending a hand, because Hervor was dead certain the head now faced the king, wherever he was. And if he moved, the head would turn to follow him, until its purpose was complete.

That success strengthened her voice. Holding out her bloody hands, Hervor said, "I turn this scorn against the king, and bid all to rise up against him. May the people ignore his words; may the spirits of the land reject his presence; may the gods themselves give him nothing but ill-will." As if they were doing anything else already. "May Ingjald find no rest, no peace, until he has been driven from the land he has drained, until he has lost the life he has stolen, until his spirit has come to Eldaskrid for its long-awaited judgement."

The mutilated head stared across the fields with a sightless, malevolent gaze. Hervor stepped back from it and wiped her hands, gathering her courage for the rest. When she looked at her sons, they were standing shoulder to shoulder, as if to draw strength from each other's presence.

"I'm sorry," she said, and the words came out lifeless. She'd said them too many times to carry much passion any more. "If I knew another way, I'd take it."

"There could still be another way," Enjarað said, but like her, he'd said it too many times. They'd looked. There was none.

Hervor gave him a sad smile. "Maybe. But odds are, it would be worse."

"How could it be *worse*?"

The question burst from him, bitter and despairing; Hervor closed her eyes against its strike. "You weren't there," she whispered. "You didn't see Heiðelt; you didn't see Auðleif. You've never had to live with the guilt of murdering two of your closest friends." Grief tightened her throat, made her voice thick. "I swore I wouldn't do that again."

Then she opened her eyes, and a measure of peace came back to her. It was like when she'd surrendered to Bolvereik's fury in the Ice Knives. She'd fought for so long – sometimes it seemed like she'd always been fighting, one way or another – but now there could be an end.

"And I won't let Ingjald live on," she said quietly, drawing Tyrfing from its sheath.

The sword's light blazed forth, rivalling the sun. Enjarað and Heiðrek flinched back, but Hervor did not. In that light, she saw peace.

"Tyrfing may never be drawn without the death of a man," she whispered, letting the sheath fall to the ground. It wouldn't be needed again. "And it will be the cause of three dishonourable deaths. Two good men have fallen already, men I cared for. My thread is done; my time has come. Let the third death be mine, and the downfall of the false king."

And, bracing the sword against the earth, she fell upon its point.

There was an ungodly impact, and Tyrfing toppled to the ground.

Hervor landed on her left hip, one hand pressed to the spot where the sword had struck, and coughed for air. Tyrfing's light went out. Its blade, glinting in the sun, was still perfectly clean.

Breath came back, and Hervor said the first thing that came to mind.

"*Fuck.*"

"What—" Enjarað stepped forward, reaching out.

"Don't touch it!" Hervor sprang up and caught him by the sleeve. "Keep away."

Heiðrek's eyes had gone very wide. "You're not dead. What in hell?"

Hervor parted the slit in her shirt and found her skin unmarked – although by the feel of it, she'd have a spectacular bruise.

"The gods wouldn't let you do it," Enjarað said wildly. "It's not your time to die!"

But having just recited some of her father's words, Hervor had no trouble remembering the rest. She swore through clenched teeth.

"I forgot something," she said bitterly, when she had enough self-control to say something other than profanity. "All my fear of poisoning myself, all that playing with knives, and I had nothing to worry about. A little side benefit of Tyrfing, although it's working against me right now. As long as I hold it, *blades won't cut me.*"

Enjarað, distraught, didn't quite follow her; Heiðrek did. "Even Tyrfing itself."

"Exactly." Hervor's heart felt like lead in her chest.

"Then we can't do this," Enjarað said, and relief rolled off him in waves.

Heiðrek, however, went very still and very quiet. When he finally spoke, his voice was almost too low to hear. "Yes, we can."

Hervor looked up, meeting her son's eyes, and knew they were both thinking the same thing.

Enjaraŏ still didn't understand. He didn't *want* to understand. "What?"

"Disaster," Hervor whispered, tears threatening to spill. This was exactly the fate she'd wanted to escape – for their sakes, if not for her own. But hadn't she thought it in the barrow? She couldn't have both, divine aid and a life free from such weight. "He said that, too. That it would bring disaster to my sons."

"It already has," Enjaraŏ said.

"And that the three deaths would – would be dishonourable." She could barely say it.

Enjaraŏ wasn't a fool. He couldn't ignore the obvious forever, no matter how much he wanted to. She felt the change in him the instant he realised. "*No.*"

"We have to," Heiŏrek said, his voice still almost inaudible.

"The *hells* we have to!"

"The only way for us to bring down Ingjald," Hervor snarled past the tightness in her throat, "is for me to become a dis. He feared that fate for me; it's why he didn't kill me. So I have to die. Neither of you brought your axes, so it has to be Tyrfing or your knives, and the rest of the curse has to be fulfilled. Since I can't kill myself with Tyrfing—"

"*I will not kill you!*" Enjaraŏ screamed.

The wind gusted across the top of the barrow. Hervor looked in the direction it blew and wished with all her heart that she could go to Aettarstað, leave this whole idea behind. But the thread of her life was done. It was time for her to die.

someday there will be peace

The voices whispered in her mind, the first time they'd spoken since the Blessed King came to her. They'd been silent since she awoke. And for once, Hervor found their presence a comfort. They understood what she had to do.

She just wished no one else had to join her.

"I'll do it," Heiðrek said.

Enjarað stared at him, eyes wild. "No. You can't do it. This is our *mother*, for gods' sake—"

"She's willing to sacrifice herself to stop Ingjald," Heiðrek shot back, iron-hard. "If she can do that—"

"You'd make us *kinslayers* – damn our souls to Kjellar—"

"Some things matter more than our own fates." Heiðrek bent before Enjarað could stop him and lifted Tyrfing from the grass. The light blazed forth once again, incongruously bright for the dark work the sword was about to do. "You don't have to do anything," Heiðrek said, and though there could have been contempt in his voice, there was only compassion. "I'll do it."

His brother shook his head slowly, but his voice had deserted him.

Hervor braced herself, feet widely planted, hands clenched into fists at her sides. That sense of peace was still with her, but *fuck*, it was harder to stand here when someone else was holding the sword. Tears ran freely down Heiðrek's face, yet his hand was steady as he levelled Tyrfing at her chest.

A second hand reached out to cover his on the hilt.

Enjaraðstood at his brother's side, gripping the sword with him. He, too, was weeping, but he hadn't come to take the blade away; he'd joined Heiðrek for the final blow.

Seeing her two sons standing there – even knowing they were about to kill her – Hervor felt all the pride of eighteen lost years. They were better heirs to Aettarstað, to Bjarmar, than she could ever have been. They would restore the holding and live in a better world than the one she was leaving behind. Hervor only wished she could be there to see it.

"You are honourable men," she whispered. "I will tell Eldaskrid so."

Her sons' fingers tightened, and Tyrfing flashed forward to take her life.

30

THE END OF STOLEN TIME

Pain lanced through her body, and she fell.

The ground gave way as if it were water; she plummeted through the earth into the chill emptiness of the barrow, and then she slammed into the stone bier she'd been laid on years ago.

Her body slammed into it. The rest of her kept going.

She fell through the darkness, then halted suddenly in a cavern.

This one dwarfed the little chamber of her barrow as the Ice Knives dwarfed an anthill. There might be a vague hint of a ceiling, high above, studded with dangling rocks like fangs, but the walls were too far away to see. Only the stone floor and the echoing emptiness gave her a sense of place.

Tiny blue flames, dancing along the floor, shed mere traces of light, and the sole thing in sight was a throne carved of ice.

Hervor took three hesitant steps towards the throne, then spun when a voice spoke behind her.

"You are brave, to face your death like that."

It took her a moment to realise how large the man standing behind her was. With the throne now at her back, she had nothing to compare him against except herself, and in the vastness of the cavern, distances were confusing. But he was, without a doubt, the largest man she'd ever seen: taller than Rannvar, taller than Enjarik, by at least a head, and built to match; his shoulders could have carried an ox without tiring.

Behind his muscled bulk she could just see the ends of a sword strapped to his back. Just the sword; no sheath covered it, and the blade was stained with fresh blood.

Hervor looked into his crimson eyes and almost choked on the name. "Bolvereik."

He smiled. It was the most frightening expression she'd ever seen. Hralthareng, that priest had called him, the Ever-Devouring One – and that was what his smile looked like.

She wondered if she should kneel.

But if she tried to move, she might collapse, so she kept standing and tried speaking again. "Is… is this your realm?"

Bolvereik shook his head. "You know better."

She did. "This is Eldaskrid's hall." The terrible fascination of his eyes had lessened enough that Hervor could manage a quick glance over her shoulder, at the throne of ice. "Where is she?"

"In the sunlit lands, seeking one who has escaped his fate." Bolvereik's voice held the growl of a wolf; Hervor's skin crawled with animal fear. "She will not return until that is done."

Hervor was no priestess, to speculate on what Eldaskrid's absence from the underworld might do, but she doubted it was good. And that thought recalled her to her task. "Bloody One – I've heard that the women you touch become disir when they die."

"They can." The god's eyes were mesmerising, twin pools of blood. "Sometimes."

Hervor swallowed her sudden doubt. "That's why I'm here. To become a dis."

Again that smile, no less terrifying the second time. "Most do not seek that fate."

"Most women aren't in my place." Her sudden flare of irritation made Hervor fear she'd overstepped her bounds – but the oppressive weight of Bolvereik's presence receded slightly.

Meekness was not a quality he valued.

Hervor clenched her fists and forged ahead with a semblance of courage. "You know about Ingjald, who calls himself the Blessed King. Meltharkatla – Eldaskrid – she wants me to bring him down. But I can't do it so long as I have a body for him to control; he's too skilled with drauðr. So I killed myself. In order to become a dis."

Bolvereik's eyes held hers again. "Killed yourself."

He was a god; he damn well knew the truth. "My sons killed

me," Hervor admitted quietly. "Knowing it might damn them to the worst of the hells after they die – but they did it because I asked them to. In order to get rid of Ingjald."

"The disir are not meant to kill kings."

"But they protect families, and get revenge. They're always linked to families; I know that much." Hervor thought of her sons, the tears streaming down their faces. "The only way to protect my sons, to bring peace to my family, is to stop Ingjald. Let alone helping the rest of the land. So what if it's a king I have to kill? He should have died long ago, and you know it."

In the silence that followed her words, Hervor realised that she'd just lectured a god.

But he smiled for the third time, and although it was still an awful expression, she knew its hunger wasn't directed at her.

Bolvereik held out his hand.

Hervor stared at it for a dozen heartbeats before she was able to make her feet move. She walked forward – and walked, and walked, for he was even further away than she'd thought, and even larger than she'd believed – until she stood in front of him.

She reached out and gripped the god's hand in a warrior's clasp.

Fire roared through her, a berserker's rage brought on all at once, and ten times hotter than anything she'd felt before—

Enjaraŏ, weeping alone in the hall when no one was there to see.

but I am here

Heiðrek, stony-faced, moving through his duties like a puppet, hardly speaking lest the stone crack and shatter.

you have the strength

People's whispers, wondering what was wrong. Murmuring about what had been seen to the south, atop a solitary barrow-mound, the mutilated head of a mare.

I set up this stake of scorn...

She was with her sons and not. She was in her barrow and not. She felt the approach of riders, hands reaching out, slowed by disgust, to grasp the rotting flesh and pull it free – but it wouldn't come.

A second attempt, a third, all failing.

Steel striking against flint, sparks falling to the brush now heaped around the stake's base, yet the flames refused to touch either stake or head.

Rising fury.

LEAVE ME BE

They fled.

Aettarstað again. Enjarað and Heiðrek, side by side at the high table, listening with hard, grim eyes to the words being spoken.

"...rumours reached his ears..."

"...accusations of sorcery..."

"...treachery against the king..."

They'd learned dignity from Jordis. They couldn't deny the presence of the mare's head on their land, and they would not flee.

She couldn't break through to speak to them – why, *why* couldn't she make her voice heard, in anything more than snatches? – and so they made the decision without her, believing themselves alone.

Horses. Wagons. The gates of Aettarstað. Then the long, desolate road, through forests dying of drought, grasslands seared dry by the unbroken summer heat.

I have been this way before, seen it in snow

Two groups of warriors, uneasily coexisting. One group nervous, semi-defiant, loyal to the end. The other cold and unfriendly: captors, though no one called them that.

And try though she would, she couldn't make herself heard. Only in dreams could she speak to her sons, try to reassure them, give them words they might remember on waking, when they rose and mounted to ride to their doom.

Finally, Svelsond, and the glorious hall of the king, blazing from its hill with a light to rival Tyrfing, to rival the sun.

we end this now

✦ ✦ ✦

The world, seen only in flashes, snapped into crystalline focus the moment Enjarað and Heiðrek walked through the doors of the hall.

Hervor wasn't alone. Angantyr stood with her, and all her brothers at his sides. But she could no more touch the world than they could; something barred her way.

She snarled in fury and flung herself forward, at the images playing out before her, but it was as if a wall of ice stood between her and her sons. She couldn't break through. She could only watch as they walked forward, alone and unarmed, Kjarvald and the rest of their scant host of housemen kept at the rear of the hall.

Ingjald sat on his throne and watched with thinly concealed smugness as they approached.

They were in danger – why couldn't she *do* anything – she was a dis now; this was exactly her purpose!

"*Our shed blood is his shield,*" Angantyr murmured. "*No ghost can get near.*"

Hervor wanted to howl. It wasn't supposed to be like this! Ingjald had feared her becoming a dis; it couldn't be true that him taking her blood meant she was powerless now. Had her sons slain her for nothing?

Ingjald had begun speaking while she fought against his magic. "Do you deny that there is a stake of scorn on your lands, carved with my name, which resists all attempts to be removed or destroyed?"

Heiðrek answered, Enjarað white-faced at his side. "No. We don't."

Horrified whispers rippled down the hall.

"Did you put this stake there?"

"No. We didn't."

Ingjald leaned forward on his throne. "Then who do you claim is responsible? Some unlettered peasant?"

Heiðrek smiled, and for a heartbeat his expression echoed Bolvereik's.

"Our mother."

His words started an uproar. Ingjald blanched and gripped the arms of his throne until his hands shook, but when he spoke, his voice was steady. He'd had centuries to perfect his control over himself. "Your mother is dead."

Enjarað raised his eyes, and Hervor saw the resolution in them. He was pale not with fear, but with determination. "We know. We killed her ourselves."

He reached under his tunic and pulled out a hidden knife.

Men leapt forward to try and disarm Enjarað, thinking he must be intending to attack the king – but he was faster, and he had a different plan. Heiðrek extended his right hand next to his brother's left, and with one motion Enjarað slashed the blade of the knife across both their arms.

"Hervor, daughter of Angantyr, chosen of Bolvereik – we call you to defend us!"

As their blood fell to the wood-panelled floor, the invisible wall between Hervor and the world melted away.

She shot through it as if hurled by a great wind, and then she was *there*, in the hall, manifested in ghostly flesh the blue of Eldaskrid's flames. She stood just in front of her sons, facing Ingjald, and her appearance brought everyone to a terrified halt.

Hervor drew strength from the blood – *her* blood, from her sons' veins – and spoke.

"*Traitor.*"

Her voice cut through the hall like a whip of ice. Even the fiercest warrior cringed back, pushing against those behind him.

Ingjald had stood up from his throne, his face deathly white.

"Blood magic," she whispered, "*is neither good nor ill. Its quality lies in what you do with it. Blood magic to lay ghosts to rest – that is one thing.*"

She advanced a step, and the crowds shied away.

"*But blood magic to extend the thread of life – drauðr to drain the life from others, so that you might live on—*"

"Lies," Ingjald hissed. "You were a madwoman when you lived, and now you seek to destroy me still. The gods will—"

"*The gods themselves have condemned you.*" Hervor didn't need to raise her voice; the cold weight of her words was enough. "*Melsafny shows her anger in the withering of the land. Eldaskrid raised me from the barrow where I slept, trapped by your spell, so I could hunt you down. Bolvereik returned me to this world as a dis, and gave me the strength to protect my sons from your evil.*"

Behind her, the blood still dripped to the floor – no charcoal circle to hold it in. She felt the air shiver as, one by one, her sons' other kinsmen appeared: Hervard, Hjorvard, all her brothers in turn. Last of all, Angantyr.

Hervor smiled wolfishly. She was a dis, and her sons' blood had broken the hold Ingjald's magic had over her. And although she'd set herself down this road for the sake of her kin, in the end, they were far from the only ones the false king had wronged.

"*You may spurn me as the shadow of a madwoman,*" she said. "*But you cannot dismiss all your victims so easily.*"

The air in the hall plummeted to the depths of winter as blue flames roared up the walls. Ringing the room were the shades of those drained by Ingjald's magic… and their numbers were beyond counting.

Screams rose as men's nerves broke and they fought to get away from the throngs of the dead.

"*You have lived on stolen time,*" Hervor whispered, lacing through the chaos. "*But no more.*" She lifted her empty palm, drawing all eyes to it – and Tyrfing materialised in her hand, shining with cold, icy light.

In desperation, Ingjald snatched out a knife and slashed his own arm, drawing blood to drive some spell, but it was no use. The power in his body was stolen from others, and it was no longer his to control.

All it did was give the ghosts the opening they needed.

Ingjald screamed as his life fled him, streaking in golden flashes back to the ghosts that filled the hall. As each struck home, the spirit smiled and vanished, and so the crowd thinned out, until the last thirteen threads leapt free of the king's body and flew past Hervor to Angantyr and his sons.

She turned to look at them. All the dire things her father had foretold... and he hadn't been wrong. But she'd chosen to take up that burden, and despite the price, she didn't regret it.

Her voice softer now, she repeated the words she'd spoken on Samsey, eighteen years and her own death ago. "*My father and brothers will rest in their graves before I am done.*"

Angantyr touched his fist to his chest. The light shining in his eyes was pride.

peace, her brothers murmured, for the last time... and then they were gone.

Of all the shades, only Hervor remained. She turned and strode down the hall, to the hideous thing collapsed on the throne, desiccated and rotten – but still alive.

Hervor looked down on him without pity. So many lies, so many ghosts, because one man was too much of a coward to face death.

There was a hell waiting for men like him.

"*Eldaskrid stands ready to greet you,*" Hervor said. Then she raised Tyrfing one final time, and brought the false king down.

EPILOGUE

A half-day's ride south of Aettarstað, in a quiet, grassy field carpeted with flowers, a solitary barrow sits in silence. Legend says a mare's head once stood atop it, impaled upon a stake, but it vanished without a trace the day the False King died.

No one was there to *see* it vanish   but details like that have never slowed legend down.

Legend also says what lies inside the mound. People *were* there to see the daughter of Angantyr laid to rest, in the armour and helm given her by the False King, but that's not what rumour claims is there today. They say Hervor lies on the stone slab in the tattered remains of clothing that was once fine, and the armour is missing.

And Tyrfing, the enchanted, cursed sword that cut down friend and foe alike on its way to the False King... that, they say, lies not in her hands, but through her heart.

No one has disturbed the barrow to see.

AUTHOR'S NOTE

This novel is the bastard child of my college thesis.

While writing *The Sword Makes the Man: Weapons and the Construction of Social Identity in Viking Age Scandinavia* – doesn't it sound exciting? – for my degree in archaeology and folklore, several times I came across a poem called "The Waking of Angantyr". In it, a young woman named Hervor goes to the barrow where her father and his eleven brothers are buried and demands that Angantyr give her his famous sword, Tyrfing. Patricia Terry's *Poems of the Elder Edda*, which is where I first encountered this, says in the commentary that she "wants the sword as an instrument of vengeance". Terry is working from the text published by E.V. Gordon, in the book my Old Norse language class used; he likewise says she is "determined to avenge her father and her uncles" – and unlike Terry, he gives the name of the saga in which the poem occurs.

Well, one of its names. The work has several, such as *Hervarar saga* (Hervor's Saga), *Hervarar saga ok Heiðreks* (The Saga of Hervor and Heiðrek), and *Saga Heiðreks konungs in vitra* (The Saga of King Heiðrek the Wise). That last is the title under which Christopher Tolkien – yes, *that* Tolkien's son – published his translation. Because I needed it for my thesis, and also because I'm a thorough-going nerd who thought "Viking woman avenges dead father" sounded like a fantastic story, I eagerly sought out a copy.

Reader, E.V. Gordon and Patricia Terry lied to me.

Hervor doesn't go to avenge her father and uncles. She basically *can't*. Hjalmar has long since died of the wounds Angantyr gave him; Örvar-Oddr (whose name, I kid you not, translates to "Arrow-Odd" or "Arrow's Point") has his own saga to go die in – which he accomplishes by tripping over the skull of his old horse Faxi, who was prophesied to kill him, whereupon a snake comes out of the skull and bites him. No, really.

What does Hervor do? She, uh, retires. Honestly, the assortment of various titles kind of reflects the scattershot nature of the manuscript: first it starts off with a brief explanation of the forging of Tyrfing, then moves on to Arngrim and his sons, including Angantyr, who dies with his brothers in the duel. Then Hervor shows up and you get "The Waking of Angantyr"... but after that she just spends a little time as a warrior, then settles down in the house of her foster-father Bjarmar before getting married and having a son.

Literally a page and a half after arguing a ghost into handing her a cursed sword, she's done. The saga moves on for a while to her son, Heiðrek – but he likewise gets killed, which leads to *his* sons (one of whom is named Angantyr; he also has a daughter named Hervor, because welcome to Old Norse literature) going to war with each other, and then there's a list of kingly descendants (the first of which is Angantyr II's son Heiðrek II, *oh my god*), the end.

This could not be permitted to stand. The poem is awesome; the saga thoroughly squanders its awesomeness. (Possibly because the poem is almost certainly older than the saga.) So naturally, being a novelist, I felt the only correct course of action was to write a novel that would deliver the blood and guts and vengeance I'd been promised.

The result hews much less closely to the source material than many of my folklore-based stories. You may have already noticed that Angantyr's brothers in the poem became Hervor's brothers in the novel, and book-Orvar isn't simply bitten by a venomous snake – though I couldn't resist saying that "Tyrfing" translates to "Serpent's Tooth," in acknowledgement of his canonical end. And of course all the stuff with the Blessed King and Meltharkatla and drauðr and so forth is entirely made up. But Hervor being a bondsmaid who goes around as a viking named Hervard – that part, I didn't have to invent.

My thanks and apologies to my professors Stephen Mitchell and Joseph Harris, who taught me about the Vikings and the

Old Norse language, for all the things I learned from them and then tossed partially out the window. As a defense I will shout "the folkloric process!" and then attempt to vanish in a puff of authorial smoke.

ABOUT THE AUTHOR

Marie Brennan is a former anthropologist and folklorist who shamelessly leans on her academic fields for inspiration. She recently misapplied her professors' hard work to *The Game of 100 Candles* and the short novel *Driftwood*, and as M. A. Carrick, together with Alyc Helms, she is the author of the Rook and Rose epic fantasy trilogy, which begins with *The Mask of Mirrors*. The first book of her Hugo Award-nominated Victorian adventure series The Memoirs of Lady Trent, *A Natural History of Dragons*, was a finalist for the World Fantasy Award. Her other works include the Doppelganger duology, the urban fantasy Wilders series, the Onyx Court historical fantasies, the Varekai novellas and more than eighty short stories, as well as the New Worlds series of worldbuilding guides. Visit her website at swantower.com, her Patreon at patreon.com/swan_tower and follow her on Twitter at @swan_tower.

For more fantastic fiction, author events,
exclusive excerpts, competitions, limited editions and more

VISIT OUR WEBSITE
titanbooks.com

LIKE US ON FACEBOOK
facebook.com/titanbooks

FOLLOW US ON TWITTER AND INSTAGRAM
@TitanBooks

EMAIL US
readerfeedback@titanemail.com